SHARP SCRATCH

By Martine Bailey

Sharp Scratch
Isolation Ward

SHARP SCRATCH

Martine Bailey

Allison & Busby Limited
11 Wardour Mews
London W1F 8AN
allisonandbusby.com

First published in Great Britain by Allison & Busby in 2024.
This paperback edition published by Allison & Busby in 2024.

Copyright © 2024 by Martine Bailey

A CIP catalogue record for this book is available from
the British Library.

10 9 8 7 6 5 4 3 2 1

ISBN 978-0-7490-3094-0

Typeset in 10/15 pt Sabon LT Pro by Allison & Busby Ltd.

By choosing this product, you help take care of the world's forests.
Learn more: www.fsc.org.

Printed and bound by
CPI Group (UK) Ltd, Croydon, CR0 4YY

For everyone who struggles to find their place
in a world of cold conformity.

'Dark, unfeeling and unloving powers determine human destiny.'

New Introductory Lectures on Psychoanalysis
by Sigmund Freud

AUTHOR'S NOTE

Personality tests like the one in this book are designed to measure traits, the habitual patterns of behaviour, thought and emotion that seem to make you 'you'. Each chapter is headed by a fictional test question intended to reflect that chapter's theme. I hope you find it entertaining to ask yourself the questions; if you agree with option 'A.' you are identifying with that trait's description written out below it. This is of course not a scientific test: if you agree with a single trait associated with depression or psychopathy, that does not mean you are depressed or a psychopath!

Any credible test would consider the combination and interaction of the different traits you identify with and their measurement on a scale from high to low. The fictional PX60 test in part reflects the thinking back in 1983, whereas today more attention is paid to the demonstration of different traits in a variety of situations – for example, 'I may be aggressive and loud at a football match but quiet and submissive at work'. Similarly, traits can change over time and our differing cultures, learning and life opportunities all contribute to making us unique individuals.

Sadism

Instructions

This is a questionnaire concerning your interests, preferences and feelings about a range of things. There is no time limit.

Be as honest and truthful as you can. Don't give an answer just because it seems to be the right thing to say.

Question 1: If people were more honest, they would admit that torture is interesting.

A. True
B. Uncertain
C. False

High score description (option A.): Cruelty, an intrinsic pleasure in hurting and humiliating others.

My past is confined in a box of steel. Though memories beg for release, I keep them carefully padlocked, deep in the cellar of my mind.

I review an old favourite: The Glen, Salford, 1963. I

watch Christie staring out from the top window of Wilkins Boarding House, one of the largest of a street of shabby villas, mostly divided into mismatched flats. She is waiting for her landlady, keeping vigil over a road that has few cars, no children, no pets. A coalman's horse and cart clops along the cobbles to the next house along. He heaves his sacks up the alley, whistling tunelessly, his eyes white in his sooty face.

Next Mrs Wilkins comes hobbling into sight, her spine bent from a life of drudgery. At the front gate she sets down two weighty shopping bags to get her breath back, admiring her smart painted sign: 'The Wilkins Boarding House – Hot and cold water. Special rates for hospital staff'. Replenished with puff and pride, she disappears up the steps and the front door bangs.

The coalman and his cart disappear. When all is quiet, Christie noiselessly descends to where Mrs Wilkins is brewing tea in the kitchen. The landlady looks up when the door opens. She's a sinewy, nervy woman, faded at sixty, her myopic eyes magnified behind round NHS spectacles.

'Oh, hello. Did they let you off early?'

An excuse is made. Then the suspicious little face peers up from the tea caddy.

'You 'aven't seen me old carpetbag, 'ave you? Last time I seen it I'm sure it were up on the wardrobe. It's got all me important papers and that locked up in it.'

Christie dolefully shakes her head, a parody of innocence.

Just then the kettle starts up like a banshee screaming a warning. The landlady rescues it from the flame, and it quiets to fitful sighs. Her big watery eyes catch sight of the bottle filched from the medicine cupboard.

'Fancy you getting hold of that health tonic from

the hospital for me,' she says, savouring a rare dose of attention. 'Go on. I could do with giving me feet a rest.'

It's quite something, Christie's Treatment Room. There's even a neat wooden sign on the door like a proper clinic. It took time to create it, to arrange the perfect setting for Christie's most private fantasies. Best of all, she arranged to take the unwanted fittings from the abandoned operating theatres when they knocked half the asylum down. She salvaged some real beauties: a rubber anaesthetic mask, and a set of original glass and steel syringes. Her pride and joy is the antique treatment couch. It's hard leather, weighty and strong, with the original straps and buckles still taut and secure.

Mrs Wilkins follows her downstairs and through the Treatment Room door like a pet lamb to the slaughter. Suddenly she spots the wax display of a brain beneath a dome of glass.

'It's a bit funny down here, in't it? All this peculiar equipment you've gone and got hold of.'

Christie gestures to the couch. Mrs Wilkins clambers up, then lies on her back, pulling her skirt down over thick stockings, preserving her pathetic modesty. Christie rolls up the landlady's sleeve and bares her withered arm. The patient needs to be quiet. To relax. To do as she is told. Only when Christie starts to bind her arm with the leather strap does she start twitching.

'Eh, what d'you think you're doing?'

It's too late. The large old-fashioned syringe looms above her. Mrs Wilkins' eyes open so wide, they might pop. The other gloved hand clamps her nose and mouth. When the old bat tries to bite the hand that restrains her,

13

the needle stabs into scrawny flesh. With the release of the syringe comes the thrill as the lethal dose surges into a vein. The old woman writhes helplessly; her glasses tumble to the floor.

She finally comprehends her fate in wide-eyed horror. The whimpering stops. Pupils shrink to pinpricks. Life ends, snuffed out, as a great black veil falls. The sensation is like nothing else, better than any sexual thrill, this extinction of another person.

On the floor the spectacles lie twisted, the cracked lenses forever dimmed.

Later, Christie returns to the kitchen with the carpetbag. One by one she removes each document and inspects them. It is mostly rubbish, ancient stuff from the war, faded letters, cheap Christmas cards. A bundle of these are shoved into the fire. Placed to one side is the Last Will and Testament of Mrs Ida Wilkins, which leaves her entire estate to The Methodist Mission for Charity in Africa.

By the light of the crackling fire Christie flattens out the will and begins to practise in a crabby, uneducated hand:

'I devise and bequeath to my dear friend the property known as The Wilkins Boarding House . . .'

Radicalism

Question 2: I am frustrated by the routine nature of normal life.

    A. True

    B. Uncertain

    C. False

High score description (option A.): Experimental, open to change, liberal, critical, free-thinking.

Sunday 13th February, 1983

What was she even doing here? Lorraine Quick was already late. And very tired. She had rushed to her mum's at noon, feeling guilty to be leaving eight-year-old Jasmine for a whole week. The bag of sweets and cheap toys felt like a bribe. Her mum had been rightly offhand with her.

And then that gig. Why had they even bothered? To be bottom of the bill at some run-down pub and circled by a few dozen snarling yobs. The longer they played the angrier the blokes became, clearly aggrieved by a nearly-all-girl band who refused to flirt or giggle or follow their suggestion to 'get 'em off for the lads'. Lily had thrown back a few cutting retorts but honestly, what was going on? Then the landlord had waved Lorraine away when she asked for their fee. Yet again, she'd have to pay for the petrol. And all the oafs around the bar had laughed.

For the last four hours her only company along the long empty stretches of the M6 had been the cassette recording of her band's last rehearsal. Christ, she felt alone. Things were not going well. Life felt like a battleground. And call it intuition but she sensed that matters were only getting worse. Now, to crown it all, she was lost in the benighted streets of Oxford.

At last her headlamps picked up a wooden board and made out the words 'Wyndham College closed'. After parking up she wondered if she'd catch any of the course introduction. She tried knocking on the ancient door of the porter's lodge that skinned her freezing knuckles. Oxford on a Sunday night in February felt like a stronghold of unclimbable walls and padlocked iron gates.

She gave the door a rattling kick for good measure. Still no answer. A few yards away a door opened in the wall and a half-dozen Sloane Ranger types emerged. Lorraine glared at them.

'How the bloody hell do I get in?' she called out.

A young guy with floppy hair and a shiny waistcoat mocked her accent, ''Ow the bluddy 'ell do a get in?'

Their hoots of laughter seemed to ascend to the city's spires. Lorraine glowered after them, her fists tightening. At last a light flickered on in the lodge, and she turned to see a uniformed porter's sour face poking through the window.

'College members only after six,' he announced in a ridiculously plummy voice.

She rummaged in her old satchel. True, she was here only for a week's study leave, but she had as much right as anyone else to pass through this gate.

'Doctor Lehman's course. Personality testing.'

'I should have guessed. A *public* course. You're late. Back of the quad.'

When she found her classroom, the entire roomful of delegates turned to stare at her peroxided hair bunched into a lopsided ponytail, biker jacket, Patti Smith T-shirt and buckled boots. They all wore their corporate best: padded shoulders and kipper ties. Some of the women sported big perms above giant blouse bows.

The course leader, Doctor Lehman, looked more interesting: fiftyish, grey bob, wearing a rainbow-coloured kaftan that might have been Zandra Rhodes. Two hawkish eyes fixed on Lorraine from behind a pair of red-framed spectacles.

'Ms Quick, I presume. We were just discussing how a negative trait like rule-breaking might reveal itself in lateness, for example.'

Nervous titters broke out around the room. She read the slide projected on the screen: a scale showing degrees of 'Self-discipline vs Rule-breaking'.

Slipping into a seat Lorraine replied, 'But didn't Professor Paston in his 1978 paper show that if we had no rule-breakers we'd all risk becoming – I'm quoting his words – "stagnant and boring". We'd have no David Bowie. No Jesus Christ.'

The room fell silent. Doctor Lehman's slightly magnified eyes fixed upon her, revealing amused approval.

'Well, well. Someone has done the background reading. On that evidence alone I'll raise your score by at least thirty per cent.' She clicked a switch and the carousel moved to the next slide.

'*To know thyself is the road to wisdom.*' *Aristotle.* The aphorism was displayed across the screen beside a portrait bust of the philosopher.

Lorraine hoped this was true. At twenty-six, she still had no idea what she wanted from life. When Doctor Lehman spoke, she concentrated hard on her closing words.

'You all have an intensive week ahead of you, even before we consider your return for the exam in just over three weeks' time. This course will change you all – and I hope guide you on the path to wisdom. Because your first, most extraordinary subject is . . . yourself.'

As the initial training days unfolded, it dawned on her that passing the course might demand more than last-minute cramming for an exam. In one group exercise, Doctor Lehman had handed out each person's scores and asked the whole group to form a line in sequence, from 1 to 100. Lorraine had the most extreme score of 94, so she got to hold a placard labelled 'Radicalism', while the guy who scored 22 stood at the other end of the line holding 'Conservatism'. Doctor Lehman had described those with high scores for Radicalism as analytical and free-thinking, with a strong desire to overthrow current customs. Though feeling like the class weirdo, she was forced to agree with the description; it felt valid, a true reflection of the life she lived.

In her free periods she wandered in the wintry college gardens, surrounded by lichen-clad statues and dead trees. She wanted to hate the place; the Marxist lecturers on her degree would say it symbolised all that was wrong with Thatcher's

Britain. Pulling her purple mohair tight against the cold, she listened to her music on new Walkman headphones. Nico's doleful Germanic tones pondered which costume to wear to a lifetime of decadent parties. Which indeed? If her future life must be a performance, she felt like an actor pushed on the stage without lines or disguise. Opening her course manual, she quailed at scary-looking equations to prove test reliability and calculate standard deviation.

One evening towards the end of the week, a rumbling organ drew her to the candlelit windows of the chapel. She sat in the shadows, succumbing to sound. The choir's voices twined and untwined, swooped and soared. She didn't flatter herself that she was much of a musician; she didn't need to be a virtuoso to play in a post-punk band. But she did have the ear of a musician's daughter. There is a reason these archaic notes are still played and sung, she mused, echoing across the days for hundreds of years.

Next day she found Blackwell's bookshop and picked up *The Warlock of Firetop Mountain*. Her daughter would love it and Lorraine was intrigued. Emblazoned across the front was 'A game book in which YOU become the hero!' Success or failure depended on how well the reader performed in a series of encounters, fights and mazes. It was a personality test, she realised, demanding all the heroic traits of a champion.

Back in her study bedroom overlooking a medieval courtyard, she ruminated over how uncomfortable she felt. She thought about norms and normality, about those people whose scores always placed them at the comfortable centre of the line-up. She guessed they must feel safe – content with their work, their spouses, their futures. She, on the other hand, was generally flung out onto the edges of the group – her brain wired to see things differently, sensitive to mental patterns and hidden possibilities. Whatever it was that made her different, she sensed its value was being utterly wasted in her job.

Sunday 20th February

On the final morning of the course, the group assembled in a classroom laid out in rows of individual desks. She breathed in the warm smell of beeswax polish, feeling scrutinised by the portraits of dozens of stiff-faced scholars. The full battery of PX60 psychometric tests took two hours, and though she enjoyed the quiz-like fun of it, she was now aware of a crafty aspect to the process. The questions were not quite what they appeared to be, and some were designed to trip up candidates who lied about themselves. It was called Motivational Distortion or 'Faking Good' – the attempt to present yourself as someone more conforming and desirable, someone who would fit in. Doctor Lehman sternly advised them to be true to themselves, answer quickly and state what they honestly believed – or the Motivational Distortion trap would catch them out.

It was late afternoon on Sunday and Lorraine was hanging around for Doctor Lehman's final feedback appointment of the day. Finding a payphone in a passageway, she dialled the only friend she'd made at work. As well as being the right side of thirty, the medical records officer had immediately struck her as being a relatively sane person considering she was a hospital middle manager. Over snatched tea breaks in the League of Friends café, they had discovered they both had a child at St Michael's. Rose didn't want to tell her work colleagues about her son Tim, just as Lorraine kept schtum about Jasmine. In a flurry of heated confidences, they had both agreed that to be labelled a working mum by some of the bigots at work would be career suicide. And their friendship was proving useful, for Tim and Jasmine liked playing together, and had just spent the morning at Rose's house.

'Just wanted to say thanks for taking Jasmine and Tim back to my mum's,' Lorraine said when Rose picked up the phone. 'I'll pay you back in time whenever you like.'

'Don't worry. When I left, Tim was having a great time. He's certainly never baked madeleines before. And I've had some actual free time on a Sunday while Phil's away at his conference.'

Lorraine was about to say goodbye and head for her tutor's office when Rose suddenly asked in a low tone, 'You had a bad relationship once, didn't you? Was he ever unfaithful to you?'

'What?' She was startled. 'Has Phil been playing around?'

Rose seemed instantly to regret her words. 'No, well, I was just wondering. Still, what would you do?'

Lorraine pictured naïve Rose, way out of her depth. Hadn't she got married straight from college? Lorraine hadn't met him, but Rose talked of Phil as a dullard, a council worker whom she had little time for.

'You really are too good for this world,' Lorraine said kindly. 'If I were you—' She considered the answer for a second or two and was punished by a violent recollection from her hellish days with Andy. 'I'd have nothing to do with that person again.'

Suspiciousness

Question 3: I suspect that people who seem friendly to me are sometimes disloyal to me behind my back.
   A. True
   B. Uncertain
   C. False
High score description (option A.): Vigilant, jealous, suspicious, distrustful.

Rose sat in front of the phone for an hour after Lorraine rang off, her thoughts black and bitter. If only Phil would come home, she could pretend everything was normal. Instead, she faced a world that was utterly changed. Obsessively, her thoughts returned to the grim bedroom at 12 Radley Road, its cheap furniture, bald carpet and nylon sheets. And yet, for nearly ten weeks, it had been her secret place, a space in which she had at last been free to express her shameful, secret self.

But now it had all been spoilt. Her lover had made that careless remark about visiting someone called Christie. The name had burnt in her brain, setting off a wildfire chain of anxieties. She had made herself miserable, weeping over imagined slights, fearful of being abandoned, certain of being betrayed.

They had made feverish love just a few hours ago; her body was still sticky and sore. Afterwards, she had dozed briefly on the ugly bed and woke to find herself alone, listening to water flowing in the bathroom. She had snatched at the diary from the opposite bedstand. Names, names, and there it was, such an old entry in faded ink. *Christie Kerr, Room 7, Wilkins Boarding House, The Glen, Salford. Telephone 061 792 3490.*

Rose had tried not to breathe, as water continued gurgling along the pipes. Groping for her handbag, she'd scribbled the details down on the back of a shopping list.

After replacing the diary she'd noticed the heavy bunch of keys and inspected them. Attached was a smaller ring labelled 'Room 7' and bearing two keys, a Yale and a mortice. It was the same room number as Christie's – proof that something was definitely going on. Hurriedly, she'd detached the pair of keys and shoved them deep inside her handbag.

Self-sufficiency

Question 4: It does not bother me if people think I am not a typical person.
- A. True
- B. Uncertain
- C. False

High score description (option A.): Self-sufficient, resourceful, solitary, prefers own decisions.

Lorraine put her concerns about Rose out of her mind as she sank into a velvet chair in the tutor's office. The psychologist leant forward and examined her through intelligent eyes slightly magnified by her trendy spectacles. 'So tell me, why are you here on this course?'

Lorraine told the truth. 'Well, deep down I want to know – who am I? And what should I do with my life?'

Doctor Lehman made a tiny retreating movement, as if this wasn't quite what she wanted to hear. 'That is a very big question. And what work do you do?' she asked, spreading out a glossy PX60 report containing laser-printed charts and graphs. Lorraine pulled closer, aware that her black nail polish had chipped and turned ugly. 'Arts or creative, surely?'

'I wish.' Lorraine explained that the last time she'd been paid for anything artistic was for three exhilarating years studying Humanities at university. Now her final grant cheque had been spent, and her songwriting ambitions had left her with nothing but debts for second-hand gear. 'So now I'm a personnel officer, a job I can't stand. I'm at a run-down hospital in Salford. And I'm out of my depth. The doctors, the managers, everyone seems like a different species to me.'

Wincing in sympathy, Doctor Lehman pointed her pen nib at a score of 9 out of 10 for Imagination. 'I doubt a bureaucracy has much call for this level of creativity. My hunch is that your colleagues are conventional, highly practical types who make you feel uncomfortable.'

'Spot on. But I have a daughter. I'm hoping my work might lead to a better life for her.'

'I see.' Frowning, the tutor studied the profile again.

'So not a great fit between me and my job?' Lorraine asked. Suddenly this was all turning out far worse than she'd expected.

'Possibly not.' Doctor Lehman's mournful tone suggested a vast understatement.

The session improved as the psychologist expanded on the details of her test results. Her scores in verbal and numerical ability were good – well, more than good. And in the personality feedback Lorraine recognised herself with some surprise at its accuracy: adventurous and unconventional, independent and imaginative, and working best in solitude. If too overwhelmed by outside pressures, she was prone to get anxious.

The tutor picked up her profile again. 'You do have a secret weapon. You can read people, can't you? I'm not saying you like what you read or necessarily empathise, but looking at your scores I'd say that beneath this bohemian persona lies a shrewd and perceptive individual. You can formulate new and penetrating insights. Tell me, why do you think they are so hostile?'

'Well. Salford has utterly shit – sorry, horrible health problems. Poverty, deprivation, drugs. No one seriously wants to tackle it. Everything feels so fake. Why can't people just be authentic?'

Doctor Lehman smiled. 'I hear your radicalism calling. You recall Doctor Faust and his pact with the devil? Most of us trade our better selves for the comforts of money and security. Over time we *become* our roles, whether administrators, teachers, or dare I say it, psychologists. Try to get past your colleagues' protective shields and help them make small changes.'

'And if I can't? Sometimes I could kill the lot of them.'

Doctor Lehman's eyebrows lifted as she checked the report. 'Your stress levels are rather high. Imaginative personalities like yours – the shadow side of your personality can jump out from nowhere.'

The sound of someone entering the room next door made them both look up. Lorraine swung back eagerly towards Doctor Lehman. 'I have a shadow side?'

'We all have. The part of us that erupts when we're not ourselves. To paraphrase Carl Jung, we all carry a shadow. And the less conscious it is, the blacker and denser it becomes. It could be an upright citizen who indulges in secret deviant acts. Or the placid-seeming personality who succumbs to a violent obsession.'

'That's disturbing.' The mirror her tutor was showing her suddenly filled with something ugly. 'What should I do?'

'Don't push it away, Lorraine. Make your shadow your friend. When you feel stuck, tune into your unconscious. Listen to its eerie suggestions.'

'But I don't know—'

A loud rat-a-tat at the door broke into her entreaty. 'Locking up now.'

Lorraine had to stop herself yelling at the man to go jump in the Isis or whatever they called it.

'We're just leaving,' Doctor Lehman called.

Rapidly, the tutor counted a set of PX60 test booklets and scoresheets and handed them to Lorraine.

'Here you are. Eight tests for you to use with a variety of personality types. Do have a go at hand-scoring some of them, but you can also fax them and I'll generate computerised reports. If you need to discuss your interpretations, ring the office and make a phone appointment. It's all part of the course fee.'

'And the shadow? Could you just explain that to me?'

With an apologetic smile Doctor Lehman stood up. 'We can talk about that next time.' She crossed to the coat stand and began wrapping herself in a snake-like turquoise scarf.

While her tutor's back was turned Lorraine slumped in frustration; she'd felt on the edge of discovering something at last. Finally reaching down for her satchel, she noticed a stray business card on the carpet. It bore Doctor Lehman's personal as well as business phone number beside a logo of a small human figure casting a giant shadow. In a flash she palmed it in her hand. She wasn't exactly sure why, whether it was a glimmer of this intuition the tutor had talked about, but she felt instantly safer once she'd slipped the card inside her pocket.

Callousness

Question 5: I do what I want. Other people's feelings are of no interest to me.

    A. True

    B. Uncertain

    C. False

High score description (option A.): Lack of empathy, disregard for others' feelings, showing no remorse or guilt.

The sound of an ancient payphone broke into my delicious reverie. I opened my eyes and there I was, still in the Treatment Room all these years later. It was a long time since I'd heard that house phone ring, a relic of the sixties, tinny and shrill. Christie didn't seem to be answering it, so I hauled myself through the door to climb the gloomy stairs to the ground floor. In the hallway I eyed the cumbersome black payphone and picked it up.

'Oh.' It was Rose, sounding breathless. 'You're there, are you? I knew it. You're at that woman's house.'

I was profoundly annoyed that she had hunted me down. I was forced to listen to a barrage of cliches: she wasn't happy. What was Christie to me? Was Christie in the house right now? How dare I betray her like this?

As she bleated on, I silently solved the puzzle of how she had found Christie's number. Earlier that afternoon we'd been at Radley Road. I had been consulting my address book and left the damn thing out while I went to the bathroom.

'Who is Christie?'

'Nobody really,' I said casually. 'We once shared digs together in the most dreadful guest house.' Smiling, I moved my gaze from the paint-flaked front door, past a stand of grotesque walking sticks, over the coat stand and its scrum of overcoats yanked up by their necks.

'And what is she to you now?'

'Just a part of my past.'

'Don't lie! Why are you with her now?' She started snivelling.

'She is ill,' I protested. 'She never gets out. There are some people who – it would be simply criminal to abandon.'

'I can't believe this is happening,' she wailed. I held the receiver away from my ear. I was not enjoying shivering in that cold hall like a paying lodger.

'There's no need to worry,' I said at last. 'I'll see you in the morning when we can talk all this nonsense over.'

There was a long silence. I thought I heard the ghost of a click sounding on the line. I gently set the receiver down and moved to peer up the stairs into the gloom. I could see nothing. The stairway yawned steep, unlit, obscure.

Returning to pick up the receiver, I could hear Rose's tiny voice still burbling on inside it. There was an unattractive wobble in her vocal cords. She was sorry but it was over. It wasn't healthy. It wasn't normal. She had to think about her little boy.

I could guess who was behind this pathetic confrontation and said her name.

'Lorraine?' she snapped back. 'No. Why would I tell her about us? Except to ask her if any of this is remotely normal.'

'Do you even know what normal means?' I challenged. 'Normal is for bores and cowards. If you carry on like this, I'll tell that husband of yours all about us. He'll drop you and keep your precious boy-child for himself.'

'I don't think so,' she shot back. 'You breathe a word to Phil and I'll ruin you. I've looked up the address. There's something not quite right about all this, isn't there?'

'Come off it, darling. You sound tired. Has that child of yours been wearing you out?'

Silence rang in my ears. When she spoke again she was frantic.

'My God. Phil's back. Let's talk tomorrow.'

'OK. How about two o'clock?'

'No, no. I've booked a flu jab. First thing? Radley Road at seven-thirty. For the last time.'

I jerked my ear away from the loud bang of the receiver and ugly burr of the dialling tone. Thank God for the frightful Phil's return, I told myself. I'd had enough of Rose's tantrums.

A telltale creak sounded from the landing. Halfway up the stairs the gloom gathered so that anything could be waiting there. The electrical wiring needed attention; the house had always been feebly lit.

'Christie? Come down and show yourself.'

She gave no reply, save for a second groan of the floorboards as she retreated further upstairs. She would detest my being telephoned like this. I waited for a minute or so, goosebumps rising on my neck from the draught whistling in from the gaps around the front door.

It was going to be a stormy night. And Christie was playing games. I returned to the parlour, turned the gas fire up and retrieved the scrapbook. Now that I'd been interrupted by Rose's nonsense it would be a pleasure, albeit a rare and clandestine one, to review her collection of clippings.

I had once heard that if a medieval man were to travel by time machine to a modern operating theatre, he would think himself inside a chamber of horrors. It was a most intelligent remark. Adjust the dial of his time machine to the Victorian age or even the early twentieth century, and the argument grows ever more convincing. Christie's collection was quite unique: experimental surgery, electrical therapies, extraordinary machines. And photographs too, forming a quite exceptional historical archive. Macabre but fascinating from a professional view. It was an outlet, I suppose, for all those unruly thoughts of hers.

An hour later I set the album down. The silence stretched ever tighter above me. I knew I should leave, sleep in my own bed, and mentally prepare myself for a demanding Monday morning at the hospital. And damn Rose – I now had to get there even earlier to coax her into silence.

In the end I bedded down in the parlour, listening to the upper storeys of empty guest rooms creaking above me as the wind worried the old house, rattling the roof tiles and snapping tree branches against the windows. Christie remained mute but the house was alive with her black thoughts. They thickened the air steadily, like the tide of darkness that swallows the earth in a solar eclipse.

It must have been after two in the morning when I heard

her tread approaching at last. She came to me and we talked, two disembodied voices whispering in impenetrable darkness. She slid her hand into mine and it felt childish and so cold, as if she'd just stepped inside from the cold winters of the past. I caressed her pitiful fingers; almost nothing and no one moves me these days, but Christie's situation is truly sorrowful. And I owe her everything. Her pain spoke to me as Rose's never could.

'I heard every word,' she said. 'I won't let that little tart ruin you. I'll sort it out. We have no choice.'

Warm-heartedness

Question 6: I feel good when I understand other people's feelings and emotions.
   A. True
   B. Uncertain
   C. False
High score description (option A.): Attentive to others, good-natured, kindly, easy-going.

Monday 21st February

It was Monday morning and Lorraine had to drag herself up and face that god-awful job again. The house had no hot water, so she shocked herself awake with a cold splash before pulling on a nylon blouse salvaged from Oxfam, an old midi-skirt of her mum's, American Tan tights and scuffed three-inch-heeled court shoes. She clattered down the uncarpeted stairs and clicked on the electric heater's orange bars. God, the place was dispiriting. After the landlord of her last flat decided to sell up, the chance to rent a condemned house had looked like a clever gamble on Salford's Regeneration Scheme.

As time passed it was feeling like a bad mistake. Each month she wrote to the council about their statutory duty to rehouse her. To date no one had bothered to reply.

A blackened cast-iron cooking range dominated the front room, so unwieldy that she rarely had the energy to light a fire. Her own stuff stood around like temporary props: the upright piano and Fender copy guitar; the poster of Rachael, the replicant from *Blade Runner*; and prints by Escher and Kandinsky. The books from her Humanities degree were arranged on brick and plank shelves, from Kafka's *The Castle* to Carter's *The Bloody Chamber*, and well-thumbed textbooks: Millett's *Sexual Politics*, Barthes's *Mythologies* and Berger's *Ways of Seeing*.

In contrast, by her armchair lay the new postgrad books she was avoiding: *Employment Law*, *Personnel Policy and Practice* and *Industrial Relations*. It was hardly the heady mix of ideas and inspiration she had enjoyed for three self-indulgent, grant-funded years. Warming her insides with hot tea and jam-smeared toast, she inspected the remains of yesterday's make-up. Cold cream melted yesterday's nubs of mascara and eyeshadows of shocking pink and peacock green. Late nights had left dark shadows which she dabbed with Hide and Heal, before brushing on lip gloss and bronze eye shadow. Finally, she tugged a brush through dry bleached hair.

The soaring melody of U2's 'New Year's Day' faded out and Dave Lee Travis announced the news for Monday 21st February. It was the same old droning resistance to seat belts and alarm at a new coin to replace the trusty green pound note. She switched it off when the announcer gave an update on that freak from the Jobcentre called Nilsen, who had been caught with a flat full of dismembered body parts.

Pulling open the curtains, she started at the reflection of her own ghostly silhouette. Fog. The usual view along Balaclava Street – dilapidated terraces, the skeletal roofless church, the corner shop advertising 'Ales & Stouts' – was hidden. She would be late for work. She hurtled upstairs in a panic.

Jasmine was a small bump beneath a balding candlewick bedspread, only her profile visible in strings of fair hair. The game book, dice and score-pad were scattered over the bed, witness to the previous night's efforts to find the correct path through the labyrinthine citadel. Even her daughter's Star Wars figures in their home-made cardboard spaceship had been abandoned for the puzzle book. The two of them had stayed up far too late, engrossed.

'It's all right, Mum.' Jas's eyes opened wide. In a few whirlwind minutes Lorraine bundled her out of bed, pulled on her daughter's clothes and set a piece of toast in her hand before hauling her out to the rusty red Metro. Peering through the misted windscreen, she steered the car slowly, trying to dodge kerbs and bollards and the sheets of flat metal that closed off half the condemned streets.

Jas was rhythmically kicking her foot against the seat. Finally, she twisted around in the passenger seat and stared solemnly up at her.

'You got my two pounds for the gymnastics trip, Mum?'

She did a quick calculation. No way. It was still five days till payday.

'Mrs Dearden said it's got to be *today*.' Jas's voice poked deep into her conscience.

'Listen, I haven't got much left till I get paid. Here's a pound note. I'll speak to your teacher if you like.'

* * *

On the main road the traffic was crawling at less than twenty miles an hour as she edged the Metro into a line of disembodied yellow headlamps. She passed the chained and padlocked entrance to Salford Docks every day, but this morning it looked especially mournful in the mist. With three million unemployed, she tried to convince herself she was one of the lucky ones driving to a job.

Clicking her band's rehearsal tape into the cassette player, the sound of Dale's jangly guitar riff absorbed her attention as she jerked the car forward in fits and starts. Words bubbled up in her mind and she began to sing, vocalising the melody line she had been struggling with:

> *'Finding my way in the dark,*
> *Trying to follow a spark.'*

'That's not bad, Mum.'

'Well thank you,' she answered gravely. This time when she sang Jas joined in:

> *'Frightened of moving,*
> *You're frightened of choosing,*
> *Finding a way in the dark . . .'*

Jas's voice was just one of the things she loved about her; together their voices harmonised beautifully.

'Hey, you wanna be in my band?' Lorraine nudged her.

'My band, my band, yeah!' Jas echoed the Gary Glitter tune.

They both giggled for a moment. At the next set of traffic lights Lorraine scribbled down her new chorus on an old envelope.

* * *

36

Guilt returned as she pulled up at the Carneys' house. It was larger but danker than her own place, its only attraction that it stood opposite St Michael's Primary. No one answered her hammering at the peeling door, though the malevolent faces of two little Carney boys watched from an upstairs window. Eventually Mrs Carney yelled from the window above, to 'Just leave 'er in front of th' telly and I'll be right down.'

Lorraine steered Jas into the grubby living room. Please, she prayed silently, let those empty cans of Special Brew not be Mrs Carney's. She looked at the foul cat litter tray and food-spattered copy of *The Sun*. Why the hell did schools not open until ten to nine, far too late for any parent with a normal job? All through her degree Jasmine had been happy and safe at a well-run council nursery. Now schools and their rigid opening times were the bane of her life.

She leant down and kissed her daughter. 'Honest sweetheart, I'll ring the council today for a new childminder.'

All along Langworthy Road she wondered how long it might take to find a new minder for Jas. Distracted, she steered into the wrong avenue. Soon she was as lost as the persona in her song, driving in circles up and down short curving streets of identical 1930s semis. The area was familiar and yet the fog cast a deceptive veil; vapour-wreathed side roads disappeared as quickly as she spotted them. The car's digital clock displayed two minutes to nine. 'No, no,' she pleaded to the Fates. 'I cannot be late.'

A pale figure sprang into view a few yards in front of the feeble headlamps. She hammered both feet down onto the clutch and brake. The car bucked, slithered a few heart-stopping feet, and then stopped only a few inches from the pedestrian.

'Rose!' Standing rigid in the road was the hospital's medical records officer, camouflaged in the kind of beige raincoat only a pensioner should wear. She was staring across the way, her face blank.

Lorraine swung the car over to some railings, clicked off the music and wound down her window.

'It's me. You OK? Get in, I'm late and I can't find the hospital in this blasted fog.'

Rose was still in some sort of daze, staring backwards.

'I'll try not to kill you, honest,' Lorraine shouted good-humouredly. 'Come on. I'm going to miss the post meeting.'

Slowly Rose manoeuvred herself into the passenger seat. As she directed Lorraine in monosyllables, the maze of avenues grew familiar.

Lorraine glanced at her colleague, whose honest, girlish face was really rather lovely. Today, however, she appeared flushed and agitated.

'You all right?' Lorraine asked quietly.

Rose exhaled wearily, turning to the window.

'Is it Phil?'

Rose shook her head.

'Not this flu? You look feverish, love.'

'I just can't stand it.' As she spoke her voice cracked. 'I've got to get away from here.' She wiped away sudden tears with the back of her hand.

'Oh, love. Here. I've got that hanky you lent me.'

Lorraine pulled the embroidered hanky she'd borrowed out of her pocket.

Rose blew her nose hard and then held the cloth against her seeping eyes.

'Shall I drive you home?'

Rose shook her head helplessly. 'No. Phil's still there. I don't know what to do.'

'If you need a break, go to see your GP and get signed off. Things always look different after you've had a rest.'

'No one can help me,' she whimpered.

'I bet they can. Come and talk to me, hey?'

She shook her head dismissively but mumbled, 'Thank you.'

'Don't thank me. Oh God, we're here.'

The bulk of the hospital had come into view on the crest of a hill – a Palladian mansion built of sooty yellow bricks in the philanthropic 1870s. Like a great ark it floated on an ocean of sulphurous fog, wakeful and bustling, rows of jaundiced lights showing at every window. Breathing in the bitter air, they climbed the steps to the entrance and stepped onto the main corridor.

A porter was manoeuvring a trolley bearing a patient so cadaverous that his skin was like mottled parchment. They both stepped aside to make way for a lad in torn trousers who limped along on a pair of crutches. Distracted and pale, Rose waved her goodbye with a bitter, 'Time to plaster my fake smile on.'

Passing through the admin office, Lorraine arrived at the hospital administrator's oak door, where the post meeting's muffled voices reached her, sounding aggrieved.

Well, I suppose they can't kill me, she thought grimly and tried to ease her way inside without making a sound.

Conservatism

Question 7: What this world needs is:
    A. To build on the past and what works well
    B. Uncertain
    C. To create a more advanced and improved future
High score description (option A.): Respecting traditional values, nostalgia, looking to the past and the familiar.

Lorraine tiptoed around the edge of Norman's office but ruined the effect by dropping her satchel. To her mortification the white bullet of a tampon tumbled out and rolled across the parquet floor. Doctor Strang and Mike McClung both spotted it and looked away. Chasing the object of shame into a corner, Lorraine whisked it into her pocket. God, if only she had the nerve to walk out and drive straight home again.

Norman Pilling, the administrator, was thankfully addressing her with his eyes characteristically closed.

'Twenty-one minutes past nine. How can you reprimand your colleagues for lateness, Miss Quick, when your own timekeeping is so appalling?'

Suddenly Norman's watery eyes opened and peered over

the top of steel spectacles. Above him hung a portrait of the Queen looking equally disapproving.

Lorraine could have recited the terms of the Employment Act, that bad weather was a mitigating circumstance for lateness, but had learnt never to answer back. The idea of the post meeting was to empty Norman's in-tray into his team's reluctant hands; a game of pass the parcel with the dreariest of forfeits. Now he pushed a bundle of heavy papers in her direction.

'We were discussing the flu crisis. Be sure all staff avail themselves of the inoculation programme.'

She glanced through the bundle: pay rates for physios, health circulars and the inoculation bulletin. She rapidly scanned the reasons to have a flu jab and a phrase jumped out at her: 'Prevent your family members from catching flu and missing school or work.' Now that was surprisingly useful. Tuning back into the administrator's speechifying, she assumed a pose of rapt attention.

'Harvey Wright, Salford's director of personnel, will be speaking at this afternoon's meeting. He tells me he has extraordinary news.'

Doctor Strang grasped the arms of his chair as if about to launch himself at Norman. 'Excuse me! What about my agenda item on this idiotic computerisation? I've told Rose Cavanagh to come along and brief us on all the disasters waiting to happen.'

Strang was head of general surgery and also the medical director, a man of forty with long hair, scruffy corduroys and scuffed shoes. He was said to be brilliant, but Lorraine only felt his presence as a series of toxic explosions she instinctively shrank away from.

An intense, bearded young man with eyes set too close together broke the silence. 'The trouble is, Doctor Strang, contractors have already connected the cables. The computer suite is ready and waiting.'

It was a rare contribution from Mike McClung, chief engineer, the loner of the group.

'We need to get the medical records loaded,' chipped in Raj Patel, the chief accountant. 'Can't have the ward clerks playing Space Invaders, eh?'

Lorraine made a point of not catching Raj's impish eye. He had a habit of pulling ridiculous faces that had cost her some excruciating fits of laughter.

'They may as well play games for all the sense those records make,' snapped Doctor Strang.

'Now, now.' Norman raised a bony hand. 'A compromise is needed. I see Rose outside. Fetch her, Lorraine.'

Even though she was sitting furthest from the door, Lorraine had to squeeze delicately past the rest of the team. It seemed incredible that only last year she had debated *The Female Eunuch* in a university tutorial and sworn never to bow and scrape to a man again.

The only other woman in the room, Chief Nurse Felicity Jardine, also remained resolute in blocking Lorraine's way. Felicity had proved to be no sisterly ally to Lorraine. She had been bemused to find that the chief nurse was considered something of a sex bomb. Her green eyes were habitually amused but the joke was not generally shared with Lorraine. She wore an auburn Bonnie Tyler perm from which large plastic earrings peeped out. All her outfits had a deeply plunging neckline that revealed two cantilevered breasts and a glimpse of lacy bra. It fascinated Lorraine that men appeared half-stunned by her full-frontal approach and generally did as they were told.

Lorraine reached the door and passed Norman's request on to Rose. 'Yes, I can do my talk straight after Mr Wright's presentation,' Rose said, lingering in the doorway without enthusiasm. 'Though I am having a flu jab at two o'clock. Or I could cancel it.'

'No, if you have an appointment you must keep it.' Norman was always excessively firm on trivial decisions. 'You must all set an example. Shall we say two-thirty prompt for your presentation, Rose? Very well, everyone.'

Keen to prevent the childcare disaster of Jasmine catching flu, Lorraine made straight for the phone in the admin office just outside and dialled the flu nurse.

'A jab for me, please, Sister Ince. No, not pregnant or allergic to eggs. Ten to two. Just before Rose, then.'

Raj gestured to speak next.

'Just a sec, Sister,' Lorraine added. 'Mr Patel wants a jab too. He might be pregnant though.' She prodded Raj's ballooning stomach.

The accountant pulled a comically affronted face and took the phone.

From nowhere Rose crept up behind her and said in a voice so quiet that no one else might hear, 'Got a minute?'

Lorraine followed her a few yards down the corridor towards the boardroom.

'Can I speak to you later, after all? You are sworn to keep confidences, aren't you?' Rose spoke in a breathless undertone. 'I've got to tell someone about what's going on.'

'Course. What about after the meeting.' She touched Rose's arm.

'Thanks a million. See you then.'

Rose disappeared and Lorraine followed in her wake. She was surprised to find Doctor Strang and Felicity huddled close behind her back. And there too was Mike McClung, waiting behind them like an abandoned child. For an instant she wondered if they might have overheard Rose's anguished words.

Erratic Lifestyle

Question 8: I enjoy taking stimulants and doing wild things.
 A. Often
 B. Occasionally
 C. Never
High score description (option A.): Undependability, thrill-seeking, recklessness, impulsivity.

A God Almighty hammering woke Rikki from the rags of a sleep he'd been clutching at. A fearsome voice thundered through the plywood door.

'Open up! Where's me fucking scratch, man?'

Rikki clung to the stained mattress, holding his breath.

'I need five hundred notes off of you, pussy boy.'

Rikki's arms and legs started shaking. To his horror the door started to move, bending beneath Buda's fist. Jesus Christ, the door handle was turning. He braced himself for a lethal kicking, his toes squirming into the sheet.

Nothing happened. He swivelled his head around and this time saw his normal bedsit again. For fuck's sake, the door lock had held tight. He was having the agonies, his eyes were seeing stuff that wasn't really there.

'I'll be back, you little ponce. You better get my cash or say goodbye to them drums of yours.'

The footsteps receded. Rikki raised his eyes to the glittering heap of his drum kit. He had to keep hold of it. Pinned above it was a cut-and-paste poster of Electra Complex that he'd torn down after a gig. Course, he wasn't in the picture himself, being the new and only lad in the band, but they would invite him pretty soon. Finally daring to move, he searched around his mattress but the only pill bottle he could find shook out empty. Just his fucking luck. He was going to have to get hold of some cash to keep his drums safe from Buda. Somehow. Anyhow. But first he needed to straighten up. He wiped warm liquid from his streaming eyes and nose. If he stayed here he'd die, either from a fit of the heebie-jeebies or on the end of Buda's steel bootcaps. It was time to get up and go. Time to feed his fucking habit.

He was glad of the fog. Rattling along on the bus, the murk felt like a mysterious force concealing his presence from a giant suspicious eye that watched from the sky. He had cadged some downers and smoked some weed with Jerry, so at least the shakes had stopped. Still, he was glad that the fog hid him till he saw the hospital lights glowing yellow.

It was like returning home, that was how he felt as he limped through the double doors onto the main corridor. It was funny how his hip started to kill him just like the old days as he hobbled along the buffed lino, mimicking the downcast faces of genuine patients. The smell of disinfectant hadn't changed, and never completely stifled the deeper stench of rot. Yet it was a comforting smell, one he knew as well as his own breath. He wondered if he could cadge a free night or two in a nice crisp bed if he kicked up a fuss in Casualty.

Then his luck turned. He was traversing a corridor punctuated by consulting rooms and waiting areas. There was that buzz of collective brainpower; the medics marching about looking hugely expert, even the clerical staff self-importantly wheeling trolleys of records about. He spotted a nurse with her back turned to her trolley. It was her drugs trolley, to be exact, a wheeled box of delights loaded up with top-class gear. Rikki stopped at a noticeboard and pretended to read the notices. The dim cow was simpering to a patient in pyjamas. From the corner of his eye he studied the packets and bottles peeping at him a few feet away. Come and get us, ready or not, they seemed to say.

He began walking, keeping his head down as he checked the time on his watch. A moment later he was directly beside the drug cart and in a flash had reached inside and transferred a big brown bottle and a plastic carton to the inside of his camouflage jacket. Keep walking mate, he told himself. Nice and steady does it.

In the gents he inspected his haul. Not bad. A carton of sleepers and sixteen dreamers. He leant back against the wall, slipped a few gritty morphine tabs into his mouth and swallowed their bitterness with saliva. He was feeling better already.

He found the canteen and had a cup of tea with piles of sugar, enjoying the school dinner clatter and wonky trays. It was as if a benevolent authority was keeping everyone comfortable, cooking their food and washing their dishes. Lighting a fag, he observed the staff closely, remembering that navy trousers meant physios, maroon was X-ray, green meant Occupational Health. The nursing sisters wore neat navy dresses and the ordinary nurses pale blue with those plasticky white hats. It was all coming back to him. He scanned the room for pharmacists but couldn't pick them out from the medics and lab technicians. He'd have to get close enough to read those name badges.

It was hours till he had to get going for band practice. He picked up a copy of *The Sun*, and after that, a staff newsletter. He skimmed over charity donations, a fun run, plans for a new computer suite. His eyes strayed over an article about a new X-ray machine for Occupational Health. Beneath a blotchy photo was a caption. And names: Norman Pilling, Unit Administrator; Doctor Victor Strang, Medical Director; Mr Harvey Wright, Director of Personnel; Felicity Jardine, Chief Nurse; Mike McClung, Chief Engineer; Raj Patel, Chief Accountant; Sister Ince, Infection Control Nurse.

As he read, he was startled by that name he hadn't seen in years. He stared at it and the job title beside it. It couldn't be. But it was. The picture was one of those poor reprographed jobs, so all you could see were over-inked outlines on the cheap paper. He hunched over the table, hiding his face in his palms.

Disturbing scenes played in his head from when he had been eight years old. Of being alone. Unable to move. Staring into a mirror. His legs were fixed tight inside a contraption. It was like a scene from *The Omen* or something. He'd struggled and twisted, desperate to be free. He wanted to be himself again, at home, running and jumping and kicking a ball. He had looked up into the mirror again. His little boy eyes were bulging, his skin was shiny. He was scared. If he didn't get free, he might stay like that for ever.

'Give us a bit of room, mate!' A patient in a wheelchair knocked into him, trying to get past with a loaded tray.

Rikki jerked backwards. He was struggling to take it in, that Diggers, the nickname everyone on the whole ward had used, worked here. That very special person who had got so close to him as a child. He remembered Diggers' hand, professionally slick in a latex glove, stroking his face.

I've found you, he muttered to himself. Looking pretty well set up these days. I wonder if you still think about me? Well, I haven't forgotten you, my friend.

A couple of nurses at the next table were staring at him, speaking with lowered voices. So what if he looked like a loony, mumbling to himself? Reopening the newsletter, he looked for any more mentions of Diggers but found none. Finally, he reached the vacancies page at the back.

Wanted – General Porter
Must be flexible for variable shifts. Good rate of pay and overtime.
Closing date: Monday 21st February.
Apply to Lorraine Quick, Unit Personnel Department.

Just after eleven, Lorraine stretched her tense shoulders and looked up from the last of a series of difficult phone calls. Her assistant Edith's earwigging presence meant she hadn't yet rung the council about a new childminder. On an impulse she decided to head for the empty boardroom with her neglected paperwork and tackle it in peace.

All was silent on the admin corridor as Lorraine passed the closed flu clinic door. A handwritten sign announcing 'Staff

Flu Jabs. Take a seat and wait' had been taped to the door. Underneath was scrawled 'Back Soon'. Simply reading the words produced queasiness in Lorraine's gut. Then she was past it. The important thing was to banish the flu jab from her mind.

The thick-carpeted boardroom was her favourite part of the hospital. Traces of Victorian Gothic remained: star-spangled lamps and heavy brass door furniture. It was magnificent but also rather sad. She settled down beneath a lovely old plaque displaying the motto 'Caring Walls for Those in Need'. It was a shame about the ugly posters sellotaped over the oak panelling: 'Rabies: Don't hesitate. Shoot!' and NUPE's demand for a '12% Pay Rise for All Staff.'

She found the phone and dialled 9 for an outside line.

'Is that Child Services? I need a list of childminders.' While she waited she chewed on a dried-up sandwich left over from an early morning meeting.

'Gone to dinner? So how long do you get for dinner at the council?'

She crashed down the phone and began to scrutinise the applications for the junior doctors' rotation scheme. In the blissful silence she even dared to congratulate herself on arranging her day rather well. After Harvey arrived she need only sit back through a few presentations before her chat with Rose. For a moment she recalled Rose's talk of resignation, her high emotion, her need to confide. It had to be that trouble with Phil. Whatever it was, she would try to be a decent friend. Then she could finally head home.

Rikki hadn't even twigged that this was Lorraine's hospital. Jesus. Another one who'd got a fancy job title, another lucky bugger who'd had everything dropped in their lap. Lighting another fag, he leant back, feeling the morphine envelop him like a comfort blanket. When he felt like this, he could do anything.

He stood up and helped himself to a map of the building. He followed the map till he found Personnel up a flight of stairs. Luck was with him: the only person in the office was a very young, very straight-looking girl typing at a desk. What he assumed was Lorraine's much bigger desk stood messy with overflowing wire baskets and stained mugs. He summoned a veneer of cheeriness and walked inside, putting on the old hyper-friendly act as he asked the girl for an application form.

'Miss Quick around?'

'Oh, her. She's gone off somewhere.'

'I want to apply for the porter vacancy.'

Ten minutes later, he came back again with the form fancifully completed.

'Thanks, love.' He gave her his special cheeky grin.

The girl really looked at him this time and gave a hesitant smile back. It was a proper result so he threw out another line. 'Wish me luck, then.'

This time her face, childish and guileless, betrayed some inner calculation.

'I'm not really supposed to say, but chances are you might want to keep Thursday free.' Then very quietly she added, 'I sent the advert off too late. And we've had some fellas drop out.'

'Thanks for the tip-off. Maybe I'll be lucky enough to see you again?'

She grinned down at her typewriter keys. It was pathetic really.

'See you then, love.'

Jubilant, he decided not to go home just yet. He told himself that now he'd applied for a job he had an official reason to hang around the corridors and offices, inspecting his new place of work. There would be easy pickings with lots more to come. With luck he'd soon be wearing a porter's jacket, making him near enough invisible. Then it would be time for the next step: to say hello to Diggers after all these years.

A sharp rap at the boardroom window made Lorraine jump and then get up to investigate. The fog still lingered, moving very slowly like a living thing. She could just discern a forbidding shape behind the glass, a figure in a dark hooded outfit. Wiping the condensation away from the window's inside with her hand, she saw it was only Mike McClung waving at her with gloved hands. She waved back at him before watching him turn and disappear in a cloud of yellowish vapour.

Shrewdness

Question 9: When at work it is wisest to:
   A. Keep my true feelings to myself
   B. In between
   C. Show my emotions as I wish
High score description (option A.): Astute, private, discreet, shrewd, polished.

Lorraine worked until Harvey Wright joined her in the boardroom at ten to one. Her former boss and mentor greeted her with the headmasterly charm that served him so well. The rest of the team arrived in good time and, at one o'clock prompt, Harvey generated a wave of agitation by handing them each a confidentiality agreement to sign and return at once. Then he rose up at the table's head, a solid figure who emanated wisdom, from the shining dome of his head to the intelligence of his steady grey eyes.

'Thank you.' He paused and gazed at each of them in turn. 'My apologies for the air of mystery. As you know, the government has brought in this chap from Sainsbury's supermarket to give his verdict on the Health Service. He's saying that if Florence Nightingale were looking around here today, she'd be searching for whoever is in charge.'

He gestured towards a bronze statuette on a shelf of Florence Nightingale carrying her lamp aloft.

'Exactly what I've been saying for years,' interrupted Felicity. 'At last, the government wants to see Matron back in charge.'

Harvey raised his palm to silence her. Raj failed to stifle a snort.

'Let's not jump ahead too fast. I am delighted to announce that this hospital has been picked to test the future of the NHS. Mrs Thatcher has decided that she wants one general manager – one man or woman in each hospital – to hold all the power. And each of you here today – administrator, chief nurse, medical director, chief engineer, chief accountant – will have an equal chance of becoming its unchallenged leader.'

'But that's my job.' Norman's mouth hung open, showing yellowing dentures.

Not for much longer, Harvey's steady gaze appeared to confirm. Out loud he replied, 'I am afraid this is a very different role, Norman.'

Lorraine kept her face deliberately immobile: the hospital administrator was for the chop. She made a rapid assessment of her colleagues' chances. It would be a pain for her if Doctor Strang got the job and continually resisted every progressive change. The medic was leaning back in his chair, mulling it over. Suddenly he sprang forward, animated.

'We doctors would never choose to become glorified pen-pushers.'

'We'll be offering three-year contracts, Victor. That's time to make all the improvements you are always telling us you

54

want. And then stand down again, job done.'

Strang lifted an eyebrow. 'Hmm.'

Raj asked the next question. 'So the pay structure has been agreed?'

Lorraine cringed. It was a typical Raj blunder, reducing the whole issue to money.

'The job will be extremely well rewarded. Plus bonuses every year.'

Mike childishly raised his hand to ask a question. 'Who decides who gets the job?'

'A very important question, Mike. There'll be a representative from Whitehall on the interview panel.'

Lorraine was watching and listening hard. The hospital did need someone who could drag it into the new era. Mike McClung seemed like a lightweight but his battles with the doctors over medical electronics were quiet victories. She'd heard that if he took his talent over to America, he could earn as much as any physician. He might be the dark horse in the group.

On the other hand, Felicity looked as smug as a cat with the cream. She kept nurse staffing levels high while urging cuts everywhere else. Lorraine wondered if Felicity might try to flirt her way into the job. Surely not.

That left Norman, who was asking Harvey about how the new salary would apply to his own pay scale, apparently deaf to the death knell ringing for his career.

'Harvey.' Felicity raised a cherry-red fingernail in Lorraine's direction. 'Lorraine's not part of the management team. What's she doing here?'

Harvey smiled back benignly. 'Lorraine will assist me in the assessment process.'

He circulated a handout titled 'In Confidence – Timetable for Appointment of General Manager'.

'I need your application forms by the third of March. With your original qualifications and registration documents, of course. There'll be a panel interview and Lorraine will be administering psychometric tests.'

Lorraine will be what? If she'd heard right and he'd said psychometrics, she still had the exam to pass and tons of maths to learn: bell curves, formulae, tables of statistics.

She wanted to protest but asked, 'This is for when, exactly?'

Her former boss was watching her with grey eyes that didn't blink.

'It's in front of you. Fourteenth of March.'

That was less than a month. Now she'd have to spend every free evening and weekend cramming for the exam and still be barely competent on the day.

'Psychometric tests?' Doctor Strang stiffened, affronted. 'Mumbo jumbo more like.'

Before going on the course Lorraine would have felt some sympathy for Strang's position, fearing that testing was merely a way to stick people in boxes and slap a label on them. Now she knew that the best tests could be uncannily accurate. Maybe this was her chance to have an influence on who would run the hospital.

Feeling quietly excited, she said, 'Psychometric tests are an excellent method of identifying leadership traits.'

Harvey nodded appreciatively. 'The panel have asked for as much detail on each candidate's leadership style as possible. Tests are the best way to predict future behaviour.'

'And if we refuse to complete such a test?' Strang asked.

'You are entirely within your rights to do so,' Harvey

replied. 'But it will leave the selection panel with – unanswered questions.'

Harvey nodded to a canteen assistant waiting at the door with the tea trolley. The group formed uneasy huddles around the gigantic steel teapot. Lorraine remained seated, doodling heavy black crosses on her notepad. The price she would have to pay for selecting the hospital's future leader was a heavy one. She would no doubt unearth all her colleagues' anxieties and ego trips and then have to find neutral language to disguise how bloody weird they all were. They would probably all hate her for it. For ever.

A hand touched her arm. Felicity had sidled up, a mischievous look on her artfully made-up face.

'Just a second.' With a tight little smile, Felicity untied a price tag from the back of Lorraine's nylon blouse. After reading it she dangled it in front of her face.

'"Oxfam 50p." What would staff think if they saw that?'

Lorraine's answer was a shrug and grin. 'That I'm the one who really needs a big pay rise?'

Thank God Raj appeared beside them. 'Don't forget your flu jab, Lorraine. It's nearly ten to two.'

Antisocial Behaviour

Question 10: If people let me down, I enjoy getting my revenge.

    A. Often

    B. Occasionally

    C. Never

High score description (option A.): Breaking rules and social conventions, hostile and aggressive impulses, episodes of assaultive violent acting out, not seeing own behaviour as problematic.

Lorraine contemplated the flu clinic entrance with unease. At the sound of a banging door she was glad of the distraction that Rose's appearance brought, though her friend still looked utterly fed up. She sank down on a chair and nervously blew her nose on her cotton hanky before pushing it up her sleeve. It looked as if she had been crying.

'I am so sorry about all this,' she whispered to Lorraine. Shaking her head, she added, 'When I tell you, you'll think I've been unbelievably stupid.'

Lorraine touched her arm. 'I bet it's not that bad.'

'It is.' Rose gestured towards the boardroom door. 'I just can't work with these people any more. I'm frightened.'

'Frightened?' Lorraine hissed.

Before Rose could answer, the flu clinic door swung open and the pair fell self-consciously silent. Sister Ince stepped outside and peered at them, then spoke in a doleful Irish accent.

'Lorraine Quick, is it now? Get along inside.'

Lorraine followed the nurse and took the seat at a Formica table. Instantly her stupid phobia made her breathless – the fear of a sharp steel needle pushing inside her body and puncturing the protective layer of her skin. Then that grazing stab of pain. And a bead of dark red blood.

The nurse laid a paper form and biro on the table. 'Pop your name down there.'

Lorraine printed her details in shaky capitals beside a vaccine serial number. A tray with rolls of tape and sachets of sterilising alcohol was waiting. And a pack of sterile needles.

'God, I hate blood, needles, all that,' Lorraine protested. 'I'll try not to faint.'

'All over in a sec. Roll your sleeve up, now. Your left arm if you're right-handed.'

The nurse selected the next ampoule of vaccine and compared it to the serial number on the sheet. She wiped the rubber seal, then drew up the plunger to suck up the dose. Lorraine closed her eyes as the spike of the needle approached.

You cannot let Jasmine catch flu, a grown-up voice insisted in her head. She felt a prick of pain and an unpleasant sensation as the plunger was slowly pressed down.

And that was the end of it. She opened her eyes to see a little ball of cotton wool sticking to her arm beneath a strip of surgical tape. She stood up, buoyant from a flood of positive chemicals.

'Thanks. All the best with the rest.'

As Lorraine left, the nurse beckoned Rose inside. Raj had arrived and she slumped down next to him and waited for her heartbeat to slow. At last she could relax and look forward to picking up Jasmine.

Gradually the sound of Sister Ince speaking behind the thin partition reached her.

'Rose, Rose! Steady now.' The sister's words were muffled but distinct.

Hearing the sudden scrape and thud of furniture, Lorraine flinched away from the reverberating wall and snapped at Raj, 'Something's happening.'

She knocked on the door and called out, 'What's going on in there?'

Getting no answer, she flung the door open and stepped inside. Rose was lying twisted on the floor, her eyes closed, her legs tangled in a fallen chair.

Lorraine felt a spasm of shock. 'Oh God. Has she fainted?' She instinctively stooped to raise her friend upright but Sister Ince blocked her way, her hands raised as if to ward off interference.

'She's not breathing,' the sister said, in a choking voice. The nurse's face was pink and her eyes protruded.

'You sure?'

The nurse feebly pushed her back through the door. 'Call the crash team. And fetch some oxygen.'

Lorraine ran back to the boardroom. Thank God the team were still there, a tableau of calm faces around the table.

Breathless, she stopped in front of Doctor Strang.

'Rose can't breathe. After her flu jab. Sister Ince wants the crash team. And some oxygen.'

Strang flung down his gold pen and sprang out towards the corridor. He spoke backwards over his shoulder to Felicity. 'Call the crash code. Do it!'

In a moment he had vanished and the chief nurse was dialling the boardroom's phone. When Felicity spoke she was clipped and precise.

'Suspected adult respiratory arrest. Oxygen and defib. The old cloakroom opposite the boardroom. Currently the flu clinic. Now.'

Setting the receiver down she discarded her jacket, flushed and alert. 'I'll go and help,' she said and strode after Doctor Strang.

Lorraine took a sip of leftover cold tea, aware that her mouth was sandpaper-dry. Rose hadn't just fainted, it was much worse than that. Rose couldn't breathe. No, that couldn't be right. Sister Ince must have got in a muddle and overreacted. Raj appeared in the boardroom with a blank, baffled expression. She felt compelled to return and check on Rose.

Lorraine watched through the half-open clinic door, her hand pressed to her mouth. Rose still lay prone on her back on the floor. She was insensible; her face greyish-blue. Felicity was kneeling behind her, supporting her head in both hands. Doctor Strang crouched over Rose's chest. Her blouse was open, showing a white bra, as he pumped his hands rhythmically up and down on her sternum, methodically counting.

'Twenty-three, twenty-four, twenty-five. Pass me the

EpiPen,' he called over his shoulder to Felicity.

Doctor Strang pulled Rose's skirt up and plunged the needle of a syringe into her girlish thigh. Lorraine winced at the sight. Rose was looking less alive every moment.

Doctor Strang's anxiety was betrayed by a tic of his head. 'No pulse for – how long now, Felicity?'

The chief nurse glanced up at the clock on the wall.

'Three minutes forty seconds since we arrived.'

'That's 0.5 epinephrine. No response.' He lifted one of Rose's eyelids with seemingly gentle fingers. 'She could almost be anaesthetised.'

Sister Ince was hanging back further down the corridor, looking as if she might collapse. Lorraine went to her and took the sister's hand and felt a weak squeeze in return.

The nurse was rambling under her breath. 'It's never happened before. I don't feel well. I just did what I—'

Lorraine felt as though time had stuck in a loop. With every moment Rose looked less like her lively self and more like one of the sinister plastic dolls used for resuscitation training. When the crash team arrived in green scrubs Lorraine pressed back against the wall. Two nurses rolled along an oxygen tank in a wheeled cart and a moment later she heard the sound of gas hissing as the valve was opened. An ugly plastic mask covered half of Rose's face.

The flu clinic door was finally closed but still she listened to the commands, 'Start CPR,' 'Charge to three hundred joules,' and the loud order to 'Clear the area!'

Lorraine hung back a few feet away, with thoughts spooling round and round. Doctor Strang had said Rose might be anaesthetised. Come on, Rose. Just take one big breath. Don't leave us. Don't leave Tim. Don't leave me here on my own.

Seriousness

Question 11: Most people I know would rate me as a quiet and deep person rather than chatty and amusing.
    A. True
    B. Uncertain
    C. False
High score description (option A.): Silent, introspective, sober, taciturn.

Detective Sergeant Diaz was silently blazing at the wheel of the police Rover, hemmed into a jam of traffic on the East Lancs. The carriageway ahead was blocked by a jackknifed lorry so he was reduced to gently nudging the car forward, though his limbs were twitchy with impatience. He was hyped up all right – just that morning he'd been washing his hands in the gents when the chief super appeared beside him in the mirror, smoothing back his own immaculate silver hair.

'There you are, Diaz. A suspicious death just came in, a female manager at the Memorial Hospital. I'll have to put Brunt in charge but I've picked you as his bagman. The thing is, I'm relying on you to point the whole thing in the right direction. Everything bagged and logged, statements neat as a pin, every link tight in the chain of evidence. Can I depend on you, lad?'

Diaz made every effort to stand up to the scrutiny of the big man's rock-steady eyes. 'You can depend on me, sir.'

The chief met his eyes in the mirror. 'Good. I've got my eye on you. I like a man who keeps his brain working and his mouth shut. Some exciting training opportunities coming up on a new Major Crime Group. Impress me and I'll put you at the top of the list.'

'Thank you very much, sir.'

'Best not say a dicky bird to Brunt, eh? Off you go then, son.'

He had no idea how Brunt had found out about the chief super's approach but the old sweat definitely had.

'There's always one, lads,' Brunt had crowed to the rest of the team on his return from the canteen. 'The smart alec. The twerp with all the funny ideas. Shoe leather and arm-twisting've kept me on top of Salford's villains for thirty years. And nowt's going to change on my watch.'

And now here he was, the old duffer's bagman on what might be a massive murder case. He'd investigated a few suspicious deaths before but nothing like this. Today's victim was a respectable wife and mother with a serious job and not even a speeding ticket. Reading between the chief super's lines, was Brunt up to the job?

His boss had just got his pipe going, filling the cab with a blue fug of sweet briar. 'The doc who rang in. He thinks this flu jab might've been tampered with. I've got the post-mortem booked for tonight.'

Brunt paused to give a loud burp and Diaz looked away.

So, the pathologist had been tracked down and a post-mortem was being rushed through. Thank God Brunt seemed on the ball. But had he looked at all the possible options?

'Right you are,' Diaz said. 'Course it could be a mix-up in the pharmacy, or at the drug company. Remember that attempted sabotage at Safeway supermarket last year, someone claiming their tins were spiked with paraquat?'

'Don't feel like that sort of goings-on to me. The doc had a quick word with the hospital pharmacy. Witnesses saw the vaccine all sealed up when the flu nurse came for them.'

On the other side of the windscreen nothing was happening. Diaz slapped the wheel in irritation.

'How long till the ruddy fire boys get here and cut a way through? I mean, there's no one hurt.' He glared at the shock-faced lorry driver whom he blamed for the delay.

He wound down his window and stuck his head out, taking in a lungful of acrid smoke as he searched for a way around mangled steel and rubber.

'Now I don't want you getting carried away with loads of pointless tests, son. Just prints and statements, all right?'

'But this could be murder, sir.'

'No one ever caught a scrote at the bottom of a microscope.'

Christ, he'd had enough. With a blast of the siren, Diaz slammed down his foot and spun the wheel through his hands, aiming to shoot forward through a narrow gap between the wreck of the lorry's cab and the steel barrier.

'Eh, watch that headlamp!' Brunt had finally woken up.

'No tests,' Diaz muttered through gritted teeth as the Rover barely missed the cab's bumper. They were through to a clear stretch of road, so he pushed the pedal down to release a satisfying roar.

Lorraine was back in the boardroom, sitting dejectedly at the table with the rest of the management team. She had managed a quick call to her mum to ask her to pick Jasmine up from the Carneys', but now the clock had worked around past five o'clock.

A flabby old man with a drinker's nose arrived and stood at the head of the table exactly where Harvey had been a short while earlier. They all looked grave: Raj, Felicity, Norman, Sister Ince, Harvey. Doctor Strang still had his necktie flung over his shoulder and sweat gleaming on his face.

The old bloke introduced himself as Chief Inspector Brunt and addressed them stonily.

'I can confirm that Mrs Cavanagh did not recover consciousness. I am afraid she died a short time ago.'

Sister Ince made a little shrieking whimper and wiped her eyes on the back of her hand.

'Good God,' Norman muttered, standing up suddenly. 'I must inform the chairman.'

'Hold your horses, sir.' Brunt looked around the room, his eyes flicking back and forth, as if the team might make a run for it. 'I'm afraid we must treat this tragedy as a sudden and unexplained death.'

Mutterings of incredulity broke out around the stuffy room. Brunt raised his palm to silence them. 'I need you all to remain here in this room until called in for questioning.'

Diaz was watching with close attention through the open boardroom door. First impressions were of a bunch of hospital managers looking grouchy at not being allowed to go home. From what he'd heard, only seven people had known the time of the victim's appointment. It was possible that one of this lot

66

had killed their colleague. And he was blowed if he'd let Brunt mess up the inquiry.

Brunt had planned their essential first hour in a tiny hospital side room.

'Key witness is the nurse who gave the jab. Ince is the name. Lives alone in one of them council flats near the Precinct. I'll take her and you take the personnel officer, Lorraine Quick. Both women hung about all through the resuscitation attempts. What did they see? Did anyone interfere with the vaccine? Quick had the previous appointment to the victim. Did she use that to switch the drugs? Don't let her go home till you've got to the bottom of it.'

When Lorraine Quick finally appeared in the makeshift fingerprint room, he had an idea that he recognised her. Her name meant nothing, yet hadn't he seen her in some pub or other? She was tall, blonde, pale, with black-lined eyes and the slightly dazed air of many witnesses to a serious crime.

He watched her give her fingerprints. Beneath the signs of shock she was keeping it together. Not remotely frightened of the Greater Manchester Police. Then Bodge, one of the scene of crime bods, ran sticky tape over her clothes for fibres. She gave him a look as black as sin.

'What are you trying to do? Take my bra size?'

He had to turn his face aside to hide his grin at that. Bodge was famous for his roving hands.

As she wiped her own hands clean on a paper hanky, he stepped forward.

'Miss Quick? I'm Detective Sergeant Diaz. If you could show me the way to Mrs Cavanagh's office.'

They processed in silence along near-empty corridors until

they descended a narrow iron staircase. Reaching the bottom, she turned and looked up at him from the basement's gloom, her face pale beneath bleached hair. As she clicked the lights on, their amber glow illuminated a low cave-like space, its walls lined from floor to ceiling with racks of suspended files.

'Looks like the paperless office is a long time coming,' she said.

She reached a low iron door, like a cell in an old lock-up. Opening it, she clicked on the light and ushered him in.

'Rose's office,' she announced. It was an oppressively low chamber full of teetering piles of paper, airless and dusty. He flicked through the drawers and picked up a government issue 1983 diary and stuck it in his pocket. There was nothing else worth sifting through tonight.

'OK then,' he said, directing her to leave.

While she locked up, he looked around the low anteroom and spotted a desk and chairs in the corner.

'I'll take your statement over there,' he said. 'That way we won't be interrupted.'

She nodded and took a seat at a forty-five-degree angle from him – avoiding going head to head, interrogation style.

'Right. Tell me, slowly and clearly, everything that happened today.'

Under the narrow beam of an anglepoise lamp, Diaz wrote in his notebook as she gave her account. The first prickle of excitement came when she described meeting Rose in the fog.

'So that was one minute to nine, you say. And where was that?'

She shook her head. 'I was lost in the fog and didn't recognise the place.' She looked up at the ceiling, frowning. 'But I'm sure I can find it again.'

'OK.'

Next, he made her run carefully through how she, Rose and Raj had made their appointments, and then Rose's appeal to her to have a private chat that afternoon. The fact that Miss Quick had then gone to the boardroom so much earlier than the others sounded suspicious to him, but she appeared unconcerned.

'You didn't try the flu clinic door?'

'No. It was closed and I knew Sister Ince was at the infection control meeting. I've just had a terrible thought. Maybe someone went down there and swapped the vaccine while I was there?'

He remained deadpan.

'So you were alone until—?'

She told him how Mike had knocked and disappeared around noon. Then Harvey arrived early, about ten to one. Then all the others came along. Rose wasn't part of it, she explained. Her eyes suddenly welled up as tears gathered.

She spent a minute with her head deep in her hands. When she raised her face she looked younger and less assured, her lashes spiked by tears. 'What about Tim?' she asked huskily. 'How's Rose's little lad doing?'

Diaz didn't have a clue. He was about to protest that welfare was for women officers when it struck him that Tim Cavanagh was the same age as he'd been when his parents died.

'I'll check he's all right as soon as we're done,' he said. 'Now take your time. Did you notice anything different about the vaccine? Yours, or the next one, intended for Rose?'

She shook her head. 'Do you think someone switched it? It could have been me who died. What do you think?'

'Did you notice the colour of the vaccine?'

She pressed her fingers against her mouth. 'No. I can't stand injections. I didn't look at the needles.'

'Do you have any idea why Rose needed to talk to you?'

She looked deep into his eyes as if urging him to help her. Her eyes were bluey-green, flecked with gold around the dilated pupils.

'She couldn't face her job. She wanted to resign. Just before she went in she said she'd done something stupid and was frightened.' With a little yelp she added, 'If only I'd taken her home.'

He watched her carefully as he framed his next question.

'Did you ever suspect she was seeing someone else outside her marriage?'

Lorraine broke eye contact to check the time. She was late and wanted to think over Rose's veiled accusation before dragging Phil into this. 'No, Rose wasn't like that. Look, it's nearly six. I have to go.'

'OK. Read your statement through and sign it when you're ready.'

He pushed it across to her and stood up, restlessly inspecting the racks of cardboard files. From the corner of his eye he watched her closely, not sure why.

'These records.' He waved his open hand up to the stacks of files. 'There must be lots of secrets down here.'

She didn't even look up. 'Sorry, those files are confidential.'

'There's nothing confidential now.'

She looked up sharply. 'I meant there are strict rules.'

If there was one thing he bloody well hated, it was being told what he couldn't do. 'There are no rules in a murder case,' he said.

He followed her upstairs to the personnel office beneath the clock tower. She was putting on her coat and packing a beat-up old satchel. The room was crammed with steel filing cabinets, leaflets and rotary phone card systems.

'Have you got everyone's personnel files?'

She checked the clock again. 'No. They're at District HQ. The building will be locked now. Will the morning do? I can call in and fetch them.'

He asked himself if it did matter; if she might tamper with the files.

'And your own personnel file? Where's that?'

'With all the others at HQ. The director of personnel is probably still downstairs if you want to check with him.'

'Bring them in first thing. We'll have an incident room set up by then.'

While she gathered her keys, something on Lorraine's desk caught his attention. A large ring binder with 'The PX60 Test Manual' emblazoned across it. It was a psychological testing manual.

'This yours?'

'Yeah, I'm just back from the training course in Oxford.'

'Oxford,' he echoed, reluctantly impressed.

He began flicking over the pages. A rare burst of excitement made him suddenly talkative. 'I love this stuff. There are some amazing ideas coming out from America, from the FBI. It's nothing like the plod work over here. They're testing murderers. Trying to get under their skin.'

She stepped around the desk to join him.

'And what is under their skin?'

'See this question?' he said. He read aloud. '"I am brought near to tears by other people's sad circumstances. A. Often,

71

B. Occasionally, C. Never." What would you say of yourself, Lorraine?'

She shrugged and said, 'You guess.'

'I'm guessing you don't cry too often, but as I've just witnessed – you do weep for a child who's lost his mother. The implication here is that you're tender-minded. Sensitive. Maybe more insecure than you think. Let's imagine that tenderness entirely wiped out. No tears. No pity for a motherless child. A soul that's cold and cruel and empty.'

She was listening to him now, her lips just parted, so he carried on. 'The Yanks use these to make what's called a criminal profile. Strange personalities, nothing like your common or garden criminal. From the outside they look to be living a normal life. But it's a mask, disguising a personality called a psychopath.' Reflexively, he touched the silver crucifix at his neck.

He found she was watching him, reappraising him perhaps.

'That's what we could have here in Rose's killer,' he added.

It had the desired effect. Lorraine stepped very close to him, suddenly tuned into his message. 'A psychopath? Here at the Memorial?'

Reputation Management

Question 12: It is wise to keep certain things private from others to preserve your own good reputation.

    A. True

    B. Uncertain

    C. False

High score description (option A.): Wearing a social mask, striving for good effect, saving face.

That last morning at Radley Road I had wanted nothing more than for Rose to remain as she had always been over the last few months: my sweet and vulnerable girl. But the silly bitch kept up the same old tune from the previous night. What did she expect if she stole a phone number from a person's private address book?

It says something for her sluttishness that I still got her into bed. With her clothes off she was like a crustacean without a shell: quivering, pliable and raw. But that morning she spoilt even sex by whining that this must be the last time. She never wanted to see me alone again. I looked down on her face with professional detachment. When she cried her porcelain skin grew blotchy and her features were really rather shrewlike. There was no point in continuing. I no longer wanted her.

I leant down and whispered in her little ear. 'You will suffer for this.'

She tried to pull back but couldn't. She was pinioned tight beneath me. 'What does that mean?'

I never answer such questions. I find the echo of silence so much more effective.

Her bloodshot eyes narrowed. 'Let me go. I want to get up.'

I let her squirm away and watched her dress, my body so unsated that I was tempted to hand out a hollow apology. Only when she was dressed and had the safe exit of the door at her back did she speak again.

'Don't you ever threaten me like that again. I drove around to see that place this morning. Has she got some sort of hold on you? I mean, why else would you spend time in that hideous slum? It's beyond belief.'

She was going to regret that little outburst. How dare she spy on me? And off she went, stamping heavily down the stairs.

I lay back on the bed and reflected. Rose was damned lucky Christie hadn't heard her speak to me like that.

Emotional Instability

Question 13: I sometimes feel upset and frustrated as I think of the day's happenings.
   A. True
   B. Uncertain
   C. False

High score description (option A.): Affected by feelings, easily upset, changeable.

Driving to Didsbury was like crossing the border into a foreign country. Lorraine parked the Metro amongst red-brick Italianate villas crowned with Gothic turrets and cupolas. But behind the ornate porches it was bedsit-land: a world of dark little landings, chipboard walls and shared kitchens, inhabited by students and deadbeats and drifters.

It was generous of Fred, an old hippy mate and electronics boffin, to let the band rehearse in his attic. But on a cold February night it had been hard to leave Jasmine in her mum's centrally heated flat and set off across town. Her mum had been irritated when Lorraine rang her at the newsagent and begged her to pick Jas up from the Carneys'. Then, when she'd reached the flat, the early evening TV news had come on and they'd both watched the item on the Memorial, appalled. Against an old photo of Rose, a grim voice announced, 'Police are questioning staff at the Memorial Hospital, Salford, after Mrs Cavanagh was given a flu vaccination . . .'

'God, Mum, whoever did it must be someone I know.'

Her mum came over and touched Lorraine's cheek. 'Poor, poor Tim. Can't you just leave that place? There's Jasmine to think of.' She looked fondly towards her granddaughter, who lay fast asleep on the settee. She was a sensitive, still-elegant woman at nearly sixty, half-French and in Lorraine's opinion, far too good for the life she now lived.

'I know. But I'm so close now to getting qualified.'

Her mum switched off the TV and hesitated over the photos of Lorraine's dad arranged on the shelves. In most of them he was playing his guitar – a lanky youth winning talent shows, and leading dance bands during her parents' happiest years just after the war.

'Someone rang about your dad this afternoon,' her mum confided later. 'Said they'd seen him playing in a club in London.'

Lorraine hated talking about her dad. The blunt fact was that one dark October night three years back he had left to play the guitar at Mr Jones's nightclub and never been seen again. He was the most natural musician she'd ever known. She hid a mix of pride, fury and – she hated to admit this – a bitter longing to see him, to know he was all right.

'How thrilling for him. Sent you some maintenance money, has he?'

Her mum shook her head.

In a rush of remorse Lorraine caught her mum's arm and

they hugged each other. It felt odd, but it was her mum who tried to reassure her. 'It'll all work out in the end, lovey,' she said gently into Lorraine's shoulder.

It felt more like midnight than eight by the time Lorraine lugged her gear up four flights of stairs lined with Red Stripe cans. By the time she'd given a rambling account of her day, every cell in her body felt drained of energy.

'I feel like I've been with the police for hours,' she told the others.

Lily, her oldest mate, shook back a tangle of black curls from her powder-white face and hugged her. They had met at Manchester Musicians Collective back in '77 and instantly bonded over the ambition to form a girl band amongst the hundreds of ramshackle DIY boy bands. The new wave meant no one needed flashy musical skills, just enthusiasm and attitude. Years of hanging out at the Electric Circus and the Factory club nights at the Russell Club had led to a string of misadventures but of fame and fortune, there was as yet no sign.

'That sounds heavy. I'd stay away from the pigs if I were you.' Lily had a justifiable reason to dislike the police after being wrongly arrested. There was no point in telling her that Diaz, at least, seemed on the ball.

'You saw, like, a real dead body? What'd it look like?' Dale was the band's newest member, a mediocre guitarist but possessor of a striking wardrobe of bandanas, pantaloons and white socks. When she answered their ad in the *NME* she had turned up in a child's frilly dress, ripped tights and surgical boots. 'With that look I can forgive her any bum notes,' Lily had said at her audition. With a few qualms Lorraine had agreed. She and Lily remained the decision-makers, the two founding members who had played their first gig with a synth and bass at Band on the Wall back in '78.

'She looked like Rose always looked, but not alive. Death isn't romantic like you think it is. Rose has a little boy. As for helping the police—' Lorraine turned to Lily. 'I'm a witness. I was standing right where it all happened.' God, she had to wipe her eyes again. Time to pull it together.

Picking up her bass, she started tuning up and remembered something. 'Any news about that tour, Lily?'

'Not yet. But listen. I've got some amazing news. There's a benefit for that missing persons charity who led the campaign to find Zeb. Gothenburg are going to be headlining so we've got to get on that bill. How about we all go to Rafters on Saturday? Talk to their manager?'

Lorraine hugged Lily, her shoulders thin beneath a black cobwebby jumper. 'Fantastic. I have a feeling this could even bring Zeb back.'

There had been something touching about the harmony between Lily and Zeb; her friend had been sweetly gentle with the volatile guitarist and steered him away from dangerous company. Lorraine remembered them as two heads of dark curly hair, huddled close together, whispering silly jokes and endearments. Then Zeb had begun to withdraw, either mumbling to himself or whispering incoherent stories about red eyes watching him through the cracks in the walls. Finally Zeb had trashed his room and disappeared back in 1980. It hadn't been the Greater Manchester Police's best moment when they arrested Lily and threw a list of charges at her, from kidnap to conspiracy to defraud her boyfriend of his royalties. She had been freed the next day, but Lily's bitterness had festered. No one wanted Zeb found as much as Lily.

'Cool,' said Dale. 'They can't say no to us being part of it, Lil, with you being Zeb's girlfriend when he went missing.'

The feminist creed imbibed during Lorraine's degree kicked in. 'That's not what we're about, Dale. That girlfriend of the band stuff.'

'Why not?' Dale shot back. 'Everyone's heard of Zeb's disappearance. It was in the *Evening News* again last week. "Lost guitarist spotted in Acapulco". Everyone's heard of Gothenburg but no one's heard of us.'

Lorraine had no answer. She pointed her guitar to the drum kit. 'Rikki not out of bed yet?'

Though Lily and Lorraine had been trying to get an all-girl band together for years, they still hadn't found a steady female drummer. Rikki was one of a handful of guys who helped out, hanging around but only half-committed.

'I wouldn't know. As of last week,' Lily said archly. Lorraine got the gist and laughed comfortably.

'Glad to hear it. You know he's a creep.'

Lily pulled a disapproving face. 'Rikki's not had it easy. He was in hospital for years when he was a kid. The medical profession got him hooked on painkillers. His parents abandoned him. That's no fun.'

'Sorry, I didn't know all that.' Lorraine still wasn't totally convinced though; to her he was a rich kid, slumming it after being expelled from some Yorkshire boarding school, all the time blaming his parents for messing him up. He'd made a play for each of them and Lorraine had slapped him away. Only Lily had apparently succumbed. Lorraine had spotted them together once in a dark corner of Piccadilly, entangled against a wall. Since then he'd worn her black plaited leather bracelet. God, Lily did love a lost cause.

They got started and gave half a dozen numbers a try-out, making the massive black speakers shake. More than ever, Lorraine could hear her own fragile hopes in those guitar riffs, keyboard lines and yearning vocals. They sounded tight; better than ever.

'I've got some lyrics to try with that new tune of yours,' Lorraine told Dale in the break. She pulled a torn envelope out of her satchel with the words to 'Path of Stars' scrawled all over it.

Dale's pixie chin jutted up, defensively. 'I was going to write those. I would have got it together, only my head's been all over the place.'

'Really?' Lorraine wondered if she sounded as unimpressed as she felt. 'But we could still try out these words. Just till you get yours together.'

Lily chipped in. 'It can't do any harm.'

Lorraine counted everyone in and began to sing the lyrics that now seemed to express all the morbid confusions of her day.

'A shadow darkens over me
I don't know where I want to be
I need a guiding hand to hold
A compass for my empty soul
Path of stars,
All lost hearts . . .'

To her amazement, it sounded OK. And then even better when Rikki slipped into the room mid-song and busked a terrific drum rhythm that lifted the song to another level.

As it ended Rikki said 'Yeah!' and tapped the cymbal with

a triumphant 'tish'. Lily nodded and grinned. 'Fantastic.'

'But it's my song,' Dale erupted, flushed and furious.

'Well, see what you come up with then,' Lorraine said.

Suddenly Dale threw down her guitar, releasing a discordant yowl. 'You've changed, Lorraine, you've gone all – fascist since you got a job. Real art is evolution. I need to evolve my art, not just stamp it out like a machine.'

Lorraine was a millisecond from giving her a piece of her mind. Then she remembered Doctor Lehman's advice, about not letting herself be needled. Go somewhere quiet. Reflect on what was happening. So she didn't reply, just took her rehearsal tape from the recorder and slipped it in her bag.

'Feel free to carry on but I've had enough for one day,' she said to Lily. 'My only work friend was murdered in front of me and I can't stop thinking about it. I should never have come here tonight.'

'Hey,' Rikki said. 'Is that your place then, the Memorial Hospital, that was on the telly?'

Lorraine nodded, heaving her bass up over her shoulder.

'Oh yeah, everything happens to Lorraine, she's where everything's happening,' Dale sniped.

Lorraine swung around and gave Dale a long vindictive stare. Go ahead, Lorraine thought, whine your way out of the band. Dale dropped her head and turned back to fiddle with her amp.

Rikki broke the tension. 'I've got a job interview on Thursday. A real easy number. With amazing perks.'

'Well, good luck,' Lorraine said. It would be good to have someone else in the band who worked for a living.

* * *

Outside, the frosty night was alive with sound systems booming from flickering windows. Lorraine had almost reached the yellow pool of streetlight beside the Metro when she heard awkward footsteps behind her. Shit. Kids often hung about round here. Purse-snatchers or muggers. Hurrying up, she rifled in her bag for her keys. She dug deeper in the satchel but found only paper hankies and sweet wrappers.

A pair of strong arms grabbed her around the shoulders. Lorraine screamed and tried to break free.

'Don't get your knickers in a twist!' The hands fell away and Rikki limped around in front of her.

'For God's sake! I nearly had heart failure.'

She backed away from him, keys finally in hand.

'Hold on a sec. Got any advice for my job interview?'

He moved far too close to her, giving off the faintly sour smell of drummer's sweat, his spiky hair slicked down on his skull. The Metro gleamed with the promise of solitude. She stopped, deciding to give him a minute.

'What's the job?'

'Oh, lifting, carrying. A kind of – meat factory.' He looked sheepish, as if ashamed that was the best he could get.

'Try to look positive, hey? Look keen. And if there's a job description, give examples of when you did similar work before. That's about it.'

'Cool.'

'Good luck. You'll probably get it.'

'You know what? I've got a feeling I will. And I've got that speed you asked for.'

He reached in the pocket of his combat jacket and produced something small and white.

'I don't remember asking. No, forget it.'

'No way. You look knackered from all this murder shit. You can owe me twenty.'

Before she could break away, he'd stuck a rectangle of folded paper in her pocket and given her a cheery thumbs up.

'Enjoy yourself, darlin'. It's trippy stuff.'

Coalition Building

Question 14: It is wise to avoid direct conflict with others because they may be useful to me in the future.
  A. True
  B. Uncertain
  C. False

High score description (option A.): Identifying potential allies and resources, forging chains of reciprocity to create a power base.

Tuesday 22nd February

Pomona House was Salford's district headquarters, a block of 340 identical windows and square concrete panels stacked into a tower of airless offices. Lorraine knew the number because in her recent junior role she had counted them while killing time on many a bored dinner break.

Oh for a few hours of boredom now, she pined, pushing through the glass doors into the beige-tiled foyer. The lift climbed ten floors to the personnel directorate, where the carpet's pile was still smoothly hoovered around neat arrangements of chairs and shrouded typewriters.

Lorraine knocked at the door titled 'Harvey Wright, Director of Personnel', and entered when she heard no reply. Thanks to her mum keeping Jas over for the night, it was still well before eight, too early for Harvey or his PA to have shown up.

The director's office was one of the largest in the building, half of it a conference area, the rest housing Harvey's vast black desk which displayed an assortment of executive toys. Accidentally, she knocked against the Newton's cradle and instinctively grabbed at the click-clacking globes. The air around her fell still. All the personnel files were kept in a filing cabinet beside Harvey's leather chair. She had soon made a pile of her own file, and those labelled with the names of Doctor Strang, Rose, Norman, Mike, Felicity, Raj, Sister Ince and Harvey himself.

Suddenly curious, she opened Harvey's file and began to read. Her former boss had come to the NHS from an international pharmaceutical company. His CV displayed his rapid rise through impressive jobs until his last role as Chief of Personnel, Valerian Pharmaceuticals.

Pharmaceuticals. Harvey's background wasn't something she'd paid much attention to. And here was more detail: 'Responsible for recruitment campaign for production of small molecule GABA receptor general anaesthetics worldwide'.

He had to know his stuff. She looked back at his qualifications. There it was: a 2:1 degree in Chemistry from Liverpool.

He had named his wife, Brenda Jane, as a beneficiary of his pension. A supplementary letter was attached, reversing a former nomination of pension benefits to a son he never mentioned, Dermott Wright. For a moment she felt disappointed that she'd never talked to him about Jasmine, nor he about this son of his. Maybe the son had died or lived abroad. It was probably for the best, she decided.

Harvey's was the sort of career she should be aspiring to: the house in upmarket Worsley with the grand title 'Mill Hall', the pile of press quotes about all sorts of boring tripe. God spare me, she thought.

Only now did it strike her that Sergeant Diaz might grab the personnel files from her the second she walked into the hospital.

She switched Harvey's photocopier on. It was a machine the size of a grey plastic sideboard that hummed and clicked like a living thing. Carefully she unclipped the pages from each file and fed them through the machine, creating photographic quality colour prints.

A few minutes later, she studied each crisply warm print, trying to interpret them as the police might. The files of the more junior staff – herself, Raj, Sister Ince, Mike and Rose – contained few surprises. True, she hadn't realised that Rose had been to boarding school, a well-advertised all-girls establishment in the far north. Her eyes filled to think of all their unspoken confidences, so she set it to one side.

Doctor Strang's was the thickest file, thanks to a succession of medical posts and endless specialist exams. His marital status was 'Divorced' but he'd not allocated any death in service benefits to an ex-wife. There was a cryptic note about an investigation by the Medical Committee that had quickly been dropped. 'Unprofessional Conduct July 1980. Decision: No need for further investigation.' There were no details of a complainant.

Felicity Jardine's career had been exemplary. Since arriving in Salford she had rapidly worked her way up the grades through a succession of mostly psychiatric nursing jobs. She had no degree, only her Registered General Nursing qualification and the prestigious Carncross Gold Medal for Nursing. She was single and lived on a new estate of executive houses near Sedgley Park. If anything, Lorraine felt her paperwork showed her as less dynamic than she was in person.

Norman's file was almost a museum piece. His background was the army and he too had unexpected honours: 'Surgical Orderly (Anaesthetics), Royal Army Medical Corps, awarded the Military Medal for conspicuous gallantry, 1944.' After the war he'd been one of the founding members of the Hospital Secretaries Association but nothing much had happened to him for decades.

Both Norman and Harvey had much more experience with anaesthetics than she had ever guessed. She wondered how long it would take the police to pick up on that.

She bundled the files inside her satchel and started to prowl around the room. Perhaps it was a sixth sense that made her notice the conference table in the far corner.

Two of the seats had been shifted from their tidy positions and drawn in close, knee to knee. Someone had met someone else here, between last night's cleaners and her arrival. The vast black ash table was empty and the kettle was stone cold. The only coat on the hook was Harvey's ancient rain mac. The waste bin was empty, save for a disposable plastic cup from the water cooler. She lifted the white plastic cup up to the light and saw a creased bow of red lipstick. Felicity Jardine alone sprang to mind. Felicity and Harvey? They were friendly enough but – no, she couldn't believe it. The lipstick mark must have been left by a thirsty cleaner.

She heard footsteps in the corridor, very close, and froze. The door swung open and Harvey walked into the room, looking not at all pleased. When she instinctively dropped the plastic cup into the bin it made a clattering sound.

'The police told me to come and collect the files.' Lorraine needlessly gestured towards the pile of folders on his table.

Harvey glanced at the bin and then at her face.

'I'm glad I caught you,' he said. 'Follow me.'

Lorraine stared at her feet as Harvey sent the lift up to the eighteenth floor. Would Harvey seriously give the chief nurse an unfair advantage to get the leader's job? Edith, whose saving grace was access to the hospital's top gossips, had told her about a white leather weekend bag Felicity brought to her office every Friday.

'Even her secretary doesn't know who she goes off with at five o'clock. A consultant probably, or someone dead high up. The chairman or someone else worth nobbling.'

Lorraine wasn't impressed. So far as she knew, sex for favours at work was rare but it did exist. Personally, she couldn't imagine anything more degrading than sleeping with the boss. For one thing, lots of men were quick to accuse any woman who climbed over their own heads of using underhand means. If she ever got anywhere it had to be on her own merits.

'Any other hanky-panky I should know about?' she'd asked Edith, trying to disguise her distaste.

Edith stifled a giggle. 'Doctor Strang is a bit of a one. A few years back he was having it off with one of the ward clerks. She made a right hoo-ha about it to Mr Pilling but as he said, she only complained after he'd stopped buying her lovely flowers and all that.'

Norman Pilling. Another example of the chauvinist pig school of management. 'So was he reprimanded?'

'Who? Not Doctor Strang, course not. No, Mr Pilling gave the clerk a talking-to. She left soon after, which he said was no better than she deserved.' A few years ago: the date fitted with the Medical Committee's ditched investigation.

Lorraine followed Harvey through a service door and emerged into bitter daylight. Harvey stopped and leant on the low balustrade, his pinstriped suit draped with an expensive-looking scarlet scarf. He inhaled from a small cigarillo, blew out a plume of blue smoke and asserted, 'Isn't that a wonderful view?'

She followed slowly, wary of the wave-like surface of the roof. Standing back from the parapet, she peered over. It was windy up here and she felt unsteady on her feet. She saw the ugly consequences of sixties town planning: gargantuan oblong flats, the concrete bunkers of a shopping precinct, a run-down bus station. She'd bet whichever architect had inflicted these monstrosities on the town was living somewhere a lot prettier.

He gestured towards the canal, a sump of metallic liquid clogged with rubbish.

'It's all about to change, Lorraine.' Harvey sniffed the air with satisfaction, though she registered only traffic fumes. 'At last the council have found a partner. It's finally going to happen – the docks cleared for new promenades, houses and businesses.'

All her life, Salford had been Manchester's runt of a kid brother and she doubted the council could ever change that. 'You think it'll actually happen this time?'

'It's the Prime Minister's vision for a new Britain. General management, computerisation, slum clearance – it's the modern world. I need to see you join the team, Lorraine.'

She wasn't going to tell him that she'd been at the demos, marching against Thatcher with Jasmine in tow, both yelling, 'Maggie Maggie Maggie – Out Out Out!' And that her life's landmarks were icons of urban decay: the Electric Circus on a bomb site in Collyhurst and the Factory club nights in the outlaw territory of Hulme.

She had been examining his leathery features closely. 'You're looking very bright. Am I your first meeting of the day?'

He didn't even blink, just gazed over the polluted landscape. 'No peace for the wicked, as they say.'

He was a wily old dog. Even when she'd worked beside him, he'd had a habit of keeping his movements under wraps.

Suddenly he started walking back to the doorway. 'Right. I need you to map out the general manager job against the psychometrics. When can I have it?'

When indeed? 'I'm snowed under. And now there's the police inquiry.'

He grimaced, smoke unfurling over his jutting bottom lip.

'Deal with it. The Whitehall guys are looking for numeracy, verbal ability, personality, the full battery. Go somewhere quiet. What about the College of Nursing library? I'll back you up if Norman starts sulking.'

Finally, he chucked the cigarillo stub over the edge of the roof and asked, 'So how did it go with the police last night?'

She pulled her thin jacket more tightly against the wind. 'Upsetting.'

He surveyed the brightening horizon, seemingly preoccupied.

'Anything on Rose's mind?'

'Not that she told me.'

Dominance

Question 15: When I make up my mind about something, I make it happen even if other people don't agree.
   A. Often
   B. Occasionally
   C. Never

High score description (option A.): Assertive, aggressive, competitive, sexual.

At seven-thirty in the morning, Diaz and Brunt walked up the admin corridor in the pre-dawn gloom, along what was now the official approach path to the murder scene.

Brunt was briefing his sergeant, shuffling along faster than Diaz had seen him move in ages. 'No leads from prints or fibres. But get this. That syringe didn't have flu vaccine in it. Popofol or summat. Enough anaesthetic to kill a horse.'

'Points to someone who works here, then?'

'Aye, fits with this notion that one of them knew the appointment time and switched the drug. Had an interesting chat with the husband last night. Insists his wife left for work at six-thirty in the morning for some meeting that no one else ever heard about. Even with the fog it leaves a bloody long time when she was off the radar. You had a shufti at the statements this morning?'

Diaz stopped just past the door marked 'Administration Office'.

'Yeah. This is where the victim asked Miss Quick for a confidential chat. Quick says Strang, McClung and Jardine all could've been listening. I'm guessing one of them wanted to shut her up and went to the flu clinic to switch the vaccine between eleven and one.'

'Right. Let's look at where everyone was between them hours.'

Ten minutes later Diaz was standing in front of a large black and white printed floor plan tacked to a blackboard in Brunt's new office. The incident room had been set up in a former isolation ward but already the smell of burnt toast and fag smoke made it feel like home.

'The crime scene,' Diaz announced, pointing to a small square labelled 'Flu Clinic'. Lifting a minuscule red paper flag, he stabbed it into that spot. 'Sister Ince didn't bother locking it while she was away at the infection control meeting. Said it was only vaccine.'

'Who were close by?' Brunt asked. Diaz drew a line with his fingertip from the flu clinic to the admin office and marked it with a green flag.

'Norman Pilling claims he didn't leave his office all morning. Apparently, there's a completed *Times* crossword that corroborates it.' He smirked and added, 'And the word of an admin clerk.'

Next, a purple flag pierced the black square labelled 'Chief Nurse's Office'.

'Miss Jardine was in her office too, on the main corridor. It was Jardine who says she saw a plump Asian man walking towards the hospital entrance. Thinks it was Patel leaving his post.'

Brunt raised his grizzled eyebrows. 'And what does Patel say?'

Diaz gave a tight smile. 'Claims he was in the accounts office, up to his eyes. Seems one of them's lying.'

Standing back, Diaz gestured over the whole plan. 'As for Doc Strang, he won't let me pinpoint him. Says he was on his ward round, flitting around all over the place. No specific sightings from eleven forty-five to twelve fifteen.'

'What, in a crowded place like this?' Brunt said. 'He could easily have nipped away for fifteen minutes. He does a spot of surgery himself, right?'

'Dead right.'

Diaz picked up one of the sheaf of statements. 'And here's another really interesting one. Mike McClung. He was changing the oxygen tanks stored in the yard outside the boardroom. Knocked on the window and said hello to Miss Quick. Then he thinks he saw someone in the flu clinic. Knocked on the flu clinic window to say hello but the light went out. When nothing happened he just carried on.'

Brunt grunted. 'Did he now? Felicity told me he sent Mrs Cavanagh some inappropriate letters. Could be he's throwing accusations around 'cos he did it. My money's on McClung.'

'Felicity, is it?' Diaz mocked.

Brunt's baggy face assumed a lecherous expression. 'Oh aye. She can give me a bed bath anytime.'

Diaz half-turned and rolled his eyes.

'What about your Miss Quick? She were there in the boardroom from when?'

Diaz reached for a blue flag and stuck it into the rectangle labelled 'Boardroom'.

'Came down from Personnel to work in peace. Arrived past the closed clinic door around ten past eleven. Says after McClung knocked she was alone till Harvey Wright arrived for the meeting at ten to one. She had the best opportunity to make the switch.'

'And she'd already met the victim on this mysterious journey of hers to work. What did Mrs Cavanagh tell her about where she'd been all morning?'

Diaz played for time by flicking through his notebook. Somehow he hadn't ferreted that much hard information out of Miss Quick last night.

'Don't just stand there in a dreamworld, sonny. Where did Patel go when he went out? Where did Quick pick the victim up from? Hop to it, lad.'

Diaz went straight out to the car park and found the attendant Jim, a lumbering jobsworth who guarded his territory like a hawk. He was a confident witness and the lead was a dead end. Patel had a red Grenada, he said, pointing out the vehicle, which was a good five years old according to its reg number.

'I remember all right. He come down from the hospital about half past eleven. I needed a space for some physios delivering their crutches and that. But he just got in his car and sat there in the driver's seat. Still there, he was, when I went for me dinner at one o'clock.'

When Diaz got back to the incident room Miss Quick still hadn't shown up. He wondered if he'd been too trusting in letting her pick up the files. He had an annoying feeling that his judgement had been subtly skewed. Well, that was understandable, the way things were for him at home at the moment – but he wasn't going to think about that while he was on duty. He was just glad to be out of the house, happy to volunteer for any shift, however unsocial the hours.

Now the personnel officer's lateness gave him the excuse to check on the inquiry's progress so far, starting with the evidence bags in the back room. There were no empty ampoules of propofol to fingerprint, only a record of two used syringes and two empty vaccine ampoules left over from the victim's and Lorraine Quick's vaccinations. Less enthusiastically he checked the contents of all the waste bins. Only one item of interest turned up. It was a paper found in the boardroom waste bin that said 'Psychometric testing of candidates – ACTION – Lorraine Quick.'

Someone shouted that he was wanted at the front desk. He got up and watched Miss Quick through the half-open door as she studied his colleagues at work. She was calm and composed but she was taking it all in. Yet there was an incongruence to her that he couldn't quite put his finger on. Far more strongly than Raj Patel, his instincts told him she might lead him to the killer. Whoever had murdered Rose was hiding behind a professional mask and this woman was using tests to catch warped personalities, tests that used the latest psychological thinking. She might not want to help him, but what he needed was more important than any petty rules. By the time he stepped up to her, he knew exactly what he wanted from Miss Quick.

'So, what do you make of it all?'

Lorraine started at the sound of the sergeant's voice. He had crept up noiselessly behind her.

'I've never seen a police incident room before. Bit scruffier than *Juliet Bravo*.'

She smiled warmly, trying to break through his stern watchfulness. He was the same height as her, with dark Mediterranean looks, conventionally handsome but carrying the suggestion of a bruiser in his leather jacket stretched over boxer's shoulders. No, the smile didn't work. That electrical charge she thought she'd picked up between them, if it had even existed, had dimmed in the daylight. No doubt she did have too much imagination, just as Doctor Lehman's tests had said. Either that or it was way too long since she'd had a regular boyfriend.

She passed him the bundle of personnel files but he didn't look at them, only dumped them on a perilously stacked desk.

'I'd like to ask you a question,' he said, pulling a photo out of a file. 'I'd rather you didn't repeat this. Have you ever seen this substance?'

It was a photograph of a cardboard carton and a glass ampoule labelled 'Propofol Injectable Anaesthetic'.

'Oh God. Is that what killed Rose?'

'Have you ever seen it or anything like it?'

'Never.'

'OK. Have you remembered it yet? The place where you saw Rose?'

She shook her head. 'I'll know it when I see it.'

He was beating his fingers on the back of a chair. 'Come on. We'll drive round now and you can show me.'

Only as they walked together to her rusty Metro did she remember the photocopies of the personnel files. So far as she could remember, they were tucked inside her band practice folder on the back seat. Yes, thank God. Glancing through the back window she saw the photocopies were out of sight, part of a heap of files and personnel textbooks.

She got inside and hastily grabbed one of Jasmine's Luke Skywalker figures. It was safely in her pocket by the time the passenger seat was invaded by Diaz. As she steered the car out of the car park he clicked on the car's cigarette lighter without asking. Flaming cheek.

When he offered her his pack of John Player Specials she declined and watched him draw in a deep draught of smoke. His black hair fell in a floppy fringe, though the back and sides were fashionably short. He caught her watching and she swivelled back to follow the road. Watch out, girl, she told herself. Even in daylight he was a good-looking bloke. Pity he was a copper. In silence she circled the looping streets, peering at regimented lines of semis. Nothing chimed in her memory.

'That reminds me,' he said, 'Brunt wants to see everyone's personal diaries. Is yours here?'

Before she could stop him he reached over to the back seat and started rooting through her folders.

'Hey. Leave my things alone.'

He raised her diary in triumph. It was a thick Filofax bound in red leather. She lifted her arm to snatch it back, then remembered she couldn't let go of the wheel in front of a policeman.

'Hold on. I'll be lost without that.'

'I'll take it now if you don't mind. Save the inspector banging on your door.'

'For God's sake,' she said, forced to keep her eyes on the road.

Next he hauled the PX60 folder over the seat back. 'Do you mind if I have a look?' Before she could protest he was leafing through the pages on his lap.

'"Following self-image",' he read out loud. 'That's exactly

what the perpetrator must be doing right now. Watching themselves, keeping control.'

She twisted her neck to check out the back seat. The photocopied files lay undisturbed. 'You honestly think it's one of us?' she asked.

He turned in his seat to face her. 'What these profilers in America are doing is – well, a murder can be organised or disorganised. So in a disorganised scene nothing is planned, the perpetrator uses any weapon he can lay his hand on and doesn't give a toss about hiding evidence. But in the other type, an organised murderer plans the whole thing. So let's say they were swapping a vaccine, there'd be no fingerprints left behind. You get my point? It's carried out by a totally different, high-intelligence type of personality.'

He was right, there could be a link to psychometrics. She laughed uncertainly. 'Flippin' 'eck. I hope you don't think it was me?'

He didn't answer, just asked, 'What if people lie in a test? Can they fake it?'

'They can try. But a warning should show up in a hidden scale. It's called Faking Good, or technically, Motivational Distortion. A high score suggests that someone has potentially been lying.'

'Brilliant.'

Distracted by him, she had driven into a cul-de-sac. From the corner of her eye she could see him turning pages, drinking in information.

Without lifting his head, he said, 'So when are you planning to use these tests?'

Flustered because Harvey had sworn them all to secrecy, she said, 'Oh, I haven't even passed the exam yet.'

He lifted his head to watch her. She was steering the car through a jerky five-point turn.

'You can come clean,' he said dryly. 'I've seen that timetable. It's pretty handy that you're going to be testing them all for the general manager job. Norman Pilling, Doctor Strang, Miss Jardine, Raj Patel and Mike McClung. Ring a bell?'

'That's confidential,' she said snappily, stopping the car by the kerb. 'I've signed a confidentiality agreement.'

'There's nothing confidential in a murder inquiry. I'm not even asking you to test them. You're doing that already. Course, hopefully, we'll have made an arrest by then. But still, I want to see the results.'

'What? I can't test candidates for a job interview and then use them for some ulterior purpose,' she said incredulously.

Diaz didn't break his gaze. 'Those guys in the FBI have tested loads of murderers. You've probably got the answer right here in these tests. Don't you care about who killed Rose?'

'Yes. But no. Don't hassle me. I need to think about it.'

Without a word she set off driving again. Then there it was – a row of green iron railings. With a jolt she swerved the car back into the kerb.

'It was here. I pulled up just here when I saw Rose.'

The previous morning the fog had blanked out the twin green doors of the electricity substation and the yellow sign warning 'Danger of Death', but she recalled those iron railings vividly.

Diaz nodded. 'OK. Switch off the engine. Talk me through what happened. Moment by moment.'

She turned the key and leant back into her seat, staring through the windscreen. Maybe it was the notion that a licensed nosy parker was itching to root through her belongings, but she couldn't concentrate.

'Sorry. I can't think straight.'

'OK. Start with the time just before you got here.'

She closed her eyes. 'The fog was pretty thick. I got lost.'

'Were there any other cues? Sounds and sights? To reconstruct the moment?'

She sighed, exasperated. 'Yeah, yeah, I know all about recall. I had some music on.'

Before she'd finished speaking Diaz had picked up a cassette and was inspecting the label. 'Echo and the Bunnymen. That is such a good album. I saw them at the Hacienda.'

'You? So did I.'

'Then we both share belting taste,' he said, his eyes meeting hers from below raised brows. 'What's this one?' It was her latest rehearsal tape. He turned it over but thankfully it was missing a label.

'What I was listening to.' He slid the cassette into the player and switched it on.

'*Taking a step in the dark . . .*' She snatched at the volume control but still her own voice filled the vehicle. For a moment it was that morning and the image of Rose – distracted and upset – was more vivid than ever.

'Not bad. What're they called?'

'Please. Shut up. I can almost see it.' She closed her eyes. Once again she felt the frustration of being late, of being mesmerised as she edged the car through a tunnel of fog.

Her eyes opened. She pointed to the middle of the road. 'Rose was standing just over there. Looking backwards.'

'Get out and show me.'

She clicked off the music. Then she stepped into the empty

road and turned her neck just as Rose had done, peering back over her shoulder. Quickly she returned and ducked through Diaz's open window.

'I know what Rose was looking at. Number 12 Radley Road. It's a hospital house.'

They both got out and walked together up the drive of a down-at-heel pre-war semi covered in mud-coloured pebble-dash. Suddenly Diaz stopped and touched her arm. With a jerk of his head he indicated the front porch. The glass-panelled front door was gaping open.

'Stay back. There's someone in there.'

She watched as he walked to the door and cocked his head to one side, listening. He called into the interior of the house and then shouldered his way inside.

A minute later he emerged looking grumpy, waving his hand dismissively.

'It's only the flaming cleaner. I reckon she's polished away every fingerprint and fibre since the year dot.' He spoke into his personal radio, summoning others to get over straight away. Signing off, he led Lorraine back to her car. Once she'd buckled herself in, he gestured that she wind down her window.

'Do you know who was living here?' he asked.

'No. When they're not rented out to staff these houses are used for meetings or to finish big reports, that sort of thing.'

'A bit cosy for a meeting room.' He was looking up at the pink curtains of the front bedroom. He thinks it's about sex, Lorraine realised. That's why he's upset that the cleaners have scrubbed all the evidence away.

'So who orders the cleaners in?'

'Anyone. You just leave a requisition in the domestic department's wire basket.'

He leant down and spoke through Lorraine's car window.

'You may as well head off now.'

'Did you check on Tim?'

She had been expecting to catch him out so was taken aback when he said, 'A female officer stayed over with him while his dad was questioned. She's looking to get him any help he needs.'

They both studied each other's faces a fraction too long. He stepped back. 'I'll be in touch. Give some thought to helping me out, eh? For Rose's sake.'

Instrumentalism

Question 16: I get a 'kick' from controlling other people.

   A. Often

   B. Occasionally

   C. Never

High score description (option A.): Exploitative stance towards others, interaction merely a means to one's own power or advantage.

The photograph of Rose they showed on the news had an unnatural, hallucinatory quality. I wondered if Christie was watching it too. No, of course, that was impossible. But it got me thinking. What had she heard from the top of the stairs? That I was meeting Rose at 12 Radley Road, yes. But what else? There had been that click on the line, on the upstairs extension. She must have heard her talking about the flu jab. And the appointment time.

I could, I should, have driven back to Christie's house and had it all out with her. Instead I rang the house but she didn't pick up the phone, because of course, she never picks up the phone. A bizarre but entirely logical suspicion began to grip me. She must have worked fast and with surprising efficiency. She had made her way to the hospital and made a simple substitution while the room was unattended. She had the knowledge. She had the necessary supplies. The answer was sublimely simple.

I sat alone in my office, tying all the uncomfortable strands into an inescapable knot. And as I did so, it dawned upon me that my problem with Rose had been conveniently solved. When she had crept down to see me in the night, Christie had as good as told me her plan. 'I'll sort it out. We have no choice.' I'd thought her words nothing but a fantastical revenge drama she was spinning. In fact, she was confiding her limitless support for me, her dearest companion. When Rose had the cheek to phone me at Christie's house, the fool had condemned herself to death.

The irony was that these past years I'd thought her quite harmless. Well, well, I smiled wryly to myself, when she wanted to help me she was unstoppable. Good old Christie. Not in a million years would the police connect her with Rose. It was beautifully, clinically, simple. She would never be suspected. She would be left alone to live without suspicion.

As for me, if I had any part in the matter it was only in providing her with playthings. It was easy for me to supply her with whatever she needed, though till now it was merely to play pretend and console herself with old routines. Nevertheless, if there was one thing I decided after Rose's death, it was this: I must control her more carefully. I must be vigilant. If I failed, she might get a taste for her old wild ways again.

Group Dependency

Question 17: To be sure I am doing the right thing, I like:
   A. To discuss the issue with other people
   B. In between
   C. To check facts in documents
High score description (option A.): Enjoyment of participation, a group joiner and follower, a need to belong.

Because of the police inquiry the post meeting was delayed until three in the afternoon. Norman glared at his depleted gathering.

'Where the devil has Mike got to?' He flapped his bony hand toward the empty chair.

Lorraine jumped to attention. 'I had a sick note from him this morning.'

'And pray what malady keeps our engineer from his duties? *Plumbum oscillans?*' the administrator enunciated smugly.

Lorraine had heard it all before, including the old windbag's term for 'swinging the lead'. 'Depression,' she said, feeling treacherous to Mike.

Norman's face wrinkled in disgust.

'Also one from Sister Ince,' she added.

'What did that one say? Guilty conscience?' Felicity gave a sour little chuckle. Felicity's lips were painted in a perfect scarlet arc. Lorraine wondered if maybe she should have kept the lipstick imprint on the plastic cup to show Diaz. What she did keep from the team's derision was the diagnosis on Sister Ince's sicknote: 'Nervous anxiety'. A fragile bond had formed between the two women as they held hands, watching poor Rose die. She could imagine how miserable Sister Ince must be feeling.

'So they haven't arrested Mike yet?' Everyone looked at Doctor Strang. He was staring at the ceiling, sardonic and superior.

Norman caved in. 'You think he's the chief suspect?'

Doctor Strang leant back, clasped his hands over his corduroy-clad stomach and shook his unruly hair. 'Sex is usually the motive in these cases. Sex and violence are intrinsically linked in the brains of some inadequate men. And we all know Mike was hopelessly pursuing Rose.'

Raj alone stood up to the medical director. 'That's unfair. I'm sure it was some random maniac who wandered in from the street.'

'Come off it, Patel. A maniac who knew how to refill a syringe?'

'And Mike did?' Raj snapped back.

Doctor Strang leant forward and spat out his words like venom. 'If Mike could assemble the latest motorised syringe pump, don't you think he could handle a basic syringe?'

Lorraine turned away. Stuff Doctor Strang. She decided she would visit Mike and offer some support.

'Whoever it is,' Norman complained to no one in particular,

'this is a dreadful blight on my record here at the Memorial.'

A loud knock at the door interrupted them. It was Diaz, looking grave. Lorraine felt peculiarly embarrassed to be spotted by him with the same group of managers that she now knew were under suspicion.

'Mr Patel. Inspector Brunt would like a word in his office, sir.'

Everyone stared after Raj as he heaved himself up awkwardly, sweat instantly beading his round face.

At ten to five Lorraine left the office with a hurried excuse to Edith and looked about for an available phone. Only the payphone on the main corridor was free, and though a cavalcade of patients and staff paraded past, the transparent acoustic hood gave at least an impression of privacy. She pulled out Doctor Lehman's business card and dialled the number. As the phone's bell rang out she watched each passer-by cast a shadow on the wall, a prancing ghoul against the fierce lights outside the operating theatres. At last Doctor Lehman picked up and Lorraine pushed a few coins in.

The psychologist did not sound pleased to hear from her. 'This is my personal number, Lorraine.'

'I know. I'm sorry. I wondered if you'd read about what's happening here at the Memorial. My friend was killed.'

Doctor Lehman's voice assumed a gentler tone. 'I have seen it. It must be difficult for you.'

'The thing is, I'm being asked to test a group of colleagues who are also police suspects. I mean, can the test pick up, you know – mental illness?'

As Lorraine listened a bulky shade like a monstrous beast grew ever larger on the wall. She twisted around and saw only a motorised wheelchair bearing a tiny gnome-like patient. God, at this rate she could scare herself to death.

'Yes it can. It is widely used in clinical settings.'

'So what do I do if I find someone I test is capable of – murder?' Her final word seemed to echo on the line.

'You will be sending the tests to me for scoring, won't you? I think it's best if we discuss them case by case. Is that OK?'

'Yes. That's good.'

'Now I do have a client waiting . . .'

'Please, wait. There's another issue. The police want me to share the results with them. Surely that can't be ethical?'

'Absolutely not. That is against the Psychological Society's regulations. Who exactly is asking you?'

'A young detective. Keen. Ambitious. Yet oddly enough, he seems the one with the most integrity.'

'So, are you saying you trust him?'

'I do and I don't.'

The tutor sounded thoughtful. 'We can be attracted and repelled at the same time by those who do not have good intentions.'

'I know. Story of my life.'

'Let's set some boundaries. If I hear you've shared confidential test results, I will report you to the society. Does that help?'

'Yes. That's incredibly helpful. I can quote the rules and be absolutely firm. But I do have this compulsion. To find out what I can about Rose. She didn't deserve to die like that.'

'Lorraine. Don't expose yourself to danger.'

'I won't,' she answered airily, without even a second's thought.

Numerical Reasoning

Question 18: Which fraction is equivalent to 5/6?
   A. 10/12
   B. 10/6
   C. 5/12

High score description (option A.): Mental agility, fast learning, adaptability.

Wednesday 23rd February

On Wednesday morning Lorraine picked up the phone and heard Felicity's voice.

'I have a nurse on a psychiatric ward who has just attacked a patient. We're about to convene the disciplinary hearing. You need to be here now.'

As Lorraine listened, she began to experience Felicity's words as mere sounds that she had no idea how to respond to. How long would this go on, this sense of floundering beyond her depth?

'The thing is,' Lorraine began uncertainly, groping for the Employment Law directory on her shelf, 'I'd need to read up—'

'I just need you here in the room,' the chief nurse broke in. 'I'll chair the whole thing.'

Arriving at the disciplinary hearing, Lorraine was ushered into a corner almost out of sight. The accused, as Lorraine privately called him, was Charge Nurse Garbutt, a lumbering giant of a bloke in his mid-twenties. As Lorraine sat down, he was whispering aggressively to an anxious-looking representative from the Royal College of Nursing.

To Lorraine's giddy relief, Felicity did not give a short introduction and then drop her in it by handing the entire proceedings over to her – a trick that a number of malicious heads of departments had played when Lorraine first took up post. Instead, Felicity conducted the hearing with absolute assurance. Two witnesses were called, who both agreed that a patient named Terry had picked up a packet of Garbutt's cigarettes, prompting the charge nurse to scream at him. When Terry didn't return them, Garbutt had knocked him to the ground and punched his head repeatedly. Terry was still in hospital with six stitches. Even the RCN rep couldn't make a defence.

Garbutt was no help to himself as a witness. 'What you don't get, Miss Jardine,' he sneered, rocking on his toes, 'is that the boys on my ward are dangerous. They need strict discipline.'

Felicity watched him as a hawk observes a worm. When his opportunity came to speak his cheeks were crimson, his finger stabbing the air in Felicity's direction. 'What you don't get is that mental illness doesn't even exist. You, and all the medics and their drug company buddies, are just prison guards trying to medicalise suffering.'

Felicity narrowed her eyes and chuckled. 'Don't try to spout anti-psychiatry at me, Mr Garbutt. Wake up, that hippy nonsense is history. It's the 1980s.'

She cocked her head to one side. 'Very well. Today I am suspending you on the grounds of gross misconduct. I will inform the police so they can investigate this grievous bodily harm to our patient, Mr Terence Ross. The Health Authority will also investigate your misconduct and take the necessary further steps. Kindly remove your possessions at once and do not under any circumstances return to your place of employment. Goodbye.'

It was an impressive performance and Lorraine thanked Felicity. The chief nurse looked relaxed and happy and Lorraine envied her that.

'It just takes time and experience, Lorraine. And remember, give any fool enough rope and they'll happily hang themselves.'

The College of Nursing was located on the campus of Salford University. As soon as Lorraine passed through the doors she welcomed the institution's air of serene dedication. A fiery rebel when she was fifteen, Lorraine had stormed out of school with scarcely a qualification to her name. At her boyfriend Andy's side she had drifted aimlessly until they split up. Only with Jasmine's birth had she felt an urgent need to get herself together and be a role model for her daughter. To her surprise she'd enjoyed zipping through her A-levels at the local technical college, a world away from the rowdy classroom at her overcrowded comprehensive school. She now understood that she was a typical studious introvert. It had made her laugh once, when reviewing her 'Obstacles to Learning' on a training course, that her own greatest obstacle to learning had been school itself.

Now, she searched out the librarian, Fran, and booked herself an empty seminar room with a window overlooking a library filled with neat bookshelves, flower vases and serious students in frumpy clothes or blue nylon uniforms. Spreading her papers across a table, she began to analyse which personality traits were crucial to the general manager's job. This was the sort of work she liked: being left alone with a mental challenge, sorting abstractions into patterns.

For a satisfying hour she sketched her ideas on a flip chart, building an ideal portrait around a stick figure labelled 'General Manager'. A good head for numbers would be crucial for debating budgets with doctors and other mathematically fluent staff. And the need to communicate ideas called for persuasive language skills. According to the new general manager's job description this paragon would also need to be a bold extrovert, mature and self-reliant, as well as tough and shrewd. Carefully, she did the maths to calculate the candidate's acceptable range of scores for Extraversion, Super-ego, Boldness, Toughness, Shrewdness, plus Verbal and Numerical Ability. She had a sudden burst of satisfaction in thinking that her work might bring a new openness and progressive thinking to the hospital.

Finally, she picked up her marker pen and cross-hatched a black shadow underneath her stick figure, showing the opposites of her chosen traits, the contraindications that had to be screened out. Low mathematical or verbal ability would sound an alarm. Signs of immaturity or traits of obsessional worry or over-submissiveness would need to be checked, along with antagonism, high risk-taking, over-suspiciousness and many more. Finally, she wrote a summary: 'Beware extremely high or low scores in any trait – especially Dominance, Paranoia, Aggression, Neurosis.'

As she worked, Diaz's conversation played out in the back of her mind. Was it really possible to catch a killer using these tests? He had talked about something called profiling. The killer was intelligent and highly organised. They would also need remarkably high self-control to project a calm facade while plotting and committing a murder – just as her ideal candidate would need high self-control to lead the hospital as a successful general manager.

She recalled the moods of those around her the day that Rose died. Sister Ince had been near hysterical from the moment Rose collapsed. Yet everyone else had appeared extraordinarily calm.

An example of high self-control was Diaz himself. Being in control was clearly part of his job. Yet it was easy to spot his aggression towards Brunt. And now he was needling her to get one over on his boss. Yet he did have a spark of something else, an intensity that wormed its way into her head in a discomfiting way. Dominant, tough-minded, self-sufficient. He was definitely in the right career for his personality.

Dreamily, she doodled a male figure on a piece of paper. Beside the dark silhouette she wrote 'Ambition'. A smile reached her lips as she added 'Adventurous?'.

The door flew open. Lorraine jumped guiltily in her chair. Thank God it was only Fran bearing a plate of biscuits.

'Do you want some of these? Leftovers from the chairman's meeting. They'll only go soft.'

'You are a lifesaver.' While Lorraine gathered a few and started eating, Fran inspected the flip chart and then sat on the edge of the table where Lorraine was working. To Lorraine's alarm she craned her neck to examine the smaller doodle.

'So who's the sexy man in black? Not this murderer, is it?'

Lorraine pulled it towards herself and then turned it over.

'God, no. Just a man who wants me to risk losing my job.'

Fran wasn't going to let her off that lightly and put on a

dramatic voice. 'Aha, by doing what exactly?'

'Oh, the usual man-thing. No,' she protested. 'No, not what you think. By doing his job for him.' They shared a chuckle, then Lorraine remembered the pressure he was putting her under.

Across the corridor a phone rang out and Fran left to answer it. Alone again, and irritated by her foolish daydream, Lorraine crumpled up the doodle of Diaz and threw it in the wastepaper bin. She stared a long time into space. Perhaps Diaz did have a point, though, that she could use tests to identify Rose's killer. She had brought eight tests back from the course, so she listed the five names of those who needed to be tested for the general management job:

1. *Norman Pilling*
2. *Raj Patel*
3. *Mike McClung*
4. *Victor Strang*
5. *Felicity Jardine*

That left three tests. If she tested suspects and sent them to Doctor Lehman without showing the results to Diaz, she wouldn't be breaking any rules. So who next? The Occupational Health physician had told her that Sister Ince was no longer fit to do her job and wanted to take her pension as soon as she possibly could. That was interesting. True, she had appeared to be terrified when Rose collapsed, but it was a fact that a tiny minority of nurses did use their knowledge to kill. Lorraine decided to try and test her, even if she had to visit her at home. She added her to the list:

6. *Sister Ince*

That left one last suspect from those who had gathered in the boardroom. She added his name, too:

7. *Harvey Wright*

Surely she could persuade her old boss to take part?

8.

Just one test left over. She left the space blank. Nothing felt predictable any more. It felt good to have one spare test remaining.

Artlessness

Question 19: I say whatever is on my mind, regardless of who is listening.
    A. Often
    B. Occasionally
    C. Never
High score description (option A.): Forthright and socially clumsy, unthinking, simple, brusque.

Thursday 24th February

After lunch on Thursday Edith started to act up.

'Here you are at last.' Her assistant jumped up from her typing, unable to contain herself as Lorraine arrived in the office. 'The phone's rung about a million times. I've got all your dictation to finish. And there's these porter interviews this afternoon. I can't do everything at once. Can't you do them?'

Lorraine threw down her satchel with a bang. She had just come from an aggressive trade union meeting and had still not received a list of childminders from Salford

Council. This morning Jasmine had balefully rolled her eyes when she'd promised her daughter she wouldn't be at the Carneys' much longer. There were some pink marks on her daughter's thin arms. Had someone pinched Jas? Those two little Carney lads had been sniggering on the stairs when she'd left the house in a cloud of guilt.

It didn't need a personality test to know that Edith wasn't suited to her job. She had inherited Edith from her predecessor and suffered from her frequent attempts to offload work.

Lorraine could feel her own teeth gritting. 'Come on, it's a chance to develop yourself. Aren't you planning to get qualified like me?'

Edith pulled a disgusted face. 'Not likely. Who'd want to do what you do? Sacking people and doing interviews and all that.'

Lorraine blinked. Well, at least the personnel profession would be spared Edith's entirely unfiltered thoughts and complete absence of empathy.

'Ancillary staff interviews are part of your job description. Are you refusing to do your job?'

Edith's freckly face turned shocked pink as she started banging objects around her desk.

'Well? Have you got your questions ready?' Lorraine demanded.

Edith almost threw the file across the desk. Inside was a piece of foolscap covered in a set of reasonably sensible questions copied out from a previous interview.

'Come on,' Lorraine said, intent on inflicting this learning opportunity on Edith whether she wanted it or not. 'I'll introduce you and you'll love it. If you're nervous just think how the candidates must feel.'

Alf, the head porter, and his deputy Darren welcomed a tearful Edith into the interview room. Lorraine patiently helped them decide which questions each would ask and that Edith would round off the interview from her question list before reading out the terms and conditions.

'Two lads have pulled out,' Alf said. 'The most promising chap broke his ankle yesterday and another fella's wife rang in and didn't give a reason. So that's just three lads to choose from. I need to cover this weekend's shifts. I haven't got time to re-advertise.'

When Darren went to fetch the first interviewee, Lorraine made her exit.

After an hour or so Edith returned in a jubilant mood. 'We got someone! It all went brilliant. I mean I got a bit tongue-twisted but Alf said I did really well.'

Edith typed the new porter's contract and left it for Lorraine in the blotter-lined pages of the signature book. There were half a dozen far more demanding letters to check over, so she quickly scanned it for typos and scribbled her signature on the contract for 'Eric Carl Fryer' without a second thought.

Friday 25th February

The next morning Lorraine heard a masculine voice call out, 'How you doing?' and looked up with a welcoming expression. Her smile vanished. Limping into her office was Rikki. He'd combed down his spiky hair and taken the hoops from his ears. But it was definitely her own drummer, Rikki. Christ, he had even ironed a shirt.

A cheery wave and 'Reporting for duty,' were directed at Edith, who beamed back up at him.

'Stop there.' Lorraine shot up from her desk and signalled at him not to take a step forward. Edith turned to her in bafflement. She saw mockery dancing in Rikki's cold eyes.

'I'll speak to you next door,' she directed. 'Edith, bring all the paperwork for this post to the interview room.'

'What's up now?'

'Just do it. And watch your tone.'

Once she was alone with Rikki in the interview room, he had the nerve to try his usual smarmy act.

'Honest, Lorraine, what's all the fuss?'

'You used me.' She mimicked a needy voice. '"Help me, Lorraine. I've got an interview."'

'I deserve a job too, you know.'

'What? And I suppose you deserve "amazing perks" as well? After drugs, are you?'

She watched him closely, this small-time dealer in weed and speed. Rikki was one of those self-dramatising drug users, forever boasting of how many horse tranquillisers he could neck, or the week-long binges that he and his mates wasted their lives on.

He stared at her, pantomiming shock, as if she'd accused Mary Whitehouse of romping in an orgy. 'No way,' he enunciated piously. 'Now I've got myself a job – I wouldn't even take a wrap of speed off a mate. You do know that's illegal?'

'So what about your attitude to hospitals?' she blurted out. 'A meat factory, wasn't it?'

'God, no, Lorraine. I think they're wonderful places. I spent years in hospital as a kid, strapped to a wooden frame with my gammy hip. I wouldn't be able to work at all without all the medical help I've had.' He lifted his weaker leg. 'It's a chance to put something good back into the system.'

'You lying git,' she hissed.

She couldn't look at his smug face for another second, so she studied his application form. On paper he had puffed up his time as a volunteer at the charity Mind, a follow-on requirement after his release from some private rehab clinic. He had also elaborated some dubious time supposedly spent helping his uncle at his hotel. That casual favour had been honoured with the title 'General Porter'.

Hoping for a reprieve, she opened Rikki's references and laid them out flat across the table. One was on Mind-headed paper, signed by another unsavoury volunteer, a long-time mate of Rikki's. The Eric Fryer described in the reference was compassionate, punctual, sensitive.

The second was a character reference purportedly written by his uncle, though possibly penned by Rikki himself. There was no phone number and an illegible signature.

The contract bore both Eric Fryer's and her own legally binding signatures. She was stumped. She couldn't tell the porters that Rikki was a druggy reprobate without owning up to his connection to her. And as their personnel officer, she really didn't want to tell them he was the drummer in her band.

'Alf wants me to clock on at nine. What's up? You worried I'll be telling everyone we're in a band together? Don't all these straight types know what you're really like?'

'Just go,' she said at last. 'But I'll be watching you. OK?'

Blame Externalisation

Question 20: I've been the victim of a lot of bad luck in my life.
   A. True
   B. Uncertain
   C. False
High score description (option A.): Inability to take responsibility for own actions, always someone else's fault, rationalising behaviour.

After the first few hours Rikki knew he wouldn't be able to work at the Memorial for long. Getting up at the crack of dawn, freezing his knackers off at the bus stop, it was fucking grim. His name was on the rota for Saturday morning but he was going to struggle; there was a party later that night. No chance of sneaking into work either; he was completely under the lash, forced to get his clock card stamped at the start of every shift. 'Three lates and you'll be up for a warning from Personnel,' another porter had warned him. Fuck that. He wasn't going to have his hands slapped by Lorraine.

The trouble was, before he walked out with a V-sign at the

lot of them, he wanted to make contact with that character he'd spotted in the staff newsletter. Since reading Diggers' name he'd seen it on noticeboards, official memos, everywhere. He hadn't actually spotted his old pal yet, but the name alone brought back a torrent of memories from when he was a kid. It was a teacher at his prep school who'd first noticed his limp and nagged his parents to take him to a doctor. Next thing, he'd been in hospital, trapped, his lower body imprisoned by a wooden frame and metal bar.

At first, he'd cried for his mum to come, but she didn't. Doctors, nurses and all sorts of experts poked at him instead. A teacher came to visit him once or twice, but he soon forgot all his school lessons: the times tables and spelling tests he already struggled to keep up with. Eventually, the mirror had been clipped above his head so he could see what was going on in the ward – a rectangle of moving shapes and colours that never seemed exactly real. He'd begged to get up and go to the toilet himself but a monster of a doctor said it wasn't allowed. Instead, he'd had to use a horrid plastic bottle or a bedpan. Some of the staff were nice and drew the curtains around him so he could sort himself out in private. Others were cruel, leaving him until he was bursting or had wet himself and then taunting him for being a baby. And where beforehand only his mum had ever seen him with nothing on, now strangers saw him with his pants down every day.

Even when his parents did come to see him, their visits were over in no time. Every time the ward bell rang he cramped with terror. One day he'd begged his mum not to go, clutching her hand as tight as he could.

'Stop it! Stop being such a crybaby.' She'd slapped him away. Her voice was so sharp everyone had been able to hear it.

He had thought things couldn't get worse – until they

did. His dad stopped coming to see him completely, and then his mum started missing visits too. Someone mentioned the word 'divorce' and someone else sneered that his dad had found another wife with two new little boys. He wanted to bash his dad with a stick then, bash him till he knelt down and begged and grovelled to have him back. He blamed his dad for everything but he also blamed himself for everything. Whichever way he thought about it, it hurt.

He lay strapped to the frame for weeks, months, one year, and eventually two long years passed. He forgot about home and lived inside strange daydreams. There were new pleasures to be found in his imagination, where he roamed in a bizarre mirror world in which doctors and nurses did all sorts of different things to him. Some of them were nice things, like feeding him jelly or petting him on their knees. Others were hot and shameful things that he knew he couldn't tell anyone about. When his day of freedom finally came and he left the hospital, he'd been so mixed-up and angry that he'd kicked his mum's leg so that she cried and said she wished she could leave him at the hospital for ever.

Now he understood there had been damage done. Slowly, he'd laid a pretend new character over the secret mess of himself. When his mum eventually dumped him in a boarding school, the other boys had called him Quasimodo when he limped behind them with the caliper dragging his leg. The thin crust of his new personality couldn't cope with ordinary stuff, like making friends or catching up with two years of schoolwork. And now here he was – stuck in a crap job after all the thousands of quid that had been spent on his education.

At first he'd been looking forward to seeing the orthopaedic wards and checking out the new kids on frames who came in with Perthes hip, the same condition as his. But Darren said they didn't do that to kids any more.

'That was only in the old days, mate. Keeping kids strapped inside iron bars. It was cruel, like medieval torture or something.'

So now they let kiddies run around at home until the hip joint fixed itself. The news set off a red-hot bolt of anger. He had been crippled in other ways to straighten his body out. These soft kids, they didn't deserve their freedom. The idiot medics had got it all wrong. It was their fault. He'd like to strap *them* inside an iron cage and let the fun begin.

Halfway through his first shift Rikki found an excuse to watch the office with Diggers' name on it. Lots of people passed by, so he had to saunter past pretending to be on his way somewhere else. But soon his patience snapped and he found an empty office with a phone. He'd learnt the extension number off by heart and dialled it, feeling a rush of excitement. It rang out a few times and then he was in luck and he got straight through.

'I'd like to make an appointment,' he said in his politest voice.

'Who is this?' The voice was flat and incurious.

'Someone you used to know very well.'

'Who is it? I'm very busy at present.'

'A patient of yours. Just started working here at the Memorial.'

'What do you want?'

'Just a chat about old times. See if you remember me. Diggers.'

There was a very long silence and he wondered if the line had gone dead.

'You do remember me, don't you, Diggers? Your best boy in the world. Harris Ward. 1962.'

Still no reply. Then finally that voice again, hushed and wary. 'I can't talk now.'

'When can you talk?'

'It's simply not possible.'

'Come off it. You can't be that busy. We've got loads to talk about.'

Rikki stiffened as a loud knock erupted on the door. Shit. When he didn't answer someone battered it again. With ghastly timing, it swung open and Darren barged in.

'What the hell are you doing in here?' Darren yelled.

Rikki covered the receiver with his hand and answered, 'Sorry, pal. I had to make an emergency call.'

He turned his back and spoke into the phone again. 'Got to go,' he said to Diggers. 'I'll ring you back.'

He crashed the phone down into the cradle.

Darren was shaking his head. 'You've got a bloody nerve. There's a taxi been waiting nearly an hour to take a very sick patient to Fairholme. I told you this morning. You got cloth ears or what?'

Rikki had to tell a sob story to Darren to shut the tosser up. He hurried to the taxi, thinking hard. The whole call had been pretty bizarre. He reran the sound of Digger's voice in his head; there had been no warmth in it at all. Surely Diggers couldn't have forgotten all that had happened between them? He felt a spasm of pain. For years he had consoled himself with the childish dream that someone had cared for him, however weird the set-up. Christ, was he really so unlovable? No, the world was fucking cruel, that was it. Well, he had learnt to be cruel, too, as Diggers was going to find out any day now.

Cynicism

Question 21: Most people are motivated by selfishness and desire for money.
- A. True
- B. Uncertain
- C. False

High score description (option A.): A negative or overly critical world view, doubt or disbelief in the motives, sincerity and goodness of others.

Here it is at last. I've always known I could be ruined by fate, springing out at me from nowhere. I've fooled myself the past is nothing but flickering images kept safe in my box of steel.

But this – invasion – has proved me wrong. It's proved the past is still alive, like a nasty bacterium, latent until it attacks, bringing weakness and collapse. That's how it felt when I heard that boy's voice on the phone. A toxin. A brain fever. The realisation that all I possessed could be snatched away.

After slamming the phone down, I locked my door and took 20mg of diazepam with a swig of cold coffee. I had to stop thinking of what I might lose. I laid my palms flat on my smooth desk and let the pills work. My advantage is, I have some knowledge of my enemy. Young, male, quite an educated English middle-class accent lurking beneath those affected glottal stops. He works here in the hospital so might be a medic, or a nurse. Or perhaps he's a lab technician working alone at a bench, a supplies assistant or even some low-grade ancillary worker.

We've probably passed each other on the hospital corridor. He must have spied on me and hunted me down. Well, now I know and I have one important clue. He is new here. 'Just started,' as he so prosaically put it.

For the first time I envy that jumped-up personnel officer with her access to boundless information. It amazes me that no one else sees how ridiculous she is, parading her 'science of the obvious' remarks. Patronising cow! I've come to loathe that bored expression on her face, as if she really should be somewhere else doing something far more interesting. A list of new starters, that's what I need. It's the sort of thing Miss Quick has at her fingertips. Yet I can't come up with a plausible excuse to ask her for it.

No. I need only stay alert behind my usual professional mask. The boy wants something from me, some money no doubt. That will prove his weakness; the little snake will need to raise his ugly head to snatch his reward. Suddenly I laugh out loud. The solution is simple. I need only arrange an appointment. And send Christie to meet him. In secret. Alone.

Anxiety

Question 22: I can depend on my memory not to let me down.
   A. False
   B. Uncertain
   C. True

High score description (option A.): Tense, overwrought, excessively worried or nervous, poor concentration.

The roar and racket of a motorbike exploded in the evening silence on Balaclava Street. Jas dashed to the window and shouted, 'It's Auntie Lily!' At last it was Friday night and Lorraine was gratefully sprawled on the settee, helping Jas with her maths homework. To her relief, the pink marks on Jas's arms were only the result of practising Chinese burns with her friends. Still, a visit from Lily. She knew she was ungrateful; if she let work grind her down she'd soon have no friends left. But still, she'd promised herself a lazy early night.

As ever, Lily made a theatrical entrance, dressed head to foot in shiny black biker gear.

'I wasn't expecting you.' Lily took off the heavy leather jacket and cumbersome helmet.

'Can I try those on?' Jas was always fascinated by Lily. There goes my plan of getting Jas's homework done early, Lorraine thought. Now it would hang over them all weekend, along with the psychometrics revision, a late college essay and a satchel full of overdue paperwork.

'Yeah, little sister. Try them on if you like.'

Lily sprawled on the settee, keen to spill her news. 'Get this. We've got a gig next Saturday at the Students' Union. It's that charity benefit for missing people. Just a support, low on the bill, but it's amazing, right?'

Lorraine raised an effortful burst of energy to answer. 'Fantastic. Well done.'

Lily was enjoying her moment of glory. 'You do get it, don't you? This could be our big break. And they're looking for someone to take on tour to Germany. Cool, isn't it?'

'That's fantastic.' She was pretty happy about it; after all, it was what they'd been working towards for years. Back in '78 she'd fallen in love with this wildfire movement that had erupted not from money-mad record companies, but from kids on the streets. Yet tonight she had to hide a yawn.

'What's up? You do get holidays, don't you?'

'Oh, yeah.' She didn't bother explaining that she only had a few days left, thanks to the long school holidays.

They talked for a while about fitting in another rehearsal and all the logistical stuff.

'Oh, I forgot to say, the charity've asked us all to waive our fees for the gig. Missing people. It's a good cause,' Lily added quickly.

'So who's paying me back for the van hire and petrol?' Lorraine knew it was mean of her but she was glad to see Lily squirm.

Lily didn't meet her eye. 'We'll all club together. Honest.'

Jas was parading about dressed in Lily's black leather jacket, the helmet like Darth Vader's on her tiny shoulders. Picking up the fireplace poker, she began jabbing the air.

'I am the Warlock of Firetop Mountain,' she said in a deep voice that made them laugh.

'It's these adventure game books.' She flung it over to Lily.

'You are a zombie. I will destroy you,' said Jas in her villain voice. Tentatively, she tapped Lily's biker boot with the poker.

'Not if I do first,' said Lily, squaring up to defend herself with the fire tongs.

Lorraine watched them play mock battles until Lily took a breather to ask, 'Any chance of a cup of tea?'

'OK.' But as she headed to the kitchen she couldn't resist saying, 'Don't forget your homework, Jasmine.'

When Lorraine returned from the kitchen, she was surprised to find Jas sitting on Lily's leather-trousered lap, poring over her maths book.

'Wow,' she mouthed silently, setting the mugs down.

'Auntie Lily's much better at Venn diagrams than you, Mummy,' Jas announced. Lorraine sank down in the armchair, overjoyed. As soon as the homework was done she put Jas's exercise book away and said, 'Time to say goodnight to Auntie Lily. And give her a big hug for helping you.'

She took her daughter upstairs, promising to read her two stories tomorrow if she skipped one tonight.

'She's a cool kid,' Lily said. She had moved to the piano and was playing rambling boogie-woogie, a fag in her mouth.

'I forgot you did maths for your degree. That was great timing.'

'Yeah. So how are you? I mean, really? Ever hear from Andy?'

Jasmine's biological father was the last person she wanted to discuss. Feeling cornered, she said, 'No, thank God. Not since he showed up at his mother's last Christmas. I'm not letting him see Jasmine.'

'She doesn't mind?'

'What she doesn't know she can't miss.'

Lily played a final melancholic chord. 'Oh, Lorraine.' Lily's pity bit deep. 'No one else on the scene?'

She gave an awkward shrug. 'It's hard. The only guy I've even noticed recently is that police sergeant who interviewed me.' She laughed slightly too shrilly.

Lily didn't laugh. 'That sounds heavy. Remember how the coppers behaved when you made that complaint against Andy?'

Lorraine still found herself blushing as if the assault had been her fault. 'Please, don't.'

'And forget the male species, too? You're a bit young for that.'

Lorraine shrugged awkwardly. 'I honestly can't see the point. Apart from, you know, a bit of practical help. It's not fair to Jasmine to get tangled up with someone again.'

'And this copper you've met?'

'He's more like me. He's after something different.'

'Has he got anywhere in catching that murderer yet?'

'No. They're still working on it. But Lily, something bloody awful has happened. I need Rikki out of the band. He's got himself a job as a porter at my hospital. I can't stand him being around me at work.'

Lily took her time to respond, getting out a ready-rolled

joint. Lorraine watched the ritual, the flame flaring in little bright cinders of hash.

'I can't believe Rikki's got a job. Wow. I thought he was up for a long service medal at the dole.' Lily released a big gust of sweetly aromatic smoke. 'So where're we going to get another drummer by Saturday?'

'Can't you ask around? He's creeping me out. Wasn't he questioned by the police over the Yorkshire Ripper stuff?'

'Oh, loads of people were questioned.' Lily cast her a sidelong look. 'Maybe it's not just about you, Lorraine,' she said tartly. 'He told me he knows someone at the hospital. Someone from years ago.'

Lorraine stalled, taking it in. Apparently, Rikki had been at the hospital the day Rose died. Maybe he'd known her friend from some past encounter. No, it was too freaky to contemplate.

'Did he say who?'

'No. But the way he talked, it was someone really big in his life.'

Lorraine put the thought to one side, sensing Lily was trying to distract her.

'Listen,' she insisted. 'Rikki's a dealer and a user. There's Jasmine to think about. I don't want her anywhere near a junkie. Can we please get rid of him?'

'OK, OK. But only when we've found another drummer.'

There was a long silence in which Lily offered her the joint. Lorraine shook her head and it felt like something bigger, like a rejection of their shared past. Suddenly she remembered one practical reason she'd wanted to see Lily this weekend. Earlier that evening Jasmine had picked out the melody line of 'Path of Stars' on the piano with her index finger. She had a musical ear. She deserved lessons. And maybe twenty quid would get her started.

'Actually, do you know anyone who wants a twenty-quid wrap of speed?'

Lily took a long draw of smoke and held it in for ages before exhaling. 'Sure.'

Lorraine went to fetch her satchel. It felt right. She needed to face the future with a clear and unsullied mind. Rummaging to the bag's bottom, she knew she'd put it somewhere safe. She checked her purse but it wasn't there. Annoyed, she began to go through the bag's inside pockets. Then the memory of where she'd put it hit her brain like a hammer.

'Oh shit. Oh God, Lily.' She stared into her empty bag.

'What's up?'

'I stuck it in my Filofax. I can't believe it.' Lorraine buried her face in her hands, struggling to digest the consequences. 'The police have taken my Filofax,' she groaned. How had she been so stupid? She could picture the moment when she'd been in the car with Diaz, when her brain had been overflowing with other stuff. Now it was only a matter of time until he found the drug and showed it to Brunt.

'I'm a personnel officer. And I just let the police know I possess illegal drugs. Jesus Christ, Lily, I think I've just blown my whole career.'

Tender-mindedness

Question 23: I am brought near to tears by other people's sad circumstances.

    A. Often

    B. Occasionally

    C. Never

High score description (option A.): Sensitive, tender, temperamental, dependent, fastidious, insecure.

Sunday 27th February

On Sunday Lorraine was up before dawn, ragged from broken sleep. Half-heartedly, she inspected a pile of post that had lain ignored while she searched the job vacancies in *Personnel Management*. She had studied each job carefully, though the adverts all described roles even worse than her current one: jobs with weekend working, overnight travel and aggressive-sounding conflict with the unions.

As she sorted the post, a small envelope fell to the floor. It bore a fancy crucifix and a postmark two days' past. Inside was a card bearing a sleepy pink-robed Madonna holding a fair, fat baby.

The message read:

Clipped to the card was a piece of blue Basildon Bond paper:

Dear Lorraine,
Rose talked about you as a friend, maybe her only
true friend at the Memorial.
We are holding a special Mass for Rose on Sunday
morning and you would be most welcome to join us.
Phil Cavanagh

An hour later, it felt like a welcome distraction from her Filofax anxieties to be driving along empty Sunday roads with her *A to Z* open on the passenger seat. Then she caught sight of St Dymphna's – the church crouched over narrow terraced streets, its lead roof rising in turrets and blackened crosses that looked more satanic than holy. She had trouble finding the entrance and wandered through a maze of semi-derelict outbuildings. When she finally got inside, an ill-kempt priest swooped down on her like a bird of omen, mumbling at her in an Irish accent.

She took a seat near the back of the nave with the intention of having an easy escape route at hand. Above her head, industrial-style ironwork supported flaking plaster. Her hymn book smelt of mildew. Why had this relic of a place been chosen to celebrate Rose's life? It didn't endear her to Phil, a character Rose had rarely spoken of, save to make mild complaints. Barely a score of people were scattered in the pews, most of them elderly and none she could believe were Rose's actual friends. If someone holds a Mass for me after I die, she thought, let me at least have friends and family and a few fresh flowers.

Then the organ struck up a wandering introit and the priest and an altar boy in a nylon surplice processed up the aisle. Behind them came a lanky middle-aged man with bowed shoulders, metal-rimmed glasses and longish greying hair. That had to be Phil. Holding his hand was Tim, wiping his face with the cuffs of his jumper.

A series of prayers and responses were chanted. Candles were lit, the censer was swung, a tinkling bell rung. The ritual meant nothing to Lorraine and she spent most of the service worrying that she shouldn't have come. At last the final amens were muttered and genuflections made. Then with a click and squeak an ancient PA system hummed on. Suddenly Elvis Costello's 'Good Year for the Roses' filled the air. It was a bit tinny but somehow just right, evoking a tumble of images of Rose's lipstick prints and cups of cold coffee. To Lorraine's embarrassment she began to sniffle. She wished she still had Rose's fancy hanky to weep into. Lacking even a paper tissue to wipe her nose, she forced back her tears.

While the priest gave a final benediction, she found herself whispering her own prayer. 'God bless you, Rose,' she muttered into clasped hands. 'I won't forget you. And I promise I won't stop searching till I've found out who stole your life.'

* * *

At the exit the priest firmly blocked her way, insisting she give her condolences to the widower. Next door, in the parish hall, she swerved away from a bereft-looking couple whom she thought might be Phil's parents. Instead, she headed for the food and helped herself to a baked custard tart and cup of strong tea.

Phil Cavanagh stood a few feet away. Poor bloke, he was having trouble stirring his tea, never mind doing justice to the refreshments. She introduced herself and felt his misery radiating like static.

'You look upset. Unlike some,' he said. Close up, he had an intelligent, beaky face, though grief left him looking dazed.

She nodded. 'It's impossible to believe.'

From nowhere, his son appeared, twining his skinny arm around his dad's trouser leg.

'Hi, Tim,' she said, sounding horribly over-bright.

'Hullo,' he said in a tiny voice, not meeting her eye.

'Do you want a custard tart? They're really nice.'

He looked up at the table and said listlessly, 'Can I have a spoon and dig out the custard?'

'Course you can. Here's a chair to sit on.'

Once Tim was settled Phil hovered closer. 'Rose talked about you. She seemed to like you.' He fixed intense, swollen eyes on her.

She lowered her voice to speak. 'I feel terrible. On that last day she wanted to speak to me. Something was on her mind.'

He pushed a strand of greasy hair behind his ear and frowned. 'Let's find somewhere private.' He gestured to the woman she'd marked as his mother, who bustled over to Tim, then Lorraine followed Phil into an empty side room where tatty hymnals and Christmas decorations were gathering dust.

Phil stood against a table and offered her a cigarette. When she refused, he lit one himself with shaking fingers.

'How are you getting on?' she asked.

'Getting by, I suppose. They're letting me work from home while I sort things out.'

'Good, good. And how's Tim?'

'OK. Sort of. A few issues. A fellow at your place, Doctor Andrews, is going to see him.'

She puzzled over the unfamiliar name.

'Child, you know, psychology. Just to – it's all a bit beyond me.'

So that was what Diaz had meant about Tim getting extra help.

'Anyway, you're right,' Phil said. 'Rose was preoccupied. Not herself for a while.'

'For a while?'

'From round Christmas, I'd say. A couple of months.'

Lorraine frowned. At that time, she'd been immersed in heavy reading for the psychometrics course – but yes, it was true, Rose had been rather distant.

'Any idea why?'

He pulled on his cigarette as if it were oxygen and tapped the ash onto a dead cactus.

'I did wonder. She said this guy McClung had pestered her. But then she laughed about it. Called it a grown-up crush.'

Mike and Rose? It definitely sounded like one of those embarrassing mid-life infatuations.

Phil peered at the grimy window, weighing something up.

'And yet, the only time she was really upset was the night before – it happened. I came home early and she was on the phone and was incredibly emotional, really having a go at

138

someone. You remember how gentle she was?'

She nodded. However much turmoil she may have felt inside, Rose had always presented her exterior as serenely unflustered.

'I told that inspector all about it but he tried to twist my words. Said it must have been this Mike. I don't think it was. I could hear her repeating a name. I went to the door and listened. The bastard's name was Chris or Christian or something like that.'

'Anything else?'

'No. I was so annoyed I slammed the door so she'd hear me. She rang off straight away.'

'Chris? I'll ask around.' The name meant nothing to her. Now Phil was watching her, his pale eyes stunned with pain.

'Can I ask you a favour?'

'Of course.'

'Please. Call round this afternoon if you can. With Jasmine. Honestly, Lorraine, it would be worth a dozen psychology sessions to Tim. My parents have to go back to Yorkshire pretty soon. They'll be back whenever we get permission for the official funeral. Say, three o'clock?'

She inwardly yelled at herself to resist. She was fast running out of time to gen up on the course. It was no use. She felt his pain.

'Fine,' she said with a weak smile. 'See you later, then.'

By three o'clock Lorraine was ringing Phil's doorbell with Jas in tow, fresh from her mum's. Rose's home was a three-storey townhouse on a housing estate where the bricks were so new they glowed bright orange. The frontage was as showy as a doll's house with fake Georgian pilasters and pediment, though Rose had restrained herself from the wishing wells and window boxes some of her neighbours had indulged in. Opening the door, Phil looked even greyer than before, though his tobacco-stained smile showed he was genuinely pleased to see them. She envied Jasmine, who ran past the adults straight to Tim and launched into an interrogation about his toys.

While Phil fetched coffee, she tried to get comfortable on the slippery leather Chesterfield. The room was saturated with Rose's presence. Vases of dried flowers stood in the cold fireplace and on the bookshelves. There were photographs too, endless pictures of Tim from baby to shy little boy.

Phil returned with surprisingly nice coffee made with hot milk. She sipped it slowly. Phil heaved himself into an armchair and stirred his coffee thoughtfully before he spoke.

'Look, I know everyone probably thinks I'm to blame. But I did try. It might not have been the easiest of marriages, but since Tim came along Rose was a lot happier.'

Lorraine nodded, wondering what exactly had been wrong with their marriage.

'You had a gorgeous wedding,' she said, and pointed to a photo in a silver frame. She wasn't remotely into weddings herself, but anyone could tell from the outfits that it was a very fancy do. Rose wore a seventies frock with mutton-chop sleeves, her head crowned with a floppy lacy hat. Phil had sported long brown hair and a kipper tie. Both looked embarrassed and awkward.

'The photographer was brilliant,' he said. 'It was one of the unhappiest days of Rose's life. She'd fallen out with her chief bridesmaid, who didn't even turn up. The whole day was overshadowed by Julie's non-appearance.'

Lorraine sat forward and tried to mirror Phil's gestures, hoping he'd keep talking.

'Rose didn't strike me as quarrelsome,' she said gently.

He tensed and looked away. 'She had her frustrations. Like I said, she put up with things – with me – and then got irritated. But she would never have risked Tim's happiness.'

'Did she have any other close friends?'

'She met a few people at keep-fit but they were on and off. She never spoke to Julie again. I wanted to meet you but Rose didn't like mixing work with leisure time. I assumed you were her new best friend, what with all the nights out you had.'

Lorraine hesitated for barely a moment. 'Phil, I'm really sorry, but I haven't ever had a night out with Rose.'

Phil grasped the arms of his chair and swallowed hard. 'I'm not totally surprised. The police asked me if she was seeing another man.' He raked bony fingers through his hair. 'Actually, I wanted to ask you another favour. You can always say no. My brother is coming to stay next weekend and I'd like to give him the back bedroom. It's just that Rose used it as a sort of – well, her own room. It's full of her things – clothes, face cream, you know. Do you think you could take it all away?'

She was genuinely lost for words.

'I mean, feel free to take anything you want for yourself. I know she'd want that. She doesn't have any family left. The Oxfam on the high street has a back porch where you can leave it all. It's just – she's not coming back, so what's the point?'

He stood up and reluctantly she followed him. 'But surely you want to keep—'

'I can't bear to touch her things myself. I've left some bin bags up there. And you and her were both similar—' His fingers clumsily traced the invisible silhouette of a woman's figure in the air.

Embarrassed, she trailed after him, towards where the children were prancing around in a front bedroom. On the threshold to Rose's room, Phil backed away downstairs.

'The police,' she called out after him. 'They won't mind?'

Over his shoulder he mumbled, 'They took everything they wanted.'

Walking into Rose's room she had the oddest feeling of déjà vu, as if she'd visited the place before. A moment later she recognised it from a page in last year's Laura Ashley catalogue, immaculately recreated by Rose. It was all there: the ruffled Austrian blinds, pink rosy wallpaper and frilly mob-cap lamps. She sank down on the floral bedspread and sadness overcame her, that all this artful endeavour had failed to keep death from Rose's door.

Think, you idiot, she told herself at last. This is the room of your friend who was murdered last week by an unknown colleague. Rose and Phil no longer shared a bedroom. Their marriage was unhappy. If Rose kept any secrets they might still be right here. When Rose retreated into this private space, who was she?

She studied her surroundings and concluded that Rose was a romantic, a seeker of rose-tinted scenarios, a deeply feminine woman. Judging by the abundance of photos, Tim fulfilled her maternal desires, but Phil's absence confirmed that he didn't feature in her romantic yearnings. She found the lingerie drawer but discovered no basques or suspenders, only neatly folded pink and white St Michael's underwear. Had Phil

142

been trying to suggest that she and Rose had similar figures? Perhaps, and they were both fair-haired, but beyond that they were polar opposites. Rose would never have touched peroxide. And the thought of wearing Rose's prim underwear was out of the question. She tipped the drawer's contents into a bin bag.

The paperbacks on the shelves were also the opposite to her own tastes. The books were all romantically inclined women's fiction: *The Mists of Avalon*, *The Thorn Birds*, and a few Victoria Holts and Georgette Heyers. Even if Lorraine didn't like the idea, Doctor Lehman had said that women on the whole tested as slightly more tender-hearted, neurotic and submissive than men. So Rose wasn't unusual, just far closer to the feminine norm than herself. And in that phone call overheard by Phil, and Rose's outburst in the fog, she had proved herself to be enmeshed in secrets. So what did Rose want beyond a frilly pink boudoir?

Lorraine stuffed four bags with the detritus of an extinguished life: Avon powder puff talc, bath cubes, St Michael make-up and Camay soaps. Her clothes smelt of citrusy Aqua Manda and occasionally Lorraine fancied she caught the odour of ancient cardboard from the medical records basement. She picked up an expensive hairbrush still tangled with golden hair. Death cast its taint over even the most prosaic of objects.

Across the landing the radio blared out Alan Freeman's weekly charts for his pop-pickers. She could hear Jasmine bossily making a tape recording of her favourite songs. So it was to the accompaniment of Annie Lennox singing '*Sweet dreams are made of this . . .*' that she found the item that made her freeze in her tracks. At the very back of the wardrobe was a white plastic handbag containing tissues and half a packet of Polo mints. Deep inside a zipped compartment was a key ring. It held two keys, a Yale door key, blackened by time, and a smaller iron mortice key. Lorraine raised it to the light and read 'Room 7' written in black ink on the ancient cardboard label. Below the number was a name written in the same old-fashioned curly italics but missing its final few letters. *The Wil-* something. The Willows or Williamses, perhaps? The two keys weighed cold and surprisingly heavy in her hand.

So did they belong to the Williamses' family house, or the Willows Nursing Home, or maybe even the Wilton Hotel? She had a vision of a seedy hotel paid for by the hour, the sort of place she presumed was used by prostitutes or married philanderers. Whatever rooms the keys unlocked, she was sure Rose had hidden them away for a reason. The white handbag went into the charity bag but she put the key ring inside her jacket pocket. Maybe if she found the Wil-something Hotel she could look at the register and identify Rose's murderer. And if she did that fast enough, maybe Diaz would trade the information for the return of her Filofax.

Downstairs, Phil was smoking at the kitchen table, an unread copy of *The Observer* open before him.

'It might be nothing, but I found this.' She laid the key ring on the pine table.

He inspected it. 'God, how sordid. A hotel bedroom key. I've never seen it before.'

'I'm wondering if I should look for a Chris Williams?'

He studied the fob closely. 'If it even says Williams? It's a really tatty label, given how it's partly torn away.'

'Probably from the NHS then,' she joked weakly. 'I'd like to try a few keyholes, if that's OK.'

Phil shrugged. 'Keep it quiet, will you? I'd rather nothing like this goes any further. Whatever gets into the papers might be read by Tim one day.'

'Of course.' Then she added, 'You mean from the police, too?'

Phil hesitated. 'Well, they didn't think it was important, did they? See how you get on first.'

'OK.'

'The kids' teacher mentioned you're looking for a new childminder.'

Thanks a million, Mrs Dearden, she thought. When she didn't reply he made a proposal that sounded very carefully designed to appeal to her.

'Jasmine can come here before and after school. I'm off work for a while. And you've seen how well the two of them get on. She'll be much happier here than at the Carneys'. Won't she?'

It was all true, and the arrangement would be immensely convenient. It was pretty perfect but nevertheless she felt reluctant to agree. It was bizarre, but there was a slight chance Phil might be tangled up in Rose's death.

'Well, if it's only temporary,' she said at last. 'Until I find a permanent solution.'

Rule Consciousness

Question 24: It is safer to follow basic rules of right and wrong than risk society's disapproval.
    A. True
    B. Uncertain
    C. False
High score description (option A.): Conscientious, responsible, determined, sense of duty, concern with moral standards.

Monday 28th February

On Monday morning Lorraine got up well before sunrise and dropped Jasmine at Phil's house, feeling relieved pleasure as her daughter hurtled up the path to greet Tim.

'Coming in for a coffee?' Phil shouted from the front door.

'Sorry,' she called through the open car window. 'I need an early start.'

In fact the post meeting had been cancelled as Norman was away, so by eight-thirty she was in the payroll section at Pomona House. She requested an urgent computer report on all staff employed at the Memorial over the last year with the names 'Chris' and/or 'Williams'.

'Could be ages before I get round to it,' the clerk spluttered, his mouth full of a bacon barm cake. 'Got a massive backlog.'

'The police need to check staff names urgently. Today. Yes, it's in relation to the murder inquiry.'

The clerk wiped his greasy mouth on his sleeve and told her he could get it sent over that morning.

At the Memorial she went in search of Diaz, hoping to beg back her Filofax. Just her luck, he was out of the office that morning and she had to wait. Crossing the hospital site, she managed to slip inside the nurses' home. It was a rambling Victorian villa subdivided into sad little cubicles. Though each cubicle bedroom had a key, she saw at once that the keys were all much smaller and fitted with red plastic fobs.

In the switchboard room she had a word with the supervisor, who pointed to shelves of dog-eared Yellow Pages. Against the incessant din from operators greeting callers and clicking jacks back and forth across the consoles, she searched 'Hotels', 'Homes', 'Rest Homes' and 'Bed and Breakfasts'. She didn't get far. There was a newly built King William Hotel and a few variations of Wilmslow Hotels far away in Cheshire but nothing worth following up.

Nevertheless, she was starting to feel better, binding her anxiety onto orderly actions, controlling her fears by taking determined steps forward. It reminded her of one of Doctor Lehman's tenets, that it was better to employ mildly anxious individuals in responsible jobs because they always turned their worry into to-do lists.

She needed to find Room 7. Back in the office a porter

delivered the report from Payroll. She took the pale green computer printout to the privacy of the interview room and unfolded its concertina pages across the table. All the relevant names had been listed but none was credible as Rose's lover.

At eleven she had an appointment with Lynn, the deputy medical records officer, to discuss the vacancy left by Rose. She found her sitting around a table with three other clerks. Lynn was a gabby redhead of about thirty-five who made it clear she resented her upgrade to manager.

'I can't stop,' she complained, looking up from clipping papers into an awkward springy clasp. 'I came in this morning to find records chucked all over the floor. Security isn't interested because nothing's missing.'

'So what do you think happened?' Lorraine asked, inspecting the mess made by the removal of a whole shelf of files.

'How should I know? That shelf over there was pulled right out.'

Lorraine picked up a random folder that, according to the cardboard cover, contained the medical history of 'Herman Woods'.

'Lynn, I need to speak to you alone.'

A few moments later they both sat on opposite sides of Rose's former desk. Trying to project relaxed friendliness, Lorraine said, 'Rose wanted to speak to me about something very personal the day she died but it didn't ever happen. Do you have any idea what it might have been?'

Lynn's hand shot to cover her mouth. 'Oh God. This is about her being murdered, isn't it? She was seeing someone, wasn't she?'

'It's one possibility,' she said casually.

Lynn's hard eyes watched her, weighing something up. 'I wouldn't have blamed her if she had been carrying on.'

Lorraine nodded in encouragement until Lynn spoke again.

'She wasn't happy at home. I think some men could tell – that, you know, she was available. Mr McClung, the engineer, was always hanging around her. She put up with his daftness but I don't think he got anywhere.'

'She confided in you?'

'Well, I could tell when she was fed up. If she talked to anyone I'd say it was Miss Jardine. I suppose being a nurse, she knew best how to advise her.'

Lorraine felt a momentary pang that Rose had confided in the chief nurse rather than herself. Then she dismissed the idea that Mike had been involved. 'You said "men", so not just Mr McClung? Did someone called "Chris" figure at all?'

'Not that I know of.'

'Or a room she had a key to?'

'No.'

'Have you heard of "Williams" or "Will-something"? A name or a place?'

'No, I can't help you. But Doctor Strang and Rose were often at loggerheads. Is his name William? You know what they say about sparks making a fire and all that?'

'It's Victor.' She paused, trying to picture Rose with the acerbic consultant, but couldn't. 'Anyway, let me know if you think of anything. And I'll place the advert for the manager's job in the journal next week.'

On her way out she took another look at the scattered files that were slowly being reassembled. 'So which letters of the alphabet were pulled out?' she asked the nearest filing clerk.

'There didn't seem to be no rhyme nor reason,' a plump woman replied. 'It were only from the end of the alphabet: some of the Vs and most of the Ws.'

Lorraine inspected the shelf that was too high up the wall to reach without a step. 'Are you sure there's nothing missing?'

'Not a page. A few got a bit crumpled, but thank God not a single record has gone missing.'

'Did they include "W-I"? Williams and so on?'

'Yeah.'

Lorraine mentally reviewed any other surnames she knew from the end of the alphabet.

'Have you got my assistant's file? Edith Woodbridge?'

One of the filing clerks rifled through the pile on the table and handed it to her. It was a notably thin file and Lorraine didn't open it.

'So was that file disturbed?'

'It were one of the ones thrown on the floor, yeah.'

It was a day when no one would leave her alone. On the way back to Personnel, a domestic assistant harangued her about missing overtime payments. Then a physio reminded her she hadn't yet sent out the new pay scales. At last she sighted the open door to Personnel and called out to Edith, 'Would you take a look at Mary Greenhalgh's overtime please?'

She stopped short to see her assistant perched on the edge of her desk, her face raised coquettishly towards a man. He had his back to her and his fingers were touching Edith's shoulder. A second glance revealed he was wearing a porter's jacket. The dyed silver hair was the final giveaway.

'Edith!' she barked. 'Get back to work.'

She jumped off her perch like a frightened bird and scurried back behind her desk.

'Don't you have a job to go to?' she said, as Rikki didn't move away.

He kept his cool, which was more than she could manage. 'Come off it, Lorraine. Even porters get tea breaks.'

That casual use of her first name stoked her anger. 'You were touching her,' she insisted.

Rikki turned an unruffled grin in her direction. 'And which law does that break?'

'My own personal law, which says you don't play creepy little games with work colleagues.'

'I only ask,' Rikki said casually, 'because you could always check the law with that policeman standing behind you.'

She turned to look. Unseen behind her back, Diaz was all eyes, watching from the open door.

'I am asking you to leave,' she said to Rikki. Edith didn't look up from where she was blushing violently behind her desk.

As soon as Rikki had gone, Diaz stepped inside. 'Am I interrupting something?'

'Not at all. You've got great timing,' she said. 'In fact, I need a word. In private.'

Diaz followed Lorraine as she climbed the stairs up from Personnel to a door that looked like a cleaner's cupboard. He had to bend low beneath the lintel to reach a further cramped set of stairs that rose high above the hospital's entrance. At the top he followed her into a shabby cube of a room that he realised was the inside of the Italianate clock tower. He was surrounded by unfaced stone, grey from the passage of time. Against one wall was a short metal ladder that ascended to the wheels and cogs of the clock mechanism.

'Like something out of *The 39 Steps*,' he said, looking around. On three of the walls the interior disc of the tower's clock face gleamed, taller than a man. Mirror-reversed images of large Roman numerals shone through. The clock didn't seem to be running so the air was dead still.

Lorraine sat down on a rough wooden bench. She nodded agreement but was obviously narked.

He lit a ciggie without asking if he was allowed. The flame from his lighter flared up like a fire in a cave and then the shadows returned.

'So what was going on down there?' he asked, exhaling slowly.

She was watching him, her head leaning back against the stone wall, appraising him so hard he could feel a current coming off her.

'That porter's making a nuisance of himself.'

'Who is he?'

'Eric Fryer. Edith appointed him last week. A mistake.'

'Is he breaking the law?'

She winced. 'He's on the edge. She's very young for her age.'

The devil in him decided to needle her. 'And you don't allow relationships at work?'

She gave him a withering look. 'Relationships at work equal problems: jealousy, favouritism, fallout when it all inevitably ends. If colleagues get frisky, I say – throw a bucket of cold water over them.'

'OK, OK.' An amused guffaw escaped him. Then,

remembering he was on duty, he rapidly assumed a scowl.

'Actually, have you questioned him?' she asked. 'Eric Fryer. You should. He was here at the hospital the day Rose died, though he wasn't even working here then. He came in to apply for the job. I noticed the date stamp on his application form. And he has a history of being a nuisance to women.'

'I'll look into him. You had any more thoughts about those tests?'

'Maybe.' She folded her arms protectively across her middle. 'Have you interviewed Phil Cavanagh?'

'Course.' Actually, Brunt had questioned him but Diaz had studied the statement. Cavanagh had been at work all that day, so it wasn't clear how he could have switched the propofol. He'd have needed an accomplice. Could it have been Lorraine herself, Rose's best workmate?

A prickle of suspicion prompted him to ask, 'And you've had a chat with him, obviously.'

'I went to a Mass in her memory. He told me Rose had been behaving oddly. He suspects an affair. It does tie in with her wanting to talk to me in confidence. And why someone wanted to shut her up.'

'Who was she seeing?'

'Rose's husband overheard her arguing on the phone, getting upset. Speaking to someone called Chris or maybe Christian. He said he'd told Brunt all about it.'

Flaming Brunt – that hadn't figured in the statement. The DCI only heard what he wanted to hear, which, at the moment, seemed confined to anything iffy about Raj Patel.

'I've checked the payroll for "Chris" or anything similar,' she continued. 'There's no one at all likely. Just sixty-five-year-old Christopher Jenkins in the lab and a Chris Ross, a fourteen-year-old schoolboy on work experience. Oh, and a Christine Baker, a fifty-nine-year-old domestic who I think we can also discount. So maybe this Chris or Christian is a personal friend?'

'Right.' This was a lot of information she was divulging. The FBI articles said you could sometimes spot a perpetrator because they tried too hard to help the police.

'He seems sincere,' she said. 'Phil, that is.'

It was Phil now, was it? 'Well, we can't rely on hearsay.'

She shrugged. 'I suppose you think he's to blame because he was her husband.'

Diaz sighed. 'It is a fact that women are far more likely to be killed by their partners than a stranger. Especially if the woman tries to finish the relationship.'

'God, I hope you're wrong.' She looked completely stricken. She was probably thinking about the little lad again. Well, at least he'd got some therapy arranged for the boy. He'd have liked to tell Quick about it but reckoned he'd already shared too much.

'Look, I get that you're trying to help, but it's hard evidence I need,' he said instead, sounding overly harsh.

She shot him a stony glance. 'Right. But I suppose you still want my soft personality testing skills?'

Jesus, he'd fallen into that one. 'Well. Yeah.'

She folded her arms and looked away. Finally, she said, 'Look, I'll help you in any way I can but I can't share the test results. I checked with my tutor. If I do, she'll report me to the Psychological Society. Can't you get a police psychologist or someone to do it for you?'

'Brunt would no more pay for a psychologist than a witch doctor.'

'I'm sorry. It's not ethical.'

'And what about Rose? Is it ethical to let someone get away with killing her? Come on, I know you want to help.'

'You really do hassle people, don't you?'

'Help me then.'

She jerked her chin up abruptly and sighed. What she said next startled him. 'I might help. If you give me my Filofax back.'

'What? It's all bagged up in the station.'

'Can't you get it out? Or can't someone just lose it?'

'Why?'

'I can't tell you.'

He gave a groan of frustration. 'I can't pull something like that out of the evidence room. It could destroy the whole case. You're a key witness. I can't let you contaminate the evidence.'

Lorraine exhaled as if the weight of the world had just sunk onto her shoulders.

'So what's all this about?' he asked, making an effort to speak more gently.

She pressed her fingers to her brow. She looked up at him beseechingly. 'Please can you give me my diary back?'

He shook his head.

She stood up. They were a similar height and for a few seconds he really looked at her, studying the contours of her face, his breathing shallow. Their gazes momentarily connected. The next moment she hurried off with a hurt expression. He hung back in the gloom, smoking another fag. He liked this weird tower room; it was good for thinking, like the silent eye at the heart of a hurricane. Emergencies and crises might be erupting only yards away, yet here the air stood still.

Well, there was only one way to sort the bugger out. He dropped the butt on the floor and stamped on it, wondering what he'd find. As soon as he had a minute, he'd go to the evidence room and take a dekko inside Miss Quick's Filofax.

Memory Disturbances

Question 25: There are times when I have trouble remembering recent events or the things I have done.
   A. Often
   B. Occasionally
   C. Never
High score description (option A.): Periods of memory loss more severe than usual forgetfulness, finding self in unusual places, memory blanks.

I was as high as a kite when I walked out of Brunt's office. For twenty entertaining minutes I'd been amused by that dyspeptic old duffer hammering away with questions so far off the truth it was hilarious.

I headed for my office and reached for my keys. Then it hit me. They were too light in my hand. Back at my desk I inspected them. The heaviest keys, the couple belonging to Room 7, were missing. They were Christie's old guestroom keys from years ago, still on their labelled ring. One of them opened the back door into the kitchen, and the other, a small iron mortice, gave access to Room 7 itself. True, I'd had a niggling sensation my keys had been light for a few days. Had they worked themselves loose? Where the hell had they got to? My memory failed me.

It was well after five before I managed to get over to Christie's house. The old place hardly looked inviting these days: two gaunt upper storeys loomed above me, the windows blinded by dirty nets. I stepped cautiously into the yard. Twisting tree roots were shoving aside the paving stones, the outgrowths of those specimens that masked the back of the house.

At least I still had my own anonymous Yale, so I got myself inside the back door.

'Christie!' I stood at the bottom of the stairs, yelling. 'Have you taken the key to Room 7?'

No answer. I checked the key hook on the kitchen wall. Room 7's key wasn't there either. In itself, it wasn't a catastrophe, for like all prying landladies Mrs Wilkins had boasted of a spare set of master keys. True, I hadn't seen them in years, but they had to be around somewhere.

I strode to the stairs again. 'Christie!'

She might well sulk. I ran upstairs, flicking on light switches, though the bulbs in those gloomy passages were as weak as water. There was fust and mustiness everywhere. I couldn't remember the last time it had been cleaned.

She wasn't in her room. Well, she wasn't a prisoner. Every now and then she wandered off and was surprised to find herself in unexpected places.

'I'm not surprised you've scarpered,' I shouted into the void. 'After all this upset. You wouldn't believe the fuss your antics have caused.'

I went back downstairs to look for the master keys, but I couldn't think where they might be in any of a dozen drawers. Time was passing – it was night outside – and now I'd got a sudden itch to make the most of Christie's being away and her whole little empire to play in. I ran my fingertips over the keys on the kitchen hooks again, then picked up the one for the basement.

Swinging the key in my hand, I descended the stairway with a burst of pleasant anticipation. I unlocked the Treatment Room and then groaning with relief, I reclined on the couch. God help me, I was tight in my deltoids, my neck was sore, I needed to forget what had happened and take a mental break. I took off my left shoe and set up the injection. Track marks need to be well hidden when you work in the field. In the glass cabinet a torn carton told me that just as I'd guessed, Christie had raided the propofol. There was still plenty left, and a lovely old cannula I wanted to try out, quite the museum piece. I slipped on the rubber tourniquet and palpated a nice springy vein. Milk of amnesia they call it. An emulsion as chalky as the antacid in those blue bottles of Milk of Magnesia, but something else entirely. A nice brisk scratch – boy, those needles were bigger in the bad old days. A jet of fire raced up my leg. One, five, ten seconds. Then I swam into that cloudy stream . . .

I woke gradually. Sleep still lapped at my consciousness, as warm and woozy as an isolation tank. I wondered for a while, Who am I? What is this life I'm forced to live? Then I remembered Rose and that she was gone for ever. I felt more inconvenienced than angry. Until those last few days I'd been enjoying our encounters.

I became aware of a presence moving above me. A momentary obliteration of the bare light bulb. All was well. Christie was here. She came to me, gazing down on me like an angel, her expression all tender forgiveness.

'Come along now. Time to wake up,' she murmured. I drifted, feeling so happy, while she tidied up the injection site and then gently tapped my hand.

Reluctantly I let her help me sit up. I slumped against the cracked leather, watching her move around me with all the grace of a trained nurse. She fetched a glass of water and we didn't even talk about Rose's death. It felt too painful to draw attention to the crime. Whatever those gasbag therapists say, there's no point in talking about unpleasantness. Best forget it. Instead, I gently warned her.

'Be careful, won't you? The police are investigating some incidents at the hospital. So if anyone calls round here, don't answer the door.'

She stared at me blankly as if she had no idea what I was talking about. She can be crafty like that.

Then another block of my memory returned. 'Have you seen the key to Room 7?'

I shouldn't have spoken. Her mood swung like a flag in the whipping wind. She stood up huffily and started seeing to the needles, crashing the delicate glass doors of the cabinet together.

'She's got my key!' she wailed at last.

'Who?' I asked blearily.

'Her. That bitch. She must have taken it. Fancy you getting involved with someone at work. I knew it, I knew it,' she muttered. 'What am I going to do? What am I going to do?'

I tried to comfort her but she was too agitated. Soon there were tears and then insults. Circular thoughts emerged in stuck-gramophone phrases. 'You've ruined everything. Ruined it. All my happy memories gone. It's all your fault!'

I was still confused but the truth of what she was saying rang true. Maybe Rose had taken the key. I grew angry because Christie might be right. I pushed her away and she bumped against the couch, giving a little scream. I stumbled out of the room. I'd had enough. I ran for my car.

'You'd love to get rid of me, wouldn't you?' she screamed after me. 'But you can't, can you? I'm a prisoner here. I've got no life thanks to you!'

I was giddy by the time I got behind the wheel. All the way home I struggled to stay calm, praying the propofol would linger in my nervous system and soothe my mind. It had to have been Rose. After she'd sneaked a copy of Christie's phone number, she must have taken Room 7's key as well.

So what the hell had Rose been planning? To confront Christie? To go there, get inside; to try to find my secret love nest? Well, maybe there was justice in the world. She'd got what was coming to her just in time.

In a panic I asked myself, where was the key now? What if the police had found it in Rose's possession? Damn her to hell and back. They might link it with Christie. They might even connect it to me.

And what made it worse than anything else was that it was Room 7, of all rooms. I couldn't let strangers see what was in there.

Depression

Question 26: There are times when my mood is too low for me to meet anyone.
   A. Often
   B. Occasionally
   C. Never

High score description (option A.): Feelings of weariness, worries, lack of energy and hope, general dissatisfaction with life.

Tuesday 1st March

The next day, Lorraine was crossing the yard on her way to find Mike when Raj caught hold of her arm.

'You want to see the new computer suite? Have a quiet chat?'

He led her into the newly upgraded building that had once been the luxurious doctors' mess. The main room still smelt of fresh paint and was stacked with furniture draped in polythene. Cables littered the floor and copper wiring poked out of holes in the plasterwork. The walls of the doctors' exclusive former sitting rooms had all been knocked through. Another sign,

Lorraine thought, of the end of centuries' deference to the medics.

She paced around, touching the smart new blinds and worktops. Raj was desperate to unburden himself.

'I'm scared stiff they're going to arrest me.'

'Why should they?'

'I lied in a statement,' he said in a flat voice. 'I told the police I was in the accounts office the morning Rose died. But really I was in my car.'

'Oh.' She wished she could unhear his words. 'What were you doing there?'

Raj flinched miserably. 'Do you ever feel you've got to escape the pressure cooker? Get away from the office?'

'Yes. But I usually just go to the loo and take a few deep breaths. Sorry, what were you actually doing in the car?'

He looked at her sheepishly – or was that a hint of craftiness in his sideways glance? The maroon shadows beneath his eyes made him look different today.

'I'm not sleeping properly. I just needed a kip. And now they think I went and swapped the vaccine. You know I didn't go near the place.'

'Not so far as I know. But you shouldn't have lied, Raj.'

'I thought it would be easier. You've got to know that sergeant chap, haven't you? Can't you tell him I'm an OK guy?'

She tried to laugh but it sounded forced. 'I don't think it's that easy.'

'This is my life, Lorraine. They've even accused my wife of being part of it. It's true she was a doctor in Delhi, but she's never practised here in Britain. So now I'm some kind of expert in anaesthetic drugs. It's barmy. All I know are the budget codes. You know it wasn't me.'

She thumped his arm. 'Just stick to the truth, hey? That way I can back you up to the hilt. Now I'd better get going.'

The blackened chimney rose above the hospital boiler house, just like the stacks of industrial mills that had crowded the skyline of Lorraine's childhood. She rang the buzzer beside his door. Waiting, she wondered how Mike could stand living in the flat that came with his job as chief engineer, living right next to the boiler's perpetually thumping heart. It started raining and she found herself looking back over her shoulder, shivering as if someone was watching her. Trust your gut instincts, Doctor Lehman had said. She carefully surveyed the hospital grounds. Nothing moved.

People often joked that she must love catching staff who claimed to be sick when they were later seen running around the football field or disembarking from a plane at Ringway airport with a suntan. On the contrary, it only added to her workload and diminished her faith in humanity. She was relieved when Mike finally appeared, looking poorly and unkempt.

'Sorry to bother you, Mike. It's not an official call. Just seeing how you are.'

Reluctantly, he gestured her inside and upstairs to the flat. The poor bloke was wearing grubby tracksuit bottoms and carried the fusty smell of sickness. He ushered her into a sitting room with woodchip wallpaper, a flocked brown three-piece suite, and an array of dismantled machinery spread out across the carpet. What did impress her was his Technics hi-fi, a gigantic tower with a famously expensive graphic equaliser. The whole place looked clean, without the usual bachelor stains and crumbs.

He didn't offer her a cup of tea, just a seat on the armchair, while he flopped down on the settee.

'It's such an awful time for everyone.' She leant forward and noticed Mike's eyes were puffy. 'I want you to know you're not alone in this mess.'

The poor fellow was hugging his middle defensively, wanting to hide inside himself. 'Right,' he said. 'Are you saying I can keep my job?'

She had learnt on Doctor Lehman's course that highly practical types responded best to blunt speech. 'Yes. So long as you aren't involved in this tragedy. And if you recover well, and come back to work when the doctors say so. Why do you think you'd lose your job?'

In the long silence she noticed the ticking of a wooden clock on his mantelpiece.

'Mike?'

'The police think I had an unhealthy interest in Rose. I didn't! It was just – I liked talking to her. That's not unhealthy, is it?'

'No. Talking to someone isn't a crime.'

To her embarrassment Mike sank his head forward into his hands and his chest started heaving.

'They made me feel dirty,' he said in a strangled voice. 'I sent her a few letters because I had to tell her how I felt. It was vile, to hear those strangers talking about it. But I never hurt her.'

'Have the police got the letters?'

He lifted a face streaked with tears. 'No. She told me she destroyed them.'

'Why? Was there anything – incriminating in them?'

Suddenly a pale fire lit his eyes. 'Have they sent you to spy on me?'

She attempted a non-aggressive pose, leaning back against the chair. 'No,' she said gently. 'It's hard, isn't it? If you really cared for Rose.'

He nodded emphatically. She waited again, wondering if he'd make another outburst.

'She was desperate to speak to me that day,' she added. 'Had something happened between the two of you?'

'Not then.' His lips were trembling, making it difficult for him to speak. 'It was all over. Long before that. I'm all churned up. I could kill whoever did that to her.' The next moment he looked up at her, terrified. 'Sorry, for God's sake don't repeat that.'

'So what was wrong with her that day?'

Suddenly he grew hard. 'Wasn't that for you to find out? I heard you put her off till it was too late.'

She nodded. 'I feel awful.'

'I suppose you told the police I knocked on the boardroom window?'

'Yes, I've tried my best to recall everything from that day.'

'Well, after I saw you I noticed another light on in the flu clinic. I looked inside and through the net curtains I could see someone. Not very clearly, though it was someone tallish, I mean an adult. So I did the same thing, I gave a sharp knock on the glass but the only thing that happened was the light went out. I waited a bit but the light stayed off. So I thought I'd probably just knocked as Sister Ince was going out. I didn't think much of it and carried on to the oxygen tank store.'

'God, Mike. I was just a few doors away. You might have seen the killer.'

He nodded, then sighed. 'I should have gone in to find out.' Suddenly he stood up and said, 'I'd like you to go now.'

She stood up too. 'If you want to talk in confidence to anyone, Mike, just give me a ring.'

With effort, he showed her to the door.

Lorraine hesitated on the threshold. 'I'm sorry to bring this up now. But there's the general manager's job. Given your sick note, do you want to withdraw?'

He nodded his head vaguely, all his aggression subsided. 'Can I do that? Say I don't want it?'

'Of course. If you're certain. There's just one thing. Everyone going for the job will be offered training if they need it. It could be a management course, or a secondment, or even a qualification. Would you be interested?'

He raised his head, looking more alert. 'I had a counselling session yesterday. I was expecting – I don't know, some sort of codswallop. But it made me think. I'd got into a state about the general manager job because I don't know the first thing about being a manager.' He released a heavy sigh. 'Maybe it's time I faced up to things. But if I don't go for the job, can I still have the training?'

'Well, I could try to sort it out for you. But any training has to be based on the psychometric test and a learning plan. I've got the test here if you want to have a go.'

She opened her satchel and offered him the PX60 test booklet. He took a step back in alarm.

'I was dreading taking that test. Dreading what it would tell everyone about the real me.'

The real Mike? She felt a frisson of apprehension but

spoke up. 'This is a chance to get feedback about yourself, Mike. I suffer from anxiety myself at times and it's hard to believe things will get better – but with help, they will.'

To her surprise he took it, opened the booklet and began to read.

Lorraine couldn't face going back to the office just yet. Mike's raw pain had got under her skin and she needed a breather. It had stopped raining so she turned her back on the hospital, and set off down a neglected path into an expanse of shrubbery. She was cold, but it felt refreshing after the airlessness of Mike's flat.

Soon she reached a forlorn area where weeds sprouted amongst rectangles of masonry. She had recently recognised the place from an engraving in Norman's office; it was the garden of the first hospital superintendent, laid out in Italian style with formal ponds and planting. Though it had fallen into neglect, it still possessed a mood of serenity. She bent to touch the caps of pristine snowdrops bravely pushing through the soil. She had a sudden fierce longing for the countryside: for long walks filling her lungs with unpolluted air as she gazed out over hills and valleys. If she missed one thing from before she started work, it was the freedom to get out into the wild.

One day, she would take Jasmine on a holiday. There would be mountains and lakes and forests to explore. As a child she'd been lucky to live near scrubby woodland and play intense games with her friends, building secret forts and dens. Somehow she had to offer those childish adventures to Jasmine, too.

She found a rickety bench and sat down to mull over

everything she had recently discovered. She was worried about Raj. It had been a bloody cheek to ask her to put a word in with Diaz. It made her question just how shallow their friendship had been. Today she had glimpsed new traits in him that she didn't much like.

And yes, she could understand how Mike, trapped in his dreary flat and subjected to lonely, monotonous work, had cultivated an infatuation for Rose. It was sad, but understandable. She recalled his depressed demeanour and wondered if the story about the light in the flu clinic could be a diversion because he had harmed Rose.

That assertion of Rose's deputy, Lynn, had bothered her, too. Lynn had told her Rose had confided her worries about Mike in Felicity. Later that day, Lorraine had approached Felicity on the main corridor. Cautiously, she had tried to draw Felicity on the subject.

'I have my own suspicions about what happened to Rose,' she'd fibbed. 'Wasn't Mike bothering her?'

'That sap,' Felicity had scoffed quietly. 'I told Rose to tell him to get lost. Didn't she tell you all about it in one of your visits to the League of Fiends café?'

Lorraine had chuckled at the notion of those earnest do-gooders in the League of Friends in reality being a clutch of devilish fiends. 'No. Apparently, Rose didn't confide that much to me.'

'Didn't she? You always looked like best chums. I wondered if there was someone new in Rose's life.'

She had reached her car and said goodbye to Felicity, adding, 'If there was, she didn't tell me.'

Now, chilled to the core, she got up from the bench to return to her office. The mid-afternoon shadows were lengthening and a couple of times she imagined the sound of footsteps following behind her. Alarmed, she went in search of a shortcut back into the main building. Amongst the rows of prefabs and medical labs, she lost her way. Frustrated, she persevered until she faced a dead end and was forced to take a nasty little ginnel back towards the hospital's electrical glow. In the deepening dusk, she dared herself to walk past a tribe of feral cats nesting by an air-conditioning outlet. It was the watchfulness of the cats that made her look up to the top of the building. A figure was perched twenty feet above her on the roof beside the stairway of a fire escape. He didn't move, just stood with arms folded, watching her. As soon as she noticed his spiky hair, she faltered and stopped. Had Rikki been following her?

He remained motionless, malevolent against the bruised sky. He didn't speak. She began to pass beneath him, making a feeble pretence of not having seen him.

Then she heard his voice, a low bass, gruff and accusatory.

'You've been a long time in that murderer's flat, Lorraine.'

She didn't reply; the only sound was her heels clicking as she dashed to the hospital entrance.

Wednesday 2nd March

On Wednesday, Mike called Lorraine into his office on the main corridor. He looked dreadful, his shoulders slumped, his face waxy.

'I told Harvey about your withdrawal from the general manager's job and that's absolutely fine,' she said. 'But should you even be here? The doctor's note means you should be taking it easy.'

Mike's office was a dingy mess of fading engineering plans and dusty Venetian blinds. The only colour glowed from the golden crest and red seal of his framed certificate conferring the title of Chartered Engineer.

'I just wanted to check some paperwork. I'll get off now. And thanks, I've done the test,' he said, holding out the completed scoresheet. 'It was good to be distracted for a while.'

At once, she put the 'Do Not Disturb' sign up on the interview room door. She had a choice between sending tests to Doctor Lehman to be computer scored or scoring them by hand. With the exam coming up fast, she opted to practise self-scoring and placed a cardboard template punched with holes over Mike's answers. After counting up the raw scores she compared them to a normative group, in this case UK middle managers. Then she plotted Mike's profile and was at once struck that his scores looked far from normal. Worst of all was an unusually high score of 9 out of 10 for Guilt-proneness. All the questions about self-reproach, worry and feelings of guilt were scored highly. She checked it again, fearful that Mike was using the test to communicate something to her, maybe that he had in fact killed Rose.

On the landing she caught sight of Diaz descending to the main corridor. His broad shoulders were set firm and he looked infinitely secure in himself. For a second she sped up, eager to share Mike's results. Then she stopped in her tracks. Doctor Lehman had banned her from sharing results and she must stand by her tutor's better judgement.

It was no use. From some sixth sense he glanced up and spotted her. He raised his arm in greeting and smiled up at her, making it hard not to respond with the same.

'I'd like to re-examine everything Rose told you over the last few months. How are you fixed for tomorrow morning?'

She felt suddenly buoyed up to be helping the investigation. 'Sorry. It's the general manager shortlist meeting. I could do Friday, though.'

They agreed on a time and she continued to the fax machine. When he forgot to scowl Diaz's eyes were darkly intense, she thought. Then returning to Mike's troubling words about his real self, she faxed her hand-scored results to Doctor Lehman with a note about her concerns and a request for the tutor's full interpretation.

Though Lorraine kept trying to phone her, Doctor Lehman was unavailable all that afternoon. As soon as she got home she pulled out her course notes. There were only a few paragraphs on personality type and crime, and those connected it with high impulsivity. Doctor Lehman had called the theory rather simplistic; it suggested that those who were impulsive and thrill-seeking were less likely to be conditioned by the rewards and punishments that stopped most citizens from breaking the law.

'Are we going to have tea soon?' Jasmine was heading for the biscuit tin.

Lorraine shoved the notes inside her bag. 'Won't be a minute. You can whisk the Instant Whip while I grill the gammon and pineapple.'

Impulsive Nonconformity

Question 27: I do risky things just for the hell of it.
   A. Often
   B. Occasionally
   C. Never

High score description (option A.): Undependability, recklessness, impulsivity, unstable mood, especially in relation to social norms.

By Wednesday's night shift Rikki was getting seriously pissed off. The only other two porters working that night had been called to Casualty and hadn't come back, so he was alone, manning the porters' office. On an impulse he took the master keys off the hook. Spinning them around his forefinger, he felt their power to open doors and uncover secrets. All around him were miles and miles of dimly lit corridors and empty rooms. He stretched and yawned, picked up the porters' pager, then shuffled his boots on over his sweaty socks.

Disembodied cries occasionally reached him as he paced the corridors. Some parts of the hospital sounded like a zoo at night. When he'd been an inpatient himself, he'd been taken on a trip to a proper zoo where he'd been pushed around on a sort of flattened wheelchair with his legs stiffly clamped. A woman had come over to Diggers and said, 'You're a saint, doing what you do.' Jesus, the old bag must have thought he was a retard. But in some ways it was true. Diggers had always come to see him, telling jokes and bringing comics and little toys – and had stayed in his bed with him too, when he was scared stiff before a procedure. If he told the authorities about that it would sound pretty heavy, a proper case of kiddy-fiddling. But to be honest, he wasn't exactly sure if it had been pervy. It had been nice; just sharing warmth and touch and the sort of real love his mum didn't have a clue about. Was it against the law, though, if the kid and the grown-up both liked each other? Maybe that made him a perv as well.

His feet gravitated towards Diggers' office. There was no one around to see him slot the master key into the keyhole. Inside, he clicked on the desk lamp and looked around. There were some impressive certificates. He studied the framed credentials on the wall, reading over the familiar dates and the hospital address that had been his home. He reached out to touch the glass and felt a pulse of connection with his own history.

He helped himself to a couple of Hobnobs from the tea tray and munched them as he began to search the desk. There was nothing of interest in the top drawers, only paperclips and all that crap. It was the bottom right-hand drawer that resisted his tugging. He began to search for a smaller key. He had done a little light housebreaking in his time and learnt that people only spent about two seconds thinking about where to hide things. He rotated the amber light of the desk lamp around the four corners of the room, looking for hidey-holes. His stubby fingers felt around the tops of the framed pictures. Then he looked through all the tea tins and packets. Nothing. Next, he noticed the bookshelves were recessed inside an outer wooden rim. His fingertips found the key on the top shelf, tucked out of sight.

As he opened the lock, he was hoping to find money or something he could sell. Instead he found ampoules of propofol. He pulled one out and inspected it under the lamplight. The liquid was opaque white, true to its street name, milk of amnesia. He knew it well enough: the stuff anaesthetists injected into your arm before telling you to count backwards from a hundred – and if you were lucky you reached ninety-seven. Everyone knew it was the drug used to kill Rose Cavanagh here in the hospital. He considered reporting Diggers for holding a secret stash. No, no. He had to keep schtum or it might mess up his own plans. But then again, it was a pretty big coincidence to find it locked away here.

He wondered if people really could change. After all, this year his mum had forgotten his birthday, for fuck's sake. Yet how could Diggers, who had held him like a baby when he was a traumatised kid, have developed a propofol habit? His thoughts veered between past and present, sending little shivers through his body that could have been anticipation, or maybe even fear. The voice on the phone had been so cold when he'd mentioned Harris Ward. What had happened to the grown-up he had worshipped? He looked around the office and began groping towards an explanation. It was there, hanging just out of reach at the back of his mind, but it wouldn't quite come into focus.

A blaring electronic alarm sounded out. He shot up

like a jack-in-the-box and looked wildly around the room. Erratically, he shone the lamp over the desk and walls looking for the source. Jesus, he was going to have a cardiac arrest himself at this rate.

Suddenly he laughed out loud. Flaming hell, it was only the unfamiliar pager in his pocket making a hideous electronic screech. Red digital letters glared out 'CALL 264' in the oblong window of the little black box. All in a rush, he shut the bottom drawer and locked it, and shoved the key back where he had found it. Later, he would come to regret how easily he had been distracted. For by the time he headed off into the night, his emerging theory about Diggers' behaviour had completely slipped his mind.

Guilt-proneness

Question 28: I feel guilty even when I know I have done nothing wrong.
   A. Often
   B. Occasionally
   C. Never
High score description (option A.): Apprehensive, self-reproaching, worrying, sense of obligation, sensitive to disapproval.

Thursday 3rd March

It was the closing date for the general manager's job. As each application form arrived, attached to impressive professional credentials, Lorraine had photocopied them for her own file and glanced through them. Doctor Strang had thrown everything he could at his bid for the job, cramming the form with masses of clinical data. She felt he'd missed the point, which was to persuade the panel that there was more to him than a clinician. Norman had presented his long career in the kind of uninspiring detail that would send the interview panel to sleep. Felicity, on the other hand, had grasped the Thatcherite concept of reform and written a terrific statement on how she would tackle the job. Reading it, Lorraine wished she were on the interview panel to probe the chief nurse more deeply. Experience had taught her that a brilliant application form didn't always lead to brilliant performance on the job. Finally, Raj had confused number-crunching with leadership. She suspected he was going to suffer badly at the hands of an inquisitorial panel.

Lorraine had asked Harvey why they even needed a shortlisting meeting, given that all the applicants already worked at the hospital. 'You have a lot to learn, Lorraine. If Whitehall thought we could manage something as simple as an interview on our own they'd all be out of a job.' He had laughed but she had shaken her head behind his back. All this kerfuffle over rubber-stamping a list of names. With a few minutes to spare before the meeting, she asked Edith to fetch the paperwork.

The sound of a little squeal made Lorraine look up. Edith had unlocked the cabinet and was ransacking through it. 'Have you gone and moved the professional certificates, Lorraine?'

'No. Of course not.'

Edith turned around, her face tight with apprehension. 'The application forms are here. But someone's moved the certificates. I locked them in a different drawer like you said. I'm sure I saw them—'

Lorraine joined her and Edith darted aside. But even when Lorraine systematically worked through the drawer from back to front, there was no sign of the contents of the file titled 'General Manager Professional Certificates'.

Trying to remain calm, together they unhooked all the

drawer's contents and laid them out across their desks. However many times she looked, Lorraine could not find the documents. Terror dawned as she remembered that the shortlisting meeting was expecting to verify the candidates' precious registration certificates – registration to practise medicine, nursing, administration and accountancy. Was it possible that she, the hospital's personnel officer, had lost all the original certificates she'd been entrusted with?

Against her better judgement, Lorraine pounced on Edith. 'That porter friend of yours. Did you ever leave him alone here in the office?'

Edith was on the verge of tears. 'No. I never. It wasn't him.'

The clock told her she was already ten minutes late for the meeting. Lorraine got out her own personal photocopies of the qualifications and sent Edith to copy them again, as carefully as she could. They couldn't pass as originals because the originals were coloured, embossed with seals and crests, while the copies were black and white and a few had emerged skew-whiff from the photocopier. Yet they were something, at least, to produce at the meeting.

By the time she arrived at the boardroom, she was twenty-five minutes late. Harvey was addressing a group of top brass from the Regional Office and Department of Health. She chose a peripheral seat, in dread of being spoken to. For a long time the men scored low-wattage points against each other. Finally, her old boss noticed her.

'Ah, Lorraine. Find out what's happened to the coffee and biscuits.'

When she returned with a catering assistant and refreshments trolley, she poured the drinks and handed them out with a smile. It was about twenty minutes later that Harvey asked her to pass round the application forms.

His interested expression puckered into a frown as soon as he'd leafed through a few pages. 'Where are the original certificates, Lorraine?' he asked.

She plastered on a humble-handmaiden smile. 'I'm keeping them under lock and key. So there's no possibility of losing them.'

'For goodness' sake,' Harvey protested. 'I told you we'd sign the professional registrations off today and return them to the candidates.'

Any second now she would have to make some pathetic excuse: she had lost the key, or the drawer was stuck. So she entreated Harvey to shut up using the silent force of her desperate gaze. At first he returned her stare in irritation, and then finally, thank God, picked up that something was wrong.

'Well, do bring them along next time,' he added lamely.

To the assembled men he said, 'Do we all agree that each candidate has their merits?'

As expected, the motion was carried that all four candidates should be interviewed. Only when the big chiefs had all left the room did Lorraine confess that the certificates were missing. 'I'm going to turn the entire office over inch by inch. And if they're not there, I think we should tell the police.'

Harvey's pouchy mouth compressed in annoyance. 'Pull yourself together, Lorraine. It's not a police matter. You've lost some documents and you're going to bloody well find them.'

By Friday morning, everyone at the post meeting knew about the lost certificates. Norman eyed her furiously through his round spectacles.

'We've had something of a crisis upstairs,' she gabbled. 'The thing is, your certificates are not where I left them.'

'What? You mean my accountancy certificate is missing?' This was from Raj. Thanks a million for your loyalty, Raj, she thought.

Out loud, she said, 'I doubt they are actually lost. The fact is, they were locked away in a cabinet and now they've disappeared.'

'Do you have any idea how difficult it will be to replace my nurse registration?' Felicity wailed. 'Unbelievable!'

'Naturally, I'll arrange for replacements straight away,' Lorraine cut in.

Norman shook his head. 'Sadly, the Hospital Officers' Association no longer exists. A replacement is out of the question.'

'I'm so sorry. I'm sure we can find—'

Doctor Strang interrupted, gripping the arm of his chair. 'If I am fortunate enough to be general manager, things are going to be run very differently in the future.'

When the meeting ended, Lorraine hugged her satchel to her body and made for the door.

'Just one moment, Lorraine.' Norman glared after her.

Before the others had even left, he leant back in his chair and began to lecture her.

'Within these four walls, I'm going to give you some personal advice. You're not really cut out for this sort of work, are you? It takes a certain kind of person. Someone with natural man-management skills.'

'Actually,' she said bravely, 'our staffing is seventy-four per cent women.'

'This habit of yours to always have the last word is exactly what I'm talking about. If I were you, I would try another line of work, before it's too late. Personnel simply isn't for your type.'

She forced her lips into a twisted smile. 'But don't you think that all these types are changing, Mr Pilling? The new general managers are being drawn from a variety of different professions and most personnel officers are now female.'

Norman's thread-veined cheeks glowed. Then he said, 'Don't think I take your insubordination lightly. If you don't find my missing certificate, I'll see you get your marching orders without delay. Understand?'

That afternoon Lorraine had a message to ring Doctor Lehman. She sent Edith to the photocopier with a huge pile of circulars and was lucky to get hold of her straight away.

'Lorraine,' her tutor answered, as unruffled as ever. 'I hope you are well. I understand you must be feeling your friend's death very deeply.'

It was ridiculous, but the older woman's sympathy touched her. Lorraine's throat burnt and she only managed a mumbled 'Thank you.'

'I read your faxed note about Mr McClung with interest. Firstly, let's look at your question about the link between crime and impulsivity. On the course I was discussing a personality type who would never attain the self-control needed by a competent chief engineer. The unredeemed criminal, the excitement-seeker who frequently reoffends, never learning from mistakes. A moody individual who finds ordinary routines strictly for the bores.'

'More of a James Dean type?'

'Yes, exactly. Or rather his character in *Rebel Without a Cause*. Of course, there are other factors beyond personality, such as the effectiveness of parenting, and the opportunity for crime. Yet the fact is that crime is mostly a phenomenon among young men. Almost all young men commit minor transgressions – and plenty of young women too. Who has not, when younger, stolen a small item or struck out at another person in anger? The question is, rather, how it is that most individuals develop the self-control that allows us to live in a civilised society.'

Lorraine warmed to her tutor's good sense, recalling her own idiocy as a teenager, when she had nicked some make-up to impress a gang of older kids.

'So Mike's score doesn't suggest criminality?'

'No. However, as you noted, his score on the Apprehensiveness scale is very high. But that doesn't mean he is a criminal, rather that he has a very active conscience. Taken with his other results we see an intelligent, rational but compulsive man. One might even say he is obsessed with his work. And he's deeply interior. Note the very low score for Warmth, a coolness suggesting he expects little support or pleasure from other people. You tell me he wrote letters to the victim. He may have failed to see the consequences and now feels mortified by the suspicion he's aroused.'

'Yes, he is. Could Mike be violent?'

'In my opinion, probably not. His results suggest he is more likely to feel anger only under intense pressure and then will usually hide it. Rather than express it, he turns it upon himself. Is he receiving any therapeutic help?'

'Counselling for his depression.'

'Good. Let us hope he can be turned away from any suicidal thoughts. More social contact would be very beneficial. Now, Lorraine, I can fully understand it if you need to defer the exam?'

'No, no. I need to do it.'

'Good. But when you come down, we should meet after the other candidates have left. We'll speak then.'

Imagination

Question 29: I am sometimes so absorbed by my inner thoughts and ideas that I am unaware of my surroundings.
   A. Often
   B. Occasionally
   C. Never
High score description (option A.): Imaginative, absent-minded, absorbed in theory and ideas, enthralled by inner creations.

It had already got to Friday and the investigation was at a standstill. The chief super's 'I'm relying on you, Diaz . . .' played on a loop in the sergeant's head. As he'd expected, Brunt couldn't get anything serious to stick to Raj Patel. A couple more witnesses had seen him asleep in his car, but the evidence wasn't stacking up. Patel's wife freely admitted she'd worked in women's health for more than ten years in India, but her medical tutors vouched that she'd never worked with anaesthetics. The goofy accountant didn't feel right for Rose's killing. After Brunt's morning briefing, Diaz retreated to his own tiny office and started to give his own lines of investigation some real welly.

Doctor Strang was proving to be a complete tosser. He'd given Brunt an initial interview but all Diaz's further requests for clarification were being met by his British Medical Association rep accusing him of time-wasting. So he had gone through Strang's background inch by inch and found an accusation of misconduct. Yvette Dobson, a ward clerk, had made a complaint that he'd molested her. The trouble was, it turned out she'd resigned before the committee had a chance to meet.

He tracked the complainant's phone number down to a remote part of Yorkshire. But when he finally got hold of Mrs Dobson she laughed it all off in a patently fake way. 'It were six of one and half a dozen of the other,' she said. 'I were flattered and then I got the huff when he cooled off.'

'Were you ever nervous around him?' Diaz asked.

'Of Victor? Not likely. Now my fella's due home any second so do me a favour, will you, and don't bother me again.'

Giving up on that line of enquiry, he next decided to take a quiet look at the flu clinic.

'I'm just going to take a dekko,' he told the bobby keeping guard at the top of the admin corridor. He'd brought along a photostat of one of his prized FBI Bulletins to try to get this ultra-modern approach right. The paper was written by two special agents – and boy, didn't that sound cool – at the FBI Academy, Quantico. It talked about the psychological profiles they created to catch suspects in homicide cases. A key part was to get access to the crime scene and try to reconstruct the crime. There were clues, the paper said, that were not physical. Traces of rage, fear, love and hatred. That was the profiler's job, to learn to read the pattern of personality invisibly etched on the walls of the crime scene.

Standing inside the cool, pale room, he felt its ordinariness, its weight of routine. Feeling a bit of a twit, he closed his eyes. He tried to conjure an image, a feeling, a portrait, anything at all. Around him the room felt cold and distinctly whiffy with disinfectant. Yet he thought he could feel something. An alien consciousness focused on the task of murder.

He cast his mind back to that first Monday and imagined the killer's movements: walking silently down the corridor, entering the room, closing the door quietly behind him. It probably only took a few furtive moments. With surgical gloves stretched tight he'd taken the top off the flu ampoule, discarded the vaccine and refilled it with propofol.

Opening his eyes, he got out his notebook to make a first attempt at a profile. At the top of the page, he wrote:

1. *Male/Female*

He hesitated. Almost all the FBI suspects he'd read about were male because chiefly young men committed violent murders. He tapped his biro impatiently against his notepad. He wasn't sure if the killer was a man or a woman, so he left the question blank.

2. *Occupation*

That was easier. The killer was practised in giving injections. And patently knew about anaesthetics and the means to acquire them. So, medically trained. Or possibly, a junkie.

3. *Crime scene emotions*

He jotted down, 'Organised'. He had been fast, efficient and cunning. Diaz had seen only a few violent murder scenes and this room was the opposite of those messy car parks and doss houses. He wrote down: 'Clinical'.

Doubtless the perpetrator had mirrored this emotion with a cool exterior as he executed his plan. Only Sister Ince had shown extreme anxiety, which was unsurprising given that she was the apparent stooge, the unwitting wielder of the murder weapon itself. Lorraine Quick had also been fretful, hanging around the crime scene. Brunt had wondered if Lorraine had been present to watch the progress of her murder plan. Diaz thought that was bullshit.

No, he was wasting time considering the women. In the pathologist's opinion Rose Cavanagh had enjoyed sexual activity within the twelve hours prior to her death. Something to do with a stain on her underwear. Unluckily, so far they had no semen to test. According to Brunt, Phil Cavanagh had admitted the couple's sex life had dwindled to nothing over the last year. It looked pretty certain that Mrs Cavanagh had been playing away from home. Returning to question 1, he pencilled in 'Male'.

He puzzled over the crime scene again. He imagined the emotions that having a bit on the side would stir up in most men. A secret thrill, passion, jealousy, fear of public exposure, possibly of being exposed as impotent. Diaz played around with a few scenarios in his head. Then he wrote down the names of his two prime suspects:

Doctor Strang
Mike McClung

Strang. He fitted every aspect of the profile, a divorced man, a belligerent surgeon with professionally chilly detachment. As for opportunity, he had tried to save Rose's life by resuscitating her – or had he? The victim's life had been in his hands and yet still she had died. When waiting in Strang's office his eyes had been drawn to the doctor's ghastly model of a plastic brain. A pair of psychedelic sunglasses had been propped on its gruesome half-flayed face. A sign of free-loving, pot-toking hippy values, perhaps? Diaz had inspected his impressively framed certificates, and shelves crammed with books about drugs, not just medical ones but street stuff: amphetamine, heroin, even marijuana.

When Strang finally breezed in he dismissed Diaz with a curt, 'Monday morning is my ward round day. If you need witnesses to my whereabouts just ask any of my juniors. Now get out of my office. I was due at a case conference ten minutes ago.'

Well, playing the big consultant act would only get him so far against the law.

What was Strang's motive? Maybe Rose had threatened to expose their affair or some other secret? He smiled slowly. It felt so right.

Nevertheless, he'd written down a second suspect: McClung.

In McClung's role as advisor on medical electronics it turned out he knew all about operating theatre equipment and the use of anaesthetics. He was the only member of the team with a proven sexual interest in Rose. And the engineer's personality, so flat and emotionless, could well have carried out the machine-like substitution of two drugs in the cold pursuit of murder.

Diaz gave him a hypothetical motive: fear of the victim exposing his sexual inadequacy. Or perhaps there had been humiliating letters, or something along those lines, that Rose had threatened to make public.

Funny really, but McClung felt right as well.

When Lorraine arrived in the afternoon, he brightened up. He noticed she'd got some nice glossy stuff on her lips and wondered if it was for his benefit. Still, they hadn't met for a date exactly, though if he had the chance he wouldn't say no. He cautioned himself not to be stupid and ploughed into his interview, probing deeper into Lorraine's recall of events. What was Rose's reputation like? Did she ever seem excited, secretive or frightened? Had she changed her habits over the previous few weeks? Lorraine answered carefully, doing her best to summon the tiniest facts. The trouble was, she told him, since Christmas she'd been distracted, busy preparing for the Oxford course and the essays for her postgrad diploma.

By the time he reached the morning of Rose's death, it was all feeling like a let-down.

Lorraine recounted it all again: Rose saying she couldn't stand her job any more, and Lorraine's advice that she signed off sick.

'That was when she started crying,' she said.

'What exactly prompted that?'

'Saying she wanted to resign. That's when I gave her the hanky back.'

'Hold on. Gave it back? A paper tissue?'

'No. She lent me a proper cloth one the week before. I had it in my bag already washed.'

Diaz bit his bottom lip, thinking. 'A cloth one? What was it like?'

'Fancy. With a curly R. Very pretty, embroidered in pink chain stitch.'

'What did she do with it afterwards?'

Lorraine looked up to the ceiling, accessing her visual memory. 'She was wearing a cardigan and she pushed it into her cuff. She still had it with her when we were waiting for our flu jabs. She blew her nose on it. Like lots of people, just before public speaking she had nervous rhinitis. A runny nose.'

He watched her fixedly. 'Look for it, will you. However unlikely, check the car and anywhere else you can think of.'

'I know it isn't there,' she insisted.

Yes, he thought, his excitement growing. She knew it with the same conviction as he knew that a cloth hanky had not been entered in the evidence book.

'Does it matter that much?'

Suddenly he gave way to the urge to share what he'd just worked out.

'A particular type of killer takes souvenirs from the scene of the crime. Things like jewellery, a lock of hair, clothing or a handkerchief.'

He didn't mention the more macabre examples he'd found listed in the FBI Bulletin: the severed fingers and sexual body parts.

Lorraine leant forward, curious. 'But why would anyone risk getting caught just to take a souvenir away?'

'Remember how I told you about different types of killers? The FBI have interviewed loads of these guys in prison and got deep inside their minds. Fantasy is a big thing with them – anticipating the acts they daydream about, imagining a bizarre fantasy world. And then, when they can't resist their compulsion any more, they act. After the act they recreate it in private. That's where these souvenirs, or mementos, come in. When the cops catch these men they often discover a secret trove, like a trophy box. Apparently, they handle these objects to relive the moment more intensely.'

Again, he restrained himself from describing the solitary sexual acts many of these killers indulged in with the souvenirs they stole – or dissected – from their victims.

'My God,' she said. 'But hold on. It's not like Rose was – you know, raped or – I don't know, assaulted. What's this moment they want to relive?'

'Some damaged people,' he said, aware he was probably saying too much, 'get turned on most by complete possession of their victim. And the ultimate power comes at the moment of death itself. That's why I think if we find this handkerchief, we might find the murderer.'

Lorraine pressed her lips tightly together. 'That must mean the murderer was present at Rose's death. The hanky must have been taken after she went in for the jab but before you collected evidence.'

Diaz didn't reply. He didn't need to spell out that it pointed to Doctor Strang. Yet there was another possibility. He needed to check which of the porters had moved the body to the mortuary. A porter. Or it could have been any imposter in a dark blue jacket.

'You said Eric Fryer was in the hospital that day?'

Lorraine nodded. 'And now all the professional certificates for the general manager job have gone missing. Eric Fryer is top of my list for nicking them. He worries me.'

He worried Diaz, too. He'd taken a look at the porter's criminal record and the guy was what he classified as a scumbag. The trouble was, officially Eric Fryer was having a couple of days off after doing some long shifts. But each time the uniforms had called at his bedsit to bring him in for questioning, no one had been at home.

'Well, let me know how you get on,' she said, but didn't move from her chair. She was watching him, waiting.

'Going to any gigs this weekend?' His attempt to sound airy came out a bit too interested.

'You could say that.' She was grinning, getting up, then carefully pushing her chair back neatly.

'What's the big secret?' he asked. She was openly laughing at him now.

'I'll tell you on Monday. Have a great weekend.' Then she was gone.

Alone again, Diaz whistled softly and allowed himself a few seconds to think about her. He wondered which gig she was going to. In a luckier world they might have got together when they both saw Echo and the Bunnymen. He felt his mood sink. Thank Christ for the distraction of work. He began to concentrate hard on what she'd said. The fact that the killer might be a souvenir-taker changed the whole profile. If he was right, the handkerchief was emotional evidence, a clue to the hidden personality of the murderer. He could recall the descriptions of this type of killer with ease. They were intelligent and yet indifferent to society, all the while faking an amiable facade in order to manipulate and use the people around them.

Unexpectedly, the door swung open. Diaz jumped in his seat as guiltily as if he'd been caught committing the sort of unspeakable act he was contemplating.

Brunt was crimson with excitement. 'Get this, lad, a new lab report just landed on me desk. That injection pen, 'ippy-pen or whatever, it didn't have any adrenaline in it. Our super-duper Doctor Strang never even gave her a shot of adrenaline. It were probably just water.'

'Ruddy hell,' Diaz replied admiringly. 'So we might be able to detain him?'

Brunt grimaced. 'He's a right prickly bugger. He won't

come voluntary. And if a magistrate don't sign every jot and tittle he'll probably get some barrister mate to challenge it. You got anything else on him?'

Nothing you'd take seriously, he thought bitterly. Instead he asked, 'Could we get a warrant to search his house?'

Brunt jutted out his flabby lower lip. 'We'd be pushing it. Course his prints are all over the pen thing. But he'll just say it's the fault of Sister Ince, or whichever minion stocked up the clinic.'

'Do you know if the adrenaline would've saved her?'

'Seems not. But it might've woken her up for a few seconds. She might have pointed the finger at someone.'

Diaz could see it all as clear as day. The killer was the organised non-social type. Fundamentally cruel but highly intelligent. The type for whom the perfect job might very well be cutting people's bodies open with a scalpel.

'Boss, I just found out the victim was in possession of a handkerchief when she went in for her jab. I think the murderer took it. It's the sort of souvenir—'

Brunt glared at him. 'We need watertight evidence against this Doctor Death fella. A lost hanky?' He shook his head sourly. 'Even if Strang picked it up I can't see that sticking. Move up a gear, lad. We're not the lost property department.'

Brunt grumbled off, on his way to HQ to have a word with the super about a magistrate's order. Diaz glowered after him, feeling like he was knocking his head against the wall. They had to search Strang's house, for starters. He would go on his own, he decided. It wouldn't be the first time he'd bent the rule book. He would find this killer on his own and make it clear to the chief super he'd had no help from Brunt.

The thing was, he wasn't quite the good little Catholic boy

most people reckoned him to be. When he and his pals seized a load of gear, he was one of that inner circle of lads who took dibs of white powder and bags of strong sweet weed. More than once he'd kept his trap shut to protect a mate whose fists had got carried away when persuading some toerag to confess. He knew he'd taken a few small steps towards what coppers joked was the dark side. But now it was all getting mad, totally off the scale. All this overtime was the perfect excuse for getting home way past midnight and creeping out again before dawn. He didn't want to think about what would happen when the case ended.

He eased his thoughts into more pleasurable channels. Lorraine totally got what he was saying. She was up to speed on psychology and soon she'd be testing Doctor Strang along with all the rest. He leant back and stretched his aching neck. He had to persuade her to share those test results. He pictured a scenario in his mind and found that he liked it a lot. He was reminded of a phrase in the FBI Bulletins. Killers fantasised until they lost contact with reality. And then they pulled their real-life victims onto the stage of their fictional dramas.

For a split second, he understood how all that fantasy shit worked. He liked Lorraine but he still wanted her to play a part for him. And the sense of power that he glimpsed – he grasped that too, how that seductive path could pull even a good man into the badlands of obsession.

Magical Thinking

Question 30: I have sometimes thought that objects have special, almost magical powers.

    A. True

    B. Uncertain

    C. False

High score description (option A.): Unusual experiences, visions, belief one can read and control minds or one's own mind is being read, sense that objects contain a living force.

I still couldn't find the key to Room 7. It was driving me mad. I couldn't break the lock and leave a room like that open. I couldn't invite a locksmith into the house because of what he'd see. I searched for the master keys in each room, one by one. Last night the kitchen, then the Treatment Room. Christie was in a state, too. She has such particular habits and can't bear any disturbance. We both like to see things done properly. We both like everything safe in its place. In the end I headed upstairs, not having checked the room for months. I turned the door handle, bracing myself. The handle resisted. Thank God. It was locked up tight.

For a long time, I leant my forehead against the solid

door, picturing what was waiting behind it, like an ocean behind a frail dam. Back in Mrs Wilkins' day she used to say she liked having lodgers from the hospital because it made her feel safe from the worst that could happen. What incredibly stupid things people say. Once the worst had actually happened to her, Christie moved out of Room 7 but kept that room for her special things. She said it felt safe and secret because the tree branches crowded so close across the window. It was the one place she could entirely be herself.

A soft footfall. Christie had come up behind me, still horribly agitated. She thrust something small and soft into my hand. I watched, baffled, as it unfurled in my palm like crushed petals unfolding. I didn't ask how she retrieved it but let her know how proud I am of her deftness and cunning. A relic is what it is, like a saint's holy knucklebone or papery skin rescued from a torturer's flaying knife. It still smells of her when I bury my face deep into it. It exudes her essence, mascara-tinted from weeping, and when held to the light it bears a watermark of tears.

The handkerchief is so pathetic. And that's what's exciting. The souvenir should have been added to the collection in Room 7 as soon as possible. But till we find the key I'm keeping it on my person. A risk, I know, but I need my small pleasures. I wash my hands before I touch it. I touch myself with it. I picture her sobbing, her begging, her anguish. I plunge my tongue into the thin fabric. It tastes of salt and the insides of pockets. It tastes of wet tears and power.

Parasitic Lifestyle

Question 31: I don't see the point of hard work, as I can always borrow or steal from other people.

    A. True
    B. Uncertain
    C. False

High score description (option A.): Manipulative, selfish and exploitative dependence on others, lack of motivation, low self-discipline, sense of being owed special favour.

Rikki was crashing at Jerry's place after another visit from that bastard money collector. He'd been trying to get the five hundred quid together that he owed, but then some really cool gear arrived in town. 'Why not double your money, mate?' Jerry had urged him. 'Earn yourself a nice little cush.'

He couldn't recollect where it had all gone – the cash or the gear. Up Jerry's nose mostly, and now he was broke again. When Buda had turned up at his bedsit, the collector's fist had nearly sent the door flying off its hinges.

He needed cash and he needed it fast. And some hard stuff to keep himself together. OK, time to push all those mushy feelings about Diggers aside. He reran that weird phone call in his head and clocked that from the moment he'd mentioned being the 'best boy in the world', that pet name had seemed to trigger the same memories in both of them. Secret night visits, hot whispers and cool hands, being kissed and stroked in the darkness. All the way to the phone box Rikki replayed the rising pitch of the voice, the wariness, the alarm. The question was – how best to use Diggers' terror of being exposed to his own advantage?

He had to ring the extension number three times before he got through.

'It's me. About our meeting,' he said impatiently. He was as jumpy as hell, what with people walking past all the time and freaking out that Buda or his mates might give him a thrashing.

'Oh. Yes.' The voice was neutral.

'Look, Diggers. We go back a long way, right? Only I'm in a bit of trouble. It's not even my fault but I need some cash.' There was a long crackling silence. 'After all, we were pretty close, hey?'

'It's been a long time,' said Diggers, slowly.

'Yeah, a long time all right. But I kept that photo, of you and me. Of you by my hospital bed.'

Another long, wary pause. 'Oh, that. I'd love you to show me that photo again. And I'm glad you're feeling better now.'

'That's just it. If you even cared about me you'd know I'm not better. I've never got better. And I know things about you. What you did. All that climbing in under the bed sheets. Times have changed. I was only a little kid, for fuck's sake!'

He heard a laboured breath being exhaled. 'I have no idea what you are talking about.'

'Oh yeah? Yeah? OK. Let's talk about what's in your

bottom right-hand drawer then. The one you keep locked. Or are you having – let's say, a rush of amnesia?'

'Have you told anyone?'

'Not yet.'

'We need to talk about that.'

'Right. So don't fuck me around. It's going to cost.'

'What do you want?'

'Five hundred quid. And a supply of the hard stuff. Morphine, right? The computer suite'll be empty for a few more weeks. It's dead quiet in there. Best if you come in at night.'

'Night. What about late tomorrow night? Just after midnight.'

'OK.'

'Good. And I want to see the photo. Don't forget the photo.'

'I won't.'

A click sounded, followed by the deadness of the dial tone.

He staggered back up the road, relieved that things were turning around at last. Letting himself back into Jerry's place, he remembered the band's gig was also tomorrow night. Bugger that, he told himself, the band were low on the billing so he could still play the gig and then make it to the meeting by midnight. He speculated pleasurably upon just how valuable the info on the propofol might be. Christ, poor old Diggers must be freaking out by now. He, on the other hand, was buzzing. A secret midnight rendezvous and the prospect of getting hold of five hundred quid *and* the hard stuff. Yeah, Saturday night sounded exactly like his favourite sort of gig.

Threat Sensitivity

Question 32: I avoid having to perform on stage in front of a large audience.

    A. Often

    B. Occasionally

    C. Never

High score description (option A.): Threat sensitive, restrained, hesitant, intimidated, emotionally cautious, belief in the negativity of others.

Saturday 5th March

Lorraine was dropping Jasmine off at her mum's on Saturday afternoon when she started to feel the usual nerves before a big gig. Though she'd managed to wangle it so that Fred would drive the band's gear back at the end of the night, she still had to pick up the van at three. Her mum looked up from the kitchen worktop where she was bashing digestives to make Jasmine's favourite chocolate and lime jelly flan.

'What's Tim's dad like?'

'Phil? He's taking long-term leave from his job in housing

to look after Tim. I think having Jasmine around helps give structure to his day.'

Her mum was giving her one of her long assessing looks. 'My concerns are not about strangers, Lorraine. What about Jasmine? How does it help her, being surrounded by these bereaved people?'

Stung, she didn't reply. Her mum had a point. Why was she exposing herself and Jasmine to this sad and sorry couple? It was guilt, that was it. She should have found time to listen to Rose that day and she hadn't.

Her mum was still waiting, her fine-boned face looking old with worry.

'It helps Jasmine learn,' she said at last, 'to be generous to people who are having a really awful time.'

Her mum digested this and then gave a sharp conceding nod of agreement. 'Yes, well. It is a moral thing that you're doing, the way you describe it. But be careful, Lorraine. This Phil had nothing to do with Rose's death, did he?'

'Of course not.'

'And Tim. How is he coping?'

The previous day she'd spotted Tim's limp figure sitting on an overlarge plastic chair in Child Psychology.

'Getting help from experts. But honestly, Mum, he and Jasmine play together just like two ordinary kids. There's nothing weird going on.'

By the time they all drew up a bunch of stools around a table in Oxford Road's Students' Union bar, Lorraine's nerves were jangling. She sipped warm cider from a sticky plastic beaker and asked, 'Anyone seen Rikki?'

Lily shrugged, tight-lipped, and Lorraine bit back a retort

202

that she'd always told them he was trouble. He'd already missed the sound check, at which each of them obeyed strict orders from the sound engineer not to touch a single wire of the headline act's gear. She had teetered at the front edge of the stage feeling unnerved by the yawning floor below her feet, picturing it dark and full. Already a queue of mostly students was forming at the ticket desk, some of them uncool kids with bad haircuts and stonewashed jeans, others Gothenburg's usual fans, dressed in faded black, their faces pallid from late nights and chemicals.

Her own band had done their best to look cool, but image never was their strong point. At home she'd rippled her hair with a crimping iron and circled her eyes with a smoky rim of black eyeliner. For luck, she was wearing one of her dad's old shirts, a purple two-tone affair, with a pair of black jeans. Dale had made more of an effort, arriving in a school tunic and Chinese silk jacket, and Lily wore her usual biker chic. God knows, feminism had left them not daring to be too glammed up but not wanting to look like dungaree-wearers either. She vaguely hoped they looked like someone off the front of the *NME* but was resigned to the fact that they didn't.

Unsettled, she wandered over to the table set up by the charity, The Disappeared. Someone had hung a backdrop printed with the famous grainy photo of Zeb performing on stage with Gothenburg, waving the broken neck of his guitar at a camera lens. She rifled through an array of missing person cards to be distributed on noticeboards, along with pleas for contributions to the charity's running costs. Seeing a flyer describing The Disappeared's most famous case, she started to read: Zebedee (or just Zeb) had made an appearance on the Manchester music scene in 1977 that was almost as extraordinary as his disappearance two years later.

It went on to describe how he had been living rough near Piccadilly Station when he first became the band's hanger-on and roadie. Then, as singer Ben Rowlands famously recalled, Zeb picked up a guitar one day and blew everyone away with his experimental, open tuning style. He composed a string of tunes to Rowlands' lyrics, later released as the album *The Fables of the North*. The flyer recalled Zeb's bouts of schizophrenia, in which his acute episodes earned him his nickname after the manically bouncing character on *The Magic Roundabout*. In interviews he recounted the hostility of his family and the nightmarish terrors he'd lived through when sleeping rough.

Lorraine had accompanied Lily and Zeb to his final live appearance at The Squat, in December '79. There had been no sense of history being made, just of a vibrant scene collapsing into chaos. A fight had broken out among some morons not far from where she and Lily had stood, and it had spread to the stage. The music press made much of Zeb's ferocious tirade, but from where she'd stood it had been pitiful, the way he smashed his beautiful guitar. Her memories were of Zeb's bewildered stare as his guitar neck hung grotesquely askew.

She read the sad details of the story's end. That at a New Year's party he became manic, jabbering of a bizarre plot to implant him with an electronic mind-reading device. Then, after two days in a private clinic, he had escaped over a wall and vanished. Though the rest of the band and their management had searched for him for months, he was never reliably sighted again.

The account of Zeb's life ended on a note of mystery:

Though spotted by fans in locations as far apart as Rio de Janeiro and Sumatra, no sighting has ever been confirmed by investigators. Since his disappearance, no representative of Zeb's family has come forward to claim his belongings, or the accrued fees from his musical works, which are currently held in trust by lawyers. At the present time his status remains as one of the UK's most enigmatic missing persons.

She looked again at the fuzzy photo. Live, the band had been raw and chaotic, and *Fables of the North* was an underground classic. Oh well, she decided, given such a good cause she could hardly grudge handing over that night's fee.

Back at the table, she saw that Rikki still hadn't shown up. After all her outbursts about wanting to be rid of him, she had a bad feeling fate had taken a hand and done her a favour. The Poly's social secretary came over and told them their slot was strictly from eight-thirty to nine and not a minute longer. The clock above the bar read ten past eight. Dale was hunched over the table tearing a beer mat into tiny shreds.

'What if he doesn't turn up?' she wailed.

'I'll try and ring him,' Lorraine volunteered. But after waiting five minutes to use the phone booth and then phoning his flat, she felt genuine panic. As she stared at handbills for the Gay Switchboard and Rock Against Racism the phone rang out unanswered thirty times.

Rejoining the band, she couldn't bring herself to say it: they'd have to pull out. And the worst of it was that the crowd was heaving now, packed four deep around the bar while the keen ones were already standing up against the stage. A local comic was making desperate efforts to warm up the audience. It sounded as if his act was winding down.

Lily leant forward on her elbows and had to yell above the noise. 'He said he was going to meet someone tonight.'

'Who?' she yelled back.

'Didn't say. I just hope he's not gone off on some trip or other and forgotten us.'

Lorraine tried again to pick at the puzzle of whom Rikki might have met up with at the hospital, but soon gave up.

They all sat in miserable silence before Lily looked at her watch and asked, 'Do you think we should tell someone?'

All the headliners were in the official dressing room, drinking and eating whatever their management had demanded in their riders. No one but themselves would be particularly bothered if they didn't play. Lorraine thought of all the time and effort Lily had put into getting this gig.

'I could kill him, I really could,' she burst out.

'You could kill whom, my dear? Not me, surely?' A pair of strong hands grasped her shoulders and she looked up to see Rikki himself, grinning down at her. He raked his fingers through his gelled hair and yawned as he waited for them to gather up their things.

'Come on then, girlies. Our moment of triumph awaits. Chop chop!'

The floor had filled up and they had to carry their guitars through the heave and swell of the audience. Clambering up on stage, they made final adjustments, picking their way across the cable-strewn boards. A few catcalls and shrieks came from the roiling mass below them. Christ, this is always the worst bit, she told herself, like sweating in the dentist's waiting room. But once Lily had counted them in, they relaxed into the familiar comfort of their set. The boom and sparkle of their music cascaded from the big black PA; their hopes and ingenuity formed into guitar riffs, drum crashes and yearning vocals. Shit, it sounded almost OK.

They got through four or five numbers and she was feeling great, telepathically communicating the changes with the others and at one with those in the audience who were cheering and whooping. Next on the set list was 'Path of Stars' and she tried to take a deep breath into her tight lungs. Jesus, why had she fought with Dale to sing her own lyrics to the number? Shakily, she took her place at the front mic. Spotlights were moving over the crowd, picking out groups of faces. Then the disc of light fell on a face she knew too well. Sergeant Diaz was standing alone at the side of the hall, pint glass in hand, staring directly at her.

Lily was counting her in. She barely had time to swallow down her fear before the cue came to open her mouth, and she prayed that a noise something like her usual voice would emerge.

Irresolution

Question 33: I sometimes get a strong urge to escape from rules and regulations and just be my natural self.

    A. True

    B. Uncertain

    C. False

High score description (option A.): Uncontrolled, lax, undisciplined self-conflict, rebellious, follows own urges.

Students. There was something ridiculous about their earnest faces, greasy hair and glasses. Diaz wouldn't have come to the Students' Union for a hundred quid, if he hadn't spotted a photo of Lorraine and her band in a local free paper. But now he was almost enjoying himself, after making an excuse to leave his mates behind at the Bierkeller and moving off alone through the urgency of the city lights. He was tuning into the rhythmic swoop of Lorraine's voice accompanying the jangly guitar number. It was like watching a completely different person from the one he knew at the hospital. She was standing spotlit and exposed, her chin raised as she sang in a warm, husky voice:

'City lights flashing by
Can't find my way, though I try – try
A galaxy too distant to find you
Path of stars
All lost hearts
Taking a step in the dark . . .'

It was the song he'd heard in her car. This time he followed the words. It was about all of them, searching for something, hoping for someone. He watched, mesmerised as she stood on the edge of the stage, guitar strap between her breasts, holding it all together for a nervy, rhapsodic three minutes. Then finally she retreated to the side of the stage and the intense knot of feeling unwound, leaving him wondering exactly where people got the guts to stand up and do that.

It was only during the next number that he recognised the band's drummer as Eric Fryer, the scrote he'd been trying to locate for days. What the fuck was going on? And there was he thinking that Lorraine couldn't stand the sight of him. Eric Fryer had come up on the National Crime Register on three counts: 1979 and again in 1981 – possession of a class B drug with intent to deal. Then, back in 1980, he'd been questioned at two different flats in Didsbury in relation to the Yorkshire Ripper inquiry. A couple of female witnesses had given statements that he'd followed them at night, then hung around their homes, watching them. Nothing had stuck but he was convinced Fryer was the sort of smart-arse who wriggled out of tight holes.

And now here he was belting out a rhythm on the drum kit, his silvery hair plastered to his sweaty face. Diaz was going to have to ask Lorraine some very awkward questions. Surreptitiously, he patted his inside pocket.

The band were euphoric once they jumped off stage. Lily had spotted the drummer who played with Gothenburg and was convinced the world would soon be at their feet. Lorraine had that rush she only ever got straight after a performance: giddy and laughing and woozy on adrenaline. The only drag on the proceedings was Diaz. She could see him hanging back by the wall, watching her. Dreading him coming over and, God forbid, introducing himself as a copper, she pulled away from the others.

Diaz's eyes were glittering like two quartz beads as she approached. He'd slung his battered leather jacket over his shoulder and didn't look too ridiculously out of place in a black T-shirt.

'You look pretty happy,' she said.

He gave her a roguish smile. 'That was good.'

She nodded. 'So what's this then. Undercover work?'

'Fancy a dance? The disco's on next door.'

'You kill me.'

'Come on. I need to tell you something and I'd rather go somewhere less visible.'

She'd forgotten that the Poly Union kept its infamous disco blaring in a side room, for the diehards who couldn't stand live music. The DJ wasn't bad and Iggy's 'The Passenger' was thumping out of the speakers. So she danced with him as she waited to hear his big revelation, standing well back, so for a while there was nothing but the beat and Iggy's imagery of a neon city and that hypnotic sense that the whole crowd was beating to one heart. Then the music changed and he nodded towards a dark uncrowded corner.

He caught her arm and sweat gleamed across his skin. 'I've been looking through the evidence.'

'And?' She felt her whole future teeter on the edge of a precipice.

He pulled out a plastic bag. Inside was something small and white. Her wrap of speed.

'Look, it's not a habit I—'

'Where'd you get it?'

She shook her head, annoyed. 'It's one of the reasons I lost it with Rikki. He virtually planted it on me.'

'You put on a pretty convincing act of hating his guts.'

'It wasn't an act.'

'So what was it? A bribe to give him the porter's job?'

'What? No chance. I didn't even know he'd applied. Edith interviewed him a few days later. It was all signed and sealed by the time I found out.'

'You do realise if Brunt finds out, he'll probably lock you up.'

She silently cursed Rikki to hell and back. Her future looked like a long dark tunnel to nowhere. And then she looked up at Diaz and wondered what the hell was going on. He wasn't behaving like his usual uptight self. And after all that blather about safeguarding evidence here he was, waving the stuff in front of her.

'OK,' she said slowly. 'So what do I have to do to get it back?'

The question hung between them as 'Suffragette City' sent everyone around them rushing back to the dance floor. Suddenly they were standing alone in the darkness.

He shook the little bag in front of her. 'First, let me try this psychometric test of yours myself. I need to understand it.'

'You take the test? Christ's sake. OK.'

'And second. Give me the suspects' results as soon as you get them.'

'You don't give up do you? What if I can't?'

'The evidence in this bag gets written up and reported to Brunt on Monday.'

She looked at the white powder. He was giving her a chance to escape a criminal record and keep her career. There was no contest. Fuck the Psychological Society.

'And is that it?'

'And help me destroy the evidence.'

This time he was eyeing her from cool, narrowed lids. Destroy it? There could only be one way. Even if she had to take a load of speed with Diaz, it had to be her way out. Jasmine would be staying happily with her mum most of Sunday. She'd have had time to come down before she picked her daughter up.

Yet something in her gut made her hang back. She recalled what Doctor Lehman had said, after asking if she trusted Diaz. 'We can be attracted and repelled at the same time by those who are not good for us.' Some instinct had held her back from the moment she'd met him. Sure, she'd picked up that they got on pretty well, that speculating on this killer was exciting. She could feel it now, as he watched her, unblinking.

But sometimes, you don't act rationally, she decided. Sometimes you're forced to confront that tar-black pit in your stomach. Like a snake shedding skin, she felt her own secret self emerge and flex its nerves. She swivelled and stretched up to whisper into his ear.

'Why are you risking everything for this?'

He slung his arms around her neck, pressing his body against hers, radiating heat.

His breath was hot in her ear. 'Sometimes the law needs to be bent to a new shape.'

A bent copper. Not just ambitious, but bending the rule book. She tried to read his mind by studying his familiar features; his hair was ruffled, his lips moist. When he dipped his mouth to try to kiss her she got it at last. At first she pulled back, uncertainly. Then she thought, why not? If they'd met in any other way they'd probably be together by now. And surely all the wrongdoing was on his side? He was the police officer while she was just a helpful witness. Whatever rules he was breaking were a million times more serious than anything she was doing.

And then she told her brain to bloody well shut up. And she let him kiss her and kissed him back and it was better than she expected, all because it felt so wrong.

But still, it sounded like the devil whispering in her ear when he clasped her bare arm and pulled her down onto a saggy settee and said, 'Here. No one'll see us.'

'OK,' she said, as he offered her a line of speed as if she were choosing an ice cream, and not an irreversible twist in her life's path.

Bubble after bubble of hysterical giggles surfaced and popped in her throat. Whatever Rikki had given her, it was like nothing she'd ever had before.

'Pretty trippy,' she said.

Diaz nodded with a spaced-out smile. Hearing Gothenburg starting up, he took her arm and she followed, oblivious to her earlier worries about the others seeing them together. Squeezing into the mass of fans, she gasped as the exertion triggered another wave of the chemical. The edges of the room had started to loom and recede; the floor was trembling like a living heart. A moment later the soar of fluidly melodic bass and the crack of drums charged her heart with explosives. Ben Rowlands reached for the mic and the room hushed. That night he sang like a voice from the other side of an abyss, communicating pain and a dreadful understanding. The first number ended and there was a pause for cheers and whoops of acclamation.

The singer stood alone, silhouetted in the white stage lights, the smoke of a cigarette twisting to the ceiling. As one of Zeb's surging riffs from 'The Dead Letter House' shook the air, the new guitarist worked up to a crescendo, eyes closed, seeming to channel Zeb, their dead hero. She closed her eyes and sank into visions of prophets and haunted eyes. All the while the music spoke to her: Zeb was a martyr with terrible knowledge that spoke through his music, telling of what lay across the gulf, on the other side, in the void.

Time flashed by on tramlines different from the everyday slog of minutes. Suddenly they were outside, the cold air drying the sweat on her skin, and for a second she wondered who she was and what she was doing. Diaz had hold of her arm and they were weaving through a bunch of bizarro night people on the pavement. Dark-socketed tower blocks crowded above them. There were lights moving fast.

'Watch out! A bus!' someone shouted. And looking up, there it was, a crazy double-decker lightship careering towards them down Oxford Road. With an electric jolt she launched herself out of its path onto the pavement. She and Diaz giggled hysterically, clutching hands.

'I'll give you a lift home,' Diaz said. And she turned back to the canine gleam of his teeth and followed him into the darkness.

Carefree Nonplanfulness

Question 34: I seem to make the same errors in judgement over and over again.
  A. True
  B. Uncertain
  C. False

High score description (option A.): Difficulty in planning ahead and considering the consequences of one's actions, absence of forethought, blaming others.

From the queue at the taxi rank Rikki watched as a seriously stoned couple nearly went under a bus. Bloody hell, the blonde was Lorraine and the dark-haired bloke was that tough-looking copper he'd seen around hospital. Now that was very interesting. He watched them walk hand in hand through the little park at All Saints. He wasn't quite sure how to do it yet, but he was going to bleed that scrap of knowledge dry.

He was pretty chuffed all round. The gig had been a dream, and according to Lily there was talk of a tour. And whatever Lorraine said, Lily had a soft spot for him and would keep him in the band. He fingered the plaited leather bracelet she'd knotted around his wrist the first time they'd slept together. And tonight he'd even made twenty quid from a big lump of incense he'd passed off as Moroccan hash to some gormless student. Up the road, the clock on the Refuge Building announced half eleven, so he was in good time for his meeting. Right on cue, a cab pulled up and he slid into the back like a playboy.

Lolling back on the slippery leather, Rikki turned his mind to the prospect of finally meeting Diggers. As the vehicle trundled and lurched over the invisible inky waters of the Irwell, up Chapel Street and past Salford Uni, it came back to him where the nickname Diggers had come from. When he'd been in hospital and seeing the world through the mirror suspended above his face, he'd listened to a programme on telly about people sailing off to live in Australia. There had been jokes doing the rounds about Ten Pound Poms being so desperate to reach the sun that they'd happily dig their way down through the centre of the earth to get there. Yeah, it was coming back to him now . . . Wasn't that the reason he'd never seen Diggers again, because the boat ticket and everything had been booked? Again he felt a revelation dangling just beyond his reach. Well, he'd find out what happened tonight. Maybe the trip to Australia had gone wrong? After all, Diggers was back again. Well, all the more reason to get something massive out of tonight's meeting.

Up on the hill the hospital glowed into view, the main arteries of its corridors phosphorescent in the night.

'Pull up round that side road, mate,' he told the driver, directing him to the black hulk of the computer suite. It would be better if no one spotted him. As soon as he got what was due to him he was going to be out of here.

He looked around for his Army and Navy bag. Shit. He hadn't picked it up; he'd tucked it inside his bass drum before he left the Students' Union. Well, no one would find it in there. Christ, he'd only gone and left his photo of Harris Ward in it too. He'd wanted to show Diggers that picture. Hold on. On second thoughts, it was probably best to keep the photo back for the time being. He'd already had a few copies made at Supasnaps as his insurance policy, in case Diggers didn't deliver the goods. Yeah, it was a tough call for old Diggers, but why should he care? His own life had been murder, too.

He paid off the taxi and headed to the deserted computer suite. It was as silent as outer space in there at night. He'd checked the place out on his last shift, and no one ever came round after the doors were locked at five-thirty. And tonight, well, maybe the moon was all blacked out or something but he had to feel his way forward like a blind man. He found the porch, groped towards the door and found it helpfully ajar. Diggers had to be inside, waiting for him already. Straight up, he was actually looking forward to their little reunion.

Clumsily, he shuffled into the main room. A faint, colourless light penetrated the windows, revealing gleaming shapes draped in thick polythene. Furniture. Then a figure stepped out from nowhere, shining a torch into his face with a painfully fierce beam.

'Get that fucking thing out my eyes,' he yelled. The beam swung down at an angle.

'Diggers can't make it.'

Rikki blinked at the figure warily. The stranger was a theatre orderly or something, judging from the scrubs, cap and mask. And whoever it was, it was not Diggers. Jesus, what a let-down. 'What's going on?'

'Like I said, tonight's a bad night for Diggers. But I've brought you a present.'

The figure set the torch on a desk so it cast eerie shapes onto the ceiling. A hand in a surgical glove offered Rikki a large plastic carton. He squinted to read the label. Morphine sulfate: 500 high-dose 200mg tabs.

'Nice,' he said coolly. 'But where's the rest?'

The figure didn't move but Rikki felt two eyes watching him forcefully.

'I haven't got it yet. Have you got the photo?'

'I'll bring it next time.'

Weird. The voice was the same as the person he'd phoned but muffled by the mask. So the person who had said they were Diggers on the phone was not really Diggers. Now they were face to face, he realised the voice he'd spoken to had never actually been the one he remembered as a boy. This whole situation was totally screwed.

Rikki rattled the tub in his hand and grinned at the masked figure. He was pissed off now and he needed to demonstrate who was in charge. He was taller and younger than this waster. 'I need five hundred quid for starters.'

'For starters? So when does it all stop?'

'Do you think I'm thick or something?' he roared.

He made a grab at the orderly's wrist and twisted it backwards, pulling as hard and fast as he could. A grunt of pain emerged from behind the mask. Rikki exulted, gaining a wrestling lock and raising his free hand to pull the mask down. His victim's head whipped back and forth like a maniac. A heavy theatre clog kicked hard against Rikki's shin. Rikki began to pummel the orderly, who cowered beneath a series of blows. Somehow the lid of the morphine carton flipped off and pills flew into the air like hailstones.

'So,' Rikki grunted, feeling a surge of triumph as his boots crunched across the polka-dotted carpet. 'If you're not Diggers then who the fuck are you?'

He became aware of a hand sliding serpent-like across his torso, under his jacket, snaking across his back.

'Ow!' Pain spiked into his body. He knew that sensation well; a jab followed by a deep and unstoppable rush, like a gush of hot lava.

'Get off me!' Rikki flung his assailant away from him and twisted around helplessly, contorting his neck to try to see what had punctured him. He reached round to grab at it but before he could, his knees concertinaed to the floor. The two eyes above the surgical mask resolved as belonging to a familiar face, one he'd often seen around the hospital. The whole situation was just bizarre.

For a few glorious seconds he was aware of the figure in green towering above him. Then like a tidal wave the anaesthetic powered through his bloodstream, halting his respiration and snuffing out his precious consciousness, as his head crunched onto hundreds of tiny hard discs scattered across the carpet.

Transliminality

Question 35: I have experienced an altered state of consciousness which I believe utterly transformed the way I look at myself.
   A. True
   B. Uncertain
   C. False

High score description (option A.): Large volumes of imagery crossing the threshold from the unconscious to conscious mind, magical or paranormal ideas, mysticism, identification of meaningful patterns, creativity.

Still unsteady from the gear, Diaz parked at the address he'd scribbled down from Lorraine's witness statement. He hadn't checked it out along with the other suspects' homes and for a moment, he wondered if he should have. In this part of Salford, the urban sprawl petered out to slum clearance: nothing but rows of crumbling houses as ugly as sin. Across the way, a skeletal church blotted out the stars. As he got out of the car a figure stepped forward and eyed him up, as thin as a girl but with an ancient sunken face.

'Lookin' for business, chuck?' she croaked.

'No, love. Take care.'

'Poor thing,' Lorraine muttered. 'What a life.'

He wondered why Lorraine lived here, in this landscape of streetwalkers and blasted brick dust. Yet above them the streetlights were like golden planets in the infinite beauty of space.

It was hard to believe he was actually out at midnight on a Saturday night, a free agent, taking a good-looking bird home. Jesus, he'd wasted all those nights watching *Blankety Blank* and *3-2-1*, vegetating on the settee like an old geezer. He'd even caught himself daydreaming as he watched those army recruitment adverts. He could quite fancy losing himself in a desert or a jungle, where drill and discipline would wipe out a million questions. Then reality would hit back. With his luck he'd probably end up as target practice in Northern Ireland.

And now he was here, with the feeling he could be eighteen again, or even fifteen, from the way his blood was hammering. They stopped at a grim-looking little terrace and Lorraine opened the door. Next thing, he was standing in the dark while she uselessly clicked the light switch.

'I think it's those, what d'you call 'ems? Blast. I was supposed to get some.'

She was absolutely out of it, puzzling over the non-functioning light switch.

He also searched for the word like a hand groping in sawdust. Then he remembered. 'The meter? Is that it?'

She started giggling. 'Yeah, yeah. You got some money?' That set her off again, doubling over with laughter. 'I didn't mean it like that! Not like, "You looking for business, chuck?" God, I'm not that desperate!'

That started him laughing too, as he uselessly searched through his trouser pockets for a fifty pence piece. 'Shit. I haven't got one either.'

'You're no good then.' It was starting to hurt to laugh now, but it felt good, like he was getting rid of all that wound-up tightness at last.

He investigated the red glow in the fireplace and she appeared with a couple of candles that they set alight. It was like igniting a spell: the little pools of radiance trembled like a furnace deep underground. Earlier, when he'd been driving, he'd daydreamed their arrival like a classic movie scene, that he'd throw her against a wall and they'd tear each other's clothes off. Yet now, after he'd walked into this magical cave, he wrapped her in his arms and they started to talk. He told her how he was keen to go places with the force; to climb over the heads of has-beens like Brunt. There were rumours of secondments to the police college at Bramshill and that had links to America. It all tumbled out of his mouth, exposing the real him far more than physical nakedness.

'What makes you do your job?' she asked.

His answer surprised even himself. 'My mum and dad died so I was brought up by my granddad Rocco in Ancoats. Little Italy, they called it. I was a bit of a runt. I had to toughen up to survive. You've got no choice when there's a ring of rock-hard Irish lads after your guts. It was a good lesson. When Granddad died, I was put in a kid's home for a few years. Had to look after myself. Now I bloody love it when I collar some thug and see him go down.'

'So I guess when I test you it's going to show you're happy in your work,' she murmured. He nodded.

'Hey, you never even told me your name.'

'Diaz,' he teased.

'No, idiot. Your other name.'

'Dani.'

'Danny. Like Daniel?'

No, it wasn't like Daniel. He usually lied, dreading anyone having a laugh at his expense. Yet the urge to be honest was unstoppable. 'Dante,' he heard himself speak out loud.

'Dante? Like the poet who wrote the *Inferno*? Wow.'

Her eyes gleamed molten gold in the firelight, staring far away. '"Midway on life's journey I found myself lost in a dark wood" – or something,' she recited softly.

His granddad had recited those very same lines. He closed his eyes and started to kiss her, lifting her hair to nuzzle her neck. Everything slowed down from lightning bolts of lust to a syrupy delight in body against body. He got a bit lost around her shoulder until his fingers found her bra strap and he slid it down, feeling a blast of desire. His tongue explored the heat of her mouth, while his hand simultaneously uncovered her left breast, warm and silky outside the cup of her bra.

He heard himself groan, floating off on a long-forgotten planet bombarded by pleasure-rays. He clambered over her, nudging himself against the taut crotch of her trousers. As he looked down, her face was a smooth cameo of amber in the candle flame, her lips parted, her eyeliner smudged around acquiescent eyes.

'Oh God,' he whispered and smelt lacquer and mustiness in her hair. He wondered if this was what people meant when they used that alien word, 'love'. The word formed on his lips and he took a breath.

Then his bloody radio crackled.

'What the fuck?' Diaz manoeuvred it out of his pocket. His tripped-out brain struggled to comprehend the message relayed by the call-room operator. He tried to digest the news and then pressed transmit and mumbled that he was on his way. She looked up at him like an unwrapped feast, her shirt hanging open, her cheeks flushed.

He gripped her fingers tightly and stroked them. 'I think it's Eric Fryer.'

'Rikki? What? He radioed you?' She sat up too, blearily pulling her shirt tight around herself.

'No. A fatality at the hospital. A porter. Young white male. The security guard just identified him.'

As Diaz drove through the night, the chemicals made him feel like an astronaut diving through mysterious galaxies. Yet painfully, an umbilical cord of common sense kept reeling him back home. His car radio repeated the urgent call from Brunt, to get straight over to the hospital. The operator announced she'd been trying his home number. His guts cringed when he realised Shirley must be awake too, wondering where the hell he was.

He had flashbacks of Lorraine standing at the front door, warming her hands around a mug of tea. Her face was unreadable, but he had a bad feeling she thought his leaving was for the best. He'd wanted to kiss her goodbye but she'd edged her lips away from his mouth.

Somehow he'd remembered to warn her. Reaching the car, he called out, 'You'll be questioned tomorrow. Best stick as close to the truth as you can. Just leave out – our little indulgence, eh?'

As the hospital rose before him like an alien city, he felt bereft. Tonight he'd told Lorraine stuff he hadn't told anyone in years. He smashed his fist against the steering wheel. What had he done to get such evil luck?

The police lights blazed with white ferocity through spears of rain. Diaz rubbed his gritty eyes and made for Brunt, who was standing with a couple of SOCOs. Shit, the gear was still distorting reality, making the DI look like a giant hog. Together they walked into the building. Soon his porcine boss began speaking.

'Security guy found him half an hour ago. Eric Fryer, a porter. Note the pills he no doubt pinched and used to merrily top himself with.'

Diaz didn't speak. He was agonising over what to say so he'd sound like his usual, die-straight self. He checked the corpse's long lean face, the eyelids so calmly closed that the drummer might have been taking a quick kip. A white plastic tub of morphine tablets had spilt all over the carpet.

'I just saw him playing the drums down at the Students' Union.'

Brunt swung his bulk around, his pig-eyes peering out from beneath his soggy trilby. 'Whoa, hold it there, Giuseppe. What exactly were you doing at this musical extravaganza?'

'Night off, boss.'

'Shirley said you'd gone AWOL. Got hold of your mate Rob. He last saw you around eight. Trailing this smackhead, were you?'

He didn't have the wherewithal to lie. And Brunt would want witness statements from everyone who had last seen Rikki alive. It cost him considerable pain to come clean.

'Not exactly, sir. Lorraine Quick is in the same band.'

'Miss Quick, eh? An associate of this scumbag? Cough up then, lad.'

He sprang to her defence. 'They're in the same band but she can't stand him. She didn't give him the job here, her assistant did and she's not happy.'

In the silence that followed, Diaz's brain plunged into a helter-skelter comedown.

'Well, we can't have Miss Quick not being happy, can we? Been whispering in your shell like, has she? See sense, laddie. They've been working a scam in the pharmacy together, just like they've been sharing the same music stand.'

'No.'

'Oh, and you know all about it, do you? Pillow talk was it? I hope you've been keeping it in your pants, lad. And you with a decent girl waiting at home.'

Diaz told himself the safest way was not to open his mouth. And then his mouth opened of its own accord and started talking.

'What do you know about anything, eh?' he said so loudly that the nearest SOCOs turned to gawp at them. 'I'm only here because the chief doesn't think you're capable on your own.'

Brunt waddled towards him and then shoved him so hard he went flying against the wall.

'Till I retire, the line of command's through me. Got that, smart-arse?'

Blazing, Diaz righted himself and straightened his jacket. He could hear his own loud breathing and he didn't like it.

'I won't suspend you this time,' Brunt was grumbling. 'Wake up, you soft git! She's got you by the short and curlies.'

He hesitated too long before his muttered, 'Sir.' Then without thinking, he blurted, 'I tell you, she wanted rid of him.'

'Aye, son.' Brunt leant forward and touched Rikki's senseless body with the toe of his shoe. 'I can see that all right.' He lifted his pouchy eyes to glare at Diaz before growling, 'You keep away from her. I don't want to see you within a dozen yards of Miss Quick.'

Brunt and his colleagues disappeared outside. Glad to be alone, Diaz lingered over the corpse. What were those magic words again? The walls of a crime scene carried rage, fear, love and hatred. If he was ever going to read those invisible clues it was now, while the walls pulsed like his own inner light show.

The dead body seemed nothing but an absence. The lad's consciousness had gone, leaving this leftover carcass sprawled across the carpet. This was death, he thought, with what felt like deep profundity: the sudden snuffing out of all speech, memory and secrets. Brunt thought Rikki had come here to steal drugs and accidentally OD'd. No way. A long-time user didn't just neck some morphine and pop his clogs. Maybe the tabs were poisoned? Maybe Rikki had picked up some dangerous knowledge that the murderer feared, some information that meant killing him was the only answer. They'd have to wait for the lab results and PM to know for sure. In the meantime, he felt he might burst from not knowing.

Diaz inspected the victim's donkey jacket, worn over a grey shirt and grubby jeans. Checking no one else was around, he slid his hand into the corpse's jacket pocket.

Nothing but a handful of grubby pound notes. Then he tried the jeans pocket, flexing his wrist awkwardly so as not to disturb the body's posture. He noticed the jacket was tented up by an object a few inches high. He lifted the jacket aside. And there it was. A rusty-looking syringe protruding from the thin fabric of his shirt. Even a contortionist of a junkie couldn't have manoeuvred a needle so far into his own back.

'Guv!' Diaz ran out into the rain and grabbed his boss's sleeve. Dragging him back inside, Diaz pointed at the victim's back. With a grunt his boss heaved himself down and inspected the syringe that dangled at an angle, its chamber nearly empty of white fluid. Diaz squatted down beside him.

Rage, fear, love, hatred. Fear. The motive for this murder had to be fear.

'What about this, boss? Fryer found out who killed Rose Cavanagh,' Diaz said in a low, almost reverential voice. 'And that put the fear of God into the perpetrator. So he stuck that' – he pointed at the syringe emptied of propofol – 'in his back to shut him up.'

Demoralisation

Question 36: I experience periods of distress when I feel hopeless about my life.

  A. Often

  B. Occasionally

  C. Never

High score description (option A.): Emotional discomfort, feeing discouraged, loss of control, overwhelmed, pessimistic, poor self-esteem.

Sunday 6th March

Grimy daylight brought Lorraine a new mood of caution. Rikki was dead. He'd been an annoying prat, but no way had he deserved to die. And he was the second person she had known who had died within a fortnight. Thank God Diaz had not stayed the night. As soon as the investigation was over, Diaz would vanish and she could get her life back on track again.

Yet still she couldn't bear to take off the two-tone shirt that smelt of him, that felt alive against her skin. She hugged it close and closed her eyes. Shit, why couldn't it have worked out for once? Her skin still felt sticky. Overheated hormones battled with common sense. God, she felt horribly alone. She risked a short walk to the phone box and rang Lily. After what must have been fifty maddening rings her friend picked the phone up with a string of sluggish curses. She went quiet when Lorraine told her Rikki was dead. And then she grew panicky when Lorraine warned her that the police would question them all. It was a relief when the beeps started and she could drop the receiver back in its cradle.

Soon after she got home, a loud rat-a-tat-tat at the door made her almost jump out of her skin. The WPC on her doorstep asked Lorraine to accompany her to the local station. She recited that it was a simple matter of speaking to everyone who knew Eric Fryer, beginning with those who had been with him at the Students' Union last night.

There was something depressingly institutional about Salford Crescent police station – a reminder of the battered corridors of her down-at-heel secondary school, save that here the windows were barred. She waited in a reception area stuck over with fuzzy photographs of wanted criminals. Taking a seat on a filthy chair, she felt a surge of pity for Rikki. With hindsight, Rikki's stories of being stuck in hospital as a kid were even more poignant: the medical team's efforts to heal his bones had all come to nothing now he'd died so young. Lorraine rubbed her damp palms against her jumper. The killer felt very close; not only watching from just behind her shoulder when Rose was killed, but drawing Rikki back to the hospital, too.

She longed for a glimpse of Diaz but instead she had to face Brunt. He looked up with a bilious expression, his bulk shoved behind a scarred Formica table with the WPC squashed in beside him. As he lit his pipe, she silently ordered herself to keep it all together. Letting herself become a suspect would waste everyone's time. More than anything she wanted to help the police find Rikki's murderer. All she had to do was stick to the truth. Well, save for just one lie.

The opening questions were straightforward. How well had she known Eric? When did he join the band? And how did he get the porter's job? She told him emphatically that her assistant Edith had appointed him. She reminded Brunt that she'd tried to warn Diaz about Rikki and given him a statement about his being in the hospital on the day of Rose's death.

Next, she told him about the gig and that Diaz had surprised her by turning up and offering her a lift home. No, she hadn't even told him where she'd be. At least that gave her a brilliant alibi for the time of Rikki's death.

'You're looking the worse for wear today,' he said, then released a cloud of blue sweetbriar smoke that made her cough.

'Last night I learnt that another person I know has died. I might not have liked Rikki but it's still a terrible shock.'

Brunt pinched his flabby lips. 'So how did it work, the set-up between you and Fryer?' he asked with sudden aggression. 'We know you've both been taking drugs from the hospital pharmacy.'

The WPC looked up from her notebook.

'That's ridiculous. Ask anyone. I don't even have access to the pharmacy.'

'But your friend was a drug dealer. And your work's been suffering. According to Mr Pilling you lost some important documents.'

'No. What really happened was that someone stole

232

some professional certificates from my office. How about investigating that?'

His big shoulders shrugged. 'Because it's not a matter of interest.'

'So the theft of medical qualifications for the black market isn't a crime?'

Annoyingly, he jumped topics. 'Did you slip an illegal substance in my sergeant's drink last night?'

All the body language theory she knew stated that a liar would displace anxiety and grow fidgety under questioning. Might touch their nose or blink fast. So she sat very still and kept her gaze in direct contact with Brunt's pouchy little eyes. Even as she did so, a niggle bubbled up in her mind: had Diaz left the empty wrap at her house? It would have her fingerprints all over it. She forced herself not to waver. She was pretty sure he'd thrown it away.

'No. I don't take drugs. Drugs are incompatible with my job.'

She had purposely draped a huge bandolero-style scarf around her neck. Like many nervous interviewees her throat turned blotchy when anxious. Brunt was looking directly at her neckline. He whispered to the WPC, who left them alone. With a grunt he leant forward across the table, two pillow-like elbows moving into her personal space. His fat knees prodded against hers.

'What were you up to when you invited young Diaz back to yours? Keeping him out of the way while Fryer was done in?'

'No. I told you. Diaz invited himself.'

He scrutinised her as if she were something revolting at the bottom of a dustbin.

'You stay away from my sergeant. I weren't born yesterday. Not like young wet-behind-the-ears miladdo. Got it?'

She mutely nodded.

'I've had a look at you. False accusation of rape back in '75.'

'It wasn't false!'

'Strung your boyfriend along and then made up a nasty little story. Luckily for him you didn't have the bottle to press charges.'

Lorraine opened her mouth to protest but couldn't form words. A spasm of grief blurred her eyes. She had tried to finish with Andy and he had forced himself on her at his flat when she went round to pick up her clothes. Egged on by a desperate phone call to the Rape Crisis Centre, she had reported it to the police. It had been one of the biggest mistakes of her life. Now she knew better. It was always on the news these days, that women were to blame if they wore the wrong clothes or gave off the wrong signals. As that judge had said last year, it was common knowledge that if you begged a man to stop attacking you, you were only a slutty tease. Cowed by Brunt, she dropped her head.

The frigid silence continued until the policewoman returned and Brunt spoke with fake courtesy. 'Right you are, Miss Quick. Just check and sign the statement.'

She was so relieved that she asked, 'I can go?'

'A car'll fetch you home once we're done.'

Machiavellian Egocentricity

Question 37: The creation of the world's great civilisations was worth the enslavement of its workers.
  A. True
  B. Uncertain
  C. False

High score description (option A.): A lack of empathy and sense of detachment from others for the sake of achieving one's own goals.

I went into work and listened for news. It wasn't long coming; an announcement that the police were hastily arranging interviews. At my interview the DCI hopelessly flailed around in search of facts until I told him where I was. He made no comment, only scowled. It was that easy.

Dear God, I learnt that my mystery caller was a porter! A brighter blackmailer would have smelt a poisonous rat but Eric Fryer – a former public schoolboy slumming it in the ancillary grades – swallowed my bait.

It is a diverting game to work out who is leading the board as chief suspect. I took my lunch in the canteen, doodling in my notebook, a cup of undrinkable coffee cooling in front of me. A gaggle of domestics settled near my table. In a hospital the cleaners are always the closest to the ground in every sense.

A fat creature with thinning hair spouted forth, 'I were telling my Frank, there's a bleeding poisoner wandering the hospital, murdering us all as we work. And the bizzies haven't got a flaming clue.'

A flood of reminiscences of the porter followed: that he was 'a lovely lad' and 'the salt of the earth'.

After these dim-witted platitudes, another woman spoke up, a creature with gold medallions strung around what looked to me like a goitre from acute thyroiditis. 'Did you 'ear who he were out with just before he were topped? Playing the drums at some student place in town. And who were up on stage at the same time? Blondie. 'Er in Personnel. Miss Quick.'

Eric Fryer and Lorraine Quick. I listened intently. I reached absent-mindedly for my coffee, but at the first sensation of wrinkled milk-skin I started to cough. The women ignored me; like gannets, they were too busy tussling over the carcass.

'She's a dark horse.'

'D'you think it were 'er what done it?'

I made my escape. This changes everything. Surely Fryer must have told her that he was returning to the hospital that night? And whom he intended to meet? Lorraine Quick is a threat to me. My first instinct is to deal with her at once. In my office I inspect the empty wall spaces that formerly held my credentials. The slightly faded rectangles make me uneasy. I thought I'd fully dealt with that girl's interference.

No, the general manager selection day is next Monday and Lorraine Quick has a crucial part to play in my success. I must keep steady. I won't discuss this with anyone, not even Christie. It would be annoying to have my promotion postponed because of yet another tragic incident.

Prudence

Question 38: I believe that the proverb 'Look before you leap' is useful advice.
    A. True
    B. Uncertain
    C. False
High score description (option A.): Cautious, self-controlled, tending to deliberate carefully, considering options, inhibiting impulses.

Monday 7th March

Back at work, Edith was gobsmacked to find out that the flirty lad she'd fancied had played in a band with – of all people – Lorraine. Since that revelation, Lorraine felt herself under Edith's constant and suspicious surveillance. It was the same everywhere in the hospital: news of the dead porter spread fast and staff congregated in whispering huddles. Anxiety generated by the second suspicious death manifested itself in lateness and minor accidents. Even the post meeting sank into a dissection of the recent tragedies.

'Strictly within these walls,' Norman announced from

238

across his desk, 'the police have told me it may be the same culprit as killed poor Rose. It was the same drug, apparently. I'm issuing a memo to all staff with details of new security precautions – all outer doors to be locked after 5 p.m., security patrols, and so on. The psychology department are also on hand to provide counselling.'

'But have the police made any progress with their precious enquiries?' Everyone, including Lorraine, looked over at Doctor Strang. There was an anxious pitch to his voice and a new low in his scruffy dishevelment. No one answered him. 'As for myself, I can assure you I was at the Palace Theatre with a girlfriend on Saturday night.'

'Have we all been asked to account for our whereabouts?' Felicity asked with a tinge of glee.

Mike nodded dolefully. 'I was at a United away weekend. Dozens of people saw me on the coach down to Ipswich.'

He caught Lorraine's eye and she returned a flash of warmth. After his counsellor had advised that he look up old friends, Lorraine had arranged cover for the chief engineer so he could take a whole weekend off. It had been tricky but news of Mike's weekend away made it worth her while.

'Same here,' said Raj. 'I was out with my brother-in-law. Then I stayed over at his place.'

Lorraine held her tongue, though Raj's alibi was not on a par with being in a distant part of the country with countless witnesses. She wondered what Diaz had made of it. It was getting to be a mental tic: almost every thought she had was about Diaz and his reactions.

Norman was next to cough up his whereabouts. 'As for me, I was at a brass band concert with my wife.'

'What about you, Lorraine?' Felicity teased. 'Weren't you

at the same concert as the dead porter? I hear it's not so much a good girl gone wrong as a bad girl found out.'

Aware of a roomful of eyes watching her, Lorraine said with a touch of double entendre, 'Don't worry about me. The police are more than satisfied with my movements on Saturday night. So how did your interview with the police go?'

Felicity addressed the whole group. 'I informed them I was at the Rotary Dinner at Swinton Civic Hall. I have a whole ballroom-full of witnesses. And a good friend has confirmed to the police that he drove me home.'

Lorraine wasn't the only person to jerk up her head in a double take at what she'd just heard. Was Felicity suggesting she had spent the night with a man? She remembered Felicity's fabled white overnight bag and wondered who on earth it could be.

Upstairs in her office, she had to sort out the nitty-gritty arrangements for Norman's extra security patrols. She'd glimpsed Diaz only once, striding in the wake of Brunt on their way to the incident room. She found it hard to switch off an internal dialogue with him that ranged from 'Don't you ever come near me again,' to 'Do you fancy a drink after work?' Still, she was blowed if she was going to seek him out after Brunt's threat.

It was the afternoon and she was deep in triple-checking the arrangements for the general manager selection day when the sergeant's dark silhouette appeared, hanging back at the door. Edith was sitting at her typewriter scrutinising them both.

'Afternoon. You said you'd give me a sample of the test questionnaire.' He spoke quietly, as she took in the height and build of this man she'd expected to take to her bed two nights earlier. His words meant nothing for a moment, until she remembered her promise to give him the PX60. So Diaz would be the recipient of her final test.

For Edith's benefit she replied in a flat voice. 'Of course.' She searched her desk and walked to the door to hand him a question booklet and scoresheet. Brunt could go jump, she thought. He'd need to catch them together first.

She was standing only a few inches from him when he passed her a piece of paper, shielded from Edith's eyes by the angle of her body. Lorraine felt the warmth of his hand brushing hers for a second.

After he'd left, Edith continued typing and Lorraine stared hard at a pile of paperwork; it took her a while to calm down. A sheet torn from the sergeant's notebook lay hidden in her palm. She glanced at it a few times.

See you upstairs in an hour. Where we met before.
Sorry about Saturday.

'He was a bit off with you,' Edith said at last. 'I thought he had his eye on you.'

'Him? You must be joking,' she said, not daring to look up from her desk.

Diaz was waiting upstairs, a darkness against the gleaming disc of the clock face. He looked away when she appeared, threw his cigarette down and ground it out on the floor. Then he held out the test sheet towards her. She had to walk right up to him to take it. Again, the paper felt overheated in her hand.

She backed away to lean against the wall. 'Brunt didn't

241

see me follow you up here. Is he guarding your virtue, or what?'

Diaz appeared to be studying the wisp of dying smoke on the floor. 'It's the inquiry. You're a witness. I can't be seen to be partial. But—' He finally looked up into her face, his dark eyes burning. 'I am so sorry about what happened.'

She shrugged, trying to play it cool. 'About what exactly?'

He looked up at the ceiling as if making a confession. 'About having to leave you like that.'

She felt a weird mixture of triumph and panic. If he'd put his arms around her at that moment, she'd have given in. But time passed.

'I haven't got long till I'll be missed. How did your interview with the boss go?'

'I didn't tell him his sergeant stole an evidence bag of speed supplied by the murder victim. And then shared it with a key witness. I lied. He seemed to believe me.'

'But – are you OK?'

'Not really. Your boss is a revolting bully. And I'm surprisingly upset about Rikki. And I feel everyone's pointing at me. But it's not just me. The whole hospital is on edge. It's called projection – mass blame-shifting, seeing wrongdoing in others. Hospitals are really prone to it apparently. And I still hate my job.'

'Why not sit down.' He gestured to the bench and when she was seated, he moved a few feet towards her.

'Is there anything to it? This job not being right for you?'

'Probably. It was one of the issues on my psychometrics course. I'm a square peg – or maybe even a polyhedron or something – in a round hole. But I think maybe all those holes need redesigning.'

He nodded. 'I know the feeling. I'm surrounded by loads of round pegs all waiting for their round hole retirements. You know, I'm really looking forward to my test results.'

'I need to get it scored. Then I should give you feedback. But I'm not supposed to have any contact with you.'

'Forget that. I'm ferrying the boss around tomorrow. What about Wednesday?'

She could say no. Then she recalled his hesitant boyishness when he'd opened up about his life. Finally, she said, 'OK.'

'Let's say one o'clock at 12 Radley Road. I've still got the door key.' He got out his notebook. 'First, I want to show you something I found in Rikki's locker.'

He passed her a six-by-eight black and white photograph. She held it up to the grey light. It showed an old-fashioned pulley device above a hospital bed frame and a skinny kid stranded on the sheets beneath it. She recognised a pathetically vulnerable version of Rikki aged about seven or eight. Around him were a group of young staff smiling for the camera in their old-fashioned uniforms and sixties hairstyles. One was a doctor with a stethoscope, his features almost hidden by long hair, a beard and moustache. Under his white coat he was wearing ludicrous big lapels and one of those flowered shirts that had been all the rage back then.

Next to him was a very attractive and vivacious nurse grinning at the camera, wearing dolly-bird make-up and a more flouncy version of the current nursing uniform. At her side stood a bespectacled serious-looking woman wearing what might have been the former uniform of a student nurse, or possibly a radiologist.

She studied each face, waiting for the proverbial penny to drop.

'I'm surprised,' she said. 'Apart from Rikki I've never seen any of these people before.'

Diaz came closer and looked, so close she could imagine warmth coming off him. 'All that face fuzz is as good as any criminal disguise. You can keep the photo. We've had copies made and we're questioning staff. I think – and I'd be interested to hear your opinion – that Rikki was a threat to Rose's murderer. Maybe he witnessed something important the day Rose was murdered. So he was killed to keep his mouth shut. What do you think?'

'It's possible. I hate to speak ill of the dead but he was always on the lookout. For drugs or cash.' She pondered a moment. 'And like I told your boss, I heard he arranged to meet someone that night. Did you find anything else in Rikki's locker? All the professional certificates for the general manager job have disappeared. I guess there must be a black market in fake credentials.'

'No, no sign of them. Are you sure it was him?'

'Well, someone stole them.'

'Got any other theories?'

'It could be someone who bears a grudge. Maybe they think they deserve the general manager's job? Or maybe someone wants to undermine Edith. Or me. My instincts say I'm being sabotaged.'

Diaz raised his eyebrows. 'Who would do that?'

She leant her head back against the wall and sighed. 'Any of the management team. Harvey's not in my fan club either.'

'Anyone else?'

She shrugged. 'Take your pick.'

'I'm sorry. It's bloody unfair.' He began to reach out a hand to touch her arm but when she pulled away, jerkily withdrew it. 'Anyway, tell me about testing the candidates. How soon can you get me the results?'

'The selection day is next Monday. Assuming I pass my exam this weekend.'

'What about Sister Ince? And Harvey Wright? Can you test them, too?'

She sighed theatrically. 'I'm seeing Sister Ince at her flat at Marlow Court near the ever-delightful Salford Precinct on Thursday. I think I can persuade her. But I don't know if Harvey will go for it. Do you really need his?'

'On the day Rose died, Harvey Wright arrived at the boardroom first. He had the best opportunity to go unseen into the flu clinic.'

Lorraine's thoughts turned to her former boss and mentor. 'He's too smart to fall for a silly ploy.' She glanced down at her watch. 'Blast, it's nearly five. I've got to go.'

He touched her hand and his fingers lingered. 'Watch yourself, hey? Whoever is doing this is getting a kick out of it. He might well do it again.'

She looked up hopefully towards him. What a sorry case she was.

'I did some self-defence back in '78. You remember when that poor woman was killed by the Ripper outside Manchester Infirmary? The Students' Union laid classes on for us, along with vigils and protests against you lot. I learnt some really evil techniques.'

'Good. Not one of the force's finer moments. Anyone waiting for you at home?'

She hadn't mentioned Jasmine before and had a sudden qualm. She didn't have time for a big explanation.

'Honest, I'll be fine.'

'The gig. It was really good.'

She stood up. 'Listen, I don't go on about it at work. I have these two completely different parts of my life. And I'd like to keep it that way.'

'I get that. Take care, Lorraine.'

So no Miss Quick this time. She tensed and waited, wondering if he might hug her.

He didn't.

As soon as Jasmine had fallen asleep, Lorraine took Diaz's test up to her bedroom. All day she had been reluctant to fax it to Doctor Lehman and now she rapidly hand-scored it in pencil. At first, she noticed only the similarities to herself. But as she inked the snake-like line on the graph, the differences between them jumped out at her. She checked a few factors twice, hoping for a better match. Reluctantly, she had to face the facts. On some crucial scales the two of them couldn't be further apart.

She pulled out her notes from Doctor Lehman's course, recalling some remarks about compatibility between married couples. Apparently, research had shown that people tended to marry those similar to themselves in education, class, religion, age, education and even physique. She had sarcastically written in the margin: 'So where's my matching clone?' Looking at these results, it certainly wasn't Diaz.

The wisest course would be to tell him so on Wednesday – that they were different, far too different, to get further involved.

Grandiosity

Question 39: I think someone should one day write my biography.
    A. True
    B. Uncertain
    C. False
High score description (option A.): Sense of personal superiority and entitlement, overconfidence, exploitation of others for self-gain, hostility and aggression when challenged.

Tuesday 8th March

At nine the next morning Lorraine was at HQ, waiting outside Harvey's office to run over the final details of the general manager selection day.

'Miss Jardine's still with him,' Harvey's PA, Janet, explained. Lorraine sat very still in the waiting area, earwigging through the door. Although she couldn't hear the exact words, the muffled surge and flow suggested an attempt at persuasion from Felicity punctuated by Harvey's cheery bluster.

When the door finally opened, Felicity emerged in a low-cut

costume of pillar-box red. Lorraine watched her totter up on spiky shoes, unsure if she loathed or admired the woman. As Felicity was the only female candidate for the top job, Lorraine had a guilty notion she should wholeheartedly support her. It was a pity, but she just couldn't do it. She was a Mae West or Cleopatra type, power-broking through men, with little time for other women.

Now the chief nurse gleefully beckoned her over, beyond Janet's earshot.

'Harvey's just taking a call. I wanted to ask, didn't I see you driving off with that good-looking young sergeant the other day?'

Lorraine tried not to squirm. 'It wasn't exactly pleasure. I had to show him where I picked Rose up that morning, the day she died.'

'I bet the police are all ears about whatever Rose told you in the car.'

Lorraine sighed. 'There was nothing to tell them. I feel awful that I put her off till later.'

'And rumour has it you've been seeing a lot of Rose's husband, too. Busy girl.'

'Who told you that?'

'Ah, so it is true.' Mischief sharpened Felicity's features.

'He asked me to a memorial service for Rose at his church. It was very moving.'

The chief nurse became instantly repentant. 'Was that it? I should have liked to attend that myself. Let me know, won't you, if there are any more gatherings. I genuinely would like to offer my respects.'

With some relief she heard Janet announcing that Harvey was ready to see her.

Inside Harvey's office, the atmosphere was ripe with cigar smoke and Felicity's Opium perfume. Harvey didn't even look up before barking, 'You found the certificates yet?'

'Not yet.'

He glanced up irritably. 'I had so much faith in you, Lorraine. Go on then. Run through your general manager profile.'

She took out her notes and pushed them towards him. 'The successful candidate will need to be highly intelligent, articulate with a good grasp of finance. Also open and outgoing, and not excessively anxious or admiration-seeking,' she explained. That last trait was a bit of a dig at Felicity.

Harvey sniffed, disgruntled. 'Sounds woolly. What about Churchill or Napoleon? Great leaders need iron in their souls.'

She knew he wasn't quite describing Hitler but still she raised her eyebrows. 'High level of dominance? It is a hospital, not wartime high command.'

'We need force and bloody-mindedness.'

All the arguments about sex difference were fresh in her mind from scoring Diaz's test. 'Isn't that all stereotypically male? Women generally score higher on warmth and agreeableness. Both excellent qualities for a modern leader. If we always look for dominance and aggression, we may never get any women leaders.'

Harvey burst out laughing and pointed to the photo of himself in white tie beside Mrs Thatcher in regal satin. 'Look. The PM has the personality to reach the top. And Felicity can hold her own against any man.'

'But what if a more conventionally feminine woman was in the running?'

Harvey grimaced. 'You women have to compete on a level

playing field or not at all. So put some backbone into that profile before Monday.'

He opened his desk drawer and pushed a schedule in front of her. Then he tipped his chair back and meditatively lit his cigarillo from a leather desk lighter.

'I want you to oversee the testing and make sure the results are ready by one o'clock at the latest. Get the printouts faxed over from your contact at Oxford. It looks better than handwritten. Then I'll give the feedback to the panel.'

It felt like an insult. 'I thought I was giving the feedback? I'm planning to brief the panel to investigate any mismatches in the interviews.'

He visibly stiffened. 'No. Only I speak to the panel.'

He wasn't going to be persuaded. In her annoyance she glimpsed an opportunity. 'But we also need to follow the Psychological Society's guidelines. I'm the only one trained in testing. So I need to, well – supervise you.'

He looked at his watch. 'You really think so?'

'I'll send you a test to complete. Then I'll run through your results with you.'

There was a sudden crack in Harvey's smooth demeanour. His ice-coloured eyes struck hers with some force.

'Not remotely appropriate. Given our difference in status.' He continued in a half-humorous, half-chastising manner. 'I can save us both precious time by telling you the results of the dozens of tests I've already taken. I'm a rare character in the personnel profession because I actually like people. I want them to enjoy their work. And I can read people's motives very easily without tests. You, for instance, Lorraine, have taken your eye off the target. You need to step back in line.'

After a puff at his cigarillo he asked, 'What else would you need to know? Whether I should have applied for the general manager job, perhaps?'

He chuckled and leant back, his eyelids half closed.

'Well, I'd enjoy ordering those smug doctors back from their private practices to attend their NHS clinics. But no, the only ambition I have left is to enjoy my retirement and tackle the best golf courses in Britain.'

Finally, he stretched his arms and clasped the back of his head, in what she knew was a fiercely domineering piece of body language. 'But if it makes you happy, send a test over.' His sarcasm rang out in warning.

'Great,' she said, trying to sound more cheerful than she felt.

'I'll see you on Monday at nine o'clock sharp. It's the biggest day of your career. Don't let anything else go wrong.'

The mood at band rehearsal that night was one that Lorraine was getting used to since Rikki's death: a mix of febrile excitement mixed with po-faced solemnity when anyone remembered to look sad. In honour of Rikki, Lily produced a bottle of Black Tower and some tea-stained mugs. Leaving their instruments untouched, they huddled around the electric bars of the portable heater and shared accounts of their police interviews. Lorraine told them what she knew: that Rikki had turned up at the hospital sometime before half past midnight and was later discovered dead from a lethal dose of propofol.

'After the gig I thought you and that copper might have been following him,' Lily said, suddenly suspicious.

'No. Did either of you keep an eye on him?'

Dale looked to Lily for back-up. 'We had a drink and then I realised he'd disappeared.'

Lily nodded. 'Asked Fred to load his kit and said he had to go.'

They all stared at the silent drum kit heaped in a corner. Dale sighed noisily. 'You know what I don't get? Why hasn't the band been mentioned on the news? I thought at least people might get to hear about us.'

Lorraine explained. 'It's a police inquiry. They keep certain facts hidden so they can weed out the time-wasters.'

Dale had put blue streaks in her hair and was momentarily checking out her reflection in the benighted window. Now she flashed a hard look at Lorraine and said, 'So they're holding back the facts? Like a conspiracy?'

'Yeah, I suppose you would think that,' she said, too weary to retaliate. The wine was even worse than the usual multi-squeezed teabags but she took a restorative gulp and then reached for her bag.

'Have either of you seen this before?' She pulled out the photo of young Rikki with his care team.

Lily studied it, then shook her head. 'No. But he told me about it. How he was abandoned by his parents and, you know, really suffered.' The unexpected crack in Lily's voice made her own throat burn too. Poor Rikki, he'd had a pretty shitty time of it.

'Did he tell you who those people were?' Lorraine asked.

'No. But he did tell me that the person he knew from the old days – he'd talked to them.'

'Someone at the Memorial who knew him as a child?'

'Suppose so.'

Dale picked up the photo and squinted at it. 'He said he'd

once had a photo of himself printed in a nursing magazine or something.'

Lorraine felt a quickening of interest. 'So it could be this one?'

Dale shrugged, then said, 'Hey, I've just remembered. Rikki put his bag in the drums before he left.'

She started poking around the drum kit, then froze and turned to Lorraine. 'I suppose you'll be ringing 999 if we find anything? Squealing to that cop you hang out with.'

'Give me a break, will you? I just want to find out who did this to Rikki.'

'Oh yeah? Rikki would still be alive if you hadn't made him work for you.'

Lorraine folded her arms tight to stop herself from slapping the girl. 'I think you've forgotten two things. One. He told lies all over his application form. Two. I would never ever have given him that job.'

Thankfully Lily distracted them both by pulling Rikki's Army and Navy bag out from the bass drum and swinging it aloft. They unpacked the contents and spread them across the top of an amp: another copy of the same photo, some spare drumsticks, a Manchester *A to Z*, a scraggy scarf and fingerless knitted gloves, some Opal Fruits and a bottle of Valium. There was an EP too – a copy of Gothenburg's first single, 'Night to Day'.

'Wow,' Dale said, hugging it to her chest. 'You could get twenty quid for that down the Underground Market.'

'What's that say in the corner?' Reluctantly, she relinquished it to Lorraine who held the sleeve up to the bare light bulb. 'FAIRHOLME?' was written very faintly, in grey pencil. He'd used his usual childishly scruffy capitals. Lorraine found the question mark perturbing.

On the front of the EP sleeve was a grainy distance shot of Lily's ex, Zeb, looking gawky and very young.

'Fairholme mean anything to either of you?' she asked.

Dale shrugged. 'I hope you're not going to hand that over to your plod friend. With our links to Zeb it's like a talisman or something. Rikki would have wanted us to have it, not the pigs.'

Lorraine picked up her mug to finish the wine but at the first tannic wince, put it down again. 'I'm going to photocopy the cover, OK? I'm serious about finding whoever killed Rikki. So how about you hold off from selling his final assets for just a day or two?'

Expedience

Question 40: There are occasions when what I want to achieve is more important than conforming to the law.

    A. Often
    B. Occasionally
    C. Never

High score description (option A.): Disregards rules, self-indulgent, oppositional, casual, resistant to group influences, especially moral values.

Wednesday 9th March

The hospital house at 12 Radley Road was still a location of interest, but Diaz had ignored Brunt's request to lodge the key at the station. He let himself in and prowled around, then climbed up to the bedroom where the double bed lay stripped to its striped pink mattress. To his frustration, the SOCOs' search for a Durex, stray hairs, fingerprints or fibres had all proved negative thanks to the efforts of the hospital's domestic department. The requisition form requesting the cleaning job could have been typed by any standard hospital typewriter and bore no signature. Again, he felt his adversary was a dozen clever steps ahead of him. Whatever had triggered Rose Cavanagh to step out of this house into Radley Road in a state of disorientation, he was sure the originating drama had been acted out here in this dreary bedroom.

At a quiet knock he went downstairs and guided Lorraine under the crime scene tape with awkward chivalry. When he had fetched her a brew from the kitchen she perched on the edge of a grubby moquette armchair.

Close up, she had made no effort with her lipstick or clothes and seemed utterly mundane. But at the same time her presence was excitingly physical and real.

'So, any news?' he asked. Goosebumps rose on his arms; the mildew lurking in the unheated walls was palpable. He got up and fiddled with the gas fire until solid orange whooshed across the corrugated radiants.

'Is it true that Felicity Jardine and Harvey Wright were together on Saturday night?'

He shook his head. 'You know I can't talk about that.'

'I'm only repeating what everyone's saying. I'm disappointed in Harvey. What about his wife?'

He shrugged, unsure if her offended expression was intentional. Had she somehow found out about Shirley? No, she couldn't have. Still, he felt it as a dig at his own treachery.

The gas fire hissed; he shifted on the ancient settee and wished Lorraine would come over and join him. He'd got over the first rage of lust. Just to put his arms around her would have been really great.

'Well, have you got my test? Are you going to commit me to the loony bin or what?'

'Got all the evidence right here,' she replied, deadpan. She got out some papers and made her way over to the settee and said, 'Shove up, then.'

He made room and she set down a paper headed 'PX60 Profile' between them on the coffee table. There was a wiggly line down the centre plotted on a graph.

'I'll give you the basic spiel. When we test people, we compare them to norms. I've compared you to other professionals, lawyers, teachers and so on rather than the general population.'

He nodded, dismayed at the prospect of being judged against what he imagined were snobby grammar school types.

'So, let's start with this cluster.' She pointed her pen at the graph. 'Your scores for Dominance and Tough-mindedness are much higher than average. That's in line with your police work.'

He perked up, feeling better already.

'But your scores for Warmth and Extraversion are unusually low. To be frank, you are far more critical and detached than most other people. You appear to prefer ideas to people. You say what you want and don't care how harsh it sounds. My advice is to watch your behaviour and how it affects other people. You always need to be right,' she said.

'I can live with that.'

'You just gave an example,' she said dryly. 'It's about being right all the time. But what about your colleagues who have to listen to you all the time?'

'They'll learn,' he quipped.

She looked disappointed. 'It's you who'll learn when you get nowhere.'

He made an effort to grasp her point. He wondered if she was telling him he'd been too cold and harsh towards her.

'OK. Let's lighten up,' she was saying. 'Amazingly, your score is above average in Intelligence.'

He laughed out loud at that.

'OK, hardly the next Einstein.' With a pencil she pointed towards two big zigzags on the chart.

'Another surprise.' Her pencil pointed to a jagged height. 'A very high score for Imagination. Another unconventional side to your personality that you keep under wraps.'

'What do you mean?'

'A powerful inner life. Absorbed by ideas in your head as much as the realities outside it.' She looked down at her paperwork. 'An active fantasy life.'

Suddenly, it was as if a searchlight was sweeping inside him, illuminating his private thoughts. No one – and he barely acknowledged it even to himself – knew that behind the hard-man image he was an intense daydreamer. At the kids' home he'd spent every second longing to be somewhere else. Was it any surprise he'd escaped into a secret dreamworld?

'This interest you have in profiling,' she continued. 'It's abstract, it's deep. It's radical compared to the police work going on around you. It's firing up your brain.'

He nodded, still reeling from the phrase 'active fantasy life'.

'You don't have to answer this, but do you feel you have to watch yourself all the time?'

'Christ. How did you pick that up from all those daft questions?' When she didn't answer he mumbled, 'Sorry. Go on.'

'And you have to keep people at a distance to function well?'

He gave a little nod of his head in surprise.

'The bad news is how far you disregard rules. That really

threw me for a so-called law-keeper. Not quite Charles Manson, but at best an outlaw, a Robin Hood type. I think you get a kick out of pushing against the status quo.'

'I can usually see a better way of doing things.'

'So can I. But it's dangerous, isn't it? You're risking your career. Other people aren't as stupid as you think they are.'

He was about to say that he had evidence to the contrary but held his tongue. Maybe he could learn from all this stuff after all.

'Your scores indicate that, to use an old-fashioned word, you struggle with morality. You told me you were very much alone as a child.'

'I had to look after myself, dead right.'

'That must have been very painful.'

When he mentioned his childhood he sensed she shifted closer. That she was supportive. But maybe that was the old Imagination playing up.

'I don't trust rules for their own sake. They work for other people, not for me. Brunt and his sort can go hang.' Suddenly he checked himself. 'Blimey. Are you enjoying getting inside my skull and having a good poke round?'

She was watching him narrowly. 'I know. It feels awkward to share the way we really experience ourselves. My tutor told me we all have a shadow inside us. Our fears, our capacity for inflicting pain and violence, all the bad stuff we repress. But it helps to talk about our authentic selves. The questionnaire helps. Otherwise it might take years to trust another person.'

'And even then, not always,' he found himself saying treacherously. He and Shirley hadn't had an honest heart-to-heart in ages. She complained that talking to him was worse than talking to the wall. 'So, are there any traits here that we – you know, me and you, both share?'

She took a while till she found the right paper. 'Imagination, for one. Like you, I live in my head a lot of the time. And we're both very private and independent. And prefer to work alone more than most.'

He felt grateful and nodded emphatically.

She put her head on one side. 'And we're both fishes out of water. We have to follow our self-image, to watch ourselves for good behaviour, because we're not really part of the club, are we?'

'Dead right.' Like bitter medicine, he grasped that this was good advice. After years of reining himself in, he was losing his cool around Brunt. He must never have another rant at the boss like the one he'd had over Rikki's corpse.

'But I'm nothing like you about the law,' she said, meeting his eye. 'That trick you played with the speed the other night. That puts you way beyond the pale of most other people. In a minority of four point four per cent of the population, to be exact. You might want to think about why you needed to do that. What were you really trying to do?'

She was waiting for an answer. Why had he done that? He'd told himself he wanted to get hold of the test results, but now he was less certain. He'd been fed up and frustrated but it had been more than that: the idea of taking the speed with her had possessed him like a devil directing his thoughts and limbs. He had lied to his colleagues, forged the evidence sheet, and risked destroying years of study and diligent behaviour.

He mumbled, 'I don't know. Couldn't stop myself.'

'I am worried for you. That's my sensitivity showing. For the record, I'm about fifty per cent more sensitive than you.'

260

'You can keep that,' he said.

'Actually, this horrible sensitivity I have – my tutor tells me it's the trait that helps me read people.'

'And what do you read in me?'

'On some traits you're almost my opposite. A bold, cold tough guy. But under the steel armour there's lots going on: fizzing ideas, dreams, plans. Lots of energy fuelled by anxiety, lots of libido.'

He laughed nervously, wondering if he'd heard that last word properly. Sex. Was she trying to remind him that that was what they both really wanted?

'OK. So what are you doing tonight?'

She stood and gathered up her papers. 'Not seeing you for a start.'

Cheekily, he reached for her hand but she pulled away. 'Come on, Lorraine. Please.'

She looked down on him severely. 'Don't underestimate me. I know your boss thinks I'm some dizzy blonde but he's a dinosaur heading for extinction. I've got to work tonight or I might fail my psychometrics exam this weekend. And I need to be in my tutor's good books when I ask her what a murderer's test results look like. So not a good time.'

'Don't go yet.' He tried to put his arms around her this time and there it was – a flash of how the killer must have felt, a surge of dominating power over a weaker victim.

She squirmed and stepped back. 'Seriously, Diaz. Behave yourself.'

'Sorry.' And for that instant he actually was. 'I just – I just want what we had before,' he added mournfully.

'Think first. Brunt will find out.' She shook her head at him. 'And I'm not sure.'

She'd reached the door when she said, 'One last thing. You're even more stressed than me. But you know how to bind it, to use it to create lots of energy. You're compulsive. I'd back you over Brunt to solve this any day. You won't give up.'

It felt like the best compliment anyone had ever given him. 'And what if I won't give up chasing you?'

He stood and moved slowly over towards her.

'I'm going.' She looked around the living room. On the wall hung a cheap gilded mirror where they both stood reflected in sulphur-tinted shadow. 'If that mirror could only speak,' she said.

He looked into it and Lorraine's gaze met his inside the glass. For an instant they stood side by side, a proper couple in another parallel and possible universe.

Then Lorraine moved out of the frame and the odd little premonition, if that was what it was, was over.

Absorption

Question 41: At times I am not sure what is fantasy or reality.
- A. Often
- B. Occasionally
- C. Never

High score description (option A.): Openness to a wide array of imaginative experiences, absorbed by sights and sounds, able to vividly re-experience the past, experiencing states of altered awareness.

I woke with a sickening lurch and felt myself alone in the darkness. Hanging onto the edge of consciousness I wondered, can we ever truly know another person? We live beside them, breathe the same air, yet never share their sunless core. Then I heard the rise and fall of a voice crying in the darkness. I set my feet down on the icy linoleum. A cat wailing, I thought. It had better find its way back outside before Christie found it. There was that incident years ago, a mess of blood and fur scattered all over the Treatment Room. I guessed it was a cat, or maybe a small dog. The cleaning up had not been pretty.

I was searching for the creature when the sound

changed. 'No, no,' it wailed. A cat cannot speak. A child, perhaps. The sound scraped my nerves. I felt my way silently to her room. She was weeping.

Opening her door, I called gently, 'Christie?'

I could hear her breathing; short little gasps weighted with resentment. The sound of all that ancient blame exhausted me.

'Can we talk sensibly?' I asked. I moved through the darkness and sat on the edge of the bed, releasing the smell of old sweat and talcum powder.

Confrontation has never been our style. Christie is damaged. I've always avoided speaking of what happened to her. But recently I've had strange thoughts, that maybe it's dangerous sheltering her here so long. That maybe it's not only her being damaged by our special bond.

'Did you do it, Christie? That boy?'

A furious sob escaped her lips.

'You did, didn't you?'

She started to rock, rhythmically, beneath the sheets. If only I could abandon her. Yet the thought of her here alone in these empty rooms, day after day, so scarred and needy. It would be kinder to save her the pain, like putting an ancient pet to sleep with a calming sedative.

Suddenly a small hand grasped my wrist, iron hard, the sharp little nails digging deep. 'It was you who made me do it.' Her voice was shrill. 'You! I'm so alone. I'm so alone. I'm so alone.'

She kept chanting the same phrase. If only I had more time to devote to her . . . But no, I had to be the responsible one, the professional worker, ever vigilant, ever controlled.

I shook her off, roughly. 'Did you do it?'

'Without me you'd be nothing,' she hissed. 'You needed

me when you were young. When I came to you, when all you wanted was to end the pain. I protected you from the world. And now you want to leave me, don't you?'

'I always thought we'd go our own ways naturally,' I said wearily.

'But I love you! You need me. It's not that simple.'

'Did you kill him?'

She threw something at me and I ducked down low to avoid it. Then scrabbling in the sheets, I found a cold and flexible strap. With a curt goodnight I took it back to my room.

The second relic was charged with a different, male potency. Returning to bed, I was acutely wakeful. I tied the strip of plaited leather tight around my wrist before I slept. It's strange that Christie's wrist is of such a small circumference and yet she so easily overcame her victim. As I pulled the strap tighter, I pictured it all: the delicious moment when Eric Fryer woke up to his own stupidity. That brief expression of dumbstruck horror. And his twitch of alarm as the needle struck. And then the release: the transmutation into nothingness – a corpse, a has-been, a vanquished enemy.

Practicality

Question 42: I am a reliable and practical worker who likes to get on with my job without needless changes.
   A. Often
   B. Occasionally
   C. Never

High score description (option A.): Practical down-to-earth concerns, regulated by external realities, conventional, unimaginative, prosaic.

Thursday 10th March

Lorraine's nan had always been full of stories of Salford's street markets manned by chirpy barrow boys and corner shops run by matriarchs in hair curlers and headscarves. Now her own generation had Salford Shopping Precinct: a ghetto of dirty concrete slabs with sewer-like underpasses. As Lorraine manoeuvred the Metro into a parking spot, a couple of scallies in torn jumpers and half-mast trousers sprang up from nowhere. The bigger lad rapped on her window.

'Fifty pence to mind your car, missus.'

She wound the window down. 'What's going to happen if I don't?'

'The Brody gang'll 'ave your tyres.'

She didn't bother asking how two little tykes were going to stop any gang doing anything.

'Maybe. If you show me the way to Marlow Court.'

They struck a bargain and her two attendants skipped ahead of her past boarded-up shops covered in balloon-lettered graffiti, up slimy steps and across scary walkways. Hard drinkers malingered outside pubs that could have been in Belfast or Beirut.

Sister Ince lived in a seventh-floor flat with a padlocked iron grate guarding its front door. Out of uniform the former nurse looked diminished, just another worn-out woman in Crimplene trousers and a buttoned-up cardi. Still, she'd got the tea things ready, and a plate of malted milk biscuits on a tray. The living room was tidy and the kitchenette had the luxury of hot water. On the downside, Lorraine could recognise the exact Black Sabbath track vibrating through the chipboard walls.

Miss Bernadette Ince, as she was now to be known, sat opposite her in an armchair, her fingers compulsively working at the frayed moquette.

'I'm not going to get my pension, am I?'

Lorraine smiled. 'Yes, you are. One thousand seven hundred pounds a year for your pension. With a lump sum of five thousand and one hundred pounds.'

The nurse gasped and then crossed herself. 'Jesus, Mary and Joseph. It's better than a win on the bingo. When do I get it?'

'If you sign the form today it'll take about two weeks, backdated to today.'

'And Miss Jardine has honestly signed it off?'

'Yes, the Occupational Health doctor has found in your favour.'

She wiped her palms on her knees and sighed. 'Well, that's a miracle. Where do I sign?'

Lorraine got out the documents and ran through her spiel. Did Miss Ince intend to work as a nurse again?

'The doctor says me nerves have gone. I'd as soon go to hell and back.'

'I'll inform the General Nursing Council that you're no longer registered.'

'Thank the saints for that.'

After she'd signed, Lorraine looked back over her service history. 'It's not surprising you've got a decent pension, looking at all the years you've done. I see you once worked at a place called Fairholme. Not part of the National Health is it? What was that like?'

Miss Ince shook her head. 'I had a loan company after me and had to do some extra shifts. It's on the site of some posh old mansion at the side of Prestwich Hospital. When the mansion burnt down they built Fairholme. For a psychie job it was the pits. No ruddy pension for the hours I did there.'

'Don't the Memorial porters sometimes go there?'

'That's right, they escort patients if the nurses are busy. Anyway, I'm well out of it now.'

'You just reminded me,' Lorraine added as casually as she could manage. 'I recently picked up this key ring by accident. The keys to a room at "The Williams" or "The Willows" or something like that. Ever heard of it?'

Lorraine passed her the keys with the tatty fob.

The former nurse frowned effortfully. 'It's not quite ringing a bell, but I am getting a little tinkle. Not the National Health.

But I heard about it, oh way back. "The Wil—". Ooh, what would that be now?' She shook her head. 'It's gone.'

'Would you ring me if you remember?'

'All right.' She didn't sound convincing. 'Is that my stuff from the office?'

Lorraine scribbled a note of Fairholme's location and then unloaded the framed certificates, yellowing Tupperware and copies of *The People's Friend* she'd found in Sister Ince's desk. It seemed a pathetic remnant of all those decades of service.

'Oh, and I'm supposed to give you this.' She lifted a Salford Health Authority plaque out of her carrier bag. 'Here's to a long and happy retirement.'

Miss Ince took it with a grimace. 'I'll hang it in the lav where it belongs.'

They both giggled. In the sudden shared warmth Lorraine decided to give her plan a spin. 'Actually, I wonder if you'd do me a favour. I'm doing some research into people leaving their posts and asking them to fill in a questionnaire. You can't exactly say you've got no time for it.'

Miss Ince looked up at the gilt clock. 'Well, I suppose I can miss *Pebble Mill* for once.'

While she completed the test Lorraine read the *TV Times* and then used the loo, involuntarily eavesdropping on a couple engaged in a screaming match just above the ceiling.

'There you are,' Miss Ince said at last, pushing over the test and answer sheet.

'Do you want me to send you the results?'

Miss Ince stood up and started clearing up the tea things. 'Save your stamps, love.' Then picking up the pension statement, she smoothed it out and reread the figures. 'I've got all I want here.'

Disorganised Cognition

Question 43: I find that I am confused about what is going on around me.
    A. Often
    B. Occasionally
    C. Never

High score description (option A.): Disorganised thoughts and behaviour, confusion, racing thoughts, loose associations, disrupted speech, difficulty following conversations.

Friday 11th March

On Friday, Lorraine told Edith she was leaving early for her exam in Oxford. But instead of heading south she let the Metro freewheel down the steep hill into Agecroft valley. Four colossal cooling towers overshadowed the road, fat-bellied grey chimneys releasing plumes of white vapour into the winter sky. As she drove she imagined that at Fairholme she might discover the reason why Rikki had been killed – by uncovering a drug gang, or a front for a massive fraud. Then she imagined surprising Diaz with her brilliant solution.

That's pathetic, she told herself. Why did she need his

bloody approval? Privately, she knew the answer. The closer they became, the more justification she'd feel to have a fling with him. Interrupting her daydream, his test scores rang a discordant warning in her mind. Watch out, sweetheart, she told herself. Beneath the surface, this person might only be out for himself.

Arriving in Prestwich, she searched for the asylum. There it was, a sprawl of mouldering red-brick arches and Italianate towers, a former workhouse of yard-blocks, wards and wash-houses. In the Victorian age it had been a small town of more than 3,000 unfortunates. If there was one place she'd always promised herself she would never work, it was there.

She drove the car along the outside of the hospital walls to the leafy avenue Sister Ince had described. Here were the elaborate villas that had once housed hospital superintendents, warders, gardeners and farmhands. Getting out of the car at a set of iron gates, she stood on tiptoes to glimpse the building. The original Victorian pile had long gone and now there was nothing but razor wire and flat prefabricated roofs in view. Fairholme – its name was certainly questionable.

She rang the buzzer and when a distorted voice asked, 'Who is it?', replied that she'd been sent from the Memorial as she needed a place for her difficult mother. The gate bleeped and creaked open. She manoeuvred the car up the drive, her hands tight on the wheel.

From a distance the four men lounging on benches might have been workers taking a break. Then, as she approached, the fellow sitting closest to her sprang up and started running blindly towards the car. With no time to swerve aside she cried out and slammed on the brakes as his body walloped into the chassis. A bony unshaven face lurched across her windscreen and gurned at her, twisting pink rubbery lips. She cringed back; he was inches from her with only thin glass between them.

He slid off the bonnet but a moment later a gobbet of phlegmy drool splattered across her car window.

She had stalled the engine and it took long moments of panic to restart it. Where the hell were the staff? She spotted a small sign for a car park and manoeuvred the car to the rear, where she switched off the ignition and sat for a while. The man's saliva was still dribbling in a stomach-churning mess inches from her face.

Scanning her surroundings for other patients, she was relieved to spot a gardener disappearing into the shrubbery behind a wheelbarrow.

'Excuse me!' She hurried out of the car to accost him. 'I'm looking for whoever is in charge here.'

'This way.' He picked the barrow handles up; he looked a peaceful, nature-loving type with long straggly hair tied back in a ponytail.

'It's a lovely garden,' she added, more politely. As soon as she spoke she saw it was true. March had brought golden sprays of daffodils to the flower beds, set off by clumps of delicate crocuses. For a moment she felt the sun on her face, shining from high in the pale blue sky. The air was sweet and warm. Maybe she too would be happier working outdoors.

As she followed the gardener she looked around for a further building where the manager must be at work. Well, an encounter out here had to be better than stepping inside the gulag-like buildings of Fairholme itself.

'Are you sure this is right?' she asked as they passed through a gap between some waxy rhododendron bushes. There was a path but also great clouds of midges that she had to slap away. To her surprise they emerged into a circle of gravel surrounding a pockmarked fountain.

'He's in charge today,' announced the gardener. He pointed at what looked like a filthy sack dumped on the ground. Slowly she identified slabs of matted hair around a face from which almost all humanity had been erased. Whether it was a result of heavy sedation or a comatose state, she had no idea.

'This lady wants to ask a question,' the gardener said.

The sack-like figure didn't stir. She took in a group of bizarre items displayed on the fountain's dry plinth. There was a Sindy doll, decapitated and painted with red felt-tip as if bleeding, a small animal skull, and a scattering of other filthy detritus ranging from broken mirrors to old toothbrushes.

The gardener began speaking in an urgent monologue. 'This is the radio control centre. There's two power sources locked in eternal conflict. The enemy is inside the radio in the therapy room and emits signals in frequency two nine five . . .'

She stood paralysed by the surreality of her surroundings. This was not the path to the manager. And this was not a gardener.

'Right,' she said awkwardly. 'Thanks. Sorry, I think I forgot something.' She turned on her heels, trying not to break into a run. Then hearing footsteps rustling ahead of her in the rhododendrons, she cried out, 'Hello. Anyone there?'

Around the bend came a nurse, a huge guy in a grubby white tunic with a swinging fob watch. He barged past her, straight up to the fountain. 'Oy, you two! Back to your rooms.'

Obediently, the gardening patient dropped the barrow and set off back towards the house. The nurse prodded the second

273

patient. 'So you can move when no one's looking, eh? How did you get yourself out here?'

She saw then that despite the creases of pain carved into the face of the tramp-like patient, he was not very old. His unfocused gaze rested on the ground, his bleary eyes framed by long crusty lashes. The outlandish scenario was suddenly painfully poignant.

The male nurse turned to her, scowling. 'What are you doing here?'

Shit. His face was familiar. Full of apologies, she stuck to her story: that she'd heard of Fairholme at work and was looking for somewhere to put her difficult mother.

'Trouble is she? The old 'uns can be the worst.' The nurse bore a name badge printed with 'John Garbutt' and was six inches taller than her and as wide as a small shed.

'Yeah,' she replied, trying to match his nonchalance. 'She loves hitting social workers.'

'We're used to trouble here. Get the referral sorted and we'll do the rest.'

'Great,' she said, attempting enthusiasm. 'Can I have a look round first?'

John pulled a disgruntled face. 'We're dead busy. Short-staffed and it's teatime in half an hour.'

She put on her most plaintive expression. 'Please. I'm desperate.'

He glanced through the bushes to dusty windows blanked out by Venetian blinds. 'Well. Just a quick dekko then.'

John Garbutt hoisted the tramp-like patient up onto a bench and told him to stay put. Then she followed him, taking the back entrance into Fairholme. Watching his barrel-sized back, she silently agonised over the last occasion she had

274

seen him. He was the psychiatric nurse Felicity had sacked for hitting a patient. Thankfully, she had sat at the very edge of the disciplinary panel while the others had done all the speaking. She hoped he met dozens of people a day and with luck, forgot them instantly.

Inside the building there was a fug of urine and old clothes inadequately disguised by pine disinfectant. Everything she looked at was cheap and grubby. The man who had run at her car was muttering as he paced a corridor in what she recognised as a lopsided Largactil shuffle. He paid her no attention. Instead a gaunt man approached them, extending a begging hand to wheedle, 'Just one little fag?' Then he recognised John Garbutt and backed quickly away.

'We'd keep your mum away from this lot,' John assured her. 'We've got a proper female ward here.'

He pulled a chain out of his pocket bearing dozens of steel keys. Behind a locked door a dozen women lay or sat on low metal beds, bereft of natural light. In a dingy-looking day room, the television bellowed. Lorraine knew the NHS had a few hellholes but at least there was a lumbering process of inspection. If this was the privatised future it had to be stopped.

'Who do I get the referral from?' she asked, struggling to maintain a rigid expression of interest.

John hesitated, then turned surly. 'You weren't sent?'

'No,' she stumbled. 'Not really. I just heard about it.'

'Who from?' His goldfish eyes fixed on her, seeming to detect her lies with ease.

'Oh, who was it? Sister Ince,' she stammered.

It was the wrong answer. His pouchy face hardened and jerked towards the door. What an idiot she was. Of course, doctors generally made referrals.

'Don't I know you? You're that one from Personnel, in't you? Come snooping around, have you?'

She didn't stay to explain, only broke away and hurried back the way she'd come, desperate to escape. Distantly, a hi-fi was playing and by some chance Gothenburg's 'Night to Day' reached her, replete with Zeb's spangly guitar riff. It felt like a clarion call to return to open air, freedom, her own precarious existence. She almost ran to the car. The tyres skidded on the gravel and only when she was back on the busy main road did she wind down the window to let in the cold air of approaching night.

Shaken by the encounter at Fairholme, Lorraine stopped at a phone box and checked with her mum that she'd picked Jasmine up safely. Grandma and granddaughter had a weekend of treats planned, so she got back in the car and hit the accelerator along the M62's Death Valley. By the time the M6 dissected Birmingham, the sun was setting and the industrial fairy lights of the power station blazed against a damson sky. Why had Rikki written down 'Fairholme' and a question mark? Maybe it was just a coincidence. Fairholme had been on the porters' runs and Rikki may simply have been querying expenses or overtime. But Lily had said he'd recently talked with a figure from his past at the Memorial, maybe someone in that photograph.

Like Diaz, she wondered if Rikki had crossed the killer's trail. Maybe the daft lad had been too doped up to feel alarm signals when the killer lured him to the computer suite. And where the hell had he hidden those stolen certificates?

Night fell fast upon unfamiliar place names flashing

276

by on blue motorway signs: Chipping Norton, Gloucester, Worcester. Who, beyond a mutilated Sindy doll, was in charge at Fairholme? And who at the Memorial managed referrals? For all her ferreting around, she was still completely in the dark.

Psychopathy

Question 44: I like looking at pictures containing lots of blood and guts.

    A. Often

    B. Occasionally

    C. Never

High score description (option A.): A syndrome that includes a lack of conscience or sense of guilt, lack of empathy, egocentricity, pathological lying, violations of social norms, law-breaking, shallow emotions and a history of victimising others.

Saturday 12th March

On Saturday morning Lorraine joined the rest of her group in a room laid out with rows of single desks to take their exam to gain accreditation by the Psychological Society. Everyone chatted nervously until Doctor Lehman told them to turn their papers over, be silent and begin. Lorraine did her best to enjoy herself, though the maths was pretty deadly, fulfilling the old student jest that 'statistics' might more aptly be renamed 'sadistics'. Maths hadn't been taught well at her crappy comprehensive, so she'd had to learn the graphs and formulae and conversion tables using visual patterns. Still, it wasn't the maths but a verbal question that stalled her:

> Give two reasons why psychometric test results should remain confidential.

The first reason was the right to privacy but trying to recall the second broke her concentration for precious minutes. Instead, the pressure from Diaz to break confidentiality sent her into a tailspin. She wanted this qualification so badly, yet even on the cusp of her success, events at the Memorial Hospital were intruding. At last, she remembered what her written notes had stated: that testing allowed a stranger to get a view into the candidate's undefended psyche, allowing a malicious person to coerce a vulnerable colleague. She checked her watch, pulled herself together and hurried to finish the paper.

She had agreed to meet Doctor Lehman last of all the students for a private appointment at four o'clock. In the meantime, she went out for a walk, rehearsing her usual socialist muddled thinking about the injustice of this academic paradise being denied to most comprehensive school leavers. She wandered around the high street, admiring gorgeous stonemasonry, gilded gateways and magnificent windows. God, she'd been an idiot to think she could find an answer to life's questions here.

A cold chill rose from the river and the charcoal clouds were gathering by the time her appointment slot arrived. Inside the seminar room Doctor Lehman lifted a haggard face from behind a desk towering with papers.

'Lorraine. Congratulations, you passed.' She handed over the printed form she'd need to claim her official certificate. She felt a jolt of relief that she wouldn't have to explain another failure to Harvey on Monday morning.

Tilting her head to one side, Doctor Lehman asked, 'Now, I need to tell you the results of that last test you sent me. After a long day it's easier for me to use visual aids.'

The tutor rose and switched on the projector. She placed a new slide in the carousel: the screen showed an oil painting of a poor working man leaning forward with his face buried in his fisted hands. Every line and shadow spoke of harrowing grief.

'*Old Man in Sorrow* by Vincent van Gogh,' Doctor Lehman announced. 'I'd like you to recall your recent profile of Bernadette Ince. Here we have a man whose face we cannot see. His conflict is internal, he visibly retreats from the world and the sight of others.

'You may recall that, like Mike McClung, Miss Ince's test results had an extremely high score for Guilt-proneness, a trait associated with apprehension, insecurity and anxiety. Yet when we look at the overall profile, Mr McClung's serious and sober attitude points us to depression, while Miss Ince is generally talkative, if rather heedless. Her responses to the anxiety scales tell us she sleeps badly, is dejected when criticised and reproaches herself for her own failings. She is also subject to unrealistic fears, seen in her high level of free-floating anxiety. Overall, the test suggests she's probably a chatty, self-centred person, and noticeably tense. However, traumatic events such as the recent murder can leave her fairly defenceless. Lorraine, would you say this is her general character, or could it simply be a reaction to recent events?'

'She did find Rose's murder unbearably stressful,' Lorraine felt compelled to say. 'But to be honest, ever since I've known her, she's been a nervy, self-apologetic person. A dedicated worker though, and almost the longest-serving member of staff.'

'Yes. I would venture she'll soon miss her work and its moral commitment to serving others. I take it she has a religious faith.'

'How could you know that?' Lorraine asked, genuinely surprised.

'Persons with these traits often practise a religion and choose what is deemed to be a virtuous profession, perhaps as a way of warding off their feelings of guilt and so-called sin. Priests, for example, have long been noted as having a fragile sense of self-worth.'

'Does her profile show a propensity for violence?'

Doctor Lehman picked up the test result sheet again. 'If she had tested as highly cynical and suspicious of mankind, perhaps. But I doubt Miss Ince could have subdued her high anxiety sufficiently to carry out a murder. And if she had committed violence I think she would have confessed by now, subject to an uncontrollable impulse. You know her in person. Would you agree?' Doctor Lehman removed her glasses and rubbed her red-rimmed eyes.

'Yes, I would. But I have another question,' Lorraine said. 'I know the test gives an accurate description of a co-operative subject. But can it honestly catch a killer who doesn't want to be caught?'

The tutor glanced up at the clock. 'Dinner is not served

till eight tonight and it's been a long day. Shall we fetch some supplies from the buttery?'

Lorraine returned with a plate of food and tried to relax, spreading a gigantic teacake with butter and jam. Doctor Lehman nibbled on a modest slice of fruitcake and took long sips of black coffee before saying, 'So, firstly, could a test actually catch a killer? Well, no test in isolation can predict future behaviour. We are speaking only of probabilities, not certainties. But specific results linked to violent or highly impulsive traits should always raise a red flag. Carl Jung wrote that personality types are like a compass to help us find our way in a wilderness. I for one prefer to carry a compass on any journey into the unknown.

'And remember, Lorraine. It is never ethical to use test scores for any purpose beyond what the subject has agreed to. Especially if the scores could have a catastrophic effect on your subjects' lives, as being accused of murder certainly could have. So tell me, if you did find unusual results, what would you do?'

This was the crux of it all and Lorraine knew it. It was the point at which she'd break the ethical code.

'I would discuss it with you.'

Doctor Lehman raised her eyebrows. 'And what about that police officer?'

Lorraine felt exposed. 'He thinks that sharing the result could be justified. I don't know what to do,' she said simply. 'On the phone you talked about being both attracted and repelled by a person. I need to understand what you said about my shadow side. How can I know who to trust?'

Her tutor switched on the slide projector again and the screen filled with the image of a marble statue of two lovers.

A winged youth stooped to embrace and kiss a sensuously waking woman.

'*Eros and Psyche* by Antonio Canova. Psyche gives her name to the soul or mind, and "ology" of course refers to the study of that subject. I often use this story to explain the danger of the shadow side in relationships. It applies to many types of relationships beyond romantic pairings, whether with mentors, teachers, friends, colleagues or family members. You are familiar with the legend?'

Lorraine shook her head.

'The shorter version, then. The young god Eros falls in love with the mortal Psyche but makes her promise she must never see his face. They must only make love in the absolute darkness. All goes well at first, for is it not more comfortable to never entirely know or be known? In the first rush of attraction we can hide our bad habits, our unacceptable histories, our shameful secrets. So the pair agree to mutual blindness.

'And thus do we project a dark veil on our prospective lovers – or teachers, or mentors, and so on. Instead of a stranger we see fragments of our parents, our ideals, those odd patchwork fantasies which we hope might make us whole. Then the fatal day comes. Our psyche is inquisitive. In the myth, the mortal Psyche lights her candle and raises it high in the darkness. She sees the face of Eros. This person we desired so strongly is not who we anticipated. He is damaged and disappointing.'

Lorraine leant back, considering, then said, 'That's a terrible story. But so perceptive. This policeman, we seemed so alike but—' She considered telling her tutor she had tested Diaz but instantly rejected the impulse.

'Now he seems damaged and disappointing?'

Lorraine laughed softly. 'How did you guess?'

'It is a very old story. What are you frightened of, Lorraine?'

She tensed as she considered. I'm still frightened of being attacked, she thought, suddenly wary of the vulnerability of Psyche's raised arms, and the ravishing entanglement of limbs and wings. That was heavenly, while she feared that what drew her to most men, from treacherous Andy to DS Diaz, was potentially hellish. Another bad man. Sex on his terms. As if she needed that now.

'Being hurt.'

'Oh, you will always get hurt. Love, authenticity, a self-directed life. The price is always pain.'

'I wish you could tell me the answer.'

The tutor smiled benevolently. 'I am a psychologist. Not a prophetess. If you want to live your life fully, go and experience it to the full.' Then lifting her forefinger in emphasis, she added, 'But remember to light your candle before being led into the woods.'

'Thank you.'

Lorraine expected to be dismissed but Doctor Lehman continued to stand by the projector, her lips pressed together, considering.

'I have hesitated over sharing this with you but have decided to do so. There is one personality type that some researchers claim is quite different from the rest. According to the definition in the new Mental Health Act, such a person has a disorder which results in abnormally aggressive or seriously irresponsible conduct. Again, it is easier to show than explain.'

She clicked on the projector and the screen was filled with a fresh image that recalled a grotesque magic lantern show;

it was a disturbing illustration from the fairy tale 'Little Red Riding Hood'. Lorraine recognised the work of the Victorian illustrator Gustave Doré. He had portrayed that moment in the story where the little girl has been joined in her grandmother's bed by the wolf, his gigantic muzzle protruding from a lacy bedcap.

'Robert Hare's work on a ground-breaking new checklist claims such psychopathic personalities reveal a propensity towards violence, often from childhood. Hare's test measures items such as manipulation, grandiosity, callousness, impulsivity and an entire lack of empathy. He or she is cool, controlled and clever. A glib and charming predator. An intelligent psychopath has the skills to pass themselves off as a normal human being. Like this grisly wolf, when questioned by Little Red Riding Hood the psychopath will echo back exactly what he thinks you want to hear.'

Lorraine looked at the disturbing image of the child, her expression capturing the moment of alarm in which she first comprehends her danger. Tucked up beside her was the sharp-toothed wolf, bedecked but not disguised in spectacles and lace. Lorraine quailed, remembering her terror of the Yorkshire Ripper who had killed a woman with a hammer just yards from her university.

'The high-intellect psychopath has a history of success in all manner of business – in banking, finance, the law and medicine. One problem is that recruiters often mistake excessive dominance for strong leadership. Callousness is mistaken for ruthlessness. There is a theory that these monsters drag us all into conflict, and even wars, that no sane person would contemplate. At the most extreme, some say the whole economic world structure relies on these monsters bullying those with more submissive personalities, fostering inequalities and exploitation.'

A flash of understanding sparked in Lorraine's mind. She recognised this phenomenon in the explosion of Porsche-owning bankers, rapacious shareholders and pension-pilfering bosses. 'What can we do to stop them?' she asked.

'Psychopaths present themselves as excellent candidates because they tell lies with exceptional ease. Personnel professionals need to insist on cleverly structured interviews that challenge any gaps or discrepancies in the candidate's history and probe a fake persona. And qualifications and credentials need to be checked rigorously.'

Lorraine had another revelation. She had failed to listen to the alarm bells in her mind.

'All the candidates' certificates were stolen. I've just realised that one of them must be false. And now I've got no time left before the interviews on Monday morning. I've been manipulated. Made to question my own ability to do the job.'

Doctor Lehman paused to reflect. 'I've never said this to a student before. But why don't you resign?'

Over the last month she'd had no time to find new work. Yet it wasn't only the lack of job prospects that made her thoughts suddenly crystallise. 'I think you've just told me why not. You see, however much my job infuriates me, the hospital doesn't deserve this. I've got to give fairness and openness a chance.'

Her tutor looked tired. Her finely wrinkled skin hung from her bones, but that only made her blue eyes appear even brighter.

'So what am I looking for?' Lorraine asked.

'Mimicry. The wolf echoes back Red Riding Hood's

questions. He enjoys playing at being her grandmother. To your face, he may be warm, but catch him unawares and you'll spot nothing but vacancy and coldness. Look for managers who clamber over their colleagues. Who destroy other people's careers.'

'And the test? How do I spot this wolf in grandma's clothing?'

Doctor Lehman touched her arm, tense with concern. 'Remember the results are at most a probability and not a prediction. If there is an unusual result you must not tell the police until we've reviewed the results together.'

'Yes.'

'To simplify matters, there are just two factors to look out for. Firstly, psychopathic personalities find taking tests irresistible because they are proud of their uniqueness. To themselves they are superior beings starring in their own exciting drama.

'So if you ask a psychopath if he loves the thrill of danger, he will admit it. He may also claim to never feel guilt at putting his own needs first, and to be one hundred per cent intelligent and self-reliant. I doubt you'll miss such an outrageous profile.'

Lorraine felt a great gulf in her knowledge. 'I don't know, Doctor Lehman. I don't feel capable of this level of interpretation.'

'Simply look for someone too extreme to be true. I'll be here waiting for the scoresheets. And the second factor is easy. It's a single number. As forensic psychologists know, too many psychopaths have been released from custody with tragic consequences simply because they lie with consummate ease. So unless the subject is trained in psychometrics they will fake so exceptional a score that the tripwire built into the test will catch them. Expect a Motivational Distortion score of at least seven and even as high as ten out of ten.'

Lorraine felt her breath growing tight. 'You mean the Faking Good score? I can't believe anyone would lie so outrageously.'

Doctor Lehman pointed at the monstrous hunter and his innocent prey on the screen.

'The wolf simply can't resist boasting about his gigantic carnivorous teeth. Yet according to the fairy tale, even an innocent child can catch him out. Seriously, I do hope you are wrong about these suspects, Lorraine. I hope you never have to encounter such a monster.'

Hypomania

Question 45: I get thoughts racing in my head that make me feel agitated and restless.
   A. Often
   B. Occasionally
   C. Never

High score description (option A.): Restless, high energy levels, irritable and dissatisfied, takes risks, tries new things.

At Saturday teatime, Bernadette Ince switched on the telly while she heated up some crispy pancakes and frozen peas to eat on a tray, washed down with a celebratory glass of stout. The sports fella was going on about how United were going to play Everton in the cup when she heard him say it again and again – 'Wilkins'. Now what did that remind her of? Her memory was like a blessed sieve these days.

She was well into *Wish You Were Here . . . ?*, thinking maybe she could go somewhere herself, spend a bit of her pension lump sum on taking some of the sick of her congregation to Lourdes – when she remembered. Wilkins wasn't only the name of that footballer; it had also been that place for nurses to stay back in the old days. And Lorraine from Personnel had asked her about it, but she'd got it all wrong. She thought it was the Williams or suchlike. No, it was the Wilkins Boarding House, down at The Glen. Some of the others at work had told stories about all sorts of scrapes they had while living there. She herself hadn't needed digs because she'd been living with her auntie in Pendleton. Still, it was a pity it was a Saturday or she could have rung Lorraine straight away.

Sunday 13th March

In the morning she went to Mass but after her dinner she just couldn't settle down with the *Sunday Mirror*. She had wanted to talk about the trip to Lourdes with Father Maguire but he'd been absent with a touch of bronchitis and no one else had wanted to know. A ragbag of ideas jostled in her mind as she paced the living room, stopping each time to lift the net curtains and look outside. The walkways were empty, the sky was grey, but it was dry outside. If only she could set off for Lourdes today. Well, if not Lourdes she could maybe catch a bus up to The Glen and take a little wander round.

Half an hour later she was rattling along on the bus, getting a fine view of the park that had used to be such a lovely place, with a bandstand and a lake and hundreds of cheery people all out for a stroll come holiday-time. She had once met a young man there called Billy, a haberdasher's assistant from Urmston, but her auntie hadn't cared for him. Looking back, she was struck how Auntie had never wanted her to have a life of her own. She'd always hinted how she'd leave her a fine inheritance if she'd stay a bit longer and be the companion of her old age.

So like a right idiot she'd stayed and when the old lady passed away Bernadette had got twenty-three pounds, nine shillings and eightpence, and the landlord had given her notice to quit. She had been forced to go begging to the council for a roof over her head. And now the park looked all spoilt and tarmacked over and not at all the sort of place to find a sweetheart.

She clambered off the bus and headed to The Glen where the big old houses were. All those fancy villas that were four and five storeys high were not so posh now. Most of them were bedsits with sheets tacked up at the windows, or those special houses where they put mental cases or ex-cons.

Still, it gave her something to do to check the names on all the stone gateposts that were engraved with the house names. It took her an age to find the name Wilkins on two blackened stumps. And after all that bother, it wasn't a very nice place at all. It was falling to bits like something off *The Addams Family*. In fact, she'd have liked to go into work and tell everyone what a dump it was now. It was going to take some getting used to, just sitting at home and twiddling her thumbs. Anyway, it gave her an excuse to ring Lorraine on Monday and she'd be glad to hear all about it.

She was standing at the empty gate – she'd certainly not be knocking on that nasty paint-blistered door – when she spotted a figure watching her from a first-floor window. Bernadette looked up and waved her arm in greeting. The woman stared back at her hatefully, not moving, as if to say, who did she think she was waving like that? Bernadette retreated guiltily away and set off walking at a fair pace, mortified at being caught out as a nosy parker. There was nothing wrong with her eyes, mind you, and she wouldn't forget the way that woman stared at her like a shop dummy. Of all things, she looked like she was wearing a nurse's uniform. Not the new blue nylon one, but the old-style one, with a rubber apron over it that you used to wear in the sluice room. Holy Mary forgive her, she didn't look to be a nice sort of nurse at all. She pitied any poor soul ending their days in there.

You could wait for ever for a bus on Sunday. Some wicked hooligans had smashed the glass in the bus shelter into hundreds of dangerous little pieces. It had started drizzling and now the wet was blowing through the gap in the glass, ruining her perm. She wondered whether to go to five o'clock Mass, hoping Father Maguire might be feeling recovered. She could do with a cup of tea and a natter.

She looked up fretfully for any sign of the bus. Something caught her eye and she flinched back behind the edge of the shelter. A figure was turning the corner and walking towards her. And she was wearing, of all things, the old-style nurse's outdoor uniform of a dark gaberdine coat and hat. Mother of God, it was one of those Bessie Bunter brimmed hats like they wore in the old days. It was pulled down very low but she was sure it was that same woman she'd seen at the window of the Wilkins place. Flustered, she looked up and down the road. There were a few cars but they were whizzing past her, throwing muck and spray at her stockings if she got too near the kerb. No one else was about. What if this woman accused her of snooping around?

She peeped around the shelter edge and the woman was still bearing down on her. She had her collar up and most of her face covered but what with that funny old rig-out the woman didn't look quite right in the head. Oh well, maybe if she ignored her she'd walk on past. Bernadette retreated deeper into the shelter and stared steadily into space, avoiding the woman at all cost.

She heard the wet footsteps slow down and only stop when they walked inside the shelter. The sound of breathing reached her, very slow and steady. She didn't dare look up. Was she imagining it, that the woman was staring at her? She resisted the urge to confront her or move an inch. It was always best not to bother a nutter.

From nowhere it seemed, a deafening noise erupted, then something massive swung in front of her face. She gasped and tottered backwards, her shoes crunching on the broken glass. Two hydraulic doors hissed and a gust of stinky heat hit her face. The bus. Still not daring to look back over her shoulder, she grasped the rail, hauled herself up and pulled her bus pass from her pocket. Thank the Saints, she was that glad to be with people again. Lots of them, crowds of young people with coloured scarves, all crushed together along the length of the bus. The shame of it was, there wasn't an empty seat in sight. Her knees had gone too weak to stand up all the way so she launched herself up the juddering stairs, clinging to the metal rail and dragging herself up to the top deck.

At last she was seated on smooth green plastic, catching her breath in the damp heat. She tried to look out of the window to see if that funny woman had gone away but she was too late. The bus had roared off from the bus stop and the window was all steamed up. That would serve her right for going off on an adventure. She would say ten Hail Marys for her deliverance when she got the chance. But not now. Now she was going straight home to get some dry shoes on and take a medicinal nip of gin.

It was starting to get dark and the rain was bucketing it down when she got off the bus at the Precinct. What a sorry fool she'd been to wander off like that. She'd forgotten night-time fell so early. She was hopeless on her own, just like Auntie always said. From now on she was going to check the newspaper for the lighting-up times before she set off anywhere. Almost home. Just the walkways to climb, remembering they could be slippery in this weather. She kept herself going with the promise of the gin and a hot-water bottle under her wet toes. And wasn't it *Country Greats* on the wireless tonight?

She was waiting for the lift inside the sour emptiness of the tower block when she heard wet footprints slapping on the concrete at the entrance round the corner. A neighbour, she told herself, but she didn't dare to look around. Just in case. She stared up the stairwell, straining her neck. It was a dizzying sight, spinning above her.

Again, some angel was listening from above. The doors to the lift opened and she rushed inside and jabbed at the button like a maniac. In maddening slow motion the graffiti-covered doors eased back together. The lift groaned its way upwards.

The front door key was ready in her hand when the lift stopped at her own landing. The twin steel doors screeched open. Making little moans of panic, she wobbled forward on her weary feet. Her breath was wheezing by the time she reached her own front door. Holy Jesus, she'd had a proper fright. If she only got inside she would never leave her flat again. She had a bad stitch now and her hands were shaking. She was having trouble finding the keyhole.

Saints above, the footsteps were coming again! They were closer, slap, slap, slap, steadily behind her. She poked the key at the keyhole. It slipped out of her cold fingers and tinkled to the floor. She bent and scrabbled on the ground. Where was the thing? She couldn't see where it had gone.

There was a warning rustle behind her. The hand, when it caught hold of her mac, pulled her backwards. And the other hand, smelling faintly of antiseptic, clamped hard over her nose and mouth.

Abstract Thinking

Question 46: Which of the following should come next at the end of this row of letters: xoooxxooooxxx?

    A. ooxx

    B. oxxx

    C. xooo

High score description (option A.): Mental agility, insightful, fast learning, adaptable.

Lorraine slept badly in the airless student bedroom in Oxford. Twice in the night she surfaced from sleep, convinced that someone had followed her up the twisting staircase. Or some thing. And that they now shared her narrow single bed. In a half-dream she smelt rancid wolfish breath on her cheek. Later, she opened her eyes in the darkness and saw a darker mass of breathing fur beside her on the pale pillow. Slowly, the creature turned towards her and its bloodstained jaws opened, razor sharp. It was a monster, yet she knew with a nightmare's logic that its black and chilling eyes were those of a malign human being. She shrieked in terror and groped for the light switch in a sweaty tangle. The room sprang up before her eyes. A blue bedcover, cheap desk and scarred pinboard. The crimson digits on the clock read 6.15.

She hunched up her pillow behind her back and tried to think. Now she had passed the exam it was time to gain a clearer perspective on everything. The police inquiries had turned up almost nothing. This psychopath, this killer, was well disguised. 'He or she will try to pass themselves off as a normal human being.' Doctor Lehman's words chilled her afresh.

She rooted in her satchel and dug out the photo of Rikki in the hospital bed. She tried to picture the long-haired man as he might be now, clean-shaven and most likely wrinkled and grey-haired. She could not detect Doctor Strang's high forehead or Mike's close-set eyes. And certainly he was too young and trendy to be Norman. As for the two young women, she saw only strangers with no resemblance to Felicity or Rose or anyone else at the Memorial. The photograph seemed devised to baffle her.

There was that other thing Lily had said. Or was it Dale? The photo had once been in a magazine, a nursing journal. Overwhelmed by work and exam prep, she hadn't yet checked out the source. Idiot. So far as she knew there was only one prominent journal, the *Nursing Times*. There must have been an article published beside the photograph, giving the names of the adults in the line-up.

Like a shot she dressed and rushed over to the dining hall and bolted down her breakfast, pleased that the early hour meant that she was alone. Soon after, she presented herself at the library and asked for directions to journal back copies.

'The *Nursing Times*?'

The old fogey on the desk recoiled as if she'd asked for a copy of *Razzle* or *Hustler*. 'This is a college library. We hold only learned academic journals here.'

For more than four frustrating hours she drove, then crawled, through miles of coned-off roadworks. At last she neared the tower blocks of Salford, a cluster of alien sentinels dominating the sky. At the university she swerved the car into the ominously empty car park next to the College of Nursing. Feeling like *Treasure Hunt*'s capering Anneka, she pelted over to the entrance and pulled impotently on the handle. A sign in front of her read, 'Library Opening Times: Sunday 9 a.m. – 1.30 p.m.' The doors had closed an infuriating ten minutes earlier.

After collecting Jasmine from her mum's she arrived home to find two letters lying on the doormat. She picked up the largest, a manila envelope with 'Sunningdale Housing Association' printed on the front. It contained a long application form and shiny brochure. Thanks to Phil's inside knowledge she had a good chance of getting a house – not a flat, but a newly built centrally heated townhouse – when she returned the form with a character and salary reference from work. She glanced through the brochure's photos of shiny kitchens and bathrooms, her hopes flying high.

The other was a creamy-white envelope bearing a Health Authority crest. Later, she was glad that Jasmine had disappeared upstairs to play before she opened it. The letter was from Norman, a frigid request that she attend a disciplinary meeting at the end of the week, to discuss her incompetence in losing a number of important documents.

It warned her that the meeting could result in her dismissal. She was therefore entitled to be accompanied by a trade union representative or friend.

She stared at it, the words blurring before her eyes. The old snake was being pushed out and wanted a last strike at those around him. A warning on her file would ruin any chance of promotion. She would be trapped at the Memorial for ever. Or even worse, if she was sacked she'd lose her place on the postgrad diploma, her small income, the chance to improve Jasmine's life. The centrally heated house near a better school would be lost for ever, too. She crumpled up Norman's letter in her fist and threw it against the wall.

Breathing deeply, she began tearing up an unread copy of the *NME* to light a fire in the grate. Someone was trying to make her lose her job. She recalled Doctor Strang's personal insults, Raj's lack of support when she needed it, Norman's mean-minded hostility. No, she mustn't take it so personally, she told herself.

'Think,' she muttered, fanning the flame until it caught. Next, she unwrapped the lamb chops and kidneys her mum had given her with the advice 'that range of yours was made for cooking hotpot.' Mechanically, she chopped up a pile of vegetables and pushed them haphazardly into the pot.

Or maybe Rikki had taken them? That was more plausible, especially if he'd acted under the direction of this secret friend of his. She turned the matter over as she retrieved Norman's scrunched-up letter from the floor. She smoothed out the Salford Health Authority crest and recalled the patterns on each suspect's certificate. The idea that someone had gone to all that trouble to humiliate her simply didn't make sense. Doctor Lehman's analysis pointed to someone covering up a problem with their professional credentials. Only as she shoved the pot into the range's cast-iron oven did she at last visualise a chain of cause and effect, from the lost certificates to a logical, if incredible, solution.

Autobiographical Memory

Question 47: Try to remember a day or situation in your past that was important to you. Could you describe it in sixty seconds?

A. Yes

B. Uncertain

C. No

High score description (option A.): The ability to construct a specific mental representation of an event from one's past, containing unique episodic memories and self-referential information.

I had found Mrs Wilkins' spare key to Room 7. It was nearly midnight and I was inside the pantry, rummaging through piles of mouldy old possessions: rusty hatpins and ration coupons, balls of string and earwax droppers.

There they lay, a set of spare keys. They were gummy with dust, lying at the bottom of a Robinson's jam jar. Not wanting to disturb Christie further, I cleaned and oiled them and said nothing to her. Climbing the stairs, I told myself it would be good to remind myself exactly what was at stake. The key turned easily. Inside Room 7 the electric light shocked the room to life. The furnishings are horribly dated: a saggy armchair with a crocheted antimacassar, a small Edwardian fireplace, a cheap desk and iron bedframe. When Christie first created her Memory Room, it had only recently been her own digs. She'd had in mind a shrine where everything could be collected together. Blinking my eyes entirely open, I turned first to the photograph. It is a large black and white print, rather fuzzy since it was blown up, but it catches the girl's image for ever. She's a poor diminished creature, her slightly protruding eyes avoiding the lens of the camera, as if she felt herself unworthy. Which she was, of course. She's wearing a shabby gaberdine coat and a hand-knitted hat. Neglected, half-starved, and cast off; the world hadn't even made enquiries when she disappeared. Next, there was a display of her records: the birth certificate with a mother's name bracketed with 'deceased' and the line for the father's name blank. And then the patchy records kept by the staff of Griseford Hall. The last clothes she ever wore hung on an ancient Woolworth's hanger. The stained blue nylon has a shiny, greasy texture.

Next, I came to the collection. I laid out the two new mementos on the pink glass tray. It felt good to secure them at last. Peace descended upon me as I arranged them in neat chronological order. At last the relics stood on their private altar. All was in its correct place in the universe.

Smiling, I lifted another gilt-framed photograph off the wall and held it close to my eyes, devouring every detail. Christie is on the left, still ungainly in cheap nylon and a hideous haircut, her expression rigid and awkward. Yet there is happiness, invisible yet radiant, suffusing her nineteen-year-old face.

And on her right-hand side, pushing in very close to her body, with her arm clasped around Christie's waist, is her first and finest love. She is smiling so radiantly that the bottomless pupils of her eyes seem to penetrate the camera's lens and connect with my own even now. It is interesting, too, that more than twenty years later the smooth vitality of her youth shines like polished silver.

I have come to understand that in our lives we can meet a single person who transforms us and whose spark of life can kindle a blaze in even the dreariest of existences.

I shivered in the unheated room. Replacing the photograph, I was renewed. The essence of the youthful Felicity Jardine never fails to renew my purpose.

Entitlement

Question 48: I will never be satisfied until I get everything that I deserve.

    A. True

    B. Uncertain

    C. False

High score description (option A.): Inflated and pervasive sense of deservingness, self-importance, exaggerated expectations to receive special treatment without reciprocation.

Monday 14th March

She was determined about one thing: the general manager selection day must run exactly to schedule without any hitch or hold-up. By eight-fifteen on Monday morning Lorraine had set up the Personnel interview room for the psychometric tests. Diaz slipped in, shutting the door quietly behind him.

'You all right?' He was hovering, scrutinising her. She was dressed more smartly than usual, in a tight black skirt suit from Richard Shops, in the vague hope of acquiring some gravitas. The last thing she needed was this interruption. She backed away, unsettled by his nearness.

'I will be so glad when today's over with,' she said with feeling.

She surveyed the four individual tables and chairs, each laid out with a sharpened pencil, working-out paper and eraser. The prospect of standing in front of the final four suspects made her stomach turn over.

'How was Oxford?'

'Good, in that I passed the exam. Not so brilliant in terms of what Doctor Lehman told me. Her briefing on psychopaths left me sleepless most of the night.' She caught sight of the clock. 'God, it's nearly twenty past. I should be greeting everyone. I honestly haven't got time now.'

'So when will you have the results?'

'The panel assemble at half nine. Tour of the hospital at ten. The tests are eleven till twelve-fifteen. Then Harvey's insisted I fax them to be scored while everyone has lunch.'

'So the results could be through by what – one o'clock?'

She felt herself blanch as she gathered a few stray papers. 'I'm sure they'll all be absolutely normal,' she insisted.

He stepped closer and his eyes studied her face. 'Relax. You'll be great.'

Relax? Easy to say it. Today had to run like clockwork. She was trying to get past him when he reached for her hand and squeezed it. It felt comforting but she shook him off.

'Listen, Lorraine.'

'Not now, please.'

'You need to know something. Brunt's got a new lead on Raj Patel. We found something in the taxi tender file. Could be fraud. Brunt's going at it like a bull in a china shop.'

The news made her feel suddenly sick. 'It can't be Raj – though the idiot might have got caught up in something stupid. I'd stake my career he didn't kill Rose.'

'Well, who did then?'

'I may be wrong, but I've got an idea.'

He exhaled impatiently. 'We're under massive pressure to make an arrest. You'll need hard evidence to counter the paper trail Patel has left behind him.'

With lips tight, she nodded and then thrust past him to get on with her job.

Downstairs in the boardroom, the interview panel had gathered in an obsequious circle around Marcus Challinor, the man rumoured to have the ear of Mrs Thatcher. Lorraine slipped into a corner of the room and watched the middle-aged men in suits as they mingled stiffly. The great man from Westminster was a preening individual with a slab of silver hair above a loose-lipped face. His voice was very soft, so that Lorraine had to pick up a few empty cups to get within eavesdropping distance. He was midway through an account of the Prime Minister's plans to rationalise the health budget.

'All a matter of eliminating waste, you understand. Of running a tight ship.' There was a moralistic edge to his opinions. Hospitals, especially in the northern regions, were frittering taxpayers' money on the undeserving sick who did nothing to help themselves. His audience replied with a chorus of 'absolutely' and 'splendid', and other emollient sounds.

Mr Challinor was also unhappy about the media attention the two murders had attracted. 'How difficult can it be to make an arrest? How do you suppose the PM feels reading all these negative accounts in the press?'

No one felt able to summon an appropriate response.

Challinor lifted his coffee to his lips and visibly winced. 'I am safe drinking this, I hope? No arsenic today?'

Too late, everyone realised this was a joke, albeit in appalling taste. A chorus of fake laughter erupted.

'On second thoughts, I'll pass on the coffee,' he said, wrinkling his nose and putting his cup down.

Norman and Harvey nodded solemnly. Lorraine watched, cringing. It was ridiculous, this kow-towing mood.

For a moment Challinor admired his own shiny gold cufflinks and said, 'Those other hospital sites, who are recruiting general managers from the open market, have had some excellent applications. Military men, merchant bankers, those sorts of fellows. That job profile you've put together—' He looked for Harvey. 'Won't do. Too airy-fairy. It's a new broom you need, not the same old dreary mop. Get the gist, do you, Wright?'

As Harvey nodded, she noticed a flush of anger beneath his golfing tan.

Ten minutes later Harvey found her. 'There you are,' he hissed. 'For God's sakes find some decent coffee. Attention to detail, Lorraine.'

From the corner of her eye she noticed Challinor jerk his head up, spotting her for the first time.

With a joyful sense of reprieve, Lorraine slipped out of the room and into the corridor. Before she had walked half a dozen steps a heavy hand dropped on her shoulder. Harvey had followed her. 'Any news from the police about this manhunt yet? It's a PR disaster.'

Treacherously, she chose not to share the confidential update on Raj. 'Not that I know of.'

'Hopeless. I take it you heard Challinor's opinion of the profiles. He wants a tough character. Military-style. Give him what he wants. And it won't hurt to crack a smile, Lorraine. A pleasant one, not a sarky one. Be nice to him.'

Yeah, and I'll slip into something more comfortable while I'm at it, she was tempted to reply. Instead, she said, 'I'm just off to fetch Mr Challinor a decent cup of coffee.'

'And have you got the certificates?'

'I've got Doctor Strang's and Raj Patel's replacements.' She searched her satchel and found the newly reprinted certificates. She had looked at them only briefly and both looked so fresh and colourful she hoped they were genuine. 'The Hospital Secretaries Association is defunct so Norman can't replace his. And Felicity says there's some sort of printing delay at the Royal College of Nursing.'

Inside Norman's deserted office, she raided his VIP cupboard and found a jar of Nescafé and a packet of chocolate Hobnobs. Passing the boardroom again, she swung into the kitchenette and checked that everything was lined up ready for the next break: decent coffee, clean tray with lacy cloth, fresh milk, bowl of sugar, plate of biscuits.

The sound of the door latch made her look round. Challinor was standing at the threshold emitting sweet cologne. He looked at Lorraine with bemusement. 'So you're the coffee girl?'

'I'm Lorraine Quick, Unit Personnel Officer. I'm administering the psychometric tests today.' Then, indicating the Nescafé, she added, 'I've just been hunting down some coffee for you.'

He smiled, showing square yellow teeth. 'Good girl. I was beginning to wonder if caffeine existed up here.'

'Well, the best coffee place around here is the Kardomah in Manchester.'

Challinor continued watching her, his pinstriped girth blocking the door.

'Mmm. Perhaps you could spare the time to show me the sights?' His voice had assumed an oily texture. 'I'm staying at the Midland Hotel tonight. A drink at this famous café perhaps? A chat about career opportunities?'

Smile, Harvey had told her. The best she could manage was a grimace that spread stiffly across her face. 'Oh, I am sorry. It's band practice tonight. I can't miss it.'

'A band? Would that be a brass band?'

Fuck smiling. She allowed herself a perplexed frown at his stupidity. What a tosser. 'No. A new wave band.'

'Ah, pity.' He was looking at the opening to her blouse. 'I could see you in some sort of – tasselled outfit.'

'Right,' she said coolly. 'I'd better go upstairs and get the tests started.'

The reptile didn't even move out of the way. It was the old trick. She would have to press her body against his to escape.

'Would you please excuse me?' she said very loudly. 'I can't get on with my job unless you let me get past.'

Faking Good

Question 49: I am never bothered by stress when I think of all my responsibilities.
    A. True
    B. Uncertain
    C. False
High score description (option A.): The test-taker may intentionally be presenting a socially desirable picture of themselves, deliberately giving false answers, 'faking good'.

As the hand of the clock reached exactly eleven, she stood in front of the four candidates in the interview room and spoke clearly from her notes.

'From now on, please do not talk amongst yourselves, but ask me if anything is not clear. We shall be doing three tests. A numerical test, a verbal test and a personality test. First, locate the numerical test in the blue booklet. Please print your name on the answer sheet provided. This test is designed to assess your ability to work with numbers. Each question has six possible answers. One and only one is correct in each case.'

'Time is short, so work as quickly and as accurately as you can. There are a total of twenty-five questions and you have twenty minutes in which to attempt them. Is everyone clear about how to do this test?'

No one spoke. Everyone had picked up their pencils. 'Please turn over the page and begin.'

As she uttered 'begin' she clicked on a stopwatch.

The invigilation period was her first chance to take a proper look at Raj. He had turned up looking a bit of a dork in a shiny suit with a blue silk tie and matching handkerchief puffed up in his pocket. She wondered if he had already been interrogated that morning; he was sweating in the way that paunchy men often did when under pressure. Sitting beside him, Doctor Strang soon had his head bowed and his pencil busy. Norman had got off to a bad start. He dropped his pencil twice and got in a fluster as he retrieved it. He had turned up in some sort of regimental tie and an ancient double-breasted pinstripe. As for Felicity, she was frowning but working steadily. Her navy-blue skirt suit had over-sized military brass buttons. The ageing cleavage was peeping out thanks to a low-cut ruffled blouse. Lorraine wondered what Challinor made of her display.

In no time the numerical test was over and she swapped it for the verbal ability test, giving another short speech and then timing the session to the second. This time Raj was in difficulty, his bitten fingernails disappearing into his mouth. She wondered if the test might be discriminatory if the candidate had been educated in Delhi. Even worse, a few questions seemed designed to upset anyone placed under police suspicion.

Then again, Norman was also squirming and continually adjusting his spectacles. No, surely fidgeting was normal? According to Doctor Lehman's analysis, if the killer was present he or she would be entirely unperturbed.

Doctor Strang was sitting in the posture of the class clever-clogs, hunched defensively, his elbow curled secretively around his work. Felicity was more poised, erect and precise, her auburn coiffured head very still as she worked down the sheets.

Lorraine had to steady her nerves as the start time of the third test approached. Here it was at last, the PX60, a series of seemingly random questions that might nonetheless catch a malign personality. Lorraine dealt out the booklets and answer sheets and then introduced the test, consciously slowing her breathing and hoping her voice wouldn't shake. This was the most important introduction of the three tests. Unsurprisingly, candidates were often deeply resistant to what looked like a mishmash of inane statements. Her tone of voice and choice of words were crucial in gaining the candidates' confidence.

'The next and final questionnaire is an objective test devised over many decades of psychological research. Most of the questions have no right or wrong answers because people have the right to their own opinions. All you have to do is answer what is true for you. Please read the examples and think about how you would answer them.'

The four preliminary examples were uncontroversial and, to her relief, no one asked any questions.

'Very well. Give the first, most natural answer that occurs to you. Please turn over the page and begin.'

Lorraine sat down again in a hot wave of relief. Downstairs Diaz would be waiting for these results. So would Doctor Lehman over in Oxford. And then there was Harvey, who was ill-tempered and snappy this morning. She guessed Harvey knew about her forthcoming disciplinary and might even have instigated it. He was slippery; he hadn't got to his dizzy position by exercising openness and honesty.

For a long time, the wall clock seemed stuck at eleven fifty-nine. She noticed the candidates were less stressed by this test, perhaps because she'd told them there were officially no right or wrong answers. Her mind wandered back to Harvey. She had sent him a test but he had not returned it. Sitting in the overheated room, she asked herself for the first time, why not?

Time crawled on until the clock displayed fourteen minutes past noon. Felicity appeared calm and good-natured, waiting to be dismissed. Doctor Strang and Raj were hastily checking through their answers, while Norman was still working feverishly. Now that she was here, about to mark the tests, it felt ludicrous to harbour any suspicions of these familiar colleagues.

'Please stop writing now,' she announced. 'Lay down your pencils and close your booklet.'

She managed a shaky smile. 'Please leave your scoresheets. You are free to go. Lunch will be served in the doctors' dining room.'

Lorraine was alone with the answer sheets. Rapidly she hand-scored the numerical and verbal tests, fearing that if the personality test told her anything too dramatic her powers of concentration might fail her. The numerical test results were roughly as she'd expected:

Raj Patel 96
Victor Strang 92
Norman Pilling 65
Felicity Jardine 51

'Good for you, Raj,' she muttered to herself. She made a note to remind Harvey that Raj and Doctor Strang had both performed exceptionally well, placing them within the top 2.4% of the population in numerical ability. Felicity's score was little better than an absolute average. To be fair, she had probably not been taught maths with any competence. Now those disadvantages were biting back at her. It was certainly a moot point whether she had the ability to argue complex budgets with the medical fraternity.

The verbal tests were slightly more surprising:

Victor Strang 92
Felicity Jardine 74
Norman Pilling 72
Raj Patel 46

Raj had performed very badly. She had no idea of his first language and could have kicked herself for not finding out if special norms existed for candidates for whom English was learnt later in life. The remaining three, especially Victor Strang, had all scored respectably well, indicating no problems with communication and persuasiveness. Her mind flashed back to Felicity's carping about Norman's declining mental capacity. According to this objective test she was dead wrong. He still had well above average ability in verbal communication.

At last she laid out the answer sheets for the PX60 personality test in a line across the table. She had arranged with Doctor Lehman to fax the scores straight to her, to be computer marked, but now the moment had come she couldn't wait that long to find out. If she scored them by hand, a secret preview would take no more than ten minutes.

Top of the pile was Norman's. By aligning a stencil over the rows of numbers she could quickly count the visible marks through the holes. Then she added up the sum of marks for each factor and compared them to a table of norms drawn up from UK strategic managers. Last of all, she plotted his scores onto a spare blank profile sheet. The familiar wiggly line emerged as she joined the dots with a black pen. From the way the line clung to the centre it was immediately clear that the profile lay within a normal range. Norman's personality was cool rather than warm, on the borderline between dominance and submissiveness. Suspiciousness was his highest score, along with a strong score for compulsive behaviour. She recognised his mistrustful nature from the daily ritual of the post meeting. He was a stickler for timekeeping and expressed anxiety if his routines were out of kilter. And last of all, the Distortion score of only 2 revealed he was apparently telling the truth.

Raj was next. She scored it with dread, uncertain how the police's accusations would have skewed his results. It was a credit to the test that the results largely confirmed the chief accountant that she knew and liked. He was fundamentally warm and sociable but had little interest in fitting in with collective goals. Even under his current duress he had reported himself as being far less conforming to rules and standards than most people. Though she once might have dismissed that as the odd fit of laziness, today it read as far more worrying. After all, standards and rules were key elements in a well-functioning hospital. His low scores also betrayed flashes of immaturity: in frequently changing interests, and his often-expressed sense of frustration. His Distortion score revealed he had been keen to impress, having tripped up on enough questions to score 4 out of 10. It was acceptable, but only just.

Lorraine made a few notes in readiness to defend her friend. Even if he was not entangled in fraud, the last thing Raj needed was a black mark on his career.

Turning over the next sheet, she noted that the candidate had forgotten to complete their name. That was unusual, yet she decided not to identify the individual just yet. Scoring was something of a guessing game that she was enjoying so far, and it would hone her skills to work out whether this was Doctor Strang's or Felicity's answer sheet.

Again Lorraine aligned the template and began to score the columns. She was about halfway through when she began checking back over her calculations. This one felt odd. Here was a person who reported themselves to be so warm, so stable and so shrewd, that their score exceeded more than ninety per cent of UK managers.

Lorraine totted up the score for Self-control and found the highest possible score. It was the same for Emotional Stability. This person was a paragon. The scores had to be false. Quickly she calculated the Distortion score to see if the candidate had been 'Faking Good'. It was a whopping 9 out of 10. She stared at it, rehearsing exactly what that meant. Here was a candidate who wanted the panel to believe they were entirely free of any faults whatsoever. No one could be that perfect. Thank God the test had been designed to catch them out.

She looked back over the questions and how the scores had been allocated. This candidate was simultaneously indifferent to what other people thought and yet forever considerate of their colleagues. They claimed to have a perfect memory, be constantly successful, and be so independent-minded that they always knew a better way. For the right cause they would tell lies with little difficulty. And would never be to blame when things went wrong. The profile revealed a character so dominant and self-willed as to be plainly hostile to others. Combined with the factor for high intelligence and a calculating nature, the portrait was of an arch manipulator. She stared at the almost complete lack of anxiety and guilt. Here was her potential wolf, her predator, her killer.

She sprang up from the desk with the urge to run downstairs and warn Harvey of the outcome. Then she remembered his disparaging digs at her that morning. No, she had to finish the job properly.

Turning over the fourth answer sheet, she could instantly work out who the previous candidate had been. Her hands began to shake as she scored the final test. Candidate four was intelligent, domineering and tough-minded.

A loud knock sounded at the door. Lorraine instinctively covered the papers with her arms.

Edith poked her head in looking worried. 'The police inspector rang for you. He wants to see Mr Patel's attendance records.'

'Give him whatever he wants,' Lorraine answered, glancing up at the clock. 'God, it's half twelve. I've got to go.'

When Edith had left, she performed one final calculation. The fourth candidate also betrayed many human foibles, by admitting to occasional loss of control in the form of disturbing dreams, fits of anger and even depression. This was a human being whose day-to-day troubles were reassuringly normal. The Distortion score was 2 out of 10.

Hurriedly, she gathered her papers and set off downstairs.

* * *

317

Harvey had set up a temporary back office in the former flu clinic. Lorraine burst into the room to find her former boss reading at the same Formica table that had once displayed Sister Ince's syringes. His leathery presence almost filled the available space.

'Harvey. Thank God I've caught you on your own. One of these tests doesn't look right.'

He barely looked up from a sheaf of papers. 'Just a moment. One thing at a time.'

There was no spare chair, so she had to stand and fidget like a disobedient child.

Finally, Harvey came to attention and unwrapped the cellophane from a cigarillo. He jerked his bald head in the direction of the boardroom. 'Remember the panel are just across the corridor. Let's not broadcast the results. Have you made the proper adjustments to the general manager profile?'

'Honestly. That doesn't matter any more. One of these Distortion scores is sky-high. That means—'

'I know what that means.'

'Don't you want to know whose it is?' Lorraine shoved it at him.

Harvey made a small grimace as he took the deviant profile and absorbed the results. He was reading so slowly her adrenaline was reaching toxic levels.

'Well. It's an excellent match to the job requirements,' he said at last.

Was that supposed to be a joke? Lorraine leant against the Formica and pointed.

'Look. The Distortion score indicates—'

'That this is probably the best candidate.' He was interrupting her again. 'And this candidate will create an excellent press story.' Finally, he put the profile down. 'Mr Challinor will be satisfied. You and I keep our jobs. And your test result supports the whole process.'

'Oh yeah, right.' Her sarcasm rang out loud and emphatic. 'But only if you don't tell them the—'

'That's enough, Lorraine.' He leant forward with chilly emphasis and hissed at her. 'Don't be a slave to procedure. Just do the job. Deliver what's needed. This will do fine.'

There followed a long silence in which she wondered if her hearing had failed. No, Harvey had actually said, 'This will do fine.' She made an almighty effort to bend to Harvey's will. Today had to run like clockwork. No hold-ups, no hitches. Her future home, her career, were in the balance.

'Thank you, Lorraine. No need to get these results confirmed by fax. I'll handle the feedback.'

He was avoiding her gaze, blowing a stream of smoke towards the ceiling.

'No,' she said, hating the tremor in her voice. 'If you think that's fine, why did you even let me get qualified?'

'Of course you needed to be qualified. But now you've got the badge you need to be pragmatic.'

'No,' she repeated. 'It's wrong.' She sounded as if she was going to burst into tears.

He scowled; his old kindly manner evaporated. 'I've been looking at the disciplinary hanging over you. And now this. I had been hoping . . .' He paused to tap a grey tip of ash into the bin. 'To offer you a new post at HQ. A more senior position. How about it?'

For a second Lorraine's hopes blazed at the prospect of a nice cushy number, well away from the pressures of the

Memorial. More money meant a chance of that house with lovely warm radiators.

She wanted to say yes. But her mouth opened again and mumbled, 'No.'

Harvey narrowed his eyes. 'It's time to grow up.' He leant towards her conspiratorially and hissed, 'No one beyond the two of us need ever know. In ten years you'll have my job. Think about the achievement. A woman and a working-class one at that.'

A picture came into her head of almost unlimited luxury and power. She could do the job, she was sure of it.

'Or you could stay here, a handmaiden to men like Norman. Right, I guessed as much. For all their wittering, most women aren't brave enough to go after the big jobs.'

She felt crushed. There was a rightness to what he was saying.

He continued. 'I'm sure you wondered why I appointed you?'

She nodded.

'You were different. Bright but unconventional. The quiet one who everyone underestimates. The one who is secretly thinking – I can do the boss's job better than him. So prove me right. You've passed the real personality test. The one that's got nothing to do with ticking the right boxes or pretending to be normal. You've worked it all out, haven't you? Now all you have to do is keep your mouth shut.'

Her breath sounded ragged as she asked, 'And if I don't?'

'Well, the job isn't really working out, is it?'

'What does that mean?' The statement came out very loud, amplified by a disbelieving gasp.

'That you're not up to it, are you? A disciplinary hearing,

refusal to follow instructions. I warned you. Today you blew your final chance.'

She felt like a pan of milk fizzing on a stove. 'That is outrageous!' It came out as a shout.

'Keep your voice down,' he shushed at her. 'Just do as you're told.'

Finally she boiled over. 'Go on. Give that monster the general manager job. Destroy the whole place. What do you care?'

He stood up abruptly, his face not at all fatherly now.

'Get out of my sight. I am dismissing you for incompetence and failing to carry out a reasonable instruction. With immediate effect. Go!'

Self-control

Question 50: Which do you believe in more strongly?
　　A. Perseverance
　　B. Personal luck
High score description (option A.): Self-sufficient, following self-image, resourceful, compulsive, obstinate, internal locus of control.

Lorraine left the hospital, trying to avoid those who stared after her as she rushed past. She couldn't face the indignity of clearing her desk. Her eyes were pricking, and a jab of pain was stabbing into her chest. With relief she reached the sanctuary of her car and buckled herself in. She had been sacked. It was sinking in now, sending rills of panic through her nerves. She needed to calm herself. Then she could get the hell out of this place.

She was waiting for her breath to slow down when a sharp rap came at her window. It was Felicity Jardine, military in navy blue and ruffles. Lorraine didn't wind the window down, but before she could slam down the lock button the chief nurse swung open the door. Involuntarily, Lorraine started back.

The witchy little smile on Felicity's face told her everything she needed to know.

'Cheer up. I thoroughly enjoyed your funny little tests.'

Felicity's bright eyes were exploring the grubby interior of her car: the snotty tissues, reused cassettes and old sweet wrappers strewn across the seats.

'I was wondering,' she continued, alight with malice, 'if you noticed our police colleagues' latest gift collection? It's for that nice Sergeant Diaz. You know him rather well, don't you? It's for his fiancée. Shirley. You do know, don't you? The baby's due this autumn.'

Felicity slammed the door in her face and disappeared.

Lorraine recoiled, then dropped her head onto her arms that rested on the steering wheel. It's all over, she repeated to herself. My career, my struggles, everything I want for Jas.

And this potential fling with Diaz was all over, too. Tears trickled over her hands. He had fucking hidden that from her. And she'd *known* there was something off about it all.

What was wrong with her? Why did she constantly fuck up? And now she didn't have the strength to start again.

She confronted a dizzy emptiness inside herself. She had no confidence left to launch herself forward. She could blame Felicity, or Diaz, or Margaret Fucking Thatcher herself, but the fault was hers. She was hopeless. It was a long, bleak time until she was able to raise her wet and swollen face. She had to get a grip of herself and get out of this place before someone else came along and harangued her. She could picture any of them ambushing her: Harvey or Norman or even flaming Edith.

She blew her nose and took some shaky breaths. Checking the car's mirror, she saw the reflection of uniformed police officers crossing the car park. Brunt's brown trilby was bobbing amongst them and then she spotted Raj's pouchy face. He was staggering between two coppers, looking blank and terrified, dabbing at his forehead with the blue handkerchief. She felt scared for him. He was a good pal and she wondered what she could do to help him.

The police cars set off in a convoy with the Rover in the lead. Lorraine steeled herself to wait a few minutes before she switched the Metro's engine on. It was only quarter past one but it felt like she'd been incarcerated in the hospital for weeks.

She drove on autopilot, fighting to prevent her emotions from surfacing and making her crash. The car was idling at a red light on the junction to Langworthy Road when a movement flickered in her mirror. Diaz was jogging down the road after her, waving his arm in the air. Lying tosser. Talk about the last person on earth she wanted to meet. He'd spotted her and was racing to catch her up.

The amber traffic light glowed on. If she waited for the philandering bastard she could tell him how she'd thrown her career away trying to help him. The green light sprang on. She put her foot down and swerved around the corner like a getaway driver.

She had a last glimpse of Diaz in the mirror, standing gobsmacked, staring after her, then doubling over to get his breath back. She drove mindlessly for a long time and then realised she still had ages before she needed to pick Jasmine up. No one knew she had lost her job yet. And if she was going to strike out on her own, it would be best if no one found out what she was up to.

* * *

Diaz turned back and walked up the hill to the hospital, sweating under his shirt and jacket. What the hell was Lorraine up to? He had to talk to her. Brunt had taken the Rover, so he couldn't jump in and tail her. Shit, he would be too late anyway. He didn't like her racing off like that. The testing must have gone badly wrong.

All morning he'd had to put up with Brunt crowing about how he'd cracked the case and got his man. Over the weekend an anonymous letter had turned up, tipping Brunt off to look at the hospital's taxi tendering process and check out the figures. They hadn't needed a fraud officer to spot the scam. Patel had collected in all the tenders from local taxi companies and put forward Top Service Cabs as the winning option. The problem was, the owner of Top Service Cabs was Patel's landlord and he was six months behind with the rent. The tip-off had further informed them that Rose Cavanagh had been on the taxi tendering subgroup and had told Patel she wouldn't cover his back for any rackets. Brunt had got a warrant to search Patel's home, found a batch of unused syringes in his wife's suitcase, and pulled him in.

'You all forgot the bleeding obvious,' Brunt had told them at the morning briefing. 'Patel was there at the flu clinic all the time, hanging around, watching and waiting. He wanted to be sure the woman who threatened to expose him never got the chance.'

An hour later it was apparent that Lorraine had left the building. Diaz tracked down Harvey Wright in the former flu clinic. He didn't think Lorraine would have been too happy about Harvey's insensitive choice of office. He tapped on the door and found the director of personnel standing motionless, staring out of the open window.

'Afternoon, sir. I need a word with Miss Quick. I believe she's assisting you today.'

'A word about what?'

Diaz wasn't going to fall for that one. 'Police business.'

'Maybe I can help you?'

He could see the profiles on the table and that Lorraine had plotted their wiggly results. He tried to read the name on the topmost profile but couldn't. So, she had done the tests and then rushed off. But why?

'I don't believe so, sir. Is she here or not?'

Harvey's colour was definitely up. Spots of crimson flushed his weather-beaten face.

'I'm afraid not, officer. She had to leave suddenly.'

'Ill, was she?'

Harvey gave him a long level stare. 'That's personal business.'

'Right you are, sir.'

As Diaz was about to leave Wright attempted heartiness. 'Well, it's a big day for you, Sergeant. I see you've pulled in the accountant. Charged him, have you?'

Diaz drained his face of all expression. 'Nothing decided yet, sir,' he said, enjoying the momentary sag in the older man's features. Wright was a weaselly sort of bloke under all that oily charm. Lorraine had told him he was the only suspect not to have returned a test.

'Would you let the incident room know, sir, if Miss Quick comes back.'

Harvey Wright released a sudden gust of false bonhomie. 'Certainly I will. You'll be the first to know.'

* * *

The mood in the incident room was demob happy, the team basking in Patel's arrest and the prospect of collecting their overtime by the month's end.

'So tell me again,' Diaz asked irritably, 'how this taxi scam was connected to the porter's death?'

Brunt gave a little shake of his head, as if to say, there's always one bloody smart alec. 'Not connected at all, sonny. Some of you got carried away looking at *modus operandi* and all that crap. In the end it was just a druggie porter whose mate shot him up in the back and then scarpered.'

Diaz had a dozen objections but kept a lid on them. When he'd seen Raj Patel earlier, he'd worn the befuddled look of a chump about to cough up a false confession.

'Coming for a bevvie?' one of his mates called out.

'Yeah, in a minute,' he said. He may as well sink a few pints and mull it all over.

The call came in a few minutes later. Diaz was trying to work at his desk when he overheard, 'Marlow Court. Female fatality. Suspected overdose.'

Marlow Court. He recognised the address as a place that Lorraine had recently visited. No, please not Lorraine. He was over at the desk in two bounds. 'Who is it?'

'No ID yet, Sarge. Despatch just called it in. Probably just another junkie.'

'What d'you mean, just another junkie? Who the fuck is it?'

The desk officer recoiled and read his notes. 'Number 72 Marlow Court. Address of a Bernadette Ince.'

'And is it her? Sister Ince? The nurse who's just retired? Or someone else?'

The bloke was young and green. He had to study his scrawled notes.

'Looks like the Ince woman. That's who the priest said it was when he found her.'

It gave him a perverse twist of pleasure to tell Brunt that Sister Ince had just been rung in as a suspicious death. The Patel connection was looking weaker every second.

Brunt slumped. The old dog had picked up Diaz's triumphant tone. The inspector called over Roy, another lad from the team, to drive him to Salford Precinct.

'As for you, Sonny Jim,' he barked at Diaz. 'You can go through the last five years' taxi committee accounts. I want to know about every penny Patel's ferreted away. And all in your neatest handwriting. Got that?'

The College of Nursing was quiet on a Monday afternoon and Fran appeared to be on leave. The loos were empty as Lorraine washed her face and tried to soothe her swollen eyes with splashes of cold water. None of the silent students gave her a second glance as she headed to the journals section of the library. She worked out the approximate date of the photograph. Rikki looked about eight when he'd had his hip treated. She had read in the paper that he had been twenty-eight years old when he died. So that put the parameters for the photograph around 1962 to 1964. That date also seemed to match the length of the guys' hair and shortness of the women's skirts.

In practice it wasn't that easy. She started by trawling through the *Nursing Times*' microfiches, loading a series of flimsy sheets into the reader and looking for the keywords 'Perthes disease' and 'Eric Fryer'. After half an hour of frustration she picked up an armful of journal boxes and found a quiet corner out of sight of the librarian on duty.

She flicked through page after page, studying slightly fuzzy photographs of crisply laundered nurses with fussy caps pinned to backcombed hair. There had been a lot of unrest back in the sixties – nurses raising banners against Enoch Powell and a 'sick government'. But there was no photo of a bedbound Rikki.

After working through the *Nursing Times* she tried other journals. Thankfully most were published only quarterly, so she stumbled across a 1962 edition of the *Journal of Orthopaedic Intervention* about an hour later. The article had the spectacularly unsnappy title 'The Pathogenesis of Perthes Disease' but it made Lorraine shake her fist in triumph. In amongst a series of gruesome diagrams and X-rays of dislocated hips was the familiar photograph of Rikki. The caption read:

Eight-year-old patient Eric Fryer immobilised by traction at Cumberland Infirmary under the care of Mr Knox-Miller.

Left to right: Patrick Knox-Miller, Orthopaedic Consultant; Felicity Jardine, Ward Sister; Jane Smith, Staff Nurse.

Even before Lorraine carefully counted from left to right she knew that neither of the women in the photo was the Felicity Jardine currently working at the Memorial. The 1962 version of Felicity had the kind of classically pretty features that made a person look twice and want to get to know her. Even allowing for heavy Jean Shrimpton make-up, this could not be a younger version of the current chief nurse. The woman in the photo was too radiant, too long-limbed, too apple-cheeked. Her even-toothed smile beamed out of the photo, conveying confidence and happiness, and her hand rested on young Rikki's shoulder in gentle reassurance. Lorraine wondered if the captioning might be wrong and looked more closely at Jane Smith. No, the staff nurse was too old. Judging from the crow's feet visible behind her specs, she had been already over thirty when the photo was taken.

Her moment of triumph was dampened by the realisation that there may well be two, or even more, Felicity Jardines. The link between the photo and Rikki's death felt suddenly more tenuous. It was possible Rikki had made the same mistake. As Diaz had reminded her, she needed hard evidence.

After photocopying the captioned photograph, she set off in search of an empty office with a phone and then dialled the General Nursing Council.

'Hello, is that Beverley in Registration? Hi, it's Lorraine Quick here at the Memorial Hospital. Yes, it is the big interviews today. I'm afraid Miss Jardine's replacement certificate hasn't turned up.'

'Oh?' The registration clerk sounded dismayed. 'Miss Jardine said she was going to send her training record in by post but nothing arrived. We can't issue a duplicate certificate without it. What a time for it to get waylaid.'

Lorraine thought fast. 'The trouble is, we've got the men from Whitehall here now. It's all very high security. We desperately need some form of identification, especially any photo ID. Bizarre, isn't it? We need something to prove exactly who she is.'

'Well, so long as she understands we're still waiting for her original nurse training record. But I'll do my best for you, today. I'll just go and fetch her file.'

When the receiver was lifted again Lorraine blurted out, 'Any photo ID?'

'Yes.'

'Brilliant. It's very urgent. Could you fax it to me straight away? They're literally waiting in the corridor. It's probably best if you send everything you've got so I don't have to bother you again.'

Lorraine gave the library's fax number. Then she went to hang around the librarian's office, praying that no one from the Memorial or HQ would stumble upon her. Ten minutes later a thick roll of shiny paper churned out of the fax machine.

Back in her quiet corner Lorraine scanned through the records. Blast. The only photograph was a poor reproduction of an already fuzzy photo. Nevertheless, Lorraine could detect a younger version of the woman currently being interviewed for the general manager job back at the hospital. There was the halo of bouffant hair and dark outline of small lips pencilled to look larger. The date below the photo on her General Nursing Council card was 1978. There was also a scan of her very first GNC card from the 1960s but back in those days it had been an amateurish job, a rectangle of cardboard without a photograph.

Lorraine tried to flatten the warm roll of paper and digest its contents chronologically, starting from Felicity's first application to Carlisle School of Nursing to the present day. She had signed her first application in a large bold hand, elaborating the looping 'y' of Felicity and flourishing the 'J' of her surname rather beautifully. By the mid-1960s her signature had changed to a smaller, more crabbed style. Exasperated, she told herself that amateur handwriting analysis wasn't going to convince Brunt or Diaz. A peculiar PX60 profile and a degenerating signature would never stand up in court.

'Doctor Knox-Miller,' she muttered, and set off to find the phone number of the General Medical Council. A short phone call later she was saddened – and frustrated – to hear that the brilliant young consultant had died of leukaemia two years earlier. As for Jane Smith, the Nursing Council had thirty-one nurses with that name but could not distinguish those whose birth names were Smith from those who had married a Mr Smith after 1962. She could spend the next week trying to track down the right woman. It felt hopeless.

She unfurled the fax paper again. She needed to speak to someone who had known the younger Felicity in person. There was a telephone number for Carlisle School of Nursing printed on Felicity's paperwork but it no longer worked. Thankfully a directory from the library soon got her through to the infirmary's switchboard. Yes, the operator confirmed, the School of Nursing had new premises. No, they weren't sure where the former nurse training records had gone. Lorraine then spent a maddening spell on a merry-go-round of phone extensions, speaking to staff that were all too new to know or care about ancient training records. Then finally, a telephonist mentioned the medical museum.

'That's where we send all the old boxes of papers. An archive they're calling it. Somewhere over Whitehaven way. Miss Worsthorne runs it, but I canna' say if it's open right now. Shall I try to connect you?'

The number rang out for more than twenty trills before the soft-spoken clerk came back on the line. 'I'm so sorry, dear. You'll have to try again later.'

'Please. Just one more try.'

Lorraine stared around the bare office with its neat shelves of folders labelled with every nursing topic from 'Addiction' to 'Wound Care'. There were so many people trying to make this service work, by teaching and supporting every new generation, and slogging away at curriculums and mentorships. So much felt in the balance, about to tilt or topple either way. And now this Miss Worsthorne wasn't even answering her phone.

A click. 'Hello.' The voice was quivering and out of breath.

'Miss Worsthorne?'

'Yes.'

Lorraine's reply was almost equally breathless as she tried to explain who she was. 'The thing is, I need to take a look at the nursing school records from the early sixties.'

'And this is concerned with . . . ?'

'A former pupil of yours. Felicity Jardine.'

There was a long pause in which she heard crackling on the line and feared it was dying. Then it righted itself again.

'Now that is a name I remember. Went off to Australia, oh it was way back. Sent me a Christmas card with a koala bear wearing a sun hat.'

Australia. Presumably taking her original record of training along with her. 'I know this is an odd question. Do you have a photo of Felicity?'

The request seemed to floor the woman. 'My goodness. I may have one somewhere. But where that might be, now that's the question.'

'If I were to fax you a photo would you recognise her?'

'I'd know her picture. Yes, I'm sure I would. But what was that word you used? You'd "fact" me?'

'Fax. Using an electronic facsimile machine. It sends documents down the phone line. I take it you don't have a fax machine?'

'No, nothing like that. Just the telephone.'

'Miss Worsthorne, may I come up to see you later today?' She checked the clock and saw it was getting on for three. She had only the foggiest idea where Whitehaven was. Somewhere very far north in Cumbria. On the coast, perhaps. 'I'll try to be with you by six o'clock.'

Diaz gave Brunt's team an hour to look into Sister Ince's death and then radioed Roy, the lad Brunt had taken with him to Marlow Court. He confirmed the victim was Bernadette Ince and the MO looked to be the same: injection by propofol. The SOCOs were still doing their stuff and Brunt was making everyone's life hell.

'Got a time of death?'

Roy broke off; he could hear him taking mumbled advice. Diaz asked himself: when was it Lorraine had gone over there? End of last week, after they met at the hospital house on Wednesday. Five days ago. Though he hated himself for it, the cop in him knew he couldn't discount her involvement without evidence.

Roy crackled back onto the radio. 'Few days, mate, is all they're saying.'

'Come on!' he found himself snapping at Roy. 'Two days? Four days?'

'Keep your hair on. Forty-eight hours, most likely.'

'Thanks, mate.'

Surgency

Question 51: Do you ever crave adventure?
  A. Yes
  B. Sometimes
  C. No

High score description (option A.): Exuberant, enthusiastic, happy-go-lucky, cheerful, dissatisfied, heedless of danger.

By the time Lorraine approached Jasmine's school she was feeling keenly out of place, like a kid wagging it from her own classroom. She had to keep reminding herself that she was right to walk out on Harvey, the job, and to get away from Diaz. She spotted Phil waiting by the school railings, ready as usual to pick up Jasmine and Tim. He was looking better these days, since he'd started working part-time.

He strolled forward, concern creasing his face. 'Everything all right?'

'Fine. Work is sending me on a long drive north. I thought I'd take Jasmine for a run-out.'

They both looked up as Jasmine and Tim came skipping out of the decrepit school entrance. 'Why don't you go and do your work in peace,' Phil suggested. 'Jasmine can stay with me and Tim.'

For a moment she brightened at the prospect. That way she could take as long as she needed to question Miss Worsthorne.

Jasmine had spotted her mum and pelted up to her, a beam of joy brightening her face. Tim raised a wan smile. 'She can stay the night.' Phil was warming to the subject. 'That would be fun, wouldn't it, kiddies?'

Jasmine sidled up to Lorraine and grasped her hand, then silently tugged it. 'What do you think, lovey-dove?' she asked.

Lorraine could speed-read her daughter's expression and the imploring flicker of her eyes meant a definite no.

'OK. Not this time.' Lorraine stroked Jasmine's hair.

'Come on, for Tim's sake,' Phil coaxed.

Good for Tim but not for Jasmine, Lorraine decided. It was time her daughter stopped being a prop to Tim. Or Phil.

'Right. Let's get off if we're going.' She swung Jasmine's small hand joyfully back and forth.

'Thanks for the offer, Phil,' she called back to him. 'You've been brilliant. But I'll be looking after Jasmine from tomorrow. I'll ring you when I get back.'

Lorraine filled the Metro with petrol using the last tenner in her purse. She was supposed to be paid in a day or two but wouldn't put it past Harvey to stop her salary. Steering the car down the slip road to the M6 North, she wondered if she should have left Jasmine with Phil or her mum to at least be sure she got a decent meal that night. All she'd managed to bag up on a whirlwind visit back home were a packet of biscuits, a couple of orange drinks and some peanut butter sandwiches. And a couple of books, too: Jasmine's game book and a road atlas of Great Britain.

'It's an adventure,' she told her daughter. 'I've got to drive all the way to Cumbria and I need you to be my navigator.'

The first hour was easy enough, heading for Preston and then the long straight run up to Lancaster. After that the landscape became refreshingly empty. Open moorland spread around them, then crags and ravines as they wound up through the Lake District before cresting the high point of Shap. As soon as they left the motorway at Penrith the demands on Jasmine's map reading became greater. They were in a maze of back roads in which the locals had no need of signposts. Using the tatty three miles to the inch road atlas, Jasmine navigated the car through a black web of unnamed roads, calling out place names that Lorraine thought might be Norse or Viking. They were in the land of 'Riggs', 'Snittles' and 'Garths', a civilisation of low stone cottages and humpbacked bridges.

They were searching for a marker, an ancient site called The Ridcross. After getting lost for a worrying half-hour, they found it at last. It was a stone stump on a high hill with what looked like runes traced into its mossy bulk. She had been driving for almost three hours; they both got out of the car and stretched, taking in the view of hills and dales, and in the slightly fading light, a silvery shimmer that promised to be the Irish Sea. Somewhere very near was their destination, Greyrigg Cottage Hospital, where Miss Worsthorne's archives awaited.

Back in the car they wound their way to an impressive gateway, then followed a curling carriage drive past park-like gardens. An attractive building of grey stone came into view, the roof studded with elaborate chimneys and low Arts and Crafts gables. The late afternoon sun cast a coppery light on two symmetrical hospital wings that embraced the oval lawn.

'It's very fancy, Mum,' Jasmine announced as they got out. Lorraine felt cotton-headed from driving the rattling Metro for so long. There was no signposting to the museum, so they approached a splendid porch where a brass lantern hung from the ceiling. A plaque announced that Greyriggs was endowed in 1899 as 'A free hospital for sick persons without restriction to rank or income'. The bell pull gave a distant jingle behind the oak door.

Lorraine's request to see Miss Worsthorne met with a sour look from the woman in an overall who answered the door. They waited in a high-beamed hall inspecting a collection of black and white photos of gawky youths in soldiers' uniforms and nurses in ankle-length dresses. Cases of medals and letters were also on proud display as testament to Greyriggs' wartime service for the Red Cross.

A hubbub reached them from the rest of the building. Someone was playing a stop-start refrain on a piano, accompanied by a reedy tenor voice. Steady hammering, bursts of laughter, the scrape of furniture and the toot of a whistle all suggested preparation for a celebration rather than the hush of convalescence.

The sourpuss woman returned through a door that provided a flash of light from the outside and a gust of salty air.

'Matron will see you now.'

A moment later, they were ushered into a room nothing at all like the schoolmarmish study she had anticipated. Matron's room was large and light with tall French doors overlooking a ravishing landscape. The hospital stood on land that dropped to form an arc around a long empty beach. Beyond, the sea shone as if alive with gold and bronze sparkles reflecting the low sun.

'I'm Barbara Fenwick, the matron here,' said a strong and imposing woman of about fifty, rising to shake Lorraine's hand. She wore the filigree silver belt buckle and starched cap and cuffs of a most traditional matron. She had risen from a table where a trio of patients were gathering up armfuls of paper chains.

'A few more lengths should do it,' she advised the little gathering. 'And don't forget the sausage rolls.'

Once the patients had left, she turned to Lorraine with a brisk smile on her neatly lipsticked mouth. 'It's Henry's one hundredth birthday party tonight. Everyone is so looking forward to it. Now, do take a seat. I hope you've not had a wasted journey. I'm afraid Miss Worsthorne fell ill this afternoon.'

Lorraine perched on a settee and kept Jasmine close beside her, circling her waist protectively. 'I'm sorry to hear that but I really must see her. I spoke to her earlier on the phone. We've driven all afternoon to get here.'

Matron returned her gaze with one of firm deliberation. 'Miss Worsthorne has a weak heart. I appreciate you've gone to a great deal of trouble but I simply can't—'

'Is that your dog?' Jasmine interrupted, pointing to a black Scottie pawing at the French doors. Matron broke off and rose to let the dog inside.

'He's called Bert. Do you want to say hello to him?'

Jasmine ran to him and crouched low, tentatively stroking the little dog's wiry coat.

'It's nearly his walk time,' Matron announced. Comically, the dog's ears swivelled like antennae and he began to scamper around the room, making excited yelps.

Lorraine knew she would shortly be asked to leave the premises. This matron inhabited the other side of an invisible boundary composed of boundless entitlement to obedience. The prospect of a dreary drive through the night was almost too much to face.

'Can I come with you and hold his lead?' Jasmine asked, oblivious to the strained atmosphere.

Matron was clearly struggling in the face of Jasmine's enthusiasm. 'Very well,' she said stiffly. Then more courteously added, 'Why don't you both come for a walk to break your journey.'

Ten minutes later, Lorraine settled down next to Matron on a bench in a cove sheltered from the wind. In the distance Jasmine and Bert were investigating rock pools. Jasmine poked around with a stick and Bert waddled comically after her and pawed in the water. Even Lorraine laughed as his square head cocked at a perplexed angle each time he failed to catch a crab.

'Miss Worsthorne had a bad fall just after you rang, at just after three o'clock,' Matron told her, with what sounded like a hint of blame. 'She had been trying to move a heavy box of documents. There's nothing broken but she is badly bruised. I can't allow any strenuous activity. I know it's disappointing but – there you are.'

Even out here she was a powerful woman. Her only concession to the wind was to swap her lace cap for a queenly headscarf and put on a splendid navy cape with a gilt chain and buttons. Disappointment barely described the dismay Lorraine felt.

'I wonder, have you heard about the police inquiry at the Memorial Hospital?'

Matron said she had and became more attentive when

Lorraine introduced herself as the personnel officer who had witnessed the first death. 'Today the police arrested the wrong person. An innocent colleague of mine. I'm here in search of evidence to uncover the true offender.'

'I am sorry,' Matron said firmly. 'But you must leave these matters to the police.'

Lorraine stared out at the vastness of the sea that was dimming closer to dark bronze each moment. Now Jasmine and Bert were being chased by the tide. Near the horizon she could just glimpse pale crests breaking on the surface. It came into her mind that the ocean was the great symbol of the mind's unconscious: a maelstrom of desires, not just for sex, but also the drive to succeed and dominate, and achieve status in the world. How could she argue her case to this woman who wore her professional role like armour, and would undoubtedly close ranks with another nurse? What type of personality was she? Conservative, dutiful, moralistic, she decided, brimming with worthy ideals.

'I've only been here for a half-hour or so,' Lorraine said slowly. 'But I understand that you have a good hospital here, a rare kind of haven. Your patients seem happy. And I'm sure your care meets the highest standards. And I fully respect your concern for Miss Worsthorne's health.'

Matron gave a little nod of her head and began to speak. 'All of this is under threat, of course. Who needs a small cottage hospital, even one that sends its patients home feeling better than ever? The philanthropist who founded Greyriggs left an endowment for the running costs but the Health Authority are taking us to court to challenge it. You see, the land can be sold for a fortune.'

'How can you stop them?'

'We have a campaign but sooner or later a property developer will line his pockets. And I will apply for retirement. It has been my privilege to help and heal those in need. But it's a sad legacy I leave behind.'

Lorraine felt drained of anything cheerful to say. This woman's life work was being swept away in just one of countless cuts. The breeze was lifting now, growing colder as the sun sank low to the horizon. But before she left she had to tell this woman exactly how their situations differed.

'The Memorial couldn't be more different from Greyriggs. The enemy in Salford isn't greed, it's poverty.' She pictured the patients she walked amongst every day. The double walking sticks, missing teeth, NHS glasses and rickety legs. 'You can look at any indicator – housing, diet, education, addiction – it seems to me they all affect each other and drag each other down. Some staff have told me it's hopeless. That drug addiction will only increase, that many psychiatric cases are incurable, and the health indicators will never improve.

'I've often thought of leaving my job,' she found herself saying. 'In fact I've scarcely thought of anything else. But the injustice I witnessed today – I can't let that go. The Memorial doesn't deserve it. As a personnel officer I see reports of disciplinary cases every day. I'm sure you also know cases of damaged personalities infiltrating the professions?'

Matron nodded. 'It's true. They do the rest of us great harm.'

'To speak openly, there is an imposter working at my hospital. And I want to stop that person wreaking further harm. She is clever, she has fooled her colleagues for two decades, from here in Cumberland to the Memorial. And the only person I've tracked down who might actually remember her true identity is your Miss Worsthorne. On my own, I can't find the evidence the police need. The truth I need is waiting for me here.'

Lorraine turned her head and gazed towards the edifice of the hospital, growing indistinct in the gathering twilight, its lights twinkling up on the headland.

'The proof is in Miss Worsthorne's archive. All I ask is the chance to see her records. To find the truth and present the facts to the police. So that when I do leave the Memorial, I have a chance of leaving it a better place.'

Altruism

Question 52: I have given money or other help to a stranger who needed it.
  A. Often
  B. Occasionally
  C. Never
High score description (option A.): Sympathetic and soft-hearted towards others, generous to the weak and needy.

Lorraine felt a burst of pride as Jasmine led Bert by his best tartan lead into the throng assembled for Henry's 100th birthday party. The mix of old and young patients fussed over her daughter and filled her plate with crisps and sandwiches from the buffet. Lorraine took a few sausage rolls for herself but soon slipped away to follow Matron up the grand wooden stairs to the East Wing. There was a modest sign for the Museum of Nurse Training but the enterprise was clearly not yet ready to receive the public. Rows and rows of document boxes stood stacked at the corridor's end, still taped up securely.

'Here she is,' said Matron softly, leading Lorraine inside a gently lit bedroom.

The slight figure lying beneath a flowery coverlet opened her eyes and tried to rise. Miss Worsthorne was not quite the decrepit creature Lorraine had anticipated. Her short fair hair was fashionably feathered, though tousled from lying in bed. And when she shuffled upright her features were alert and attractive; the face of an intelligent woman not yet sixty.

'Miss Quick?' she asked in the same breathy tone as on the telephone. 'I'm so glad you finally arrived. My memory isn't quite what it was. It's been good to have a few hours to think this matter over.'

Once Matron had propped the patient up against a pile of pillows, she left them alone, after insisting that Miss Worsthorne must not be overtaxed. Lorraine settled beside her with notebook and pen in hand, as the patient recalled all she knew of Felicity Jardine.

'She was one of our finest young nurses. Brilliant A-levels. She could have gone to any of the London training schools. Such a shame we lost her to a handsome Australian. They met at a cousin's farm and our loss was his gain.'

'You said she sent you a Christmas card. Do you still write to each other?'

The former tutor winced as if in pain. 'No. Sorry. She had to move around with her husband's job and when my health failed we lost touch.'

'Is it possible she returned to Britain?'

'You know, I'm sure that if she had, she would have come to visit me.'

Lorraine opened her satchel and took out the picture of Rikki in the hospital bed.

'This is a picture taken at Cumberland Infirmary in 1962.

Note the woman on the left. The ward sister.'

'How lovely. Yes, that's Felicity.'

Next, Lorraine pulled out the tightly wound roll of fax paper. 'Here are Felicity Jardine's current records at the General Nursing Council. This is the woman I work with now. Felicity Jardine.'

Miss Worsthorne peered at the photo of the identity card dated 1978. Puzzlement creased her face. 'Good gracious. What a terrible photo. I don't think it's even the same person.'

'I'm sure it isn't. Yet it's fresh from the GNC today.'

'There must be two Felicity Jardines who both trained as nurses.'

'That's exactly what I thought. But how could two Felicity Jardines both have won the Carncross Gold Medal?'

Miss Worsthorne asked Lorraine to pass her a magnifying glass from the dresser. For a long while she peered through the glass at the crudely printed image.

'It's no use. What with my eyes going all blurry. I'm so sorry.'

She handed the shiny roll of paper back. Lorraine groped for another way forward. 'Is there anyone else I might ask?'

Miss Worsthorne shook her head, then said, 'Actually, you have put me in mind of another girl who might have kept up with Felicity. Christie Kerr, her best friend at the time.'

Lorraine felt the thrill of the chase surge through her nerves. *Chris*. Phil had talked about Rose repeating a name like 'Chris' on the phone and getting upset. This could be the missing link. Somehow Rose might have got to know this Christie Kerr.

'Who is Christie? Is she local?'

'Yes, she was from up here on the coast. Just pass me that shiny black book over there.'

Lorraine went to the bookshelf and found a hardback compendium of local history.

'Look it up in the index, would you? Griseford Hall. It was closed down about ten years ago and a lot of people were glad to see it go. There were always bad rumours about the place.'

Lorraine flicked through the pages and found a black and white photograph of a forbidding edifice titled 'Griseford Community Home for Orphaned Children'.

'That was where Christie came from. I don't believe she ever knew her parents. The children's home managers were keen that we took her on as a cadet and everyone tried to help her – at first, anyway. After all, she'd had a rotten start in life. She could be sweet to your face but most of the other girls didn't take to her. She was definitely odd. I think her anatomy tutor put her finger on it. She was rather too fond of the grislies. You know, animal dissections and the horrid pictures you find in surgical books. But she didn't have the self-discipline to become a theatre nurse. She was an enrolled nurse working at the county asylum when she was told to leave.'

'What happened?'

Miss Worsthorne leant her head back and stared up at the ceiling. 'Now what was it? A scandal. It came to light that Christie had been bothering a rather immature student nurse. Betty something or other, she was called. Kept ringing her up at all hours and spreading gossip about how she had cheated in her exams. We tutors were very close to the students back then when we all lived together in the nurses' home. But somehow everyone missed the fact that Christie, who was the elder of the two, was having an unhealthy relationship with a younger student.'

Miss Worsthorne sighed and shook her head. 'I don't

mean for a moment that a relationship between two women is unhealthy. But in those days, girls were more discreet about keeping romantic attachments private. Look at me and Barbara, we've kept house together for decades and are far happier than most hetero couples. And now I've got this problem with my ticker, the dear thing has taken me in here.' She shrugged and smiled good-humouredly at Lorraine.

'No, it seems Christie pursued this younger girl when Betty tried to break the liaison off. And then the threats overwhelmed the poor student and she killed herself. Stole some tablets from the pharmacy and overdosed. A terrible tragedy. A dear friend of mine had to tell the parents.'

Lorraine didn't say anything, but turned the story over in her mind, then asked, 'Does Christie still live in the area?'

Miss Worsthorne's watery eyes met her own. 'I'm afraid I don't know.'

A burst of raucous singing reached them from downstairs.

'Felicity and Christie were close friends? They sound an unlikely pair.'

'They do, don't they? Felicity had all the altruism of youth and always liked a lost cause. Christie was in danger of failing her exams and Felicity coached her. In return Christie hero-worshipped her. Yes, if Felicity had a weakness, she enjoyed that sort of adulation.'

'Yet despite all that help Christie left nursing?'

Again, Miss Worsthorne sighed. 'Oh, yes. Matron insisted on an inquiry after Betty died and Christie was struck off the nursing register. Didn't even turn up for the hearing. She can't ever have worked as a nurse again.'

A tap came at the door, and Matron popped her head around and gave them both a stern nod before withdrawing.

Lorraine was sure that her allotted half-hour had expired long ago. She stood and shook the patient's hand.

'I really can't thank you enough. I wonder, could you point me to the student files so I can show them to the police?'

Miss Worsthorne shrank back, the lines and hollows of illness more apparent upon her face.

'I've spent the last few hours recalling all I could because I haven't got much else to give you. When you phoned I'm afraid I discovered Felicity's file isn't where it should be. I don't know how or why. The only paper evidence I have left is her index card.'

She waved a feeble hand towards the table at her bedside. 'And there's precious little on that.'

Lorraine picked up a cardboard index card that bore only Felicity Jardine's name, her date of birth, and the dates her nurse training had commenced and ended. Under 'Forwarding Address' was written, 'Gone to Australia.'

She hid her disappointment and asked, 'Do you have anything on Christie Kerr?'

'I can't say. The two girls were in different years. Christie was at least a year older and began training earlier, so she'd have been with us from when she was sixteen, in about '59. If there is anything, it should be in one of those blue boxes on the landing. The admission years are written on the lids in felt-tip. You're welcome to take a look.'

The boxes had clearly not been inspected for years, judging from the dust and desiccated spiders inside them. Lorraine spent an hour searching through them. She found no personal file for Christie Kerr, either. But she did find one item, Christie Kerr's index card. According to that rectangle of faded cardboard, Christie had been dismissed in October 1963, just after Felicity emigrated. And more importantly, in order to return the cheque for £14 held as deposit against her room in the nurses' home, the accounts department had recorded a forwarding address:

C/o Mrs I. Wilkins, The Wilkins Boarding House, 43 The Glen, Higher Broughton, Salford.

Narcissism

Question 53: Nothing will stop me getting the status I deserve.
- **A. True**
- **B. Uncertain**
- **C. False**

High score description (option A.): Self-centredness, inability to love, lack of empathy, emptiness, an unremitting search for power.

Back in '63 Christie was suspended from the wards while Matron Devaux investigated that Betty McBride business. She was made to carry out clerical duties in a little cubbyhole next to Matron's office. The poor creature couldn't take much more harassment. Matron had been stupid enough to leave some notes in her desk drawer, so Christie knew the bitch was going to report her to the General Nursing Council. She was furious at the injustice of it all. Looking back, what she did next was a stroke of brilliance.

One day a large yellow packet of paperwork arrived for Matron containing Felicity's emigration papers to be forwarded to Australia. A gigantic bulldog clip held her original documentation, from her brilliant A-levels to the certificate for the Carncross Gold Medal awarded to the student with the highest exam mark in the county. Unlike Christie, a mere enrolled nurse about to be abandoned and struck off, Felicity was a star nurse, recruited to an exciting-sounding hospital in Brisbane. Christie hid the packet in her shopping bag. When Matron went out to a meeting she read every word, spellbound by the details of Felicity's perfect life. Then she fully grasped that her best friend would be disappearing to Australia the following week. Abandoning her. She was never going to hear from her ever again.

She reread the instructions to Matron in the covering letter. Devaux was requested to write a character reference for the authorities on an enclosed form. Then the whole packet was to be posted by special mail to the Immigration Department in Brisbane, Australia. Christie realised that if she didn't record the packet's arrival in Matron's post book, she had at least twenty-four hours in which to work on Felicity's papers. Quickly, she began extracting the necessary documents from the clipped sheaf.

By lunchtime everything she needed was inside a plain brown envelope hidden in her shopping bag. She rubbed some talc on her face so she looked sick, then told the other staff she had vomited and needed to go home to bed.

Instead, she caught the bus to Carlisle and found her way to the most prestigious printers in the city. There were adverts in the newspapers back then, for a new technological wizardry called xerography. Presenting herself at the counter, still dressed in her nurse's cap, black stockings and cape, she charmed the middle-aged printsman. She told him her grandmother had been a *famous nurse in the war and decorated for her bravery. The old lady would love a set of facsimile copies of all her granddaughter's nursing qualifications to be framed and hung in her living room. The only trouble was that it was her grandmother's seventieth birthday that weekend and because of her hospital shifts she needed a terribly speedy job. When he saw Felicity's documents he was impressed. He fell for the whole story and everything was ready by five o'clock that evening.*

It was as easy as that. The next morning she removed her own and Felicity's personal files from the training school's shelves and resigned. She boarded the first red Ribble bus leaving for a big city and never looked back again.

There were just two flies in the ointment. Felicity's nurse training record from Cumbria had been missing from the immigration papers. And so was her original certificate of registration with the General Nursing Council. There was a photocopy of the registration certificate but that would never pass as the real thing. It seemed Felicity had sent those two originals away to Australia to get her job. The trouble was, registration was the key to the whole plan.

The printer had done as good a job as he could, but the mustard yellow and black certificate didn't bear too close a scrutiny. The signatures and the curlicued name and date were acceptable but the all-important Seal of the Council was a mere photocopied shadow, where an original would have been stamped and embossed on the paper. Anyone who knew what to look for would spot it was a fake.

She's had plenty of time to work on it, of course. There was that jiggery-pokery with a scalpel and glue for instance, cutting out a crimson seal from a conveniently deceased nurse's certificate so it looked good enough under glass in a frame. But not good enough to pass scrutiny by an official panel of busybodies. That was why she had taken all the candidate certificates from Personnel one quiet evening and thrown them on a bonfire. They were all nothing but ash now, blown away by the wind.

Adventurousness

Question 54: I would find it exciting to volunteer for a dangerous mission.
   A. True
   B. Uncertain
   C. False

High score description (option A.): Venturesome, thick-skinned, uninhibited, active, impulsive, ignores danger signals.

Without any fuss Matron showed Lorraine and Jasmine up to a bedroom high up in Greyriggs Hospital's eaves. It was after eleven when they both fell into the twin beds, Jasmine brimming with cake and pop and excited recollections of the party. Within minutes Jas sank into the sleep of the innocent but Lorraine lay awake, listening to the steady rush and heave of the sea. Her eyes were open as she struggled with the urge to phone Diaz. There was a payphone downstairs in the hall. She had his number and a fifty pence piece. He was probably working late and would welcome hearing from her. Then she worried that she might be put through to his home number and be confronted by his fiancée. Shirley. Even the name sounded like a fifties housewife. God, she couldn't do it.

And even if she did get through to Diaz and they managed to talk together like two human beings, he'd probably snap at her, and tell her she hadn't yet found any proof. She had pictured herself returning with fat files of information, containing incontrovertible evidence of the genuine Felicity's true identity. Instead, someone had long ago created a dead end to the paper trail.

She wondered how Rose had got to know Christie Kerr. There was only one realistic route: through Felicity Jardine, or at least through the woman who worked at the Memorial under that name. She pondered the connection. Rose had perhaps been more than an acquaintance to the older Christie. Lovely, romantic Rose, with her Laura Ashley frills and her secret yearnings, must have met her outside of work on those evenings when Phil thought she was with Lorraine. Rose, with her best friend who was her bridesmaid, the same bridesmaid who had somehow ruined her wedding day by not turning up. Rose, who had laughed off Mike's attentions and been detached and cool towards Phil. Rose, whose desire to confess all her troubles to Lorraine had almost certainly been overheard by Felicity. As for Felicity, she felt oddly unsurprised to discover she was probably gay and still in touch with this old girlfriend, Christie. Long ago, Christie had bullied a reluctant girlfriend to death. Lorraine realised they had all been looking in the wrong direction entirely.

She had memorised the forwarding address on Christie's index card: C/o Mrs I. Wilkins, The Wilkins Boarding House. The coincidence of Christie moving to an address just a few miles from the hospital had shocked her. Could Mrs Wilkins still be living there? Why not, it was less than twenty years ago. Mrs

Wilkins might even have some information on Christie Kerr's current whereabouts. She got up in the dark and rummaged in her satchel. It was there, where she'd always kept it, inside an inner zipped compartment. The key to Room 7. Only now, when she carried it to the moonlit curtains, it was laughably easy to see that the word 'Wil' might be followed by 'kins' on the cardboard fob. Maybe this Mrs Wilkins had allowed Rose and Christie to use a guest room at the boarding house? She couldn't think of any other reason why Rose would have kept this key ring hidden in the back of her wardrobe. As soon as it grew properly light she got up and consulted her Manchester A to Z, and dug the edge of her fingernail into the flimsy paper to mark the exact spot where the Wilkins Boarding House stood.

Tuesday 15th March

Far away in Cheetham Hill, Diaz swung himself silently out of bed and went downstairs. He opened a bottle of beer and sat hunched on the settee to think it all over. On the way home last night he'd not been able to stop himself from driving to Balaclava Street. He had checked out her visit to Marlow Court last week, though she wasn't a suspect for Sister Ince's death. Her fingerprints were present at the flat, but only on the Salford Health Authority retirement plaque hanging in the toilet. So, that was entirely consistent with her visit to the nurse last Thursday. Had Sister Ince known something crucial about the case? If she had been killed to shut her up, didn't that put Lorraine in danger, too?

Lorraine's house looked even grimmer than he remembered it. The demolition trucks were only two streets away, the wrecking ball pounding like some alien attack on *Doctor Who*.

He wondered if she'd got on the list for a new house yet. She deserved it for doing time in that dump, without central heating or hot water.

He'd knocked a dozen times but she wasn't home. The dust-smeared windows were empty. No sign of the red Metro, either. The way she'd raced off like that, just when she'd planned to share which of her colleagues was capable of murder – Diaz had a very bad feeling about where Lorraine might have got to.

He took a long swig of Boddingtons and rubbed his eyes. He hadn't been himself at all since that night he'd gone back to Lorraine's. Shirley was driving him mental. Just the sound of her voice, the things she said, they all scraped his nerves raw. And that made him hate himself even more.

He thought about fetching his bag of weed from where he hid it in the lining of his duffel bag. No, it was time to face facts, not tune out. He had made a promise to marry Shirley at St Mary's and that was the end of it. But it couldn't be the end of it because that would be the end of any life worth living. Since he'd met Lorraine, a great crack had opened in the monotony of his days. He revisited the night of her gig constantly in his mind, talking to her, tasting her, elaborating the fantasy. He knew now what it meant to be delusional. Something had exploded in his mental landscape and the damage wasn't going away.

There had been that edgy look of hers, of course – the smudgy eyes and even better, the pliable warmth of her body beneath his hands. There was also a half-remembered message in the music that seemed to speak to him. It said that something more lay beneath the crappy loop of work, TV, sleep, cycling round on endless repeat. She hadn't completely given up. That song of hers, the one about being lost in the dark. It had stuck in his head. It was about all of them. Trying to find something worth relying on, when you couldn't even work out the right bloody way forward.

He made a rare effort to confront the truth. There was something more than Shirley keeping him from Lorraine. When he tried to picture a future with Lorraine, he sensed an abyss of unknown proportions gaping between them. Could he even do this relationship stuff? He wasn't thick, he knew that people learnt to get on with each other by growing up in families and he'd had no training in that at all. And Lorraine was smart; she might want more from him than he could give. It would be like living in a foreign country without a phrase book. The prospect of failure left him feeling diminished.

So where the hell was she? He stared up at the clock, willing it to move faster. It was only five o'clock. All week he'd been reviewing his suspects' homes. From what he'd read in the FBI Bulletins, killers characteristically looked for access to secluded, private spaces where they could let their illicit thoughts, and sometimes their illegal activities, roam free. It could be a garage but was more likely to be a basement or lock-up.

Norman Pilling hardly fitted the bill, living in a small 1920s semi-detached in Middleton with his elderly wife and pet spaniel. Also unlikely was Felicity Jardine's newly built executive home on an exclusive housing estate in Sedgley Park. Raj Patel lived in Bolton with his busy wife and three kids in another substantial but overlooked house.

On the other hand, Harvey Wright had an elegant Georgian detached mill house in Worsley. There were electric wrought-iron gates and rows of smart conifers that screened off the back of the house.

Mike McClung was more intriguing. Though he lived in a small hospital flat, he appeared to have the whole of the extensive boiler house to himself. There was a very private basement containing a furnace. He was a loner and was having some sort of breakdown since the victim's death. And of course, he was already one of Diaz's prime suspects.

Then there was Doctor Strang's home. Considering his whopping great salary of £25,000 a year, it was surprising to find him living in a vast and ugly terrace in Urmston. Strang had previously taken in other medical students as lodgers but now he lived alone.

All week he'd had that restless itch to go round and investigate Strang's house. So what if Brunt had told him not to? He settled back down on the too-short settee and tried to doze. He decided nine o'clock was the earliest he could take a secret shufti around to Strang's house.

Resilience

Question 55: When I promise to do something myself, I take pride in doing it alone and seeing it through to the end.
　　A. True
　　B. Uncertain
　　C. False
High score description (option A.): Emotionally stable, mature, stoical, calm, not quitting in the face of adversity.

Finding Jas still fast asleep, Lorraine dressed rapidly and walked down to the beach. It was a glorious sunrise, the bay curving around an expanse of seawater that twinkled as if it were sprinkled with crystals. She tried to take a mental impression of the moment, to retain the gusts of oxygen invigorating her lungs after all those months spent in the overheated hospital. All around her was living nature, in the crunch of shells and egg-like pebbles slithering beneath her feet. White-winged birds glided on invisible thermals in the big and breezy sky. If she could ever indulge her creativity, it had to be somewhere vast and open like this.

　　She felt almost happy as she strolled back inside and helped herself to a cup of tea in the morning room. Refreshed, she felt a resurgence of the stoicism that had carried her through many a past difficulty. Yes, the world was unfair and unjust, but if she battled on in support of what was right, she might bring about small victories. Soon, a few early risers joined her and someone switched the television on to watch the much-heralded new *Breakfast* show. Then a familiar voice reached her from the TV.

'—new era at the Memorial Hospital. Now the culprit has been arrested, I look forward to leading our staff in a return to the highest standards, both medical and moral.'

Lorraine caught a glimpse of a figure captioned as *Felicity Jardine, The Memorial Hospital General Manager*, speaking to the camera beneath the portico entrance of the hospital. Felicity was standing beside Challinor and still wearing the navy suit with brass buttons, so Lorraine guessed the clip had been filmed the previous day. Wrapping a couple of pieces of toast in a serviette, she scurried upstairs to find her daughter.

They were up and off before the M6 rush hour had even started. As she drove, Lorraine puzzled over what she knew. It was incredible that in this modern age an imposter had never been challenged. Partly, it had to be the fault of her predecessor as personnel officer taking the false Felicity's qualifications on trust. Yet Lorraine hadn't done much better. She hadn't inspected anyone's credentials, just handed them over to Edith. The only evidence she had was a photo in an obscure journal and the testimony of a sick woman with failing eyesight. There was the personality test, she supposed, but any defence lawyer could completely ignore that as unethical. And as well as no records, she had no witnesses: Rose, Rikki and even Rikki's

Perthes consultant, Mr Knox-Miller, were all dead. It could take months to track down the real Felicity Jardine, even if she was still alive and living in Australia, even if she hadn't changed her name.

There was this Christie woman, of course. Last night Lorraine had checked the local phone directory but she wasn't listed. And if her hunch was right and Rose had got involved with Christie, of course she wasn't still up here in Cumbria. If anyone might have some answers, it would be Mrs Wilkins.

Lorraine put her foot down and soon left the high open country unblasted by industry and headed back to Salford. The closer she got to home the darker the wintry sky grew, echoing the smoke-stained shells of industrial warehouses, grimy railways and all the ugliness sprawling around her. The infamous graffiti above the M1 was dead right: it truly was grim in this part of the north.

The rumble of the car had sent Jasmine back to sleep again. Lorraine looked over her shoulder at her daughter's small body, curled up along the back seat, a woolly scarf scrunched beneath her head as a pillow. Lorraine's sensible side told her to drive straight home. Fate had forced her hand and at last her nightmare job at the Memorial was over. There would be time to write songs, get back into the band and sort out somewhere other than the housing association house where she and Jasmine might live. It will be fantastic, she told herself. Soon, when the hurt at being sacked had subsided, she would start to scour the jobs section in the *Evening News*.

Suddenly, the fact that her daughter had fallen back to sleep struck Lorraine as an unlooked-for opportunity. She pulled off the East Lancs and instead of heading for Ordsall, swung the car in the opposite direction towards Higher Broughton. It could do no harm to have a quick word with Mrs Wilkins first thing this morning if she was still around.

Jasmine was still motionless when Lorraine parked the car a few doors along from number 43, where the name Wilkins stood engraved on the gatepost. The boarding house was a four-storey Edwardian villa of the type once owned by a large middle-class family with a team of servants housed in the attic. It was asymmetrical, like a lopsided face, with a half-timbered gable end here, and a dormer window there, and most of it painted in thick oxblood paint. A few leafless trees blocked a full view, but she could see enough to wonder what had stopped the owner selling it off to developers. There was a closed aspect to the frontage; the curtains and blinds weighed heavily, like closed eyelids. It was the sort of house that edged away from attention, accumulating grime.

A movement of shiny green forced Lorraine to duck her head down low behind the steering wheel. The bonnet of a car was emerging from a back alley she had failed to notice. Now that was odd. It was the car owned by the woman she still thought of as Felicity. The Volvo was standing motionless, sending up clouds of exhaust fumes as it warmed up with the choke out. Peering carefully up over the dashboard, Lorraine could even glimpse Felicity's reddish hair through the windscreen. She bobbed back down again, urging Felicity to get on her way to work. Finally, she heard the engine rev and the gradual diminuendo as it was driven away towards Bury New Road.

It was bizarre. Felicity lived on a new estate in Sedgley Park, so what was she doing here? Surely she hadn't been visiting this Christie Kerr, living on here since the sixties? Call it pursuing the chase, or simply the raw need to know –

now was the perfect moment to have a word with the former landlady. And if she got the merest hint of evidence from Mrs Wilkins, she need only walk a few yards over to the red phone box on the corner and ring Diaz.

After laying her jacket over Jasmine she hesitated, watching her daughter. Jasmine continued to breathe without making a sound, her face as smooth as a pearl. As a test, Lorraine got out of the car and shut the door with a loud click. She studied Jasmine through the glass as she momentarily flinched and then relaxed again, her eyelids fluttering in a dream. It was only nine-thirty in the morning. She would try the bell, have a quick word with whomever answered, and be back in two minutes. No one else was about on the lane so Lorraine hurried up to the front door.

She rang the front door bell and listened, studying the dusty letterbox and cracked paint. Not a sound emerged from the house. She waited, looking over her shoulder towards the car, and then took a few steps backwards to stare up at the uninviting facade. She neither heard a footstep on the stair nor saw a flicker of movement at any window. Her fingers reached in her pocket and checked she still carried the key ring. The feel of cold metal tempted her. Telling herself it was nothing but a test, she tried to jam each of the two keys into the brass lock on the front door. Neither key would even slide inside it. Of course, the lock had probably been changed years ago.

As she returned to the car, Jasmine still lay motionless. Lorraine pictured driving home, calling at the corner shop and spending the fifty pence she had saved from not phoning Diaz. She could buy a loaf and make a pile of toast and spend the morning considering her future. It would be a relief to get home. Her early start and long drive had left her spaced out and jittery.

As Lorraine hesitated, a powerful intuition gripped her: that if only she could gain entry to the house she would find the answer. There was still no movement behind the blank windows. Setting off towards the alley from which Felicity had emerged, she soon passed the car's pull-in and found a narrow cobbled ginnel at the rear. The next street's row of villas should have had a good view of her approach, but their outlook was obscured by trees.

The backyard was behind an eight-foot brick wall with shards of broken glass cemented into the coping. The green wooden door was locked, naturally. She looked back over her shoulder, hoping Jasmine still slept on. Though it felt far longer, her watch confirmed she had left her daughter alone for just over one minute.

Again she reached in her pocket and selected the Yale key. This time it slid into the lock in the green wooden door and turned easily. She entered a stone-flagged yard. Now she was very close and the house reared above her. She could see a back wall covered with scabrous maroon paint, a zigzagging iron fire escape. Her eyes finally settled on a dormer window set high into the roof. A window blind masked the glass like a milky cataract across an eye.

She knocked hard on the back door half a dozen times. Save for the rattling of the wood, the air was still. Another Yale lock fastened the back door. Did it look uncannily similar to the one she had just opened? Yes. Lorraine eased the same key into the keyhole and again it turned easily. Stepping into the dingy kitchen, she found nothing alive – only the clunking tick-tock of an unseen clock.

Exhibitionism

Question 56: Those with superior talents and good looks should not hide them.

    A. True

    B. Uncertain

    C. False

High score description (option A.): Desiring the centre of attention, showing off, seeking compliments.

I had blow-dried my hair especially beautifully, just in case the TV people wanted me to make another announcement. Then I put on my make-up with extra care, powdering my face to keep it matte for the cameras. I set off to work late, which is my prerogative, given that I'm now in charge.

I spotted the red car parked on my road and knew it at once. It was that rust-bucket Metro that Lorraine Quick drives. My foot lingered on the Volvo's accelerator while I planned what to do next. I couldn't quite see if she was in the car or not. I was sick to death of that girl and all the trouble she'd caused.

My test results had been perfect, I'd charmed the panel and Challinor had paraded me like a trophy. Then Harvey told me there was an entirely biased trap inside the scoring system. It only showed up if a person like me was just too far above the average. He called it a lie detector, which annoyed me because I hadn't even been lying. Still, Harvey had done what he had to. He'd got rid of Lorraine Quick on the spot. Fired her and sent her packing. Oh, I laughed when I heard about that. And now here she was, rolling back like a bad penny, nosing around Christie's house.

I set off towards Bury New Road without a backward glance. Just before the junction I pulled over and did a three-point turn. Then I switched off the engine and waited. Terry Wogan was blathering away on the radio but I made myself sit patiently for ten minutes, all through Lionel Richie and one of Wogan's tedious stories. When the next record came on I got out and locked the car, and then took my time as I walked back up the lane. I was barely halfway to Christie's house when the sky took on a black and yellow tinge. Sure enough, a sprinkling of icy hail fell like tiny darts on my bare hands. That's good, I told myself. That will keep people tucked up inside their houses and out of my way. As the hail melted it destroyed all the efforts I'd made with my hair. It didn't matter. Nothing mattered. If Lorraine Quick had come visiting she was going to get a rare treat. I was going to make sure she met Christie herself.

Then there it was, Lorraine Quick's Metro dumped like a red flag for all to see. I couldn't see her so I walked to the end of the lane to be sure she wasn't hanging around. Not a sign. Returning, I screened myself behind the car to get a clear view of the house. It was as I stood there behind the hatchback that I noticed the coat on the back seat. It was moving. I walked around the car and tried the back

door handle. Yes, the stupid cow had left it unlocked. I
scrambled inside and pushed the door lock down behind
me.

'Who are you?' said a scruffy little brat. 'Where's my
mum?'

Dissociation

Question 57: I have had the experience of finding objects among my belongings that must be mine, but I cannot remember collecting them.

    A. Often

    B. Occasionally

    C. Never

High score description (option A.): Dissociation, or disconnection, from oneself or one's surroundings. A sense of unreality, detachment from one's body.

'Mrs Wilkins?' The musty air carried no reply. Lorraine took a few tentative steps forward.

'Anybody there? Mrs Wilkins? I only want a word with you.'

The kitchen was a slatternly place of rusty knives and stained melamine. Lorraine hurried through the odour of blocked drains to the hallway, glancing into a living room in which nothing appeared to have changed since the 1950s. On the other side of the hall was a closed door. If she was going to find Room 7, she needed to check each room. She turned the handle and found a short flight of stone steps. At the bottom was another door bearing a wooden sign: 'Treatment Room'. The interior was dominated by a hideous treatment couch placed at the room's centre. Suddenly Lorraine was taking in all sorts of things she didn't want to see. Leather straps hanging off the couch. Antique locked cabinets full of worrying blue bottles. A display of a human brain covered in a glass bell jar. An obsidian cremation urn. Objects that looked as if they belonged in a funeral parlour.

She ran back upstairs and slammed the door shut. Whatever Felicity was getting up to here, it was a matter for the police. And yet – the key to Room 7 weighed heavy in her pocket. She would scout around for just one more minute. Then she would go back to the car, wake up Jas and phone the police. Reaching the front hallway, she did not like the look of the steep stairs leading up into dizzy-looking darkness. She climbed them slowly, setting off uneasy creaks despite the dust compounded in the carpet. She was halfway up the first flight when a violent rattling sound filled her ears and she started, nearly toppling backwards. She clung to the banister, breathing fast. Slowly the high-pitched sound resolved into something familiar. It was only a hailstorm rattling crazily against the windows.

Idiot, she reprimanded herself. Get a move on. She rushed up the stairs and explored the first landing, finding nothing but rooms numbered 1 to 4 containing high-framed beds and ghoulish sheet-draped furniture. She guessed they had once been guest rooms but no one had lived in them for years. The final room was a bathroom with a stained tub and giant sink, and in the corner some vast heating apparatus reminiscent of an iron lung. She cursed her imagination that seemed to magnify her fear.

The next set of stairs was narrower. She wondered if she would feel better with the lights on. A primitive instinct told her not to draw attention to her presence. As fast as she could, she propelled herself up, step by step, into deepening darkness. She needed to leave fast. But no, the dormer room at the back of the house with the pale blind lured her onwards. She rushed past Room 5 and hesitated at the final door. Room 6 showed signs of habitation. Cosmetics on the dressing table, dingy clothes on a hanger, an unwashed sheet on the bed. She had no time to look closer. The hailstorm was even louder up here, rattling like clattering bullets against the roof tiles. Then there it was, Room 7. An intuition jabbed at her. Surely Jasmine was awake by now. Wasn't it criminal neglect or some such crime, to lock your child in a car and leave her? Only she hadn't locked it, had she? In the rush of wanting to get into the house she could no longer remember.

Here was the room. She tried the handle and it was locked. In the low light the brass keyhole winked. Felicity was away, far away at work. She could take a quick peek inside. Then she would fly down the stairs, run to the car and fetch Diaz as fast as she could.

I bundled the coat over the child's head and held her so tight that only puppy-like squeaks emerged. There was no one else on the lane, so with my free hand I pulled out my keys and simply carried the child up to the front door and got her inside.

It is amazing how unobservant most people are. And how utterly dense. It made me laugh again to remember Mrs Wilkins' refrain about how much safer she felt with a nurse in the house. She was as proud as punch about the Treatment Room.

It was dear Felicity who taught Christie the efficient use of a needle. It's one of those great miracles, the way innocents offer you their veins, their most vulnerable routes to life or death. Till that point in Christie's life other people had always been monsters to run away from, telling her she should have died at birth, taking what she wanted, hitting and cursing her. It was Felicity – or dear old Diggers as the patients called her – who taught her to make her first injection. She copied everything about her. That soothing voice, that coaxing manner, casting the sweet spell of submission.

People talk about magic. That's what sedatives are. They shut other people up. Their griping and carping. For a few precious minutes. Or for ever.

Giving Mrs Wilkins an intravenous shot of what she called her super-rejuvenating tonic was a genuine thrill. There had been the usual soothing subservience to a registered nurse with a gold medal to her name. There had been the landlady's readiness to lie down on the couch and bare her scraggy arm. She simply needed to be quiet. To relax. And the magic worked.

The child wriggled like an eel but it had no strength. I secured it in the Treatment Room without any trouble. Then I loaded Christie's syringe. But I couldn't let her play with the child just yet because that bitch, Lorraine, was still wandering around somewhere.

'Mummy!' it was wailing. 'Where are you?'

I mimicked it with a feeble whine. 'Mummy. Where are you?'

I laughed to see it writhing about, cringing away from

me and pulling on the leather strap that held it. Interesting. So it was Lorraine's child. Christie doesn't like children. She knows what they get up to when the so-called responsible adults disappear off home.

As for its mother. I stepped out into the hall and listened at the bottom of the stairs. I heard the faint but wary tread of steps on the upper landing. She was up there. As quietly as the best of trained nurses, I secured the lock on the front door. Then returning to the Treatment Room, I pulled on Christie's theatre smock and rubber apron.

The noise of the storm thundered like kettledrums across the roof. For a moment the key to Room 7 caught in the lock and Lorraine felt reprieved. She twisted it again and this time the door swung slowly open onto darkness. Her outstretched hand groped forward along the wall, searching for the light switch. When the single light bulb came on the room flashed into visibility. What she saw was reminiscent of a museum of pathetically worn-out objects. She blinked at fuzzy photographs and papers displayed on the walls. An oak coffin of a wardrobe held an ancient nylon dress on a hanger. A girl's greying underwear was neatly folded on the shelf. Everything was discoloured, as if tinted by the treacle-like passage of time.

Lorraine studied a large photograph of the genuine Felicity, smiling warmly and dolled up with false eyelashes and an Alice band. At her side stood an enthralled-looking youngster with butchered hair and wearing a hand-me-down jumper. Lorraine studied the thin lips and worshipful eyes. Though she lacked the hard definition of age and expertly painted make-up, she recognised that face. It was the woman the world knew as Felicity Jardine. She shook her head. Here was the real Felicity standing beside the false one. So, the brilliant Felicity and downtrodden Christie had indeed become unlikely friends.

And after Felicity sailed away? Of course, like a parasite, Christie had hatched inside her host's identity and started a new and vicarious life. Lorraine queasily grasped that the woman she had worked beside as Felicity Jardine had imprisoned her original self, Christie Kerr, inside these four dreary walls. That was what Room 7 was: a shrine to an awkward, unwanted child. The malignant child who would not be smothered and now survived inside the woman known as Felicity Jardine.

Lorraine moved over to the dressing table that held an old-fashioned tray of pink cut-glass. A mishmash of junk objects were arranged neatly upon it. Ancient metal spectacles. A pair of gold hooped earrings. A bracelet of black plaited leather. She picked up the bracelet and slipped it over her hand. It was far too large for her yet it looked dimly familiar. In a flashbulb of memory she recalled Lily giving Rikki just such a bracelet and it circling his wrist as he thrashed the drums. She dropped it as if it were a scorpion.

It fell beside a lace-trimmed handkerchief. Scarcely daring to breathe, she inspected it and found a capital 'R' embroidered in pink thread. This wasn't a tray of junk. These were mementos of murder.

Lorraine caught sight of her own face reflected in the triple mirrors of the dressing table. Her face was ashen, a stunned stranger's face. Here was the end of Christie's story. The repression of her secret former self. The slow intensification of the dark shadow at her core. Lorraine stared into her own eyes brimming with loathsome knowledge.

Was Christie insane? The patients at Fairholme were like broken toys, their mental motors had malfunctioned.

Compared with them, the woman who had created this had kept up the appearance of a normal human being. Yet inside her brain a key area – call it normality, empathy or plain humanity – had vanished long ago.

She started at a loud bang from downstairs.

Depersonalisation

Question 58: I have had the experience of looking in a mirror and not recognising myself in the face I see.

    A. Often

    B. Occasionally

    C. Never

High score description (option A.): Fragmentation of identity or self into separate streams of consciousness, the presence of other identities or 'alters' within a personality, each with their own names, voices and personal histories.

Diaz got out of his car and surveyed the towering facade of the house. The windows were mostly blanked out, giving the property a closed-up feeling. It was definitely big enough to take in lodgers. Maybe it was not just Lorraine who had intuitions, he told himself. He inspected the house front, disappointed to see the level of security was excellent. He might have to break a window to get inside.

He went back to the car to fetch a roll of tape and a few tools. Leaning into the boot, he felt the wind suddenly gusting, bringing a spatter of hailstones. Glancing up, he saw the sky was turning stormy grey.

The hail stung his face as he slipped up a pathway to the rear of the house and up a few steps inside the back porch. He made a rapid search for a spare key. For once, luck was with him and he found it dangling from a hook inside the gas meter cupboard. 'Getting careless, aren't you, mate?' he muttered. He let himself in through the back door.

There it was again. A distant noise from downstairs. Lorraine had been in the house too long. Jasmine must have woken by now. She switched off the light and stepped quietly onto the landing. A rat-a-tat barrage of rain hammered the roof as if raging to get inside. The wind circling the house was swooping down the chimney too, like the yowling of a cat. Lorraine suddenly froze stock-still. Beneath the wailing sound rose a high-pitched cry. It was almost like words.

She ran to the top of the stairs. For a vertiginous moment she stood on the top step, alert and listening.

The sound drifted up the deep well of the stairs. 'Mum!'

Fear vanished in a mercurial explosion of energy. She ran pell-mell down and down towards her daughter. On the final turn of the stairs Jasmine's voice sounded tantalisingly close.

In the hallway she stopped, terror rising at the prospect of what she might find. More quietly she crept towards the doorway through which Jas's voice emerged.

'Mum, Mum. I'm here!' Her daughter was shrieking with panic.

Jas was down there in the basement. In the worst place. Lorraine tiptoed down the stone stairs and listened outside the door with its crude sign declaring 'Treatment Room'. There was no sound from Jasmine. All Lorraine could hear was water running and the tinkle of glass and metal. From nowhere, fear stunned her, her limbs suddenly too weak to move. Every cell in her body urged her to run back upstairs and not face what lay inside. She found she was shaking.

'Mummy!' the thin voice cried. Lorraine pushed open the door to that nightmare room. Her daughter was curled up pitifully on the treatment couch.

'Jas!' She hurried to her daughter. It was the little girl's round-eyed stare that directed her gaze to the figure standing motionless at the sink. The woman had her back to them both, showing a nurse's green uniform issued in some far-off age. The nurse blinked at her reflection in the tarnished mirror above the sink. She appeared to wake from a silent fugue and turned to face Lorraine. Her mask of flesh carried no human expression. Her eyes, thick with heavy make-up, were blanks of animal dumbness. Her mouth was slack. She was no longer Felicity Jardine. She was Christie Kerr.

'When it's you or your attacker,' Lorraine's self-defence trainer had told her, 'never play fair.'

Lorraine grasped a stone mortar bowl off the shelf and threw it hard against the side of Christie's skull. The nurse raised her hand just in time to absorb the worst of the blow. Still, she sagged and dropped to her knees. Lorraine threw herself on top of her and punched her face with her balled fist.

Though Lorraine hit her so hard that her own knuckles burnt, Christie recovered and struggled to break free. She was strong and slippery, her wet hair dripping and her rubber apron slick. From nowhere, Lorraine felt a blow deep in her stomach and involuntarily bunched up and gasped. Christie rolled free and scrambled to her feet. Lorraine grabbed the woman's legs and yanked her back down to the floor.

'Mum!' Jasmine's voice was high-pitched with terror.

Another surge of desperation drove Lorraine to scoop up the stone bowl and smack it into the woman's face. Blood oozed over Christie's hair and brow. Her eyelids drooped. She sank backwards to the floor.

Panting, Lorraine climbed over Christie towards her daughter. Jasmine reached for her with open arms and Lorraine tried to lift her up towards her heart. It was impossible. She couldn't free her daughter.

'Stop it! It's that,' Jasmine wailed, pointing to her ankle. A tough leather strap circled an ankle as fragile as a bird's bone. The knot looked hard to unpick but Lorraine would do it. And then she would—

'Mummy!' Jasmine screamed and pointed towards the sink. 'She's coming.'

Lorraine spun around and took in Christie Kerr bearing down on them, scarlet blood streaming across her face. In her hand was a syringe, the needle pointing towards them.

Lorraine's phobia gave her no time to think. She grabbed the biggest weapon in her line of sight: the grotesque Victorian bell jar. It was heavier than she anticipated and it slithered dangerously through her damp fingers as she raised it. With all her strength she swung it up into the air and hurled it at Christie Kerr and that approaching needle.

The nurse raised her hands to shield her face and staggered backwards towards the stairs. With an explosive crack the glass shattered into glittering shards. Lorraine ran at her attacker and rammed her outside with the door, then slammed it hard, sending Christie tumbling backwards against the stone stairs. Her plan was working; she almost pushed it closed. Then the door's stubborn resistance told her something was shored up under the door frame. Lorraine paused to kick a small heap of broken glass aside. In that distracted moment a hand reached through the gap and jabbed at Lorraine's arm with the needle. With an almighty effort Lorraine shoved the door closed. Gasping for breath, she dragged a chair across the room and jammed it beneath the door handle. Next, she hauled the heavy cupboard up against it. She prayed it would hold for a while.

Jasmine was cringing in a ball of shock. Her face was white, her eyes huge.

'We're OK,' Lorraine muttered. She tried to undo the leather knot with fingers that trembled uncontrollably. She had to get Jasmine out of here. There had to be some cutting implement in the room. She began searching wildly. Opening a cabinet, she started back from a horrific rubber face mask. She slammed the door shut. Opening a cupboard, she glimpsed a human skull with its top removed. And a human eye with floating nerve endings glaring from a jar of fluid. She yelped in fear.

The drawers contained a few paper files: buff folders titled 'Felicity Jardine' and 'Christie Kerr'. It was too late for all that now. She threw them on the couch.

Shock was making her shiver. What was she looking for? She noticed the strap holding Jasmine's leg and recalled that she needed something sharp. She was surrounded by what she needed. Stretching her jacket sleeve down over her hand, she gingerly picked up a curved shard of glass. She sawed back and forth along the ancient strap until it severed, leaving Jasmine with an anklet and a few ragged inches of leather hanging from her foot.

At last Lorraine pulled her daughter into her arms and hugged her tight, chafing her stiff little hands. Setting her down again, Lorraine began searching for a means of escape. There were no windows down here. There was no other exit. She inspected the sooty stone-tiled floor. No trapdoor either. There was only one way out and that was the way she had come in. Past Christie.

The first impression Diaz had was that the house was entirely deceptive. He trod cat-like through black and white rooms of shiny cleanliness. The kitchen was glossy white, fitted with kitchen cupboards of the sort he had only ever glimpsed in that poncy Habitat catalogue. The study, living room and dining room were all arranged in black leather, white sheepskins and tubular steel. Upstairs were cool-looking bedrooms with those puffy rainbow-patterned eiderdowns everyone was calling duvets. The cellar had been kitted out as a private gym with a sleek black Bang and Olufsen hi-fi, telly and video machine.

Doctor Strang was living in a dream bachelor pad. It was a dead cert to impress any girl he managed to bring home. It made Diaz feel sick with envy, as well as relieved that he'd not hassled Brunt to get a search warrant. He let himself out and put the key back where he'd found it. His so-called intuition had got him nowhere. And now he felt the grip of panic. If she wasn't here, then where the hell was Lorraine?

Lorraine's heart thumped as she inspected each wall and found only solid whitewashed stone. Well, except for one small section at the back of a tall cabinet. Peering behind it, she glimpsed a rectangle of whitewashed plywood nailed high into the wall. With a massive effort she pushed the cabinet aside. Clambering onto a chair, she knocked her knuckle against the plywood and heard a hollow sound. Again she searched the room, this time for a sharp tool. A shallow drawer contained medical tools: intestinal-looking tubes, amputation saws and nightmarish forceps. A pincer-like tool did the trick and she loosened the rusty nails holding the panel in place. The cover came down after half a dozen fierce tugs. She was rewarded by a fall of sooty leaves from a dark void stretching up into the solid wall. It was a coal chute that sloped up a few feet towards a panel of rusty metal. Her head began to ache with the effort of thinking. Perhaps her disorientation was the result of more than simple shock? When she moved too fast a whooshing sensation sloshed inside her skull. Something was happening to her vision, too.

When she stood on her toes on the chair, the tips of her fingers could just touch the metal cover that communicated with the outside world. No, she could not budge it. She clambered down and found a mop with a long wooden handle. She pushed it against the metal cover with all her might. It was jammed shut. She looked down at Jasmine and drew more strength into herself. Groaning with effort, she rammed the handle against the metal plate. At last, with a crack, it sprang open, as she tumbled off the chair. Damp air wafted down from the outside world. Getting back on the chair, she peered up at a letterbox view of grey air and hailstones. The opening at the top of the chute was no more than two feet wide and perhaps eighteen inches high. Even if Lorraine could have squeezed through the gap, she would never gain the propulsion to lift herself up at such an angle. She took a draught of fresh air and glanced at the door but heard no sound. If Christie Kerr came back she would kill her even if she died in the attempt. Her own life didn't matter. But Jasmine had to get away.

Lorraine sat down next to her daughter. Jasmine didn't

even look up. She was curled up, seeming insensible. And she, Lorraine, had brought this horror down upon them both.

'Sweetheart,' she said softly. Her daughter's body felt cold and clammy to the touch.

'Jasmine,' she tried again. 'You know how in your game books, the hero has to do one last big brave thing to win?'

Jasmine nodded very weakly, though her eyes didn't lift to meet hers.

'I want you to try to do that last big brave thing.'

Though she was a deadweight, Lorraine half carried, half dragged her daughter to the coal hole.

'Smell that,' she whispered in her daughter's ear. 'It's the outside. Can you be my hero, sweetheart? I want to help you get away into the yard. OK?'

Jasmine's eyes flickered and she swallowed hard. 'I'm too scared,' she said in a tiny voice.

'So am I, lovey-dove. But we need to get the police, don't we?' Her daughter gave a nervy little nod.

'You need to cross the yard to the green door. Use the key to open the door. Then go down the alley back to the road and go to the red phone box. Ring 999. And tell them to hurry to 43 The Glen. Can you remember all that?'

Jasmine repeated the instructions mechanically.

'But if you see *her*—' Mother and daughter's eyes met and locked in fear. 'Just run. And scream as loudly as you can for help.'

Lorraine tied the key to the belt on Jasmine's dress so she wouldn't lose it. Then she stood on the chair and hauled Jasmine up in her arms. 'Grab the edge of the opening. Pull yourself up,' she entreated in a low voice. Carefully, she raised her daughter head first into the chute.

Miraculously, the little girl sprang to life, her monkey arms dragging herself up the chute. Lorraine held her legs steady as Jasmine's shoulders, and then her chest, disappeared into the narrow opening. Next, she wriggled her hips through. For a scary moment her legs seemed stuck and Lorraine nearly toppled backwards until Jasmine dragged them slowly up through the gap. Finally, her feet, trailing the leather strap, vanished from sight. Lorraine clutched the wall, her head spinning, wondering how much longer she could stand upright. Jasmine's face suddenly appeared far away at the upper opening, smudged with soot and already wet with rain.

'Tell me what to do again.'

Lorraine struggled to remember as wooziness overcame her. 'Open the green door with the key. Run to the phone box. Ring 999. Tell them it's 43 The Glen. Say your mum is a prisoner and to come quick.'

There was a sound outside the door of footsteps crunching on broken glass. Lorraine clutched the edge of the hole in the wall.

'Go! Quick as you can.'

Lorraine sat on the treatment couch and hugged her knees. Giddiness rose in unstoppable waves. She inspected the scratch from Christie's needle and guessed that a tiny but potent amount of anaesthetic had entered her nervous system. Dully, she wondered how long she had left until unconsciousness struck, or even death. Her eyelids drooped. Surely she deserved to sleep at last?

No. She shook her head and slapped her own face. She had to stay alert. Doggedly, she opened the cardboard folders. It was all there. Inside Felicity Jardine's and Christie Kerr's files were black and white passport-sized photos of the two student nurses. One was open-faced, smiling and attractive. The other's mouth was uplifted too, but the expression was blank and unknowable.

She had also picked up a third file quite different from the first two. This one was a male patient with an address given as 'No Fixed Abode'. There was only one flimsy sheet inside, the carbon copy of a referral letter. It was addressed to Fairholme Secure Unit and signed by Felicity Jardine. There was no photograph but even as Lorraine's eyes irresistibly closed, she knew exactly which inmate the file belonged to.

Manipulation

Question 59: I admire cunning people who create a really clever scam.
   A. True
   B. Uncertain
   C. False

High score description (option A.): Desire to exploit, control or otherwise influence others to one's advantage; use of force, blackmail and intimidation.

Someone was trying to get into the Treatment Room. Lorraine opened sticky eyes and saw only cracked leather. A cold draught reached her from the open hole high in the wall. For an elastic space of time the devastation of shattered glass and broken plywood meant nothing. Then, what felt like a hundred volts of memory charged into her brain.

Jasmine. Since her daughter had escaped Lorraine had sunk in and out of consciousness. Now only phantasmagorical traces danced in her mind. The doorbell had rung. Had kept ringing. Then voices. The words unclear but urgent. And now someone was forcing their way through the defences she'd piled against the door. Was it Christie Kerr? Lorraine was too weak to stop her. Or could it please, please, be the police?

Lorraine watched the door shove open a few inches wider. A hairy male hand reached inside. Had Diaz come to rescue her?

When she saw the man's face, he was almost the last person on earth she wanted to see. Harvey Wright kicked broken glass and debris aside and crunched his way towards her.

'No,' she whispered. She could barely raise her arm, never mind stop him coming near her.

He towered above her. 'What the fuck were you thinking, Lorraine? Coming here?' He wore a stony scowl as he appraised her amidst all the wreckage.

Lorraine looked nervously towards the door. 'Where's Christie?' she mumbled.

'She killed herself.'

Even with the drug still dragging at her consciousness she wasn't stupid enough to believe that. There had been voices. Harvey and Christie. And now there was only Harvey.

Fear battled against the sedative, creating bilious panic. She raised her hand, which felt as heavy as cement. 'Syringe caught me. Call an ambulance.'

He ignored her. Instead he leant down close and spoke so softly that she smelt his cigar-tainted breath. 'Fairholme. I heard you went visiting.'

If only her brain wasn't in a fog. 'My mum, she—'

'Stop fucking around. Who knows about Fairholme?'

The sensitive hairs on her neck sprang up. 'Rikki,' she mumbled.

'That cretin. Who else?'

She couldn't summon any words. Two iron-hard hands grasped her shoulders. Harvey shook her so hard that her teeth clattered together.

'Who else knows?' he shouted, his face flushed with fury.

If he thought that only she knew, then . . . what? Her thoughts clashed confusedly against each other.

Suddenly, like a prompt in a play the words came to her. 'My daughter's escaped. Through the hole. She rung the police.'

'What?' His jolt of anxiety gave her hope.

'They're coming. Diaz knows.'

Harvey threw her hard back onto the couch. He struck his mouth with his fist.

'Fuck,' he muttered, screwing up his face. 'No one will understand.' He stared at her as if it were all her fault. 'Stuck with a child like that.'

Lorraine tried unsuccessfully to sit up and failed. 'What?'

'You know he attacked my wife? Broke her jaw when he was twelve, stabbed me when I wouldn't hand over my gold watch. You can call it delusions or psychosis or anything you like. Labels didn't stop me wishing him dead. He arrived that New Year to suck us dry of money. I'd worked out who Christie was so I called in a favour. She knew psychiatry; she knew how to pull strings. Brenda and I got our lives back. And then you stuck your nose in. This is not how my career ends, Lorraine. Public shame. Prison.'

A stinging slap sent her head walloping hard against the couch.

Lorraine cringed away from him, waiting for him to do whatever he'd done to Christie.

So this was it. She squeezed her eyes tightly shut and

thought about her mum, and her dad, wherever the hell he was, and how she needed to stay alive to be a parent to Jasmine, to grow old beside her daughter as her guide and defender. The distant wail of a siren reached her too late. Her mind drifted to all the wonderful moments she'd not yet experienced in her life. The songs she hadn't yet composed, the poems and stuff unwritten, unmet friends and unknown lovers. Her eyelids refused to reopen. If Harvey killed her now, it would be bizarre and cruel but at least she could finally sleep . . .

She didn't even startle when a hand shook her gently.

'Lorraine. Wake up. Come on, love.'

Love? She unglued her eyelids with difficulty. Standing over her was a shape familiar in a dark unsettling way. Lorraine struggled and Diaz helped her up. Her brain felt adrift from her skull. Then a miraculous comfort enveloped her as Diaz slung his jacket around her shoulders, and she relaxed in the scent of warm leather and tobacco.

'Jasmine?' she croaked.

'She's in the ambulance. No injuries, just being checked over. Great little girl. Did as she was told and waited in the phone box.'

Suddenly it hurt to look at him. 'I must see her.' She tried to scramble up but her head spun like a top.

'We just need to get you checked out. The medics are outside. We'll take a statement later. And hey . . .' Diaz's warm gaze was all over her. The next moment she could hardly breathe as her face nestled against the solid heat of his chest. He was squeezing her tight and running his big hands down her spine. She had a dim memory of being flaming mad with him but for now she clung to him, never wanting to let go.

Busy sounds reached them from the corridor and they broke apart.

There was so much she had to tell him.

'Harvey was here. I think he killed Felicity.'

'What's that? What the 'ell would he do that for?' Brunt was making his way precariously across the glass and rubble.

'To cover up this,' Lorraine said, batting the three files towards Diaz. 'The chief nurse's real name is Christie Kerr. Harvey used her to get his son incarcerated in Fairholme. Now can I see my daughter?'

There was no other way out of the house save through the kitchen. She was glad to be leaning on Diaz's shoulder when she faced Christie for the last time. She was slumped at the kitchen table with a pill carton and a bottle of whisky and glass laid out neatly before her. Her head was tilted gawkily, the jade stones of her eyes open and clownish, streaked with make-up and drying blood. Looking away, Lorraine wondered what grisly tableau Harvey might have created for her own demise, if he hadn't taken flight from the police.

Then she was outside in the rain and a paramedic was offering her a blanket.

'Keep my jacket,' Diaz said. 'I'll come and get it later when I take your statement.'

Lorraine was scarcely listening. She was hobbling towards the van with flashing blue lights, where a small white-faced figure was smacking her palm against the window.

'Mum!'

Lorraine hauled herself up the ambulance steps and gathered Jasmine into her arms.

'You did it,' she said, looking at her daughter through amazed tears. 'My hero. My big brave girl.'

Detachment

Question 60: I feel uncomfortable when other people express strong feelings and emotions.

    A. True

    B. Uncertain

    C. False

High score description (option A.): Detached, impersonal, critical, aloof, cool, distrustful, discomfited by inability to fix problems.

Whitsuntide

The garden dedicated to Rose's memory had been Doctor Lehman's idea. She had tracked Lorraine down to her mum's flat after news spread about the case, keen to check how her erstwhile student was coping. Lorraine had reassured her that she had been signed off sick and was recovering well after a few days in hospital.

'I'm pleased you didn't confide the results to the police,' the tutor told her.

Lorraine's voice wobbled; she still couldn't speak about

that day. All she said was, 'I want to forget it all now. But I do want to remember Rose.'

'Good. It's important not to bury tragic events by failing to speak about them. Organisations have memories as well as people. I suggest you bring everyone together to celebrate Rose's life in a manner that she might have chosen.'

It was the last thing Lorraine felt like doing. Yet as the newsrooms moved on to other big stories, she realised that all their memories of Rose were slipping away. Her mind drifted to the abandoned garden at the rear of the hospital and how Rose would have loved it, too. Yes, she had to do something before Rose's spirit faded and died, like a failing torch.

The next day Lorraine contacted a local heritage charity. Soon the dank ponds and tangles of brambles and briars were being enthusiastically restored back to the glory displayed in the Victorian engravings she'd seen on Norman's wall. A few weekends later, Lorraine and Jasmine turned up to see decades of weeds and rubble being dug from the hard ground. Nestling deep in the earth the volunteers had also found old corms and bulbs, not only of snowdrops but windflowers, lilies and daffodils. It felt like a wonderful sign. Then together she and Jasmine planted two rows of tight-budded rose standards.

'Welcome all. It is humbling to witness all the help, hard work and creativity gathered here today in this extraordinary project.'

The hospital's new general manager was speaking at the subdued opening ceremony. Gareth Miller was a serious but approachable chief nurse from the Midlands with a wide circle of connections and some impressive new ideas. Lorraine's first impressions were of a stern introvert but he was also an academic, decisive and fair, with a career in research and useful experience as manager of a vast general hospital. Most importantly, Gareth had immediately enthused about Lorraine's garden idea and found money in a contingency fund to cover the charity's expenses.

Lorraine edged away from the crowd and watched from the sheltering trees. There was Phil, looking sober in a dark suit and tie. He was a friend now, though she saw him less often since he'd returned to work. As two lone parents they helped each other out, Lorraine minding Tim when Phil worked at weekends, and Phil still overseeing Lorraine's attempts to get rehoused. Her old house on Balaclava Street had been flattened, so at least she was now inching to the top of the housing list.

'Though I never knew Rose myself,' Gareth Miller was saying gravely, 'I have heard only good of her, not only of her dedication but her kindness and generosity.'

Of the former management team, only Doctor Strang and Mike McClung were present, both listening attentively. The charges against Raj had been dropped. The police had struggled to find hard evidence of him gaining pecuniary advantage from falsified records, though he had certainly favoured his landlord by promoting his taxi company. Raj had immediately resigned and though currently working as an accountant to a private firm, her old friend had chosen not to return her calls.

Norman Pilling had also gone, clutching an engraved gilt clock and the promise of a tidy pension. The next day his office had been cleared out, producing trolley-loads of obstinate bureaucracy.

Now Gareth Miller wound up his speech. 'It is important that both our staff and the patients in our care find a space for healing and renewal. May the fruitfulness of nature live on in the seeds and flowers of this delightful garden. Thank you.'

Lorraine joined in the ripple of applause and then drifted away from familiar faces, all of them keen to talk about her ordeal. She was still under orders from Brunt to tell no one about Harvey's presence at Christie's house. At times that final encounter with Harvey felt like a terrifying hallucination. Still vivid in flashbacks was that long moment when she had expected him to kill her. And her instincts had been right: Harvey's lie that Christie had committed suicide was soon disproved by the forensics team. He was wanted for Christie Kerr's murder.

Doctor Lehman's words still haunted her, that some psychopaths targeted positions of power from which to manipulate their gullible underlings. Christie Kerr had exhibited textbook traits: a history of cruelty, lack of remorse and a shallow charm. More confusing were her memories of Harvey. She should have guessed he had plenty to hide when he had refused to take the PX60 test. Instead, he had given her that impromptu account of himself, describing himself as a people-loving, benevolent, golf-playing old chap. And she had almost believed him.

She slipped away from the memorial garden into a glade of beech trees. Firstly, she searched out a particular bench overlooking an ornamental pond. There she read the brass plaque on the seat: 'Sister Bernadette Ince – devoted nurse for more than 40 years'. No one knew why Christie had gone to Marlow Court and killed Sister Ince, but an incriminating strand of dyed auburn hair had proved that she had done so.

Lorraine paused at the bench and murmured a few words of farewell.

In a darker, shadier corner stood another bench dedicated to 'Eric Fryer, 1955–1983'. Officially, there had been no words of tribute to the drug-fuelled porter. It was Lily who had pressed for this small remembrance. Touching the plaque, she murmured, 'I'm so sorry, Rikki. Be at peace. Wherever you are.'

A figure appeared through the trees, stocky and uncharacteristically hesitant. He waited a dozen paces away from her.

'You ready to go?' Diaz asked.

They walked together to his car, Lorraine bracing herself against what they might yet face, relieved that Diaz had suggested he'd give her a lift. As they crossed the hospital site Lorraine silently marvelled at being back at the Memorial again. The bruises and glass-cuts from her confrontation with Christie Kerr had slowly ceased to hurt and then faded away. Then, surreally, she had returned to work. The odd thing was that she hadn't minded too much about coming back in. At first she told herself it was the promise of a change for the better in Gareth Miller's appointment. He had called her into his office and disdainfully picked up Norman Pilling's threat of disciplinary action, torn it into pieces, and dropped the shreds in the waste bin.

'I'm not interested in raking over some cloudy past.'

Lorraine gave her heartfelt thanks.

He leant forward and steepled his fingers below his direct, intelligent gaze. 'It's only fair to tell you, your name came up at a regional review meeting. There's an idea that we need to give a push to these psychological techniques, to recruit and promote the best – and be sure we weed out any dangerous personalities. What do you think?'

'It sounds a brilliant job.'

Gareth cocked his head to one side, smiling. 'Write yourself a job description and send it to the regional director. The work will be based in Manchester, developing projects across the North West. I'm making no promises, but I know there's a budget and your name came up.'

From the moment she'd left his office her brain had been fizzing with excited ideas.

Nevertheless, as she walked up the main corridor at Diaz's side, she felt a stirring of fondness for the tatty old hospital as they dodged dinner trolleys and wheelchairs, avoiding patients hobbling behind Zimmer frames, or people hurrying from appointments that had delivered joyful relief or devastating news. Amongst them were the hospital's staff – hugely annoying, often belligerent, exhausted, but the living heart of the service's success. She had used to wonder why they turned up for such punishing shifts. The answer wasn't only in their shields of professional epaulettes and badges. In the language of the PX60 a good few of them were ideals of Dutifulness, Toughness and Self-reliance. If Christie Kerr had taught her anything, it was that the urge to heal that Christie lacked was thankfully possessed by plenty of her colleagues. The regional project would give her the chance to make the service better – as well as being the sort of challenge she'd genuinely like to tackle.

She dared a direct glance at Diaz as they were getting into the police Rover. She'd barely seen him since he'd taken her statement in hospital, and never alone. He had been busy tying up the case, while she had requested that her own and Jasmine's part should be kept out of any press reports. Then he had been sent away on a residential course about new developments in policing. And now the time had come when they must surely be able to talk freely. She had found it hard to forget him, despite the differences in her own and Diaz's personalities. Instead she'd recalled their attraction the night of the gig and her subsequent devastation when she'd learnt he had a pregnant fiancée all along.

When Doctor Lehman had phoned, Lorraine had asked her: 'Do you think I can ever trust a man who has lied to me?'

'Did you ever lie to him?' her tutor replied waspishly.

Lorraine reflected on that. She hadn't told him about Jasmine or very much at all about her own life. 'Well, not so much lied as – sort of deflected him.'

'Maybe you both put up a false front,' Doctor Lehman said. 'Only by learning about vulnerability can we give any relationship a chance. By admitting negative feelings: bottled-up anger or disappointment, fears or vulnerabilities. These are the genuine emotions that true friends or a loving couple risk sharing. Think of Psyche's courage in lighting her candle and raising it to see the true face of her lover. Try it.'

That had sounded easy back then, but now, as she watched him driving, Diaz looked distracted, even moody.

'Any news of Harvey?' she asked.

He kept his eyes on the road. 'The official line is that we're looking for him to assist in our enquiries. But he and his wife have definitely done a bunk. He had arranged to have his pension paid early and it's been cleared out of his account, along with a fortune in savings. Nothing came back from the alerts at ports and airports. Could be he took a private boat to the continent. I reckon he's somewhere far, far away by now.

'I did find something interesting, mind. Remember when

we first looked around the medical records basement? I had a hunch the answer was down there. I took a look at Harvey Wright's medical file. I reckoned there had to be a link to Christie Kerr.'

She remembered the morning the clerks had found medical files scattered all over the floor. 'What did you find?'

'Not a dicky bird in Harvey's file. So I got hold of his wife's records. The only unusual item was a newly filed coding letter from Carlisle Infirmary. It looked suspicious, as if everything about a health issue in Carlisle had been stripped out of the file. So I rang them up. Bingo. 1962, Mr and Mrs Wright were at a golf tournament in Carlisle. Brenda Wright fell from a grandstand and broke her ankle. She turned up in Casualty at Carlisle Infirmary. Fortunately for us the nurse signed the admissions card. Staff Nurse Felicity Jardine.'

'So he knew her,' Lorraine grasped excitedly. 'Hang on – '62. This is the real Felicity Jardine. Harvey met her before she emigrated.'

Diaz's face grew serious. 'Yes. So years later when he found a nurse with the same name and nursing medal had been appointed at the Memorial, he spotted the deception.'

'To Harvey management was all about "trading favours",' Lorraine said. 'And he got a pretty big favour in return for keeping quiet. She made his son disappear into Fairholme. Harvey told me he and his wife had been desperate. But it's no excuse. Do you know who tampered with the file?'

'Harvey. His prints were on it.'

He steered the car down to the traffic lights and waited at a red, and tapped nervously on the wheel before suddenly turning to face her.

'I also got hold of the real Felicity Jardine in Australia. Just before midnight last night.' He released his breath in a puff of disbelief. 'I'm still gobsmacked. It must have been an Oscar-winning impersonation by Christie Kerr. The genuine Felicity is her complete and utter opposite. She's a really decent woman, married to a cattle farmer, mum to four children. Resigned from nursing in Australia years ago. I told her Christie Kerr was dead and had stolen her identity. She was surprised right enough, hearing it out of the blue. And disappointed at being used. When I told her Christie had been murdered she said, "I did wonder if she was on a dark road."'

Lorraine wondered who could ever have guessed that road's destination. Alone of them all, she had seen that waxen reflection in the Treatment Room's mirror. The Felicity Jardine they had all known had worn a mask of silvered glass: shallow and reflective and hiding God knew what damage beneath it.

'Then a totally weird thing happened,' Diaz continued, pushing his foot down as the lights changed. 'When I mentioned Eric Fryer, she said she thought about him nearly every day. I told her it was Christie who killed him. That he must have been expecting to meet up with her. You know what she said? "Now you've told me that, I wish to God I'd never helped that girl. I'll carry this on my conscience for ever."'

Diaz shook his head, pondering. 'There was the obvious question of course, because of the morphine at the crime scene. Was Fryer trying to blackmail Jardine about something dodgy in her past?'

'Yes, I thought about that too,' Lorraine said. 'You do hear about cases of bedridden children being molested. Rikki must have been very vulnerable. But surely women don't do that?'

'Well, the real Felicity wanted to talk about it. Said

400

she knew it wasn't acceptable nursing practice nowadays, but she'd allowed what she called a deep affection to form between her and the boy. Strapped in that frame, he was scared witless and alone. She felt passionately that being taken from his home and family was causing more mental damage than physical benefit. So she tried to show him what maternal love and affection were.'

Lorraine recalled the good-natured nurse in the photograph standing beside Rikki, her reassuring hand on the boy's skinny shoulder.

'"I'd have got sacked on the spot nowadays," she said. "Been called a pervert for holding him in my arms in his bed." Said he'd broken her heart. Talked about the psychology she'd learnt on her nurse training – the theory that a child deprived of its mother's affection would likely turn into what they called a juvenile delinquent.

'There was no question of anything inappropriate, she insisted, or at least not by the rules back then. But it was proper, powerful love on both sides. He was her "best boy in the world". She even looked into adopting him, but they wouldn't allow it with him having a mother of his own. And then she met her husband and moved on. Rikki was due to go home soon and she hoped she'd done enough to give him a secure start in life. "But I failed him, didn't I?" was the last thing she said. "It was all my fault."'

Lorraine took a while to reflect on what she'd heard. She shook her head and said, 'Looks like the road to Hell is paved with good intentions, after all. Who would have thought love could prove so dangerous?'

By the time they turned off the East Lancs, the phrase still echoed in the silence and their exuberance seemed to have vanished. She knew there was something wrong.

'Are you going to tell me what's up?' she asked.

They were approaching the car park at the rear of the sheltered housing units. A moment later he switched off the engine and only a gentle ticking broke the silence. She had imagined this moment over the past few weeks. The secret part of her wanted to make a go of it with him. In fact, she felt she bloody well deserved him.

He reached for her hand and gripped it hard. 'My life's complicated.'

'I heard about Shirley.'

He had the grace to look stricken. 'She's pregnant. Well, she's miscarried before. I made a promise to marry her. And she's just so – desperate at the moment.'

All the good things that had happened to Lorraine turned instantly to dust. 'Oh, and everything's just hunky-dory for me,' she managed to say without choking up.

He gave an irritated shake of his head. 'You are completely different. Opposites. You're strong. I want to do the right thing. When the kid's born and things have settled down, then we'll get together. In the meantime it's going to be hard. The odd evening, when I can see you. OK?'

She removed her hand from his. This was not how it should be. Had Doctor Lehman honestly given her permission to say what she thought? She most certainly had. Lorraine lifted the metaphorical candle up to his face and told him what she saw: his coldness, his detachment from his emotions, his unsuitability as any sort of partner to her.

'No,' she said steadily. 'It's not OK. You've just proved you don't in any way understand the real me. I sympathise with your predicament. But this plan of yours. That I get the dregs of your time after your girlfriend, your new baby, your job, have all had their share. You think I'll stand on the sidelines while you play happy families? I mean, I knew you had an overactive imagination but you're living in a fantasy world.'

The shock and pain on his face was surprisingly satisfying.

'What's the matter with you?' he protested. 'This is bloody killing me, Lorraine. Give me a chance to do the right thing.'

She looked down into her lap and spoke slowly and shakily. 'I am so proud of Jas and so ashamed of the danger I placed her in. But it was me who found out the truth, about Christie and Harvey, and you know what else I learnt? When I had to face that – insane creature, I found out about me. I discovered that I'm not scared of blood or murder or anything, not if my daughter's life is at stake. Yes, I am strong. So I'm going to ask you a question. Why are you choosing to live a life that's a sham? Why are you binding yourself to someone when it's obvious you won't ever be happy together?'

She opened the car door and got out, feeling the cold air like liquid oxygen. Then she slammed the door hard and loud. God, where had all that come from? Yet her words had at least had the dignity of being true. She regretted nothing.

With perfect timing the roar of a motorbike engine decelerating made the air vibrate. Lily was on time for once.

The sheltered housing units were newly built and painted in primary reds and yellows that clashed with the neighbourhood's soot-stained brickwork. Lorraine walked with Lily to number 5 and rang the bell. A moment later Diaz caught up with them and Lorraine ignored him.

'I feel sick,' Lily said. 'Everyone says not to expect much.'

The resettlement officer, a motherly grey-haired woman

with an easy, laid-back manner, came to the door. 'He's doing fine,' she said in a low voice, ushering them inside. 'At least, he's not tried to do a runner yet.'

Lorraine went into the tidy living room. Zeb was huddled in the furthest armchair, as motionless as a corpse, his head in his hands.

Lily pushed past and knelt down in front of him. 'Hi, love. It's me. Lily.'

They all watched Zeb for any sign of recognition, but none came. Even when Lily took his hands in hers, he didn't respond and his limbs remained stiff and claw-like.

Lorraine tuned into the conversation the resettlement officer was having with Diaz at a table on which official paperwork was laid out. 'I doubt very much he'll be able to give evidence. He's been institutionalised in the worst way,' she muttered. 'A regime like Fairholme could only do damage. I'm just grateful that place has been closed down, pending this inquiry. Thankfully, the doctor here isn't bad. And the staff are on call night and day.'

Zeb's expression was entirely vacant, just as it had been when she saw him in Fairholme's garden. He seemed the empty shell of the man he had once been, hollowed out by pain, as if his vital spirit had shrivelled away. Perhaps Harvey hadn't been quite as cruel as they'd all believed. Perhaps his son had genuinely been too confused to comprehend the worst aspects of Fairholme's regime.

'By all means get victim support involved. Any human company will help,' the resettlement officer was explaining. 'But we must insist that now he's off drugs, no one ever—'

She stopped, her attention caught by Lily.

'I brought you something,' Lily was intoning in a low

voice. Alarmed, they all turned to see what she was handing over. 'Shit, the trouble I had getting the broken frets just right again,' she murmured.

Lily laid the big black case in front of Zeb, springing open the clips. Inside, Zeb's restored silver Les Paul lay cushioned in plush red velvet. Lily lifted it out and offered it to him, but he made no move to take it. She set the guitar on her own knees and strummed a few simple chords. Then she smiled up at Zeb and handed him the guitar again, this time slotting it onto his knees and guiding his left hand to hold the neck.

Lorraine never forgot the way Zeb sprang to life, awkwardly at first, like an automaton whose long-abandoned mechanism has finally, painstakingly, been repaired. His fingers slid onto the neck and his right hand jerked to the strings. His head lifted so that the black tangle of his hair parted to reveal the familiar heart-shaped face, ravaged but rapturous.

The music that filled the room was the same melody that Lorraine had thought she'd heard playing on the radio, that miserable day back at Fairholme. It was the same haunting tune she had heard a hundred times in Manchester's clubs and bars. Only now the spangled beauty of Zeb's music took her to another place, free of anger and disappointment, somewhere more lofty and forgiving.

And yes, here was her reward. She looked to Diaz and his brown eyes met hers, wet with emotion. At once their bodies seemed to understand a connection their overworked minds couldn't grasp. Without thinking, they reached out their hands and locked their fingers tightly, warmly, together.

Afterword

Which parts of this book are based on reality? Back in the early 1980s I was indeed looking for a job; like Lorraine, I was a lone parent in need of a wage, but far more interested in playing in my band. In time, I found a job in the personnel department of Salford Health Authority, and as Morrissey of The Smiths had predicted, it was a case of 'Heaven knows I'm miserable now'. My first impressions of the NHS were of dusty files of bureaucratic memoranda and endless meetings in former Victorian workhouses. I knew almost nothing about being a personnel officer, save a description in a Careers Service leaflet that suggested a role somewhere between a welfare officer and the 'middleman' between management and workers. In fact, the job had more in common with an internal police officer: checking vast rule books and issuing warnings, suspensions and dismissals. Shortly after my promotion to the role of hospital personnel officer, Margaret Thatcher's *Griffiths Report* arrived, insisting that the Health Service's problems would be solved by strong leadership. Each hospital was to be run on a business model by a single general manager, whose remit was to challenge inefficiency and cut costs.

Although not involved in selecting my own hospital's general manager, I did jump at the chance to train in psychometric testing. Like Lorraine, I was hoping for an insight into my own personality and what my future might hold. As it turned out, I worked in the Health Service for a further seventeen years, moving through paediatrics, community services, nurse education, and psychiatric and acute hospitals through the 1980s and 1990s. Personnel became Human Resources and over the years I was confronted with cases of serious fraud, sexual abuse, addiction and violence. The idea for this book arose from a question I was asked by a chief nurse: could a multiple murderer such as Beverley Allitt have been identified as dangerous by a psychometric test? It's a fascinating question and I was intrigued to return to it here.

As my character Doctor Lehman explains, in the 1980s David Hare was working on the Psychopathy Checklist (PCL-R), a checklist generally administered by a trained psychologist. Psychopathy is a controversial mental disorder characterised by callous self-centredness allied with a remorseless use of others. From my own experience visiting secure units and special hospitals, the wards housed many 'psychopaths' detained by the courts. The concept was used as something of a catch-all for mentally disordered offenders, and also popularised in crime fiction, notably by Thomas Harris in the first of the Hannibal Lector series, *Red Dragon* (1981). Around the same time, the Law Enforcement Bulletins that fascinate Diaz were being published by the FBI, some penned by John Douglas of the *Mindhunter* book and Netflix TV series fame.

Today secure units still contain many individuals with personality disorders linked to offending or seriously irresponsible behaviour. These are now more likely to meet the definition of Antisocial Personality Disorder. Hare's research suggests that around eighty per cent of UK criminals could receive a diagnosis of Antisocial Personality Disorder. Of these, he has stated that between three and thirteen percent were assessed as psychopaths. Further work has since appeared on psychopathy, for example Paulhus's research on the 'Dark Triad' of psychopathy, narcissism and Machiavellianism, followed by a further proposal of a 'Dark Tetrad' incorporating sadism.

The premise of this book is that a non-clinical 'public use' test might flag up a malevolent personality. Firstly, I trawled the research and found correlations between Hare's test and the type of public use tests used for staff selection, such as Cattell's 16PF. I must stress that no test can perfectly predict future performance, only suggest probable behaviour. Nevertheless, I construed that if a person whom Hare describes as a psychopath completed a standard personality test, they might also (if telling the truth) report traits such as very low agreeableness and low conscientiousness, observed in a lack of empathy and in antisocial behaviour. However, some high-functioning psychopaths are said to self-regulate their behaviour by reining in their antisocial impulses and presenting a false persona to facilitate their 'success'. When tested, this might prove their undoing, for by denying they possess any negative traits, the test's Motivational Distortion score ('Faking Good') should reveal a warning to investigate further. (See, for example, S. Karson and J. W. O'Dell, *Clinical Use of the 16PF*, Illinois, 1976).

I confess to deliberately moving from fact into fiction by creating a violent psychopath who also suffers from the controversial diagnosis of Dissociative Identity Disorder.

Readers and filmgoers have long been fascinated by stories of multiple personality, from Robert Bloch's *Psycho* to Chuck Palahniuk's *Fight Club*. It seems to me that Jung's notion of the demonic 'shadow inside' has entertained us for centuries: from the shape-shifting gods of myth to the haunting bogeyman, and their modern counterpart, the sadistic serial killer. This novel is an attempt to follow in that tradition and I hope readers can allow that any stigmatisation of those with mental disorders is unintended.

As a historical novelist it was a pleasure to write about a time I can vividly remember. In 1978 I'd been drawn to the liberating call of punk rock and started performing thanks to an eclectic gathering called the Manchester Musicians Collective. After learning the simplest basslines from Tony Friel of The Fall, I co-founded all-girl bands Property Of . . . and Electra Complex with Louise Alderman, along with stints playing bass in The Passage and God's Gift. I may not be living off my music royalties today, but I have never regretted being a tiny part of an exciting moment in Manchester's musical history.

Once the scene of run-down Victorian hospitals, abandoned docks and alienating tower blocks, Salford has now been utterly transformed. Thankfully, we have also moved on from what I remember of the 1980s as a callous, coarse and deeply unequal decade. It was a time when women were still dismissed as 'birds', and currently unimaginable language was used around race, gender and disability. As Lorraine was aware, in one notorious rape trial in Cambridge, a male judge could pronounce that 'Women who say no do not always mean no.'

So much for real life; many other aspects of the book are entirely imaginary. In the service of crime fiction my cast of characters ignores the many warm and generous colleagues I worked alongside. There was no 'Memorial Hospital' in Salford, or a Balaclava Street that I can locate. Lorraine's home is an amalgamation of the terraced streets of many parts of the North. The idea of a 'pilot scheme' recruiting only from internal candidates for a new general manager is fictional but not impossible. Obviously, a trainee discussing test subjects as potential suspects with a tutor is a plot device but, again, hopefully acceptable in a work of fiction.

'Path of Stars' is an imaginary song inspired by the music of Electra Complex.

Finally, I owe a deep debt to my training in psychometric testing because I did, after all, find it useful in forging a path into my future. I had a rare epiphany when a psychometric test confirmed that my own personality was, as I suspected, not well matched to working in Personnel – but primarily suited to being a writer.

I would like to thank the many former bandmates and characters on the Manchester scene who stirred in my imagination as I wrote this book. In our girl bands Property Of . . . and Electra Complex: Louise Alderman, Lynne Howe, Lyndsay Turner, Cath Caroll, Paulette Story, Penny Collins and Vicky Richardson, along with occasional drummers Tony Tabac and Jeff Bridges.

In The Passage, Dick Witts and my sister Lol (Lorraine) Hilton, and in God's Gift, Stephen Murphy and the late Steve Edwards.

To everyone who turned up at those early meetings of Manchester Musicians Collective, from Joy Division and The Fall to those who played only a few nervous gigs. Also, Tony Friel, ever-helpful Frank Ewart, Steve Solomar (and Maggie), plus Brendan Chesterton and, forever missed, Jeff Bridges, both of If Only.

There has been some gratifying interest in the Collective's music and it can be heard on:

A Manchester Collection (Bands of the Manchester Musicians Collective) (Object Music, 1979)
Messthetics #106 Manchester Musicians Collective 1977–82 (Hyped to Death, 2012)

Most recently, thanks to John Reed and all at Cherry Red Records for a great selection on the 3-CD set *Keeping Control – Independent Music From Manchester 1977–1981* (2023).

I used some excellent books and online collections from the era:

Peter Ainsworth and Ken Pease, *Police Work: Psychology in Action* (British Psychological Society, 1987)
Peter Ainsworth, *Offender Profiling and Crime Analysis* (Willan, 2001)
S. Karson and J. W. O'Dell, *Clinical Use of the 16PF* (Illinois, 1976)
H. C. Cattell, *The 16PF: Personality in Depth* (Illinois, 1989)
Andy McSmith, *No Such Thing as Society: A History of Britain in the 1980s* (Constable, 2011)
Helen Reddington, *The Lost Women of Rock Music: Female Musicians of the Punk Era* (Routledge, 2007)

John Robb, *The North Will Rise Again: Manchester Music City 1976–1996* (Aurum, 2010)

Ian Livingstone and Steve Jackson, *The Warlock of Firetop Mountain: A fighting fantasy gamebook in which YOU become the hero!* (Puffin, 1982, www.fightingfantasy.com)

Manchester Digital Music Archive is a rich source on Manchester Music and its social history held at www.mdmarchive.co.uk.

The FBI's archive of Law Enforcement Bulletins can be found at https://leb.fbi.gov/file-repository/archives.

The early readers of this manuscript gave me helpful feedback: Louise Alderman and her daughter, psychotherapist Sarah Price, research psychologist Valerie Lawson and musician Abi Woods. My wonderful writer friends, Alison Layland and Elaine Walker, again gave me invaluable feedback, support and friendship over the long gestation of this book. Also, huge encouragement from my friends in The Prime Writers, a group of writers who have all had their fiction debuts commercially published at the age of forty or more.

A retreat in lockdown at Ty Newydd Creative Writing Centre in Wales was made possible by the generosity of a grant from the Francis W. Reckitt Arts Trust.

Huge thanks to my agent, Charlotte Seymour of Johnson and Alcock literary agents, for help and advice in refining the early draft and keeping faith in sending it out into the world.

Thank you to all at Allison and Busby, especially Lesley Crooks, Daniel Scott and Susie Dunlop for your crucial enthusiasm for this book and its forthcoming sequel.

And finally, I'm grateful to my son Chris, and to my sisters Marijke and Lorraine, for their ceaseless positive encouragement. My late father, composer Derek Hilton, was often in my thoughts, as was his distinctly northern musical legacy at Granada TV. Finally, thanks to my ever-supportive husband Martin, for reading and critiquing my early drafts.

MARTINE BAILEY studied English Literature while playing in bands on the Manchester music scene. She qualified in psychometric testing and over her career, assessed staff for a top security psychiatric hospital and dealt with cases of sexual abuse and violence. Having written historical crime fiction, Bailey's writing has jumped to a modern setting. She lives in Chester.

martinebailey.com
@MartineBailey